IT WAS AFTER one A.M. on the second week of September when Barbara Clayton cut across the lawn of the Washington Cathedral. The air was warm, the stars brilliant, but she wasn't in the mood to enjoy it. As she walked, she muttered bad temperedly. A shooting star exploded and trailed across the sky in a brilliant arch. She never even noticed.

Nor did the man who watched her. He'd known she'd come. Hadn't he been told to keep watch? Wasn't his head, even now, almost bursting from the pressure of the Voice? He'd been chosen, given the burden and the glory.

"Dominus vobiscum," he murmured, then gripped the smooth white material of the priest's amice tightly in his hands.

And when his task was complete, he felt the hot rush of power. His loins exploded. His blood sang. He was clean. And so, now, was she. Slowly, gently, he took his thumb over her forehead, her lips, her heart, in the sign of the cross. He gave her absolution, but quickly. The Voice had warned him there were many who wouldn't understand the purity of the work he did.

Leaving her body in the shadows, he walked on, eyes bright with the tears of joy and madness.

NORA ROBERTS

SACRED SINS

BANTAM BOOKS

SACRED SINS
A Bantam Book

PUBLISHING HISTORY
Original Bantam paperback published December 1987
Bantam hardcover edition published September 2000
Bantam revised paperback edition / August 2001
Bantam mass market reissue / June 2007

Published by Bantam Dell
A Division of Random House, Inc.
New York, New York

This is a work of fiction. Names, characters, places, and incidents either are the product of the author's imagination or are used fictitiously. Any resemblance to actual persons, living or dead, events, or locales is entirely coincidental.

ISBN 978-0-553-26574-3

Printed in the United States of America
Published simultaneously in Canada

www.bantamdell.com

OPM 42 41 40 39 38 37 36 35 34

For my mother,
with thanks for the encouragement to tell this story

Chapter 1

AUGUST FIFTEENTH. IT was a day following other days of sweat and hazy skies. There were no puffy white clouds or balmy breezes, only a wall of humidity nearly thick enough to swim in.

Reports on the six and eleven o'clock news glumly promised more to come. In the long, lazy last days of summer, the heat wave moving into its second, pitiless week was the biggest story in Washington, D.C.

The Senate was adjourned until September, so Capitol Hill moved sluggishly. Relaxing before a much touted European trip, the President cooled off at Camp David. Without the day-to-day shuffle of politics, Washington was a city of tourists and street vendors. Across from the Smithsonian, a mime performed for a sticky crowd that had stopped more to catch its collective breath than in appreciation of art. Pretty summer dresses wilted, and children whined for ice cream.

The young and the old flocked to Rock Creek Park, using the shade and water as a defense against the heat. Soft drinks and lemonade were consumed by the gallon, beer and wine downed in the same quantity, but less conspicuously. Bottles had a way of disappearing when park police cruised by. During picnics and cookouts people mopped sweat, charred hot dogs, and watched babies in diapers toddle on the grass. Mothers shouted at children to stay away from the water, not to run near the road, to put down a stick or a stone. The music from portable radios was, as usual, loud and defiant; hot tracks, the deejays called them, and reported temperatures in the high nineties.

Small groups of students drew together, some sitting on the rocks above the creek to discuss the fate of the world, others sprawled on the grass, more interested in the fate of their tans. Those who could spare the time and the gas had fled to the beach or the mountains. A few college students found the energy to throw Frisbees, the men stripping down to shorts to show off torsos uniformly bronzed.

A pretty young artist sat under a tree and sketched idly. After several attempts to draw her attention to the biceps he'd been working on for six months, one of the players took a more obvious route. The Frisbee landed on her pad with a plop. When she looked up in annoyance, he jogged over. His grin was apologetic, and calculated, he hoped, to dazzle.

"Sorry. Got away from me."

After pushing a fall of dark hair over her shoulder, the artist handed the Frisbee back to him. "It's all right." She went back to her sketching without sparing him a glance.

Youth is nothing if not tenacious. Hunkering down beside her, he studied her drawing. What he knew about art wouldn't have filled a shot glass, but a pitch was a pitch. "Hey, that's really good. Where're you studying?"

Recognizing the ploy, she started to brush him off, then looked up long enough to catch his smile. Maybe he was obvious, but he was cute. "Georgetown."

"No kidding? Me too. Pre-law."

Impatient, his partner called across the grass. "Rod! We going for a brew or not?"

"You come here often?" Rod asked, ignoring his friend. The artist had the biggest brown eyes he'd ever seen.

"Now and again."

"Why don't we—"

"Rod, come on. Let's get that beer."

Rod looked at his sweaty, slightly overweight friend, then back into the cool brown eyes of the artist. No contest. "I'll catch you later, Pete," he called out, then let the Frisbee go in a high, negligent arch.

"Finished playing?" the artist asked, watching the flight of the Frisbee.

He grinned, then touched the ends of her hair. "Depends."

Swearing, Pete started off in pursuit of the disk. He'd just paid six bucks for it. After nearly tripping over a dog, he scrambled down a slope, hoping the Frisbee wouldn't land in the creek. He'd paid a lot more for his leather sandals. It circled toward the water, making him curse out loud, then hit a tree and careened off into some bushes. Dripping sweat and thinking about the cold Moosehead waiting for him, Pete shoved at branches and cleared his way.

His heart stopped, then sent the blood beating in his head. Before he could draw breath to yell, his lunch of Fritos and two hot dogs came up, violently.

The Frisbee had landed two feet from the edge of the creek. It lay new and red and cheerful on a cold white hand that seemed to offer it back.

She had been Carla Johnson, a twenty-three-year-old drama student and part-time waitress. Twelve to fifteen hours before, she had been strangled with a priest's amice. White, edged in gold.

DETECTIVE Ben Paris slumped at his desk after finishing his written report on the Johnson homicide. He'd typed the facts, using two fingers in a machine gun style. But now they played back to him. No sexual assault, no apparent robbery. Her purse had been under her, with twenty-three dollars and seventy-six cents and a MasterCard in it. An opal ring that would have hocked for about fifty had still been on her finger. No motive, no suspects. Nothing.

Ben and his partner had spent the afternoon interviewing the victim's family. An ugly business, he thought. Necessary, but ugly. They had unearthed the same answers at every turn. Carla had wanted to be an actress. Her life had been her studies. She had dated, but not seriously—she'd been too devoted to an ambition she would never achieve.

Ben skimmed the report again and lingered over the murder weapon. The priest's scarf. There had been a note pinned next to it. He'd knelt beside her himself hours before to read it.

Her sins are forgiven her.

"Amen," Ben murmured, and let out a long breath.

IT was after one A.M. on the second week of September when Barbara Clayton cut across the lawn of the Washington Cathedral. The air was warm; the stars brilliant, but she wasn't in the mood to enjoy it. As she walked she muttered bad-temperedly. She'd give that ferret-faced mechanic an earful in the morning. Fixed the transmission good as new. What a crock. Damn good thing she only had a couple more blocks to walk.

Now she'd have to take the bus to work. The ugly, grease-smeared sonofabitch was going to pay. A shooting star exploded and trailed across the sky in a brilliant arch. She never even noticed.

Nor did the man who watched her. He'd known she'd come. Hadn't he been told to keep watch? Wasn't his head, even now, almost bursting from the pressure of the Voice? He'd been chosen, given the burden and the glory.

"Dominus vobiscum," he murmured, then gripped the smooth material of the amice tightly in his hands.

And when his task was complete, he felt the hot rush of power. His loins exploded. His blood sang. He was clean. And so, now, was she. Slowly, gently, he ran his thumb over her forehead, her lips, her heart, in the sign of the cross. He gave her absolution, but quickly. The Voice had warned him there were many who wouldn't understand the purity of the work he did.

Leaving her body in the shadows, he walked on, eyes bright with the tears of joy and madness.

"THE media's crawling up our backs with this one." Captain Harris slammed a fist on the newspaper spread over his desk. "The whole goddamn city's in a panic. When I find out who leaked this priest business to the press . . ."

He trailed off, drawing himself in. It wasn't often he came that close to losing control. He might sit behind a desk, but he was a cop, he told himself, a damn good one. A good cop didn't lose control. To give himself time, he folded the paper, letting his gaze drift over the other cops in the room. Damn good ones, Harris admitted. He wouldn't have tolerated less.

Ben Paris sat on the corner of the desk, toying with a

Lucite paperweight. Harris knew him well enough to understand that Ben liked something in his hands when he was thinking. Young, Harris reflected, but seasoned with ten years on the force. A solid cop, if a bit loose on procedure. The two citations for bravery had been well earned. When things were less tense, it even amused Harris that Ben looked like the Hollywood screenwriter's version of an undercover cop—lean-faced, strong-boned, dark, and wiry. His hair was full and too long to be conventional, but it was cut in one of those fancy little shops in Georgetown. He had pale green eyes that didn't miss what was important.

In a chair, three feet of leg spread out before him, sat Ed Jackson, Ben's partner. At six-five and two hundred fifty pounds, he could usually intimidate a suspect on sight. Whether by whim or design, he wore a full beard that was as red as the curly mane of hair on his head. His eyes were blue and friendly. At fifty yards he could put a hole in the eagle of a quarter with his Police Special.

Harris set the paper aside, but didn't sit. "What've you got?"

Ben tossed the paperweight from hand to hand before he set it down. "Other than build and coloring, there's no connection between the two victims. No mutual friends, no mutual hangouts. You've got the rundown on Carla Johnson. Barbara Clayton worked in a dress shop, divorced, no kids. Family lives in Maryland, blue collar. She'd been seeing someone pretty heavily up to three months ago. Things fizzled, he moved to L.A. We're checking on him, but he looks clean."

He reached in his pocket for a cigarette and caught his partner's eye.

"That's six," Ed said easily. "Ben's trying to get under

a pack a day," he explained, then took up the report himself.

"Clayton spent the evening in a bar on Wisconsin. Kind of a girls' night out with a friend who works with her. Friend says Clayton left about one. Her car was found broken down a couple blocks from the hit. Seems she's been having transmission problems. Apparently, she decided to walk from there. Her apartment's only about half a mile away."

"The only things the victims had in common were that they were both blond, white, and female." Ben drew in smoke hard, let it fill up his lungs, then released it. "Now they're dead."

In his territory, Harris thought, and took it personally. "The murder weapon, the priest's scarf."

"Amice," Ben supplied. "Didn't seem too hard to trace. Our guy uses the best—silk."

"He didn't get it in the city," Ed continued. "Not in the past year anyway. We've checked every religious store, every church. Got a line on three outlets in New England that carry that type."

"The notes were written on paper available at any dime store," Ben added. "There's no tracing them."

"In other words, you've got nothing."

"In any words," Ben drew smoke again, "we've got nothing."

Harris studied each man in silence. He might have wished Ben would wear a tie or that Ed would trim down his beard, but that was personal. They were his best. Paris, with his easygoing charm and surface carelessness, had the instincts of a fox and a mind as sharp as a stiletto. Jackson was as thorough and efficient as a maiden aunt. A case was a jigsaw puzzle to him, and he never tired of shifting through the pieces.

Harris sniffed the smoke from Ben's cigarette, then

reminded himself that he'd given up smoking for his own good. "Go back and talk to everyone again. Get me the report on Clayton's old boyfriend and the customer lists from the religious outlets." He glanced toward the paper again. "I want to take this guy down."

"The Priest," Ben murmured as he skimmed the headline. "The press always likes to give psychos a title."

"And lots of coverage," Harris added. "Let's get him out of the headlines and behind bars."

HAZY after a long night of paperwork, Dr. Teresa Court sipped coffee and skimmed the *Post*. A full week after the second murder and the Priest, as the press termed him, was still at large. She didn't find reading about him the best way to begin her day, but professionally he interested her. She wasn't immune to the death of two young women, but she'd been trained to look at facts and diagnose. Her life had been dedicated to it.

Professionally, her life was besieged by problems, pain, frustrations. To compensate, she kept her private world organized and simple. Because she'd grown up with the cushion of wealth and education, she took the Matisse print on her wall and the Baccarat crystal on the table as a matter of course. She preferred clean lines and pastels, but now and again found herself drawn to something jarring, like the abstract oil in vivid strokes and arrogant colors over her table. She understood her need for the harsh as well as the soft, and was content. One of her top priorities was to remain content.

Because the coffee was already cold, she pushed it aside. After a moment she pushed the paper away as well. She wished she knew more about the killer and the victims, had all the details. Then she remembered the old saying about being careful what you wished for because you just might get it. With a quick check of her watch, she rose from the table. She didn't have time to brood over a story in the paper. She had patients to see.

EASTERN cities are at their most splendid in the fall. Summer bakes them, winter leaves them stalled and dingy, but autumn gives them a blast of color and dignity.

At two A.M. on a cool October morning Ben Paris found himself suddenly and completely awake. There was no use wondering what had disturbed his sleep and the interesting dream involving three blonds. Rising, he padded naked to his dresser and groped for his cigarettes. Twenty-two, he counted silently.

He lit one, letting the familiar bitter taste fill his mouth before he went to the kitchen to make coffee. Turning on only the fluorescent light on the stove, he kept a sharp eye out for roaches. Nothing skidded into cracks. Ben set the flame under the pot and thought the last extermination was still holding. As he reached for a cup he pushed away two days' worth of mail he'd yet to open.

In the harsh kitchen light his face looked hard, even dangerous. But then, he was thinking about murder. His naked body was loose and rangy, with a leanness that would have been gaunt without the subtle ridges of muscle.

The coffee wouldn't keep him awake. When his mind was ready, his body would just follow suit. He'd trained himself through endless stakeouts.

A scrawny dust-colored cat leaped on the table and stared at him as he sipped and smoked. Noting he was distracted, the cat readjusted her idea about a late-night saucer of milk and sat down to wash.

They were no closer to finding the killer than they

had been the afternoon the first body was discovered. If they'd come upon something remotely resembling a lead, it had fizzled after the first miles of legwork. Dead end, Ben reflected. Zero. Zilch.

Of course, there had been five confessions in one month alone. All from the disturbed minds that craved attention. Twenty-six days after the second murder and they were nowhere. And every day that went by, he knew, the trail grew colder. As the press petered out, people began to relax. He didn't like it. Lighting one cigarette from the butt of another, Ben thought of calm before storms. He looked out into the cool night lit by a half-moon and wondered.

DOUG'S was only five miles from Ben's apartment. The little club was dark now. The musicians were gone and the spilled booze mopped up. Francie Bowers stepped out the back entrance and drew on her sweater. Her feet hurt. After six hours on four-inch heels, her toes were cramping inside her sneakers. Still, the tips had been worth it. Working as a cocktail waitress might keep you on your feet, but if your legs were good—and hers were—the tips rolled in.

A few more nights like this one, she mused, and she might just be able to put a down payment on that little VW. No more hassling with the bus. That was her idea of heaven.

The arch of her foot gave out a sweet sliver of pain. Wincing at it, Francie glanced at the alley. It would save her a quarter mile. But it was dark. She took another two steps toward the streetlight and gave up. Dark or not, she wasn't walking one step more than she had to.

He'd been waiting a long time. But he'd known. The Voice had said one of the lost ones was being sent. She was coming quickly, as if eager to reach salvation. For days he had prayed for her, for the cleansing of her soul. Now the time of forgiveness was almost at hand. He was only an instrument.

The turmoil began in his head and spiraled down. Power rolled into him. In the shadows he prayed until she passed by.

He moved swiftly, as was merciful. When the amice was looped around her neck, she had only an instant to gasp before he pulled it taut. She let out a small liquid sound as her air was cut off. As terror rammed into her, she dropped her canvas bag and grabbed for the restriction with both hands.

Sometimes, when his power was great, he could let them go quickly. But the evil in her was strong, challenging him. Her fingers pulled at the silk, then dug heavily into the gloves he wore. When she kicked back, he lifted her from her feet, but she continued to lash out. One of her feet connected with a can and sent it clattering. The noise echoed in his head until he nearly screamed with it.

Then she was limp, and the tears on his face dried in the autumn air. He laid her gently on the concrete and absolved her in the old tongue. After pinning the note to her sweater, he blessed her.

She was at peace. And for now, so was he.

"THERE'S no reason to kill us getting there." Ed's tone of voice was serene as Ben took the Mustang around a corner at fifty. "She's already dead."

Ben downshifted and took the next right. "You're the one who totaled the last car. *My* last car," he added without too much malice. "Only had seventy-five thousand miles on it."

"High-speed pursuit," Ed mumbled.

The Mustang shimmied over a bump, reminding Ben that he'd been meaning to check the shocks.

"And I didn't kill you."

"Contusions and lacerations." Sliding through an amber light, Ben drove it into third. "Multiple contusions and lacerations."

Reminiscently, Ed smiled. "We got them, didn't we?"

"They were unconscious." Ben squealed to a halt at the curb and pocketed the keys. "And I needed five stitches in my arm."

"Bitch, bitch, bitch." With a yawn Ed unfolded himself from the car and stood on the sidewalk.

It was barely dawn, and cool enough so you could see your breath, but a crowd was already forming. Hunched in his jacket and wishing for coffee, Ben worked his way through the curious onlookers to the roped-off alley.

"Sly." With a nod to the police photographer, Ben looked down on victim number three.

He would put her age at twenty-six to twenty-eight. The sweater was a cheap polyester, and the soles of her sneakers were worn almost smooth. She wore dangling, gold-plated earrings. Her face was a mask of heavy makeup that didn't suit the department-store sweater and corduroys.

Cupping his hands around his second cigarette of the day, he listened to the report of the uniformed cop beside him.

"Vagrant found her. We got him in a squad car sobering up. Seems he was picking through the trash when he came across her. Put the fear of God into him, so he ran out of the alley and nearly into my cruiser."

Ben nodded, looking down at the neatly lettered note pinned to her sweater. Frustration and fury moved through him so swiftly that when acceptance settled in, they were hardly noticed. Bending down, Ed picked up the oversized canvas bag she'd dropped. A handful of bus tokens spilled out.

It was going to be a long day.

SIX hours later they walked into the precinct. Homicide didn't have the seamy glamor of Vice, but it was hardly as neat and tidy as the stations in the suburbs. Two years before, the walls had been painted in what Ben referred to as apartment-house beige. The floor tiles sweat in the summer and held the cold in the winter. No matter how diligent the janitorial service was with pine cleaner and dust rags, the rooms forever smelled of stale smoke, wet coffee grounds, and fresh sweat. True, they'd taken up a pool in the spring and delegated one of the detectives to buy some plants to put on the windowsills. They weren't dying, but they weren't flourishing either.

Ben passed a desk and nodded to Lou Roderick as the detective typed up a report. This was a cop who took his caseload steadily, the way an accountant takes corporate taxes.

"Harris wants to see you," Lou told him, and without looking up, managed to convey a touch of sympathy. "Just got in from a meeting with the mayor. And I think Lowenstein took a message for you."

"Thanks." Ben eyed the Snickers bar on Roderick's desk. "Hey, Lou—"

"Forget it." Roderick continued to type his report without breaking rhythm.

"So much for brotherhood," Ben muttered, and sauntered over to Lowenstein.

She was a different type from Roderick altogether, Ben mused. She worked in surges, stop and go, and was more comfortable on the street than at a typewriter. Ben respected Lou's preciseness, but as a backup he'd have chosen Lowenstein, whose proper suits and trim dresses didn't hide the fact that she had the best legs in the department. Ben took a quick look at them before he sat on the corner of her desk. Too bad she was married, he thought.

Poking idly through her papers, he waited for her to finish her call. "How's it going, Lowenstein?"

"My garbage disposal's throwing up and the plumber wants three hundred, but that's all right because my husband's going to fix it." She spun a form into her typewriter. "It'll only cost us twice as much that way. How about you?" She smacked his hand away from the Pepsi on her desk. "Got anything new on our priest?"

"Just a corpse." If there was bitterness, it was hard to detect. "Ever been to Doug's, down by the Canal?"

"I don't have your social life, Paris."

He gave a quick snort then picked up the fat mug that held her pencils. "She was a cocktail waitress there. Twenty-seven."

"No use letting it get to you," she murmured, then seeing his face, passed him the Pepsi. It always got to you. "Harris wants to see you and Ed."

"Yeah, I know." He took a long swallow, letting the sugar and caffeine pour into his system. "Got a message for me?"

"Oh, yeah." With a smirk, she pushed through her papers until she found it. "Bunny called." When the high, breathy voice didn't get a rise out of him, she sent him an arch look and handed him the paper. "She wants to know what time you're picking her up. She sounded real cute, Paris."

He pocketed the slip and grinned. "She is real cute, Lowenstein, but I'd dump her in a minute if you wanted to cheat on your husband."

When he walked off without returning her drink, she laughed and went back to typing out the form.

"They're turning my apartment into condos." Ed hung up the phone and went with Ben toward Harris's office. "Fifty thousand. Jesus."

"It's got bad plumbing." Ben drained the rest of the Pepsi and tossed it into a can.

"Yeah. Got any vacancies over at your place?"

"Nobody leaves there unless they die."

Through the wide glass window of Harris's office they could see the captain standing by his desk as he talked on the phone. He'd kept himself in good shape for a man of fifty-seven who'd spent the last ten years behind a desk. He had too much willpower to run to fat. His first marriage had gone under because of the job, his second because of the bottle. Harris had given up booze and marriage, and now the job took the place of both. The cops in his department didn't necessarily like him, but they respected him. Harris preferred things that way. Glancing up, he signaled for both men to enter.

"I want the lab reports before five. If there was a piece of lint on her sweater, I want to know where it came from. Do your job. Give me something to work with so I can do mine." When he hung up, he went over to his hot plate and poured coffee. After five years he still wished it were scotch. "Tell me about Francie Bowers."

"She's been working tables at Doug's for almost a year. Moved to D.C. from Virginia last November. Lived alone in an apartment in North West." Ed shifted his weight and checked his notebook. "Married twice, neither lasted over a year. We're checking out both exes. She worked nights and slept days, so her neighbors don't know much about her. She got off work at one. Apparently she cut through the alley to get to the bus stop. She didn't own a car."

"Nobody heard anything," Ben added. "Or saw anything."

"Ask again," Harris said simply. "And find someone who did. Anything more on number one?"

Ben didn't like victims by numbers, and stuck his hands in his pockets. "Carla Johnson's boyfriend's in L.A., got a bit part on a soap. He's clean. It appeared she'd had an argument with another student the day before she was killed. Witnesses said it got pretty hot."

"He admitted it," Ed continued. "Seems they'd dated a couple of times and she wasn't interested."

"Alibi?"

"Claims he got drunk and picked up a freshman." With a shrug, Ben sat on the arm of a chair. "They're engaged. We can bring him in again, but neither of us believes he had anything to do with it. He's got no connection with Clayton or Bowers. When we checked him over, we found out that the kid's the all-American boy from an upper-middle-class family. Lettered in track. It's more likely Ed's a psychotic than that college boy."

"Thanks, partner."

"Well, check him out again anyway. What's his name?"

"Robert Lawrence Dors. He drives a Honda Civic and wears polo shirts." Ben drew out a cigarette. "White loafers and no socks."

"Roderick'll bring him in."

"Wait a minute—"

"I'm assigning a task force to this business," Harris said, cutting Ben off. He poured a second cup of coffee. "Roderick, Lowenstein, and Bigsby'll be working with you. I want this guy before he kills the next woman who happens to be out walking alone." His voice remained mild, reasonable, and final. "You have a problem with that?"

Ben strode to the window and stared out. It was personal, and he knew better. "No, we all want him."

"Including the mayor," Harris added with only the slightest trace of bitterness. "He wants to be able to give the press something positive by the end of the week. We're calling in a psychiatrist to give us a profile."

"A shrink?" With a half laugh, Ben turned around. "Come on, Captain."

Because he didn't like it either, Harris's voice chilled. "Dr. Court has agreed to cooperate with us, at the mayor's request. We don't know what he looks like, maybe it's time we found out how he thinks. At this point," he added with a level glance at both men, "I'm willing to look into a crystal ball if we'd get a lead out of it. Be here at four."

Ben started to open his mouth then caught Ed's warning glance. Without a word they strode out. "Maybe we should call in a psychic," Ben muttered.

"Close-minded."

"Realistic."

"The human psyche is a fascinating mystery."

"You've been reading again."

"And those trained to understand it can open doors laymen only knock against."

Ben sighed and flicked his cigarette into the parking lot as they stepped outside. "Shit."

❦

"SHIT," Tess muttered as she glanced out her office window. There were two things she had no desire to do at that moment. The first was battling traffic in the cold, nasty rain that had begun to fall. The second was to become involved with the homicides plaguing the city. She was going to have to do the first because the mayor, and her grandfather, had pressured her to do the second.

Her caseload was already too heavy. She might have refused the mayor, politely, even apologetically. Her grandfather was a different matter. She never felt like Dr. Teresa Court when she dealt with him. After five minutes she wasn't five feet four with a woman's body and a black-framed degree behind her. She was again a skinny twelve-year-old, overpowered by the personality of the man she loved most in the world.

He'd seen to it that she'd gotten that black-framed degree, hadn't he? With his confidence, she thought, his support, his unstinting belief in her. How could she say no when he asked her to use her skill? Because handling her current caseload took her ten hours a day. Perhaps it was time she stopped being stubborn and took on a partner.

Tess looked around her pastel office with its carefully selected antiques and watercolors. Hers, she thought. Every bit of it. And she glanced at the tall, oak file cabinet, circa 1920. It was loaded with case files. Those were hers too. No, she wouldn't be taking on a partner. In a year she'd be thirty. She had her own practice, her own office, her own problems. That's just the way she wanted to keep it.

Taking the mink-lined raincoat from the closet, she shrugged into it. And maybe, just maybe, she could help the police find the man who was splashed across the headlines day after day. She could help them find him, stop him, so that he in turn could get the help he needed.

She picked up her purse and the briefcase, which was fat with files to be sorted through that evening. "Kate." Stepping into her outer office, Tess turned up her collar. "I'm on my way to Captain Harris's office. Don't pass anything through unless it's urgent."

"You should have a hat," the receptionist answered.

"I've got one in the car. See you tomorrow."

"Drive carefully."

Already thinking ahead, she walked through the door while digging for her car keys. Maybe she could grab some take-out Chinese on the way home and have a quiet dinner before—

"Tess!"

One more step and she would have been in the elevator. Swearing under her breath, Tess turned and managed a smile. "Frank." And she'd been so successful at avoiding him for nearly ten days.

"You're a hard lady to pin down."

He strode toward her. Impeccable. That was the word that always leaped to Tess's mind when she saw Dr. F. R. Fuller. Right before boring. His suit was pearl-gray Brooks Brothers, and his striped tie had hints of that shade and the baby pink in his Arrow shirt. His hair was perfectly and conservatively groomed. She tried hard to keep her smile from fading. It wasn't Frank's fault she couldn't warm to perfection.

"I've been busy."

"You know what they say about all work, Tess."

She gritted her teeth to keep herself from saying no, what did they say? He'd simply laugh and give her the rest of the cliché. "I'll just have to risk it." She pressed the button for down and hoped the car came quickly.

"But you're leaving early today."

"Outside appointment." Deliberately she checked her watch. She had time to spare. "Running a bit late," she lied without qualm.

"I've been trying to get in touch with you." Pressing his palm against the wall, he leaned over her. Another of his habits Tess found herself detesting. "You'd think it wouldn't be a problem since our offices are right next door."

Where the hell was an elevator when you needed it? "You know what schedules are like, Frank."

"Indeed I do." He flashed his toothpaste smile and she wondered if he thought his cologne was driving her wild. "But we all need to relax now and again, right, Doctor?"

"In our own way."

"I have tickets to the Noel Coward play at the Kennedy Center tomorrow night. Why don't we relax together?"

The last time, the only time, she'd agreed to relax with him, she'd barely escaped with the clothes on her back. Worse, before the tug-of-war, she'd been bored to death for three hours. "It's nice of you to think of me, Frank." Again she lied without hesitation. "I'm afraid I'm already booked for tomorrow."

"Why don't we—"

The doors opened. "Oops, I'm late." Sending him a cheery smile, she stepped inside. "Don't work too hard, Frank. You know what they say."

Due to the pounding rain and traffic, she ate up nearly all of her extra time driving to the station house. Strangely enough, the half-hour battle left her rather cheerful. Perhaps, she thought, because she had escaped so neatly from Frank. If she'd had the heart, and she didn't, she would simply have told him he was a jerk and that would be the end of it. Until he pushed her into enough corners, she'd use tact and excuses.

Reaching beside her, she picked up a felt hat and bundled her hair under it. She glanced in the rearview mirror and wrinkled her nose. No use doing any repairs now. The rain would make it a waste of time. Still, there was bound to be a ladies room inside where she could dig into her bag of tricks and come out looking dignified and professional. For now she was just going to look wet.

Pushing open the door of the car, Tess grabbed her hat with one hand and made a dash for the building.

"Check this out." Ben halted his partner on the steps leading to headquarters. They watched, heedless of the rain, as Tess jumped over puddles.

"Nice legs," Ed commented.

"Damn. They're better than Lowenstein's."

"Maybe." Ed gave it a moment's thought. "Hard to tell in the rain."

Still running, head down, Tess dashed up the steps and collided with Ben. He heard her swear before he took her shoulders, pulling her back just far enough to get a look at her face.

It was worth getting wet for.

Elegant. Even with rain washing over it, Ben thought of elegance. The slash of cheekbones was strong, high enough to make him think of Viking maidens. Her mouth was soft and moist, making him think of other things. Her skin was pale, with just a touch of rose. But it was her eyes that made him lose track of the glib remark he'd thought to make. They were big, cool, and just a bit annoyed. And violet. He'd thought the color had been reserved for Elizabeth Taylor and wildflowers.

"Sorry," Tess managed when she got her breath back. "I didn't see you."

"No." He wanted to go on staring, but managed to bring himself around. He had a reputation with women that was mythical. Exaggerated, but based on fact. "At the rate you were traveling, I'm not surprised." It felt good to hold her, to watch the rain cling to her lashes. "I could run you in for assaulting an officer."

"The lady's getting wet," Ed murmured.

Until then Tess had only been aware of the man who held her, staring at her as though she'd appeared in a puff of smoke. Now she made herself look away and over, then up. She saw a wet giant with laughing blue eyes and a mass of dripping red hair. Was this a police station, she thought, or a fairy tale?

Ben kept one hand on her arm as he pushed open the door. He'd let her inside, but he wasn't going to let her slip away. Not yet.

Once in, Tess gave Ed another look, decided he was real, and turned to Ben. So was he. And he was still holding her arm. Amused, she lifted a brow. "Officer, I warn you, if you arrest me for assault, I'll file charges of police brutality." When he smiled, she felt something click. So he wasn't as harmless as she'd thought. "Now, if you'll excuse me—"

"Forget the charges." Ben kept his hand on her arm. "If you need a ticket fixed—"

"Sergeant—"

"Detective," he corrected. "Ben."

"Detective, I might take you up on that another time, but at the moment I'm running late. If you want to be helpful—"

"I'm a public servant."

"Then you can let go of my arm and tell me where to find Captain Harris."

"Captain Harris? Homicide?"

She saw the surprise, the distrust, and felt her arm released. Intrigued, she tilted her head and removed her hat. Pale blond hair tumbled to her shoulders. "That's right."

Ben's gaze skimmed the fall of hair before he looked back at her face. It didn't fit, he thought. He suspected things that didn't fit. "Dr. Court?"

It always took an effort to meet rudeness and cynicism with grace. Tess didn't bother to make it. "Right again—Detective."

"You're a shrink?"

She gave him back look for look. "You're a cop?"

Each might have added something less than complimentary if Ed hadn't burst out laughing. "That's the bell for round one," he said easily. "Harris's office is a neutral corner." He took Tess's arm himself and showed her the way.

Chapter 2

FLANKED ON EITHER side, Tess walked down the corridors. Now and then a voice barked or a door opened and closed hollowly. The sound of phones ringing came from everywhere at once; they never seemed to be answered. Rain beat against the windows to add a touch of gloom. A man in his shirtsleeves and overalls was mopping up a puddle of something. The corridor smelled strongly of Lysol and damp.

It wasn't the first time she'd been in a police station, but it was the first time she'd come so close to being intimidated. Ignoring Ben, she concentrated on his partner.

"You two always travel as a pair?"

Genial, Ed grinned. He liked her voice because it was pitched low and was as cool as sherbet on a hot Sunday afternoon. "The captain likes me to keep an eye on him."

"I'll bet."

Ben made a sharp left turn. "This way—Doctor."

Tess slanted him a look and moved past him. He smelled of rain and soap. As she stepped into the squad room, she watched two men drag out a teenage boy in handcuffs. A woman sat in a corner with a cup in both hands and wept silently. The sounds of arguing poured in from out in the hall.

"Welcome to reality," Ben offered as someone began to swear.

Tess gave him a long steady look and summed him up as a fool. Did he think she'd expected tea and cookies? Compared to the clinic where she gave her time once a week, this was a garden party. "Thank you, Detective . . ."

"Paris." He wondered why he felt she was laughing at him. "Ben Paris, Dr. Court. This is my partner, Ed Jackson." Taking out a cigarette, he lit it as he watched her. She looked as out of place in the dingy squad room as a rose on a trash heap. But that was her problem. "We'll be working with you."

"How nice." With the smile she reserved for annoying shop clerks, she breezed by him. Before she could knock on Harris's door, Ben was opening it.

"Captain." Ben waited as Harris pushed aside papers and rose. "This is Dr. Court."

He hadn't been expecting a woman, or anyone so young. But Harris had commanded too many women officers, too many rookies, to feel anything but momentary surprise. The mayor had recommended her. Insisted on her, Harris corrected himself. And the mayor, no matter how annoying, was a sharp man who made few missteps.

"Dr. Court." He held out his hand and found hers soft and small, but firm enough. "I appreciate you coming."

No, she wasn't quite convinced he did, but she had worked around such things before. "I hope I can help."

"Please, sit down."

She started to shrug out of her coat, and felt hands on her arms. Taking a quick look over her shoulder, she saw Ben behind her. "Nice coat, Doctor." His fingers brushed over the lining as he slipped it from her. "Fifty-minute hours must be profitable."

"Nothing's more fun than soaking patients," she said in the same undertone, then turned away from him. Arrogant jerk, she thought, and took her seat.

"Dr. Court might like some coffee," Ed put in. Always easily amused, he grinned over at his partner. "She got kind of wet coming in."

Seeing the gleam in Ed's eyes, Tess couldn't help but grin back. "I'd love some coffee. Black."

Harris glanced over at the dregs in the pot on his hot plate, then reached for his phone. "Roderick, get some coffee in here. Four—no three," he corrected as he glanced at Ed.

"If there's any hot water . . ." Ed reached in his pocket and drew out an herbal tea bag.

"And a cup of hot water," Harris said, his lips twisting into something like a smile. "Yeah, for Jackson. Dr. Court . . ." Harris didn't know what had amused her, but had a feeling it had something to do with his two men. They had better get down to business. "We'll be grateful for any help you can give us. And you'll have our full cooperation." This was said with a glance, a telling one, at Ben. "You've been briefed on what we need?"

Tess thought of her two-hour meeting with the mayor, and the stacks of paperwork she'd taken home from his office. Brief, she mused, had nothing to do with it.

"Yes. You need a psychological profile on the killer known as the Priest. You'll want an educated, expert opinion as to why he kills, and to his style of killing. You want me to tell you who he is, emotionally. How he thinks, how he feels. With the facts I have, and those you'll give me, it's possible to give an opinion . . . an opinion," she stressed, "on how and why and who he is, psychologically. With that you may be a step closer to stopping him."

So she didn't promise miracles. It helped Harris to relax. Out of the corner of his eye he saw Ben watching her steadily, one finger idly stroking down her raincoat. "Sit down, Paris," he said mildly. "The mayor gave you some data?" he asked the psychiatrist.

"A bit. I started on it last night."

"You'll want to take a look at these reports as well." Taking a folder from his desk, Harris passed it to her.

"Thank you." Tess pulled out a pair of tortoiseshell glasses from her bag and opened the folder.

A shrink, Ben thought again as he studied her profile. She looked like she should be leading cheers at a varsity game. Or sipping cognac at the Mayflower. He wasn't certain why both images seemed to suit her, but they did. It was the image of mind doctor that didn't. Psychiatrists were tall and thin and pale, with calm eyes, calm voices, calm hands.

He remembered the psychiatrist his brother had seen for three years after returning from 'Nam. Josh had gone away a young, fresh-faced idealist. He'd come back haunted and belligerent. The psychiatrist had helped. Or so it had seemed, so everyone had said, Josh included. Until he'd taken his service revolver and ended whatever chances he'd had.

The psychiatrist had called it Delayed Stress Syndrome. Until then Ben hadn't known just how much he hated labels.

Roderick brought in the coffee and managed not to look annoyed at being delegated gofer.

"You bring in the Dors kids?" Harris asked him.

"I was on my way."

"Paris and Jackson'll brief you and Lowenstein and

Bigsby in the morning after roll call." He dismissed him with a nod as he dumped three teaspoons of sugar in his cup. Across the room Ed winced.

Tess accepted her cup with a murmur and never looked up. "Should I assume that the murderer has more than average strength?"

Ben took out a cigarette and studied it. "Why?"

Tess pushed her glasses down on her nose in a trick she remembered from a professor in college. It was meant to demoralize. "Other than the marks of strangulation, there weren't any bruises, any signs of violence, no torn clothing or signs of struggle."

Ignoring his coffee, Ben drew on the cigarette. "None of the victims were particularly hefty. Barbara Clayton was the biggest at five-four and a hundred and twenty."

"Terror and adrenaline bring on surges of strength," she countered. "Your assumption from the reports is that he takes them by surprise, from behind."

"We assume that from the angle and location of the bruises."

"I think I follow that," she said briskly, and pushed her glasses up again. It wasn't easy to demoralize a clod. "None of the victims was able to scratch his face or there'd have been cells of flesh under their nails. Have I got that right?" Before he could answer, she turned pointedly to Ed. "So, he's smart enough to want to avoid questionable marks. It doesn't appear he kills sporadically, but plans in an orderly, even logical fashion. Their clothing," she went on. "Was it disturbed, buttons undone, seams torn, shoes kicked off?"

Ed shook his head, admiring the way she dove into details. "No, ma'am. All three were neat as a pin."

"And the murder weapon, the amice?"

"Folded across the chest."

"A tidy psychotic," Ben put in.

Tess merely lifted a brow. "You're quick to diagnose, Detective Paris. But rather than *tidy,* I'd use the word *reverent.*"

By holding up a single finger, Harris stopped Ben's retort. "Could you explain that, Doctor?"

"I can't give you a thorough profile without some more study, Captain, but I think I can give you a general outline. The killer's obviously deeply religious, and I'd guess trained traditionally."

"So you're going for the priest angle?"

Again she turned to Ben. "The man may have been in a religious order at one time, or simply have a fascination, even a fear of the authority of the Church. His use of the amice is a symbol, to himself, to us, even to his victims. It might be used in a rebellious way, but I'd rule that out by the notes. Since all three victims were of the same age group, it tends to indicate that they represent some important female figure in his life. A mother, a wife, lover, sister. Someone who was or is intimate on an emotional level. My feeling is this figure failed him in some way, through the Church."

"A sin?" Ben blew out a stream of smoke.

He might've been a clod, she mused, but he wasn't stupid. "The definition of a sin varies," she said coolly. "But yes, a sin in his eyes, probably a sexual one."

He hated the calm, impersonal analysis. "So he's punishing her through other women?"

She heard the derision in his voice, and closed the folder. "No, he's saving them."

Ben opened his mouth again, then shut it. It made a horrible kind of sense.

"That's the one aspect I find absolutely clear," Tess said as she turned back to Harris. "It's in the notes, all of them. The man's put himself in the role of savior.

From the lack of violence, I'd say he has no wish to punish. If it were revenge, he'd be brutal, cruel, and he'd want them to be aware of what was going to happen to them. Instead, he kills them as quickly as possible, then tidies their clothes, crosses the amice in a gesture of reverence, and leaves a note stating that they're saved."

Taking off her glasses, she twirled them by the eyepiece. "He doesn't rape them. More than likely he's impotent with women, but more important, a sexual assault would be a sin. Possibly, probably, he derives some sort of sexual release from the killing, but more a spiritual one."

"A religious fanatic," Harris mused.

"Inwardly," Tess told him. "Outwardly he probably functions normally for long periods of times. The murders are spaced weeks apart, so it would appear he has a level of control. He could very well hold down a normal job, socialize, attend church."

"Church." Ben rose and paced to the window.

"Regularly, I'd think. It's his focal point. If this man isn't a priest, he takes on the aspects of one during the murders. In his mind, he's ministering."

"Absolution," Ben murmured. "The last rites."

Intrigued, Tess narrowed her eyes. "Exactly."

Not knowing much about the Church, Ed turned to another topic. "A schizophrenic?"

Tess frowned down at her glasses as she shook her head. "Schizophrenia, manic depression, split personality. Labels are too easily applied and tend to generalize."

She didn't notice that Ben turned back and stared at her. She pushed her glasses back in their case and dropped them in her purse. "Every psychiatric disorder is a highly individual problem, and each problem can only be understood and dealt with by uncovering its dynamic sources."

"I'd rather work with specifics myself," Harris told

her. "But there's a premium on them in this case. Are we dealing with a psychopath?"

Her expression changed subtly. Impatience, Ben thought, noting the slight line between her brows and a quick movement of her mouth. Then she was professional again. "If you want a general term, *psychopathy* will do. It means mental disorder."

Ed stroked his beard. "So he's insane."

"*Insanity* is a legal term, Detective." This was said almost primly as Tess picked up the folder and rose. "Once he's stopped and taken to trial, that'll become an issue. I'll have a profile for you as soon as possible, Captain. It might help if I could see the notes that were left on the bodies, and the murder weapons."

Dissatisfied, Harris rose. He wanted more. Though he knew better, he wanted A, B, and C, and the lines connecting each. "Detective Paris'll show you whatever you need to see. Thank you, Dr. Court."

She took his hand. "You've little to thank me for at this point. Detective Paris?"

"Right this way." With a cursory nod he led her out.

He said nothing as he took her through the corridors again and to the checkpoint where they signed in to examine the evidence. Tess was silent as well as she studied the notes and the neat, precise printing. They didn't vary, and were exact to the point that they seemed almost like photostats. The man who'd written them, she mused, hadn't been in a rage or in despair. If anything, he'd been at peace. It was peace he sought, and peace, in his twisted way, he sought to give.

"White for purity," she murmured after she'd looked at the amices. A symbol perhaps, she mused. But for whom? She turned away from the notes. More than the murder weapons, they chilled her. "It appears he's a man with a mission."

Ben remembered the sick frustration he'd felt after

each murder, but his voice was cool and flat. "You sound sure of yourself, Doctor."

"Do I?" Turning back, she gave him a brief survey, mulled things over, then went on impulse. "What time are you off duty, Detective?"

He tilted his head, not quite certain of his moves. "Ten minutes ago."

"Good." She pulled on her coat. "You can buy me a drink and tell me why you dislike my profession, or just me personally. I give you my word, no tabletop analysis."

Something about her challenged him. The cool, elegant looks, the strong, sophisticated voice. Maybe it was the big, soft eyes. He'd think about it later. "No fee?"

She laughed and stuck her hat in her pocket. "We might have hit the root of the problem."

"I need my coat." As they walked back to the squad room, each of them wondered why they were about to spend part of their evening with someone who so obviously disapproved of who and what they were. But then each of them was determined to come out on top before the evening was over. Ben grabbed his coat and scrawled something in a ledger.

"Charlie, tell Ed I'm engaged in further consultation with Dr. Court."

"You file that requisition?"

Ben shifted Tess almost like a shield and headed for the door. "File?"

"Damn it, Ben—"

"Tomorrow, in triplicate." He had himself and Tess out of earshot and nearly to the outer door.

"Don't care much for paperwork?" she said.

He pushed the door open and saw the rain had turned to a damp drizzle. "It's not the most rewarding part of the job."

"What is?"

He gave her an enigmatic look as he steered her toward his car. "Catching bad guys."

Oddly enough, she believed him.

Ten minutes later they walked into a dimly lit bar where the music came from a jukebox and the drinks weren't watered. It wasn't one of Washington's most distinguished night spots, nor one of its seamiest. It seemed to Tess a place where the regulars knew each other by name and newcomers were accepted gradually.

Ben sent the bartender a careless wave, exchanged a muffled word with one of the cocktail waitresses, and found a table in the back. Here the music was muted and the lights even dimmer. The table rocked a bit on one shortened leg.

The minute he sat down, he relaxed. This was his turf, and he knew his moves. "What'll you have?" He waited for her to ask for some pretty white wine with a French name.

"Scotch, straight up."

"Stolichnaya," he told the waitress as he continued to watch Tess. "Rocks." He waited until the silence stretched out, ten seconds, then twenty. An interesting silence, he thought, full of questions and veiled animosity. Maybe he'd throw her a curve. "You have incredible eyes."

She smiled, and leaned back comfortably. "I would have thought you'd come up with something more original."

"Ed liked your legs."

"I'm surprised he could see them from his height. He's not like you," she observed. "I imagine you make an impressive team. Leaving that aside, Detective Paris, I'm interested in why you distrust my profession."

"Why?"

When her drink was served, she sipped it slowly. It

warmed in places the coffee hadn't touched. "Curiosity. It comes with the territory. After all, we're both in the business of looking for answers, solving puzzles."

"You see our jobs as similar?" The thought made him grin. "Cops and shrinks."

"Perhaps I find your job as unpleasant as you find mine," she said mildly. "But they're both necessary as long as people don't behave in what society terms normal patterns."

"I don't like terms." He tipped back his drink. "I don't have much confidence in someone who sits behind a desk probing people's brains, then putting their personalities into slots."

"Well." She sipped her drink again and heard the music turn to something dreamy by Lionel Richie. "That's how you term psychiatrists?"

"Yeah."

She nodded. "I suppose you have to tolerate a great deal of bigotry in your profession as well."

Something dangerous flashed in his eyes, then it was gone, just as quickly. "Your point, Doctor."

She tapped a finger on the table, the only outward sign of emotion. He had an admirable capacity for stillness. She had already noticed that in Harris's office. Yet she sensed a restlessness in him. It was difficult not to appreciate the way he held it in check.

"All right, Detective Paris, why don't you make *your* point?"

After swirling his vodka, he set it down without drinking. "Okay. Maybe I see you as someone raking in bucks off frustrated housewives and bored executives. Everything harks back to sex or mother hating. You answer questions with questions and never raise a sweat. Fifty minutes goes by and you click over to the next file. When someone really needs help, when someone's desperate, it gets passed over. You label it, file it, and go on to the next hour."

For a moment she said nothing because under the anger, she heard grief. "It must've been a very bad experience," she murmured. "I'm sorry."

Uncomfortable, he shifted. "No tabletop analysis," he reminded her.

A very bad experience, she thought again. But he wasn't a man who wanted sympathy. "All right, let's try a different angle. You're a homicide detective. I guess all you do all day is two-wheel it down dark alleys with guns blazing. You dodge a few bullets in the morning, slap the cuffs on in the afternoon, then read the suspect his rights and haul him in for interrogation. Is that general enough for you?"

A reluctant smile touched his mouth. "Pretty clever, aren't you?"

"So I've been told."

It wasn't like him to make absolute judgments of someone he didn't know. His innate sense of fair play struggled with a long, ingrained prejudice. He signaled for another drink. "What's your first name. I'm tired of calling you Dr. Court."

"Yours is Ben." She gave him a smile that made him focus on her mouth again. "Teresa."

"No." He shook his head. "That's not what you're called. Teresa's too ordinary. Terry doesn't have enough class."

She leaned forward and dropped her chin on her folded hands. "You might be a good detective after all. It's Tess."

"Tess." He tried it out slowly, then nodded. "Very nice. Tell me, Tess, why psychiatry?"

She watched him a moment, admiring the easy way he sprawled in his seat. Not indolent, she thought, not sloppy, just relaxed. She envied that. "Curiosity," she said again. "The human mind is full of unanswered questions. I wanted to find the answers. If you can find the answers, you can help, sometimes. Heal the mind, ease the heart."

It touched him. The simplicity. "Ease the heart," he repeated, and thought of his brother. No one had been able to ease his. "You think if you heal one, you can ease the other?"

"It's the same thing." Tess looked beyond him to a couple who huddled laughing over a pitcher of beer.

"I thought all you got paid to do was look in heads."

Her lips curved a little, but her eyes still focused beyond him. "The mind, the heart, and the soul. 'Canst thou not minister to a mind diseased. Pluck from the memory a rooted sorrow. Raze out the written troubles of the brain, and with some sweet oblivious antidote cleanse the stuff'd bosom of that perilous stuff which weighs upon the heart.' "

He'd lifted his gaze from his drink as she'd spoken. Her voice remained quiet, but he'd stopped hearing the juke, the clatter, the laughter.

"*Macbeth.*" When she smiled at him, he shrugged. "Cops read too."

Tess lifted her glass in what might have been a toast. "Maybe we should both reevaluate."

IT was still drizzling when they turned back into the parking lot at headquarters. The gloom had brought the dark quickly, so that puddles shone beneath streetlights and the sidewalks were wet and deserted. Washington kept early hours. She'd waited until now to ask him what she'd wondered all evening.

"Ben, why did you become a cop?"

"I told you, I like catching bad guys."

The seed of truth was there, she thought, but not the whole. "So you grew up playing cops and robbers, and decided to keep right on playing?"

"I always played doctor." He pulled up beside her car and set the brake. "It was educational."

"I'm sure. Then why the switch to public service?"

He could've been glib, he could've evaded. Part of his charm for women was his ability to do both with an easy smile. Somehow, for once, he wanted to tell the simple truth. "All right, now I've a quote for you. 'The law is but words and paper without the hands and swords of men.' " With a half smile he turned to see her studying him calmly. "Words and paper aren't my way of handling things."

"And the sword is?"

"That's right." He leaned over to open her door. Their bodies brushed but neither acknowledged the physical tug. "I believe in justice, Tess. It's a hell of a lot more than words on paper."

She sat a moment, digesting. There was violence in him, ordered and controlled. Perhaps the word was *trained,* but it was violence nonetheless. He'd certainly killed, something her education and personality completely rejected. He'd taken lives, risked his own. And he believed in law and order and justice. Just as he believed in the sword.

He wasn't the simple man she'd first pegged him to be. It was a lot to learn in one evening. More than enough, she thought, and slid aside.

"Well, thanks for the drink, Detective."

As she pushed out of the car, Ben was out on the other side. "Don't you have an umbrella?"

She sent him an easy smile as she dug for her keys. "I never carry it when it rains."

Hands in his back pockets, he sauntered over to her. For reasons he couln't pinpoint, he was reluctant to let her go. "Wonder what a head doctor would make of that?"

"You don't have one either. Good night, Ben."

He knew she wasn't the shallow, overeducated sophisticate he'd labeled her. He found himself holding her door open after she'd slid into the driver's seat. "I've got this friend who works at the Kennedy Center. He passed me a couple of tickets for the Noel Coward play tomorrow night. Interested?"

It was on the tip of her tongue to refuse, politely. Oil and water didn't mix. Neither did business and pleasure. "Yes, I'm interested."

Because he wasn't sure how he felt about her agreement, he just nodded. "I'll pick you up at seven."

When he slammed her door shut, she rolled down the window. "Don't you want my address?"

He sent her a cocky smile she should've detested. "I'm a detective."

When he strolled back to his car, Tess found herself laughing.

❧

BY ten the rain had stopped. Absorbed in the profile she was compiling, Tess didn't notice the quiet, or the dull light from the moon. The take-out Chinese had slipped her mind, and her dinner of a roast beef sandwich was half eaten and forgotten.

Fascinating. She read over the reports again. Fascinating and chilling. How did he choose his victims? she wondered. All blond, all late twenties, all small to medium builds. Who did they symbolize to him, and why?

Did he watch them, follow them? Did he choose them arbitrarily? Maybe the hair color and build were simply coincidence. Any woman alone at night could end up being *saved*.

No. It was a pattern, she was sure of it. Somehow he selected each victim because of general physical appearance. Then he managed to peg her routine. Three killings, and he hadn't made one mistake. He was ill, but he was methodical.

Blond, late twenties, small to medium build. She found herself staring at her own vague reflection in the window. Hadn't she just described herself?

The knock at the door jolted her, then she cursed her foolishness. She checked her watch for the first time since she'd sat down, and saw she'd worked for three hours straight. Another two and she might have something to give Captain Harris. Whoever was at the door was going to have to make it quick.

Letting her glasses drop on the pile of papers, she went to answer. "Grandpa." Annoyance evaporated as she rose on her toes to kiss him with the gusto he'd helped instill in her life. He smelled of peppermint and Old Spice and carried himself like a general. "You're out late."

"Late?" His voice boomed. It always had. Off the walls of the kitchen where he fried up fresh fish, at a ball game where he cheered for whatever team suited his whim, on the floor of the Senate where he'd served for twenty-five years. "It's barely ten. I'm not ready for a lap robe and warm milk yet, little girl. Fix me a drink."

He was already in and shrugging his six-foot lineman's frame out of his coat. He was seventy-two, Tess thought as she glanced at the wild mane of white hair and leathered face. Seventy-two and he had more energy than the men she dated. And certainly more interest. Maybe the reason she was still single and content to be so was because she had such high standards in men. She poured him three fingers of scotch.

He looked over at the desk piled with papers and

folders and notes. That was his Tess, he thought as he took the glass from her. Always one to dig in her heels and get the job done. He didn't miss the half-eaten sandwich either. That was also his Tess. "So." He tossed back scotch. "What do you know about this maniac we've got on our hands?"

"Senator." Tess used her most professional voice as she sat on the arm of a chair. "You know I can't discuss this with you."

"Bullshit. I got you the job."

"For which I'm not going to thank you."

He gave her one of his steely looks. Veteran politicians had been known to cringe from it. "I'll get it from the mayor anyway."

Instead of cringing, Tess offered her sweetest smile. "From the mayor, then."

"Damn ethics," he muttered.

"You taught them to me."

He grunted, pleased with her. "What about Captain Harris? An opinion."

She sat a moment, brooding as she did when gathering her thoughts. "Competent, controlled. He's angry and frustrated and under a great deal of pressure, but he manages to keep it all on a leash."

"What about the detectives in charge of the case?"

"Paris and Jackson." She ran the tip of her tongue along her teeth. "They struck me as an unusual pair, yet very much a pair. Jackson looks like a mountain man. He asked typical questions, but he listens very well. He strikes me as the methodical type. Paris . . ." She hesitated, not as sure of her ground. "He's restless, and I think more volatile. Intelligent, but more instinctive than methodical. Or maybe more emotional." She thought of justice, and a sword.

"Are they competent?"

"I don't know how to judge that, Grandpa. If I went

on impression, I'd say they're dedicated. But even that's only an impression."

"The mayor has a great deal of faith in them." He downed the rest of his scotch. "And in you."

She focused on him again, eyes grave. "I don't know if it's warranted. This man's very disturbed, Grandpa. Dangerous. I may be able to give them a sketch of his mind, his emotional pattern, but that isn't going to stop him. Guessing games." Rising, she stuck her hands in her pockets. "It's all just a guessing game."

"It's always just a guessing game, Tess. You know there are no guarantees, no absolutes."

She knew, but she didn't like it. She never had. "He needs help, Grandpa. He's screaming for it, but no one can hear him."

He put a hand under his chin. "He's not your patient, Tess."

"No, but I'm involved." When she saw the frown crease his brow, she changed her tone. "Don't start worrying, I'm not going to go overboard."

"You told me that once about a box full of kittens. They ended up costing me more than a good suit."

She kissed his cheek again, then picked up his coat. "And you loved every one of them. Now I've got work to do."

"Kicking me out?"

"Just helping you with your coat," she corrected. "Good night, Grandpa."

"Behave yourself, little girl."

She closed the door on him, remembering he'd been telling her the same thing since she was five.

THE church was dark and empty, but it hadn't been difficult for him to deal with the lock. Nor did he feel he'd sinned in doing so. Churches weren't meant to be locked. God's house was meant to be open for the needy, for the troubled, for the reverent.

He lit the candles, four of them—one for each of the women he'd saved, and the last for the woman he hadn't been able to save.

Dropping to his knees, he prayed, and his prayers were desperate. Sometimes, only sometimes, when he thought of the mission, he doubted. A life was sacred. He'd taken three and knew the world looked on him as a monster. If those he worked with knew, they'd scorn him, put him in prison, detest him. Pity him.

But flesh was transient. A life was only sacred because of the soul. It was the soul he saved. The soul he must continue to save until he'd balanced the scales. Doubting, he knew, was a sin in itself.

If only he had someone to talk to. If only there were someone to understand, to give him comfort. A wave of despair washed over him, hot and thick. Giving in would have been a relief. There was no one, no one he could trust. No one to share this burden. When the Voice was silent, he was so alone.

He'd lost Laura. Laura had lost herself and taken pieces of him with her. The best pieces. Sometimes, when it was dark, when it was quiet, he could see her. She never laughed anymore. Her face was so pale, so full of pain. Lighting candles in empty churches would never wipe away the pain. Or the sin.

She was in the dark, waiting. When his mission was complete, only then would she be free.

The smell of votive candles burning, the hushed silence of church, and the silhouettes of statues soothed him. Here he might find hope and a place. He'd always found such comfort in the symbols of religion, and the boundaries.

Lowering his head to the rail, he prayed more

fervently. As he'd been taught, he prayed for the grace to accept whatever trials were ahead of him.

When he rose, the candlelight flickered over the white collar at his throat. He blew them out, and it was dark again.

Chapter 3

WASHINGTON TRAFFIC COULD tear at the nerves—especially when you'd woken up sluggish, primed yourself with coffee, then handled back-to-back appointments. Tess inched along behind a Pinto with a faulty exhaust, and simmered through another red light. Beside her a man in a big blue GMC revved his engine. It disappointed him when she didn't bother to glance over.

She was worried about Joey Higgins. Two months of therapy and she wasn't any closer to the real problem, or more accurately, the real answer. A fourteen-year-old boy shouldn't be clinically depressed, but out playing third base. Today she'd felt he'd been on the verge of really opening up to her. On the verge, Tess thought with a sigh. But he hadn't yet crossed the line. Building his confidence, his self-esteem, was like building the pyramids. Step by agonizing step. If she could just get to the point where she had his full trust . . .

She fought her way across town while concern for a sullen young boy with bitterness in his eyes weighed on her. There were so many other things. Too many other things.

Tess knew she didn't have to sacrifice her lunch hour and hand deliver the profile to Captain Harris. She had been under no obligation to work on it until two A.M. either, but found it impossible not to.

Something pushed at her—instinct, hunch, superstition, she couldn't have said which. All she knew was that she was involved with the faceless killer as deeply as with any of her patients. The police needed whatever assistance she could give to help them understand him, and needed to understand him in order to catch him. He had to be caught so he could be helped.

As she pulled into the station's lot she took a quick scan. No Mustang. But then, she reminded herself as she stepped out of her car, that wasn't why she'd come. Then again, she wasn't sure why she'd agreed to go out with Ben Paris, since she considered him arrogant and difficult, and her workload was jamming up with the extra time she was taking on the homicides. She knew if she put in a couple of hours that evening, she could have things running fairly smoothly again. Several times that day she had thought about phoning him and begging off.

What's more, dating wasn't something Tess approached with much enthusiasm. The singles' scene was a tough, nasty circle that usually left everyone involved frustrated or frazzled. She was automatically put off by the slick here-I-am, aren't-you-lucky type. Frank. Nor did she have any illusions about the fanatically casual, let's-not-talk-commitment sort. Like the public defender she'd seen occasionally last spring.

It wasn't that men didn't interest her, it was simply that most of the men she'd met couldn't hold her interest. When your expectations were high, disappointment came easily. All in all it was easier to stay home with an old movie or a fat briefcase.

But she wasn't going to beg off. Tess told herself it

would be rude to break a date on such short notice—even a date she knew had been made on impulse by both parties. She'd go, enjoy the play, then say good night. She'd work over the weekend.

When she walked into Homicide she took a quick look at who was sitting at a desk, who was walking from place to place. Someone had his head stuck in a small, scarred refrigerator, but when he straightened, he was a stranger.

Ben wasn't there, but she saw a variety of styles in the cops who were. Suits and ties, jeans and sweaters, boots and sneakers. The one thing that seemed universal was the shoulder holster. It seemed to her to fall far short of the glamor of the sword.

A glance at Harris's office showed her it was empty.

"Dr. Court?"

She stopped and looked over at a man just rising from a typewriter. "Yes."

"I'm Detective Roderick. If you're looking for Captain Harris, he's in a meeting with the chief."

"I see." He was the suit-and-tie sort, she observed. Though his jacket was slung over the back of his chair, his tie was neat and straight. She decided Ben would never wear one. "Is he expected back?"

"Yes. If you'd like to wait, he shouldn't be too much longer." He grinned, remembering the day before. "I can get you some coffee."

"Ah . . ." She looked at her watch. Her next patient was due in forty minutes. It would take her half of that to get back to her office. "No, thanks. I don't have much time myself. I have a report for the captain."

"The profile. You can give it to me." When he saw her hesitation, he went on, "I'm assigned to the case, Dr. Court."

"Sorry. I'd appreciate it if you could see Captain Harris gets this as soon as he comes in." Unzipping her briefcase, Tess drew out the file. "If he has any questions, he can reach me in my office until five, then at home until seven. I don't suppose you can tell me if there's been any progress?"

"I wish I could. At this point we're going back over the same ground, hoping we missed something the first half-a-dozen times."

Tess glanced at the file and wondered if he could really understand the man she'd written about. Could anyone? Dissatisfied, she nodded and handed over the file. It looked harmless, but so did a bomb at rest. "Thank you."

A lady, he thought. You began to miss seeing the real thing in this line of work. "Sure. You have a message for the captain?"

"No. Everything's in the file. Thanks again, Detective."

Lowenstein waited until Tess was out of earshot. "That the psychiatrist?"

Roderick ran the folder through his fingers before he set it on his desk. "Yeah. Brought in the profile for Harris."

"Looks like *Harper's Bazaar,*" Lowenstein murmured. "Classy, though I heard she left with Paris last night." With a chuckle she gave Roderick a pat on the arm. "She raise your blood pressure, Lou?"

Embarrassed, he shrugged. "I was thinking of something else."

Lowenstein stuck her tongue in her cheek. "Sure. Well, I hope she knows her stuff. Better than a Ouija board, I guess." She flung her bag over her shoulder. "Bigsby and I are going to interview some of the regulars at Doug's. Keep the home fires burning."

"Bring back a lead, Maggie." Roderick dropped back in his chair. "Or we might just have to haul out the Ouija board."

Tess had turned the second corner when she heard someone cursing. When she looked back, she saw Ben giving a vending machine a hefty kick.

"Sonofabitch."

"Ben." Ed put a hand on his shoulder. "That's stuff's poison to your system. Forget it. Your body'll thank you."

"I've got fifty cents in there." Putting his hands on either side of the machine, Ben shook it and swore again. "Fifty fucking cents is robbery in the first place for a skinny piece of chocolate and a few nuts."

"You oughta try raisins," Ed suggested. "Natural sugar. Full of iron."

Ben gritted his teeth. "I hate raisins, nothing but dried grapes."

"Detective Paris." Unable to resist, Tess had backtracked down the corridor. "Do you always have fights with inanimate objects?"

He turned his head but didn't loosen his grip on the machine. "When they hassle me." He gave the machine another violent shake, but he looked at her.

She wasn't wet today, he noticed. And she'd pinned her hair up and back in a cool, sleek style that made him think of elegant pastries under crystal. Maybe she thought it was professional, but it made his mouth water.

"You look good, Doc."

"Thank you. Hello, Detective Jackson."

"Ma'am." He put a hand back on Ben's shoulder. "I can't tell you how embarrassed I am for my partner."

"That's perfectly all right. I'm used to behavioral problems."

"Shit." Ben gave the machine one last shove, then turned away from it. The first chance he got he was going to pick the lock. "Were you looking for me?"

Tess thought of her scan of the parking lot, then the squad room. She decided on tact rather than truth. "No, I brought in the profile for Captain Harris."

"You work fast."

"If I'd had more to work with, it would've taken longer." With a movement of her shoulders, she expressed both acceptance and dissatisfaction. "I don't know how much help I've been. I'd like to do more."

"Our job," Ben reminded her.

"Hi, guys." Lowenstein passed by and stuck change in the vending machine. In fact she wanted a closer look at the psychiatrist more than she wanted candy. She would have bet a week's pay the rose-colored suit was silk.

"That sucker's defective," Ben told her, but when she pulled the handle, two candy bars dropped into the tray.

"Two for one," Lowenstein said, plopping both in her bag. "See you later."

"Wait a minute—"

"You don't want to make a scene in front of Dr. Court," Ed reminded him.

"Lowenstein's got my property."

"You're better off. Sugar'll kill you."

"This is all fascinating," Tess said dryly as she watched Ben glare at Lowenstein's back. "But I'm pressed for time. I want you to know that I had a suggestion. It's included in my report to the captain."

Ben stuck his hands in his pockets and looked back at her. "Which is?"

"You need a priest."

"We've gone that route, Doctor. Ed and I've interviewed a dozen of them."

"With experience in psychiatry," Tess finished. "I've given you what I can, but I'm not qualified to probe deeply into the religious angle. And that, in my judgment, is the key." Her glance skimmed over Ed, but she knew whose opinion she had to sway. "I could research Catholicism, but it would take time. I don't think any of us wants to waste that. I know of a doctor at Catholic University, Monsignor Logan. He has an excellent reputation in the Church and in psychiatric medicine. I want to consult with him."

"The more people we consult with," Ben put in, "the more chance there is of a leak. We can't let the specifics get to the press."

"And if you don't try something else, your investigation's going to stay right where it is. Stagnant." She saw the annoyance and rolled over it. "I could go to the mayor, put on the pressure, but that's not the way I want to handle it. I want you to back me on this, Ben."

He rocked back on his heels. Another shrink, he thought. And a priest at that. But as much as he hated to admit it, the investigation was stagnant. If she wanted to pull a rabbit out of her hat, they might as well look it over. "I'll talk to the captain."

The smile came easily after victory. "Thanks." She pulled out her wallet and dropped change into the machine behind him. After brief consideration, she pulled a handle. With a quiet plop a Hershey bar dropped into the tray. "Here you go." Solemn-eyed, she handed it to Ben. "You really broke my heart. Nice to see you again, Detective Jackson."

"My pleasure, ma'am." A grin split his face as he watched her walk away. "Handles herself real well, doesn't she?"

Scowling, Ben tossed the candy bar from hand to hand. "Oh, yeah," he murmured. "Like a pro."

❧

IT wasn't like her to fuss about clothes. The truth was, her wardrobe had been meticulously chosen, down to the last cashmere sweater and linen blazer, for the specific reason that Tess didn't have the patience to debate each morning about what to wear. For the most part she stuck with classic styles and blendable colors because they looked best on her and it made it simple to put her hand in her closet and draw out the next thing in line on harried mornings.

But she wasn't dressing for the office. As Tess shoved the third dress back on the hanger, she reminded herself she wasn't dressing for Prince Charming either. At twenty-nine she knew there were no princes, nor did a rational woman want an ivory tower. An uncomplicated date with an attractive man who made you think on your feet was a different matter, and Ben Paris certainly made her think.

A glance at her watch warned her she was doing so much thinking she was going to be late. Standing in a brief flesh-colored teddy, she took out a black silk dress and gave it a critical study. Simple but elegant. A wise choice, she decided, and she didn't have time to fool around anymore. She slipped it on and did up the range of buttons that ran from waist to neck.

Another long survey in the cheval glass brought a nod of approval. Yes, she thought, this was better than the ice blue she'd started with or the raspberry georgette she'd just rejected. She settled on her mother's diamond studs and the thin gold bracelet her grandfather had given her when she'd earned her degree. She debated about sweeping her hair up, but the knock on the door decided for her. It had to stay down.

She hadn't expected he could look elegant. But when she opened the door, his steel-gray suit and salmon-colored shirt proved her wrong. Still, she'd been right about the tie. His collar was open. She started to smile at him, then saw the clutch of violets in his hand. It wasn't like her to be tossed so off balance, but when she looked back up at him, she felt like a teenager with her first handful of wilted flowers.

"Peace offering," Ben told her, feeling every bit as

unsettled and out of character as Tess. He shouldn't have been, he told himself, since he was used to making grandiose or impulsive gestures with the women he dated. It was his way. Tracking down a nosegay of violets in October hadn't seemed a foolish thing to do until he'd stood there, offering them.

"They're lovely. Thank you." Regaining her balance, she smiled at him, accepting the flowers as she stood back to let him in. The scent reminded her of the spring that was so far on the other side of winter. "I'll get a vase."

As she walked into the kitchen, Ben looked around. He saw the Matisse print, the Turkish rugs, the neat petit point pillows. Soft, pretty colors, and old distinguished wood. It was a room that spoke of quiet, generational wealth.

What the hell are you doing here? he asked himself. Her grandfather's a senator. Yours was a butcher. She grew up with servants, and your mother still scrubs her own john. She graduated with honors from Smith, and you crammed your way through two years of college before the Academy.

Oh, he'd researched her all right. That was also his way. And he was dead sure they'd run out of conversation after fifteen minutes.

When she came back in, she carried the violets in a small Wedgwood vase. "I'll offer you a drink, but I don't have any Stolichnaya."

"It's all right." He made the decision without weighing pros and cons. He'd learned to trust his instincts. While she set the violets in the center of a table, he walked to her and took her hair in his hand.

She turned slowly, no jerking, no surprise, and met the long silent look with one of her own.

She smelled of Paris. He remembered the five days he'd spent there in his twenties, going on a shoestring and optimism. He'd fallen in love with it—the look, the smells, the air. Every year he promised himself he'd go back and find whatever it was he'd been looking for.

"I like it better down," he said at length, and let his fingers linger a moment longer. "When you had it up this afternoon, you looked remote, inaccessible."

Tension snapped into her, the ripe man-woman tension she hadn't felt with anyone in years—hadn't wanted to. She still didn't want to. "Professional," she corrected, and took an easy step back. "Would you like that drink?"

He thought about making a long, thin slice through her control. What would it be like? But if he did, he might find his aim off and slice his own. "We'll get one at the theater. There's enough time before the curtain."

"I'll get my coat."

HE seemed as familiar with the staff at the Roof Terrace as he'd been with those in the smoky little bar the night before. Tess watched the way he spoke to this one, greeted that one, the ease, the casual intimacy. So he wasn't a loner, she concluded, except when he chose to be.

She admired someone who could be at ease with people, without worrying about impressions, opinions. To be that way you first had to be at ease with yourself. Somehow, as content as she was with her life-style, she'd never quite gotten there.

Ben picked up his glass, stretched out his legs, and stared back at her. "Got me figured out yet?"

"Not completely." She picked up an almond from the bowl on the table and chewed it thoughtfully. "But I think you do. If more people understood themselves the way you do, I'd have to look for a different line of work."

"And you're very good at what you do." He watched her choose another almond with long, slim fingers. An antique pearl gleamed dully on her right hand. "Class valedictorian," he began, and watched her hand stop. "A private practice that's growing too fast for you to keep up with it. You just turned down an offer to join the psychiatric staff at Bethesda Naval, but you work once a week in the Donnerly Clinic in South East for no fee."

His mild rundown annoyed her. Tess was accustomed to knowing more about the people she associated with than they knew of her. "Do you always do background checks on a date, Detective?"

"Habit," he said easily. "You spoke about curiosity yourself last night. Senator Jonathan Writemore's your maternal grandfather, a little left of center, outspoken, charismatic, and tough as nails."

"He'll be pleased you said so."

"You lost your parents when you were fourteen. I'm sorry." He lifted his drink again. "It's always hard to lose family."

She caught the tone, the empathy that told her he'd lost someone too. "My grandfather made a difference. I may not have recovered without him. How did you find out so much?"

"Cops don't reveal a source. I read your profile."

She stiffened a bit, expecting criticism. "And?"

"You feel our man's intelligent."

"Yes. Cunning. He leaves what he chooses behind, but no trail."

After a moment Ben nodded. "What you said made sense. I'm interested in how you came to the conclusions."

Tess took a sip of her drink before answering. She wouldn't ask herself why it was important she make him understand. It simply was. "I take facts, the pattern he leaves behind. You can see it's almost identical each time, he doesn't vary. I suppose in your business you call it an M.O."

He smiled a little as he nodded. "Yeah."

"The pattern forms a picture, a psychological picture. You're trained to look for clues, evidence, motives, and apprehend. I'm trained to look for reasons, causes, then to treat. To treat, Ben," she repeated, meeting his eyes. "Not to judge."

He lifted a brow. "And you think that's what I'm doing?"

"You want him," she said simply.

"Yeah, I want him. Off the streets and in a cage."

He crushed out a cigarette, slowly, methodically. It was a measure of control. But his hands were strong.

"You want him punished. I understand that, even if I don't agree."

"You'd rather open his head and make him all better. Christ." He tossed back his drink. "You don't want to let your heart bleed over a man like this."

"Compassion's part of my business," she said tightly. "He's ill, desperately ill. If you read my profile, and understood it, you'd know what he does, he does in pain."

"He strangles women. If it hurts him to tie a knot around their necks, it doesn't make them any less dead. I've got compassion, Tess, for the families of those women I've had to talk to. I have to look at their faces when they ask me why. I don't have an answer."

"I'm sorry." She reached for his hand without thinking. Her fingers closed over his. "It's a hideous job. One that wakes you up at night. I've had to talk to families—the ones left stunned and bitter after a suicide." She felt his hand tense, and soothed automatically. "When you lie awake at three A.M., you still see the questions in their eyes, and the grief. Ben . . ." She leaned toward him, needing to draw him closer. "I have to think like a doctor on this. I could give you clinical terms—impulse disorder, functional psychoses. Whatever label we use, it equals illness. This man isn't killing for revenge or for profit, but in despair."

"And I have to think like a cop. It's my job to stop him. That's the bottom line." He was silent a moment, then pushed his drink aside. "We talked about your Monsignor Logan. Harris is checking it out."

"That's good. Thank you."

"Don't. I haven't a lot of faith in the idea."

She drew back with a little sigh. "We don't have any common ground, do we?"

"Maybe not." But he remembered how small and warm her hand had been on his. "Maybe we just haven't found it yet."

"What do you like to do on a Saturday afternoon?" she asked abruptly.

"Sit down with a beer and watch the ball game."

She wrinkled her nose. "That won't work. What about music?"

He grinned. "What about it?"

"What do you like?"

"Depends. I like rock when I'm driving, jazz when I'm drinking, and Mozart on Sunday mornings."

"We're getting closer. How about Jelly Roll Morton?"

Surprised, he grinned again. "Yeah."

"And Springsteen?"

"He caught me with *The River*."

"Marvin Gaye?"

Ben sat back and took another long look. "Maybe we've got a start." His leg brushed hers under the table. "Wanna go back to my place and listen to my record collection?"

"Detective Paris . . ." Tess chose one last almond. "Trained psychiatrists don't fall for shopworn lines."

"How about fresh ones?"

"Such as?"

"Have a late supper with me after the theater and we'll see who can remember more old Beatle lyrics."

She flashed him a grin, quick, impulsive, and totally unlike the careful smiles she'd given him before. "You'll lose, and you're on."

"Do you know a guy with two thousand dollars worth of caps on his teeth and a Brooks Brothers suit?"

Her brows drew together. "Is this a quiz?"

"Too late, he's coming over."

"Who . . . oh, hello, Frank."

"Tess, didn't expect to see you here." He patted the hand of the pencil-slim, exotic woman at his side. "Lorraine, this is Dr. Teresa Court, an associate of mine."

Obviously bored, and earning Tess's sympathy, the woman held out a hand. "So happy to meet you." Her gaze slid easily over Tess and latched on to Ben. "Hello."

His smile was slow, and though his eyes never left her face, he took in every detail. "Hello, I'm Ben."

"Tess, you should've told me you were coming. We'd have made a party of it," Frank said.

Lorraine tilted her head as she looked at Ben. Maybe the night could be salvaged after all, she thought. "There's always after the play," Lorraine said.

"There certainly is," Ben murmured, and earned a swift kick from Tess under the table. His smile never wavered. "But Tess and I have to make an early night of it. Business."

"Sorry, Frank, we'll have to do it another time." Knowing escape was always in doubt, Tess was already up. "See you around the office. Bye, Lorraine."

"Here's your hat, what's your hurry?" Ben mumbled as he followed her out.

"If you knew what I knew, you'd thank me."

"Your, ah, colleague has better taste in women than he does in ties."

"Really?" Tess made a business of brushing her coat smooth as they walked. "I thought she was rather obvious."

"Yeah." Ben cast a look over his shoulder. "Uh-huh. Obvious."

"Some men like cleavage and mink eyelashes, I suppose."

"Some men are animals."

"She was his second choice," Tess heard herself saying. "I turned him down first."

"Is that so?" Intrigued, Ben slowed her down by swinging an arm over her shoulders. "He asked you to the Coward thing and you turned him down?"

"That's right."

"I'm flattered."

She shot him a look. His ego didn't need any help from her. "I only said yes to you because you're not perfect."

"Hmm. When did he ask you?"

"Yesterday afternoon."

"It didn't seem to put his nose out of joint that you turned him down and were here with me."

Uncomfortable, Tess shifted under his arm. "I told him I had a date."

"Oh. You lied."

He said it with such pleasure, she laughed. "I'm not perfect either."

"That makes things easier."

❧

THE early night Ben had spoken of ended at two A.M., when they walked down the corridor to Tess's apartment.

"I'm going to hate myself in the morning," Tess said over a yawn.

"I haven't even asked you to go to bed yet."

The yawn ended on a muffled laugh. "I was thinking about drinking a half bottle of wine and five hours' sleep." She stopped at her door and turned to lean against it. "I didn't expect to have such a good time."

Neither had he. "Why don't we try it again? Maybe we won't."

She thought about it for three full seconds. "All right, when?"

"There's a Bogart festival tomorrow night across town."

"*The Maltese Falcon?*"

"And *The Big Sleep.*"

She smiled, comfortably sleepy. "Okay." When he stepped closer, she waited for him to kiss her. If the idea warmed her, she thought it only natural. The desire to be held and touched was a human one. Her eyes half closed and her heart beat just a little faster.

"You've got to replace this Mickey Mouse lock."

Her lashes fluttered up again. "What?"

"Your door lock, Tess, is a joke." He traced a finger down her nose, pleased to see confusion. "If you're going to live in a building without security, you'd better make sure you've got a dead bolt on your door."

"Dead bolt." With a half laugh she straightened and reached for her keys. "I can't argue with a cop."

"Glad to hear it." He put his hands over hers and kissed her before she'd prepared herself again. Later, when she could think straight, she'd wonder if he'd planned it that way.

It was silly to believe that a kiss as gentle, as easy as this one could send shock waves through the body. Blood didn't really heat and the mind didn't really swim.

She knew better, but felt it anyway. Touching nothing but her hands, he took her under.

His mouth was clever, but she'd suspected as much. His lips were warm, soft, and he used his teeth to add a nip of excitement. They scraped over her lip before his tongue slid over hers. She told herself it was the late hour, the wine, the relaxation, but she gave herself to the moment without any of the caution she was prone to.

She was supposed to be cool, a little aloof. He'd expected it. He hadn't expected the heat, the passion, or the sweetness that poured from her into him. He hadn't expected the immediate intimacy of longtime lovers. He knew women well—or thought he did. Tess was a mystery to him that demanded solving.

Desire was familiar to him, something else he'd thought he understood well. But he couldn't remember ever having it ram into him and take his breath away. He wanted her now, instantly, desperately. Ordinarily he'd have followed through. It was natural. For reasons he couldn't begin to understand, he backed away from her.

For a moment they just stared at each other.

"This could be a problem," he managed to say after a few seconds.

"Yeah." She swallowed and concentrated on the cool metal of the keys in her hand.

"Put on the security chain, okay? I'll see you tomorrow."

She missed the keyhole by a quarter inch on the first try and swore as she stuck it in on the second. "Good night, Ben."

"Good night."

He waited until he heard the click of the lock and the rattle of chain before he turned and walked down the hall. A problem, he thought again. One hell of a problem.

HE'D been walking for hours. When he let himself into his apartment he was almost too tired to stand. In the past few months he found he slept dreamlessly only if he exhausted himself first.

It wasn't necessary to turn on a light; he knew the way. Ignoring the need to rest, he went past his bedroom. Sleep would come only after he'd completed this last duty. The room beyond was always locked. When he opened it he drew in the faint, feminine scent of the fresh flowers he put there daily. The priest's robe hung by the closet door. Draped over it, the amice was a slash of white.

Striking a match, he lit the first candle, then another and another, until the shadows waved on the pristine surface of the altar cloth.

There was a picture there in a silver frame of a young woman, blond and smiling. Forever she'd been captured, young, innocent, and happy. Pink roses had been her favorite, and it was their scent that mixed with the burning candles.

In smaller frames were the carefully clipped newspaper prints of three other women. Carla Johnson, Barbara Clayton, Francie Bowers. Folding his hands, he knelt before them.

There were so many others, he thought. So many. He'd only just begun.

Chapter 4

THE BOY SAT across from Tess, quiet and sullen. He didn't fidget or look out of the window. He rarely did. Instead, he sat in the chair and looked down at his own knees. His hands lay spread on his thighs, the fingers slender, the knuckles a bit enlarged from nervous cracking. The nails were bitten down below the quick. Signs of nerves, yet people often go through life well enough while cracking and snapping and chewing on themselves.

It was rare for him to look at the person he was speaking with, or more accurately in his case, the person speaking to him. Every time she managed to get him to make eye contact, she felt both a small victory and a small pang. There was so little she could see in his eyes, for he'd learned at a young age how to shield and conceal. What she did see—when she was given even that rare, quick chance to look—was not resentment, not fear, only a trace of boredom.

Life had not played fair with Joseph Higgins, Jr., and he wasn't taking any chances on being slipped another shot below the belt. At his age, when adults called the plays, he chose isolation and noncommunication as defense against a lack of choice. Tess knew the symptoms. Lack of outward emotion, lack of motivation, lack of interest. A lack.

Somehow, some way, she had to find the trigger that would push him back to caring first about himself, then the world around him.

He was too old for her to play games with, too young for her to meet on the level of adult to adult. She had tried both, and he'd accepted neither. Joey Higgins had placed himself firmly in an in-between space. Adolescence wasn't simply awkward for him, it was miserable.

He was wearing jeans, good, solid jeans, with the button fly raved about in the slick commercials, and a gray sweatshirt with the Maryland terrapin grinning across his chest. His leather high-top Nike's were trendy and new. Light brown hair was cut into moderate spikes around a too thin face. Outwardly he looked like an average fourteen-year-old boy. All the trappings were there. Inside he was a maze of confusion, self-hate, and bitterness that Tess knew she hadn't even begun to touch.

It was unfortunate that instead of being a confidante, a wailing wall, or even a blank sheet of paper to him, she was only one more authority figure in his life. If just once he'd broken out and shouted or argued with her, she would have felt the sessions were progressing. Through them all, he remained polite and unresponsive.

"How are you feeling about school, Joey?"

He didn't shrug. It was as if even that movement might give away some of the feelings he kept locked so tightly inside. "Okay."

"Okay? I'd guess it's always kind of tough to switch schools." She'd fought against that, done everything in her power to persuade his parents not to make such a dramatic move at this point in his therapy. Bad companions, they had said. They were going to get him away from the people influencing him, those who'd drawn him toward alcohol, a brief flirtation with drugs, and an equally quick but more uneasy courtship with the occult. His parents had only succeeded in alienating him, and hacking away a little more at his self-esteem.

It hadn't been companions, bad or otherwise, who had taken Joey on any of those journeys. It was his own spiraling depression and search for an answer, one he might believe was completely and uniquely his own.

Because they no longer found joints in his dresser drawers or smelled liquor on his breath, his parents were confident he was beginning to recover. They couldn't see, or wouldn't, that he was still spiraling down quickly. He'd simply learned how to internalize it.

"New schools can be an adventure," Tess went on when she received no response. "But it's tough being the new kid."

"It's no big deal," he murmured, and continued to look at his knees.

"I'm glad to hear that," she said, though she knew it was a lie. "I had to switch schools when I was about your age and I was scared to death."

He glanced up then, not believing, but interested. He had dark brown eyes that should have been eloquently expressive. Instead they were guarded and wary. "Nothing to be scared of, it's just a school."

"Why don't you tell me about it?"

"It's just a school."

"How about the other kids? Anyone interesting?"

"They're mostly jerks."

"Oh? How's that?"

"They sort of stand around together. There's nobody I want to know."

No one he did know, Tess corrected. The last thing

he'd needed at this point was to feel rejected by the school after losing the classmates he'd been used to. "It takes time to make friends, friends who count. It's harder to be alone, Joey, than it is to try to find them."

"I didn't want to transfer."

"I know." She was with him there. Someone had to be. "And I know it's hard to feel as though you can be yanked around whenever the people who make the rules feel like changing them. It's not all that way, Joey. Your parents chose the school because they wanted the best for you."

"You didn't want them to pull me out." He glanced up again, but so quickly, she hardly caught the color of his eyes. "I heard Mom talking."

"As your doctor I felt you might be more comfortable in your old school. Your mother loves you, Joey. Transferring you wasn't a punishment, but her way of trying to make things better for you."

"She didn't want me to be with my friends." But it wasn't said with bitterness, simply flat acceptance. No choice.

"How do you feel about that?"

"She was afraid if I was around them, I'd start drinking again. I'm not drinking." It was said not resentfully, again not bitterly, but wearily.

"I know," Tess said, and laid a hand on his arm. "You can be proud of yourself for pulling out, for making the right choice. I know how hard you have to work every day not to."

"Mom's always blaming things that happen on somebody else."

"What things?"

"Just things."

"Like the divorce?" As usual, a mention of it brought no response at all. Tess backtracked. "How do you feel about not riding the bus anymore?"

"Buses stink."

"Your mother's taking you to school now."

"Yeah."

"Have you talked to your father?"

"He's busy." He looked at Tess with a touch of resentment mixed with a plea. "He's got a new job with this computer place, but I'm going to be spending the weekend with him probably next month. For Thanksgiving."

"How do you feel about that?"

"It's going to be good." The little boy was there briefly, shining with hope. "We're going to go to the Redskins game. He's going to get tickets on the fifty-yard line. It's going to be like it used to be."

"Like it used to be, Joey?"

He looked down at his knees again, but his brows had drawn together in anger.

"It's important to understand that things won't be like they used to. Different doesn't have to be bad. Sometimes change, even when it's hard, can be the best for everyone. I know you love your father. You don't have to stop because you're not living with him."

"He doesn't have a house anymore. Just a room. He said if he didn't have to pay child support, he could have a house."

She could have damned Joseph Higgins, Sr., to hell, but kept her voice firm and soft. "You understand that your father has a problem, Joey. You are not the problem. Alcohol is."

"We have a house," he muttered.

"If you didn't, do you think your father would be happier?"

No response. He was staring at his shoes now.

"I'm glad you're going to spend some time with your father. I know you've missed him."

"He's been busy."

"Yes." Too busy to see his son, too busy to return the

calls of the psychiatrist who was trying to heal the hurts. "Sometimes adults can get pretty wrapped up in their lives. You must know how difficult things are for your father now, in a new job, because you're in a new school."

"I'm going to spend a weekend with him next month. Mom says not to depend on it, but I'm going to."

"Your mother doesn't want you to be disappointed if something comes up."

"He's going to come get me."

"I hope so, Joey. But if he doesn't . . . Joey . . ." She touched his arm again and through sheer force of will drew his gaze to hers. "If he doesn't, you have to know that it isn't because of you, but because of his illness."

"Yeah."

He agreed because agreeing was the quickest way to avoid a hassle. Tess knew it, and wished not for the first time that she could convince his parents he needed more intensive therapy.

"Did your mother bring you today?"

He continued to look down, but the anger, at least outwardly, was gone. "My stepfather."

"Are you still getting along with him?"

"He's okay."

"You know, caring for him doesn't mean you care less for your father."

"I said he's okay."

"Any pretty girls at your new school?" She wanted a smile from him, any size, any kind.

"I guess."

"Guess?" Maybe it was the smile in Tess's voice that had him looking up again. "You look like you have good eyes to me."

"Maybe there's a couple." And his lips did curve a little. "I don't pay much attention."

"Well, there's time for that. Will you come back and see me next week?"

"I guess."

"Will you do me a favor in the meantime? I said you had good eyes. Look at your mother and your stepfather." He turned his head, but she took his hand and held it. "Joey . . ." She waited until those dark, unreadable eyes were on hers again. "Look at them. They're trying to help. They may make mistakes, but they're trying because they care about you. A lot of people do. You still have my number, don't you?"

"Yeah, I guess I do."

"You know you can call me if you want to talk before next week."

She walked to the door of her office with him and watched as his stepfather rose and gave Joey a big, bluff smile. He was a businessman, successful, easygoing, and well mannered. He was the antithesis of Joey's father. "All done, huh?" He glanced at Tess, and there was no smile, only tension in his expression. "How'd we do today, Dr. Court?"

"Just fine, Mr. Monroe."

"That's good, that's good. Why don't we pick up some Chinese, Joey, surprise your mom."

"Okay." He bundled into his school jacket, the school he no longer attended. Leaving it unsnapped, he turned back and looked at a point beyond Tess's right shoulder. "Bye, Dr. Court."

"Good-bye, Joey, I'll see you next week."

They were feeding him, she thought as she shut her office door. And he was starving. They were clothing him, but he was still cold. She had the key, but she had yet to be able to turn it so that it opened the lock.

With a sigh, she walked back to her desk. "Dr. Court?" Tess answered her intercom as she slipped the Joey Higgins file into the briefcase beside her desk.

"Yes, Kate."

"You had three calls while you were in session. One from the *Post*, one from the *Sun*, and one from WTTG."

"Three reporters?" Tess slipped her earring off to gently rub her lobe.

"All three wanted confirmation of your assignment to the Priest homicides."

"Damn." She dropped the earring on her blotter. "Not available for comment, Kate."

"Yes, ma'am."

Slowly, she fastened the earring again. She'd been promised anonymity. That had been part of her deal with the mayor's office. No media, no hype, no comment. The mayor had given her his personal guarantee that she would be able to work without pressure from the press. No use blaming the mayor, Tess reminded herself as she rose to pace to the window. It had leaked, and she would have to deal with it.

She didn't care for notoriety. That was her problem. She liked her life simple and private. That, too, was her problem. Common sense had told her the whole business would come out before it was over, but she'd still taken the job. If she'd been advising one of her patients, she would have told him to face the reality and deal with it one step at a time.

Outside, rush hour traffic was starting to heat up. A few horns blasted, but the sound was muffled by the window and distance. Joey Higgins was out there, riding for Chinese takeout with the stepfather he refused to allow himself to trust or love. Bars were ready to serve the let's-have-a-quick-one-before-dinner crowd. Day care centers were emptying, and throngs of working mothers, single parents, and frazzled daddies were packing up preschoolers and threading their Volvos and BMW's through packs of other Volvos and BMW's with one thought in mind: to get home, to be safe and warm behind the doors and windows and walls of the familiar. It was unlikely that any one of them gave any real thought to someone else who was out there. Someone with a small, deadly bomb ticking away inside his head.

For a moment she wished she could join them in that easy nightly routine, thinking only about a warm supper or the dentist bill. But the Priest file was already in her briefcase.

Tess went back and picked up her briefcase. The first step was to go home and make sure all her calls were screened by her answering service.

"WHO leaked it?" Ben demanded, and blew out a stream of smoke.

"We're still working on it." Harris stood behind his desk, studying the officers assigned to the task force. Ed slouched in a chair, passing a bag of sunflower seeds from hand to hand. Bigsby, with his large red face and burly hands, tapped his foot. Lowenstein stood beside Ben with her hands in her pockets. Roderick sat straight in his chair with his hands folded in his lap. Ben looked as though he would bare his teeth and snarl at the first wrong word.

"What we have to do now is work with the situation. The press knows Dr. Court is involved. Instead of blocking them, we use them."

"We've been getting hammered in the press for weeks, Captain," Lowenstein put in. "Things were just starting to ease off."

"I read the papers, Detective." He said it mildly. Bigsby shifted, Roderick cleared his throat, and Lowenstein shut her mouth tight.

"We'll set up a press conference for tomorrow morning. The mayor's office is getting in touch with Dr. Court. Paris, Jackson—as heads of the team, I want you there. You know what information we've cleared for the press."

"We don't have anything new for them, Captain," Ed pointed out.

"Make it sound new. Dr. Court should be enough to satisfy them. Set up the meeting with this Monsignor Logan," he added, shifting his gaze back to Ben. "And keep this one under wraps."

"More shrinks." Ben ground his cigarette out. "The first one hasn't told us anything we didn't know."

"She told us he's on a mission," Lowenstein said quietly. "That even though things have been quiet for a while, he isn't likely to be finished with it."

"She's told us he's killing young, blond women," Ben snapped back. "We'd already figured that out."

"Give it a break, Ben," Ed murmured, knowing the temper would be deflected on to him.

"You give it a break." The hands in Ben's pockets balled into fists. "That sonofabitch is just waiting to strangle the next woman who's in the wrong place at the wrong time, and we sit around talking to psychiatrists and priests. I don't give a damn about his soul or his psyche."

"Maybe we should." Roderick looked to the captain first, then to Ben. "Look, I know how you feel, how I guess we all feel. We just want him. But we've all read Dr. Court's profile. We aren't dealing with somebody who's just out for blood, for kicks. If we're going to do our job, I think we'd better understand who he is."

"You get a good look at the morgue photos, Lou? We know who they are. Who they were."

"All right, Paris. You want to let off any more steam, you go down to the gym." Harris waited a moment, drawing the room together with his sense of authority alone. He'd been a good street cop. He was a better desk cop. Knowing it only depressed him occasionally.

"Press conference is being set up for eight A.M., mayor's office. I want a report on the meeting with Monsignor Logan on my desk tomorrow. Bigsby, you keep working on where those damn scarfs came from. Lowenstein, Roderick, go back and work on the family and friends of the victims. Now get out of here, go get something to eat."

Ed waited until they'd signed out, covered the corridors, and were crossing the parking lot.

"It's not doing you any good to take out what happened to your brother on Dr. Court."

"Josh has nothing to do with this." But the pain was still there. He couldn't say his brother's name without it hurting his throat.

"That's right. And Dr. Court's just doing a job, like the rest of us."

"That's fine. I don't happen to think that her job has any connection with ours."

"Criminal psychiatry has become a viable working tool in the—"

"Ed, for Christ's sake, you've got to stop reading those magazines."

"Stop reading, stop learning. Want to go get drunk?"

"This from a man carrying sunflower seeds." There was still tension along the back of his neck. He'd lost one brother, but Ed had come along and nearly filled the void. "Not tonight. Anyway, it embarrasses me when you have them pour all that fruit juice in with the vodka."

"A man's got to think of his health."

"He's also got to think of his reputation." Ben opened his car door, then stood jingling his keys.

It was a cool night, cool enough so that you could just see your breath. If it rained before morning, as the starless skies indicated, it would come down in sleet. In their tidy, high-ceilinged row houses, Georgetown's affluent would be setting logs in the fireplace, sipping Irish coffees, and enjoying the flames. The street people were in for a long unpleasant night.

"She bothers me," Ben said abruptly.

"A woman looks like that, she's bound to bother a man."

"Not that simple." Ben slid into his car and wished he could put his finger on it. "I'll pick you up tomorrow. Seven-thirty."

"Ben." Ed leaned over, holding the door open. "Tell her I said hi."

Ben shut the door the rest of the way then gunned the engine. Partners got to know each other too well.

TESS hung up the phone, and with her elbows on the desk, pressed the heels of her hands against her eyes. Joe Higgins, Sr., needed therapy as much as his son, but he was too involved with destroying his life to see it. The phone call had resolved nothing. But then, conversations with alcoholics on a binge rarely did. He'd just wept at the mention of his son and slurred a promise to phone tomorrow.

He wouldn't, Tess thought. Odds were he wouldn't even remember the conversation in the morning. Her treatment of Joey hinged on the father, and the father was glued to the bottle—the same bottle that had destroyed his marriage, lost him countless jobs, and left him alone and miserable.

If she could get him to an AA meeting, get him to take the first step . . . Tess let out a long breath as she dropped her hands. Hadn't Joey's mother explained how many times she'd tried, how many years she'd devoted to prying Joseph Higgins, Sr., away from the bottle?

Tess understood the woman's bitterness, respected her determination to resume her own life and bury the past. But Joey couldn't. All through his childhood his mother had protected him, shielded him from his father's illness. She'd made excuses for the late nights and the lost jobs, believing the truth should be hidden from the boy.

As a child Joey had seen too much, heard more, then had taken his mother's explanations and excuses and built a wall of lies around his father. Lies he was determined to believe. If his father drank, then drinking was okay. Okay enough that at fourteen Joey was already being treated for alcohol addiction. If his father lost his job, it was because his boss was jealous. Meanwhile Joey's grades in school slid down and down as his respect for authority and himself diminished.

When Joey's mother had no longer been able to tolerate the drinking and the break had come, the lies, broken promises, and years of resentment had poured out. She'd heaped the father's faults on the son in a desperate attempt to make him see the mistakes and not to blame her. Joey hadn't, of course, nor had he blamed his father. There was only one person Joey could blame, and that was himself.

His family had broken apart, he'd been taken out of the home he'd grown up in, and his mother had gone to work. He'd floundered. When Mrs. Higgins had married again, it was Joey's stepfather who had pressed for counseling. By the time Tess had begun to see Joey, he'd had thirteen-and-a-half years of guilt, bitterness, and pain to wade through. In two months she'd barely made a dent in the armor he wore—in their private sessions or the family counseling twice a month with his mother and stepfather.

The rage swept through her so quickly, she had to sit for several minutes and fight it off. It wasn't her function to rage, but to listen, to question, and to offer options. Compassion—she was allowed to feel compassion, but not anger. So she sat with the anger backing up in her, fighting against the control she'd been born with then honed to a professional tool. She wanted to kick something, hit something, strike out somehow at this hateful sense of hopelessness.

Instead she picked up Joey's file and began to make further notes on their afternoon session.

Sleet had begun to fall. She picked up her glasses, but didn't look out of the window, didn't see the man across the street standing on the curb and watching the light in her apartment. If she had looked, had seen, she would have thought nothing of it.

Just as when the knock came she thought of nothing but the annoyance of being interrupted. Her phone had rung incessantly, but she'd been able to ignore that and leave it to her answering service. If one of the calls had been a patient, the beeper beside her would have sounded. The calls, Tess had guessed, had all been connected with the article in the evening's paper, linking her to the homicide investigation.

Leaving the file open, Tess walked to the door. "Who is it?"

"Paris."

A lot could be gleaned from the tone of a voice, even in one word. Tess opened the door, knowing she opened it to a confrontation. "Detective. Isn't it a little late for an official call?"

"Just in time for the eleven o'clock news." He walked over and switched on her set.

She hadn't moved from the door. "Haven't you got a TV at home?"

"It's more fun to watch a circus with company."

She shut the door, peevish enough to let it slam. "Look, I'm working. Why don't you say what you have to say and let me get back to it?"

He glanced over at her desk, at the files open and

her big-framed reading glasses tossed on them. "This won't take long." He didn't sit, but stood with his hands in his pockets, watching the news team's intro. It was the pretty, heart-shaped-face brunette who read the evening's top story.

"The mayor's office confirmed today that Dr. Teresa Court, noted Washington psychiatrist, has been assigned to the investigation team of the Priest homicides. Dr. Court, granddaughter of veteran Senator Jonathan Writemore, could not be reached for comment. The murders of at least three women are suspected to be linked to the killer termed the Priest because of his use of an amice, a scarf used in ceremony by Roman Catholic priests, to strangle his victims. The police continue an investigation begun last August, now with the assistance of Dr. Court."

"Not bad," Ben murmured. "Got your name mentioned three times." He didn't even blink when Tess strode over and slammed the button to off.

"I'll repeat, say what you have to say."

Her voice was cool. He drew out a cigarette, determined to match her. "We have a press conference at eight tomorrow in the mayor's office."

"I was notified."

"You're to keep your comments general, stay as far away from the specifics of the case as possible. The press knows about the murder weapon, but we've managed to keep the notes and the contents of them from leaking."

"I'm not a fool, Ben. I can handle an interview."

"I'm sure you can. This one happens to be on departmental business, not personal glory."

Her mouth opened, but all that came out was a hiss of breath. She knew it was both undignified and useless to lose her temper. She knew that such a ridiculous and bitter statement deserved no answer. She knew that he, standing there in judgment, deserved nothing but the coolest, most controlled dismissal.

"You bigoted, small-brained, insensitive ass." Her phone rang again, but they both ignored it. "Who the hell do you think you are, barging in here and tossing out your little gems of idiocy?"

He glanced around for an ashtray and settled on a small hand-painted dish. There was a vase of fresh, autumnal mums beside it. "Which gem was that?"

She stood straight as a soldier, while he stood at ease and flicked ashes into the dish. "Let's just get something straight. I didn't leak this business to the press."

"Nobody said you did."

"Didn't they?" She stuffed her hands in the pockets of the skirt she'd worked in for fourteen hours. Her back hurt, her stomach was empty, and she wanted what she struggled so hard to give her patients—peace of mind. "Well, I interpret this little scene differently. As a matter of fact, I was promised my name would never be linked with this investigation."

"Got a problem letting people know you're cooperating with the police?"

"Oh, you're clever, aren't you?"

"As hell," he returned, fascinated by the complete annihilation of her control. She paced as she spoke, and her eyes had deepened to purple. Temper in her was rigid, and icy, unlike the venom-spitting, plate-throwing sort he was more accustomed to. It was all the more interesting.

"Either way I go, you've got an answer. Did it ever occur to you, Detective, that I might not care to have my patients, my colleagues, my friends question me about this case? Did it ever occur to you that I didn't want to take the case in the first place?"

"Then why did you? The pay's lousy."

"Because I was persuaded to believe I could help. If

I didn't still think so, I'd tell you to take your case and choke on it. Do you think I want to waste my time arguing with some narrow-minded, self-appointed judge about the morality of my profession? I have enough problems in my life without you adding to them."

"Problems, Doc?" He took a slow sweep of the room, the flowers, the crystal, the soft pastels. "Things look pretty tidy around here to me."

"You don't know anything about me, my life, or my work." She walked over to her desk, leaning her palms on it, but still didn't regain control. "Do you see these files, these papers, these tapes? There's a fourteen-year-old boy's life there. A boy who's already an alcoholic, a boy who needs someone who can open him up enough to see his own worth, his own place." She whirled back again, eyes dark and impassioned. "You know what it is to try to save a life, don't you, Detective? You know how it hurts, how it frightens? Maybe I don't use a gun, but that's just what I'm trying to do. I've spent ten years of my life trying to learn how. Maybe, with enough time, enough skill, enough luck, I'll be able to help him. Damn." She stopped, realizing how far she'd allowed herself to be pushed by a few words. "I don't have to justify anything to you."

"No, you don't." As he spoke, he crushed out his cigarette in the little china dish. "I'm sorry. I was out of line."

Her breath came out with two hitches as she struggled to bring herself back. "What is it about what I do that makes you so bitter?"

He wasn't ready to tell her, to bring that old, fleshed-over scar out in the open for inspection and analysis. Instead he pressed his fingers to his own tired eyes. "It's not you. It's the whole business. Makes me feel like I'm walking a very thin wire over a very long drop."

"I guess I can accept that." Though it wasn't the

whole answer, or the one she'd wanted. "It's hard to stay objective right now."

"Let's take a step back for a minute. I don't think much of what you do, and I guess you don't think much of what I do."

She waited a minute, then nodded. "Agreed."

"We're stuck with it." He walked over to her desk and picked up her half cup of coffee. "Got any of this hot?"

"No. I could make some."

"Never mind." He brought his hand up to knead at the tension just above his eyebrows. "Look, I am sorry. It seems like we've been running on this treadmill, and the only progress we've made is a leak to the press."

"I know. You might not be able to understand, but I'm as involved as you are now, and I feel as responsible." She paused again, but this time she felt an affinity, an empathy. "That's the hard part, isn't it? Feeling responsible."

She was too damn good at her job, Ben thought as he leaned back against her desk. "I've got this feeling I can't shake that he's about through waiting to hit again. We're no closer to finding him, Doc. We can bullshit the press some tomorrow, but what we have to swallow is that we're no closer. You telling me why he's killing isn't going to help the next woman he homes in on."

"I can only tell you what he looks like inside, Ben."

"And I have to tell you I don't give a damn." He turned away from her desk to face her. She was calm again. He could see it just by looking at her eyes. "When we get him, and we will, they're going to take this psychiatric profile of yours. They're going to get other ones done, then they're going to put you or some other psychiatrist on the stand, and he's going to get off."

"He'll be confined to a mental hospital. That's not a picnic, Ben."

"Until a team of doctors diagnose him cured."

"It's not as simple as that. You know the law better." She dragged a hand through her hair. He was right, and so was she. That only made things more difficult. "You don't lock someone up because he has cancer, because he can't control the disintegration of his own body. How can you punish someone without taking into consideration the disintegration of his mind? Ben, schizophrenia alone disables more people for a longer time than cancer. Hundreds of thousands of people are confined to hospitals. We can't turn our backs on them or burn them as witches because of a chemical imbalance in the brain."

He wasn't interested in statistics, in reasons, only in results. "You said it once, Doc—insanity's a legal term. Crazy or not, he's got his civil rights and he'll be entitled to a lawyer, and his lawyer will use that legal term. I'd like to see you sit down with those three families after it's done and talk about chemical imbalances. See if you can convince them they've gotten justice."

She had counseled victims' families before, knew too well the sense of betrayal and bitter helplessness. It was a helplessness that without control could spill over to the healer. "You're the one with the sword, Ben, not me. I only have words."

"Yeah." He'd had them, too, and he'd used them in a way he wasn't proud of. He had to get out, get home. He wished he had a brandy and a woman waiting for him. "I'm setting up an appointment with Monsignor Logan tomorrow. You'll want to be there."

"Yes." She crossed her arms and wondered why a bout of temper always left her so depressed. "I have appointments all day, but I can cancel my four o'clock."

"Not too crazy?"

Because he'd made the effort, so did she, and smiled. "We'll let that pass."

"I'll see if I can schedule for four-thirty. Somebody will call you and set it up."

"Fine." There seemed to be nothing left to say, and perhaps more to say than either of them could deal with. "Are you sure you don't want that coffee?"

He did, and more than that, wanted to sit with her and talk about anything other than what was bringing them together. "No, I've got to go. The streets are a mess already."

"Oh?" She glanced toward the window and noticed the sleet.

"Working too hard, Doc, when you don't see what's out your own window." He walked to the door. "You haven't gotten that dead bolt."

"No, I haven't."

He turned with his hand on the knob. He wanted to stay with her more than he wanted that brandy and imaginary woman. "Bogart was okay the other night?"

"Yes, Bogart was fine."

"Maybe we should do it again sometime."

"Maybe."

"See you, Doc. Put on the chain."

He pulled the door closed, but waited until he heard the rattle of the chain lock being fastened.

Chapter 5

ED TOOLED DOWN Sixteenth Street at a sedate pace. He enjoyed cruising as much—well, nearly as much—as he enjoyed sending the tires screaming. For a simple, relatively easygoing man, racing the streets in hot pursuit was a small vice.

Beside him, Ben sat in silence. Normally Ben would have had a few smart remarks to make about Ed's driving, which was a departmental joke. The fact that Ben said nothing about it, or the Tanya Tucker tape Ed was playing, were signs that his thoughts were elsewhere. It didn't take a mind as methodical as Ed's to figure out where.

"Got papered on the Borelli case." Ed listened to Tanya wail about lying and cheating, and was content.

"Hmm? Oh, yeah, got mine too."

"Looks like a couple of days in court next month. D.A. ought to nail him pretty quick."

"He'd better. We worked our asses off to get the evidence."

Silence trickled back like thin rain. Ed hummed along with Tanya, sang a few bars of the chorus, then hummed again. "Hear about Lowenstein's kitchen? Her husband flooded it. Disposal went out again."

"That's what happens when you let an accountant go around with a wrench in his hand." Ben took the window down an inch so the smoke would trail out when he lit a cigarette.

"That's fifteen," Ed said mildly. "You ain't gonna get anywhere if you keep stewing about that press conference."

"I'm not stewing about anything. I like to smoke." As proof he drew deep, but resisted blowing the smoke in Ed's direction. "It's one of the few great pleasures of mankind."

"Right up there with getting drunk and throwing up on your own shoes."

"My shoes are clean, Jackson. I remember someone toppling like a goddamn redwood when he downed half a gallon of vodka and carrot juice."

"I was just going to take a nap."

"Yeah, right on your face. If I hadn't caught you—and nearly given myself a hernia in the process—you'd have broken that big nose of yours. What the hell are you smiling at?"

"If you're bitching, you're not feeling sorry for yourself. You know, Ben, she handled herself real good."

"Who said she didn't?" Ben's teeth ground into the filter as he took another drag. "And who said I was thinking about her anyway?"

"Who?"

"Tess."

"I never mentioned her name." Ed gunned the engine as a light turned amber, and blinked through it as it switched to red.

"Don't play games with me, and that light was red."

"Yellow."

"It was red, you color-blind sonofabitch, and someone should take your license away. I take my life in my hands every time I get in the same car with you. I ought to have a suitcase full of commendations."

"She looked good too," Ed commented. "Great legs."

"You're in a rut." He turned the heater up as the air coming in through the crack of the window cut like a knife. "Anyway, she looked as though she could freeze a man at twenty paces."

"Clothes send out signals. Authority, indecision, composure. Looked like she was shooting for aloof authority. Seems to me she had those reporters in hand before she opened her mouth."

"Somebody should cancel your subscription to *Reader's Digest*," Ben muttered. The big, old trees dotting the sides of the road were at their peak of color. Leaves were soft to the touch and vibrant in reds, yellows, and oranges. In another week they would be dry, littering the sidewalks and gutters, making scratching, empty sounds as they trailed along the asphalt. Ben pushed the cigarette through the crack, then closed it tight.

"Okay, so she handled herself. Problem is, the press is going to have this meat to chew over for days. Media has a way of bringing out the loonies." He looked at the old sedate buildings behind the old sedate trees. They were the kind of buildings she belonged in. The kind he was used to seeing from the outside. "And damn it, she does have great legs."

"Smart too. A man sure can admire a woman's mind."

"What do you know about a woman's mind? The last one you dated had the IQ of a soft-boiled egg. And what is this crap we're listening to?"

Ed smiled, pleased to have his partner back on track. "Tanya Tucker."

"Jesus." Ben slid down in the seat and closed his eyes.

"You seem to feel much better today, Mrs. Halderman."

"Oh, I do. I really do." The dark, pretty woman didn't lie on the couch or sit in a chair, but almost danced around Tess's office. She tossed a sable coat over the arm of a chair and posed. "What do you think of my new dress?"

"It's very becoming."

"It is, isn't it?" Mrs. Halderman ran a hand over the thin, silk-lined wool. "Red is so eye-catching. I do love to be noticed."

"You've been shopping again, Mrs. Halderman?"

"Yes." She beamed, then her pretty, china-doll face drew into a pout. "Oh, don't be annoyed, Dr. Court. I know you said maybe I should stay away from the stores for a little while. And I did really. I hadn't been to Neiman's for almost a week."

"I'm not annoyed, Mrs. Halderman," she said, and watched the pout transform into another beaming smile. "You have wonderful taste in clothes." Which was fortunate, as Ellen Halderman was obsessive. She saw, she liked, she bought, often tossing it aside and forgetting it after one wearing. But that was a small problem. Mrs. Halderman also had the same routine with men.

"Thank you, Doctor." Like a little girl, she twirled in a circle to show off the flare of the skirt. "I did have the most marvelous time shopping. And you'd have been proud of me. I only bought two outfits. Well, three," she amended with a giggle. "But lingerie shouldn't count, should it? Then I went down to have some coffee. You know that marvelous restaurant in the Mazza Gallerie where you can look up at all the people and the shops?"

"Yes." Tess was sitting on the corner of her desk. Mrs. Halderman looked at her, caught her bottom lip between her teeth, not in shame or anxiety, but in suppressed delight. Then she walked to a chair and sat primly.

"I was having coffee. I'd thought about having a roll, but if I didn't watch my figure, clothes wouldn't be so much fun. A man was sitting at the table beside mine. Oh, Dr. Court, I knew as soon as I saw him. Why, my heart just started to pound." She put a hand to it, as though even now its rhythm couldn't be trusted. "He was so handsome. Just a little gray right here." She touched her forefingers to her temples as her eyes took on the soft, dreamy light Tess had seen too often to count. "He was tanned, as though he'd been skiing. Saint Moritz, I thought, because it's really too early for Vermont. He had a leather briefcase with his little initials monogrammed. I kept trying to guess what they stood for. M.W." She sighed over them, and Tess knew she was already changing the monogram on her bath towels. "I can't tell you how many names I'd conjured up to fit those initials."

"What did they stand for?"

"Maxwell Witherspoon. Isn't that a wonderful name?"

"Very distinguished."

"Why, that's just what I told him."

"So, you spoke with him."

"Well, my purse slid off the table." She put her fingers to her lips as if to hide a grin. "A girl's got to have a trick or two if she wants to meet the right man."

"You knocked your purse off the table."

"It landed right by his foot. It was my pretty black-and-white snakeskin. Maxwell leaned over to pick it up. As he handed it to me, he smiled. My heart just about stopped. It was like a dream. I didn't hear the clatter of the other tables, I didn't see the shoppers on the floors above us. Our fingers touched, and—oh, promise you won't laugh, Doctor."

"Of course I won't."

"It was as if he'd touched my soul."

That's what she'd been afraid of. Tess moved away from the desk to sit in the chair opposite her patient. "Mrs. Halderman, do you remember Asanti?"

"Him?" With a sniff Mrs. Halderman dismissed her fourth husband.

"When you met him at the art gallery, under his painting of Venice, you thought he touched your soul."

"That was different. Asanti was Italian. You know how clever Italian men are with women. Maxwell's from Boston."

Tess fought back a sigh. It was going to be a very long fifty minutes.

❧

WHEN Ben entered Tess's outer office, he found exactly what he'd expected. It was as cool and classy as her apartment. Calming colors, deep roses, smoky grays that would put her patients at ease. The potted ferns by the windows had moist leaves, as though they'd just been spritzed with water. Fresh flowers and a collection of figurines in a display cabinet lent the air of a parlor rather than a reception room. From the copy of *Vogue* left open on a low coffee table, he gathered her current patient was a woman.

It didn't remind him of another doctor's office, one with white walls and the scent of leather. He didn't feel the hitch in his gut or the sweat on the back of his neck as the door closed behind him. He wouldn't be waiting for his brother here, because Josh was gone.

Tess's secretary sat at a neat enameled desk, working with a single-station computer. She stopped typing as Ben and Ed entered, and looked as calm and easy as the room. "Can I help you?"

"Detectives Paris and Jackson."

"Oh, yes. Dr. Court's expecting you. She's with a patient at the moment. If you won't mind waiting, I could get you some coffee."

"Just hot water." Ed drew a tea bag out of his pocket.

The secretary didn't show even a flicker of reaction. "Of course."

"You're a constant embarrassment to me," Ben muttered as she slipped into a small side room.

"I'm not pumping caffeine into my system just to be socially acceptable." With his bag of herbs dangling from his hand, he looked around the room. "How about this place? Classy."

"Yeah." Ben took another look around. "Fits her."

"I don't know why that gives you such a problem," Ed said mildly as he studied a Monet print, sunrise on the water, all softly blurred colors with a touch of fire. He liked it as he liked most art, because someone had had the imagination and skill to create it. His views on the human race were pretty much the same. "A good-looking, classy woman with a sharp mind shouldn't intimidate a man who has a strong sense of his own worth."

"Christ, you should be writing a column."

Just then the door to Tess's office opened. Mrs. Halderman came out, her sable tossed over one arm. Seeing the men, she stopped, smiled, then touched her tongue to her top lip the way a young girl might when she spotted a bowl of chocolate ice cream. "Hello."

Ben hooked his thumbs in his pockets. "Hello."

"Are you waiting to see Dr. Court?"

"That's right."

She stayed where she was a moment, then let her eyes widen as she studied Ed. "My, my, you're a big one, aren't you?"

Ed swallowed a small obstruction in his throat. "Yes, ma'am."

"I'm just fascinated by . . . big men." She crossed to

him, letting her eyes sweep up and flutter. "They always make me feel so helpless and feminine. Just how tall are you, Mister . . . ?"

Grinning, with his thumbs still hooked in his pockets, Ben walked to Tess's door and left Ed to sink or swim.

She was sitting behind her desk, head back, eyes closed. Her hair was up again, but she didn't look unapproachable. Tired, he thought, and not just physically. As he watched, she lifted a hand to her temple and pressed at the beginnings of a headache.

"Looks like you could use an aspirin, Doc."

She opened her eyes. Her head came up again, as though she didn't find it acceptable to rest except in private. Though she was small, the desk didn't dwarf her. She looked completely suited to it, and to the black-framed degree at her back.

"I don't like to take pills."

"Just prescribe them?"

Her back angled a little straighter. "You weren't waiting long, were you? I need my briefcase."

As she started to rise, he walked over to the desk. "We've got a few minutes. Rough day?"

"A little. You?"

"Hardly shot anybody at all." He picked up a chunk of amethyst from her desk and passed it from hand to hand. "I meant to tell you, you did good this morning."

She picked up a pencil, ran it through her fingers, then set it down again. Apparently the next confrontation would be postponed. "Thanks. So did you."

He hitched himself onto the corner of her desk, discovering he could relax in her office, psychiatrist or not. There were no ghosts here, no regrets. "How do you feel about Saturday matinees?"

"Open minded."

He had to grin. "Figured you would be. They're playing a couple of classic Vincent Price films."

"House of Wax?"

"And *The Fly*. Interested?"

"I might be." Now she did rise. The headache was only a dull, easily ignored throb in one temple. "If it included popcorn."

"It even includes pizza after."

"I'm sold."

"Tess." He put a hand on her arm, though he still found the trim gray suit she wore intimidating. "About last night . . ."

"I thought we both already apologized for that."

"Yeah." She didn't look weary or vulnerable now, but in control. Untouched, untouchable. He backed off, still holding the chunk of amethyst in his hand. It matched her eyes. "Ever make love in here?"

Tess lifted a brow. She knew he wanted to shock, or at the very least, annoy her. "Privileged information." She plucked her briefcase up from beside her desk and headed for the door. "Coming?"

He had an urge to slip the amethyst in his pocket. Annoyed, he set it down carefully and followed her out.

Ed stood beside the secretary's desk, sipping tea. His face was nearly as red as his hair.

"Mrs. Halderman," she said to Tess, sending Ed a sympathetic look. "I managed to nudge her along before she devoured him."

"I'm terribly sorry, Ed." But Tess's eyes glistened. "Would you like to sit down a minute?"

"No." He sent his partner a warning look. "One word, Paris."

"Not me." All innocence, Ben walked to the door and held it open. As Ed walked by, Ben fell into step beside him. "You are a big one, though, aren't you?"

"Keep it up."

MONSIGNOR Timothy Logan didn't look like Ben's childhood conception of a priest. Instead of a cassock, he wore a tweed jacket over a pale yellow turtleneck. He had the big, broad face of an Irishman, and dark red hair just beginning to go wiry with gray. His office wasn't like the hushed quiet of a rectory with its somehow sanctified fragrances and old dark woods. Instead it smelled of pipe tobacco and dust, like the den of an ordinary man.

There were no pictures of the saints or the Savior on the walls, no ceramic statues of the Virgin with her sad, understanding face. There were books, dozens and dozens of them, some on theology, some on psychiatry, and several more on fishing. Instead of a crucifix there was a mounted silver bass.

On a stand rested an old Bible with a carved cover; a newer, though more well-used one was open on the desk. A rosary with fat wooden beads lay beside it.

"It's a pleasure to meet you, Monsignor Logan." Tess held out her hand in a colleague-to-colleague manner that made Ben uncomfortable. The man was a priest, tweed or not, and priests were to be revered, even feared a little, and respected. God's proxies, he remembered his mother saying. They handled the sacraments, forgave sins, and absolved the dying.

One had come to Josh after he was already dead. There had been words of comfort, sympathy, and kindness for the family, but no absolution. Suicide. The most mortal of the mortal sins.

"And you, Dr. Court." Logan had a clear, booming voice that could easily have filled a cathedral. Yet there was an edge to it, a toughness that made Ben think of an umpire calling strike three. "I attended the lecture you gave on dementia. I wasn't able to speak to you afterward and tell you I thought you were brilliant."

"Thank you. Monsignor, Detectives Paris and Jackson—they're heading the investigation team."

"Detectives."

Ben accepted the handshake and felt foolish for expecting, even for an instant, something more than flesh and blood.

"Please be comfortable." He gestured to chairs. "I have your profile and report on my desk, Dr. Court." He swung around it with the free, easy strides of a man on a golf course. "I read them this morning, and found them both disturbing and intuitive."

"You agree?"

"Yes, with the information from the investigator's report, I would have drawn up a reflecting profile. The religious aspects are undeniable. Of course, religious allusions and delusions are common in schizophrenia."

"Joan of Arc heard voices," Ben murmured.

Logan smiled and folded his broad, capable hands. "As did any number of the saints and martyrs. Some might say fasting for forty days might have anyone hearing voices. Others might say they were chosen. In this case we can all agree we're not dealing with a saint, but a very disturbed mind."

"No argument there," Ed murmured, his notebook in hand. He remembered feeling a little . . . well, spiritual, after a three-day fast.

"As a doctor, and a priest, I look on the act of murder as a sin against God, and as an act of extreme mental aberration. However, we have to deal with the mental aberration first in order to prevent the sin from being committed again."

Logan opened Tess's file and tapped his finger on it. "It would appear that the religious aspects, and delusions, are rooted in Catholicism. I have to concur with your opinion that the use of the amice as a murder weapon could be construed as a strike against the Church, or devotion to it."

Tess leaned forward. "Do you think he might be a priest, or have been one? Perhaps wanted to be one?"

"I believe it's more than possible he had training." The frown came slowly, and seemed to lodge between his eyes. "There are other articles of a priest's habit that would be as effective for strangulation. The amice is neckware, and therefore, grimly accurate."

"And the use of white?"

"Symbolizing absolution, salvation." Unconsciously he spread his hands, palms facing, in the age-old gesture.

Tess nodded agreement. "Absolving a sin. Against himself?"

"Perhaps. But a sin that may have resulted in the death or spiritual loss of the woman he continues to save."

"He's putting himself in the role of Christ? As Savior?" Ben demanded. "And casting the first stone?"

Because he was a man who took his time, watched his footing, Logan leaned back and rubbed his earlobe. "He doesn't perceive himself as Christ, at least not yet. He's a laborer of God in his mind, Detective, and one who knows himself to be mortal. He takes precautions, protects himself. He would realize that society would not accept his mission, but he follows a higher authority."

"Voices again." Ben lit a cigarette.

"Voices, visions. To a schizophrenic they are as real, often more so, than the real world. This is not split personality, Detective, but a disease, a biological dysfunction. It's possible that he's had the illness for years."

"The murders started in August," Ben pointed out. "We've checked with homicide divisions all over the country. There haven't been any murders with this M.O. It started here."

Detailed police work interested Logan but didn't sway him. "Perhaps he was in a period of recovery and some kind of stress brought the symptoms back, resulting in violence. At the moment he's torn between what is and what seems to be. He agonizes, and he prays."

"And he kills," Ben said flatly.

"I don't expect compassion." Logan, with his dark, priest's eyes and capable hands, spoke quietly. "That's my territory, and Dr. Court's, and can't be yours with your dealings in this case. None of us wants to see him kill again, Detective Paris."

"You don't think he has a Christ delusion," Ed interrupted as he continued to make methodical notes. "Is that just because he takes precautions? Christ was destroyed physically."

"An excellent point." The clear voice took on a richness. There was nothing he liked better than to have one of his students question his theories. Logan looked from one detective to the other and decided they made a good pair. "Still, I don't see him as perceiving himself as anything but a tool. Religion, the structure, the barriers, the traditions of it, loom more predominantly than theology. He kills as a priest, whether he is one or not. He absolves and forgives as God's proxy," he continued, and saw Ben wince. "Not as the Son of God. I developed an interesting theory you missed, Dr. Court."

She came to attention instantly. "Oh?"

He smiled again, recognizing professional pride. "Understandable enough. You're not Catholic, are you?"

"No."

"The investigation team overlooked it as well."

"I'm Methodist," Ed put in, still writing.

"I'm not trying for a conversion." Taking up his pipe, he began to fill it. His fingers were blunt and wide, with the nails neatly trimmed. A few flakes of tobacco fell on and clung to his yellow turtleneck. "The date of the first murder, August fifteenth, is a Church holy day."

"The Assumption," Ben murmured before he realized it.

"Yes." Logan continued to fill his pipe and smiled. Ben was reminded of answering correctly in catechism.

"I used to be Catholic."

"A common problem," Logan said, and lit his pipe.

No lecture, no pontifical frown. Ben felt his shoulders relaxing. His mind started ticking. "I didn't put the dates together. You think it's significant?"

Meticulously, Logan removed tobacco from his sweater. "It could be."

"I'm sorry, Monsignor." Tess lifted her hands. "You'll have to explain."

"August fifteenth is the day the Church recognizes the Virgin's assumption into heaven. The Mother of God was a mortal, but she carried the Savior in her womb. We revere her as the most blessed and pure among women."

"Pure," Tess murmured.

"Of itself, I might not have paid too much attention to the date," Logan continued. "However, it jogged my imagination enough to check the Church calendar. The second murder occurred on the day we celebrate Mary's birth."

"He's picking the days she's—excuse me—Mary's honored by the Church?" Ed stopped writing long enough to look up for an acknowledgment.

"The third murder falls on the feast of Our Lady of the Rosary. I've added a Church calendar to your file, Dr. Court. I don't think the odds for three out of three rate a coincidence."

"No, I agree." Tess rose, anxious to see for herself. She picked up the calender and studied the dates Logan had circled. Dusk was falling. Logan switched on the light and the beam shot over the paper in her hands.

"The next one you have here isn't until December eighth."

"The Immaculate Conception." Logan puffed on his pipe.

"That would put eight weeks between the murders," Ed calculated. "He's never gone more than four."

"And we can't be sure he's emotionally capable of waiting that long," Tess added in a murmur. "He could change his pattern. Some incident could set him off. He might pick a date personally important to him."

"The date of birth or death of someone important to him." Ben lit another cigarette.

"A female figure." Tess folded the calendar. "The female figure."

"I agree that the stress he's under is building." Logan put his pipe down and leaned forward. "The need for release could be enough to make him strike sooner."

"He's probably dealing with some sort of physical pain." Tess slipped the calendar into her briefcase. "Headache, nausea. If it becomes too great for him to carry on his normal life . . ."

"Exactly." Logan folded his hands again. "I wish I could be more helpful. I would like to discuss this with you again, Dr. Court."

"In the meantime, we have a pattern." Ben crushed out his cigarette as he rose. "We concentrate on December eighth."

"IT'S only a crumb," Ben said as they stepped out into a chilled dusk. "But I'm ready to take it."

"I didn't realize you were Catholic." Tess buttoned

her coat against the wind that was whipping up. "Maybe that'll be an advantage."

"Used to be Catholic. And speaking of crumbs, are you hungry?"

"Starved."

"Good." He slipped an arm around her. "Then we can outvote Ed. You're not in the mood for yogurt and alfalfa sprouts, are you?"

"Ah . . ."

"Ben'll want to stop and get a greasy hamburger. What the man puts in his system is revolting."

"How about Chinese?" It was the best compromise she could come up with as she slipped into the car. "There's a great little place around the corner from my office."

"Told you she was classy," Ed said as he took the driver's seat. He fastened his safety belt and waited with the patience of the wise and determined for Ben to follow suit. "The Chinese have the proper respect for the digestive system."

"Sure, they keep it stuffed with rice." Ben glanced over his shoulder and saw Tess already spread out on the backseat, her file open. "Come on, Doc, take a break."

"I just want to check over a couple of things."

"Ever treated a workaholic?"

She glanced over the file, then back again. "I may decide I have a craving for yogurt after all."

"Not Tanya Tucker!" Ben pushed the reject button before the first bar of the song was out. "You had her this afternoon."

"I wish."

"Degenerate. I'm putting on some—ah, shit, look at that. The liquor store."

Ed slowed down. "Looks like a five-oh-nine in progress."

"A what?" Tess straightened up in the back and tried to see.

"Robbery in progress." Ben was already unhooking his belt. "Go back to work."

"A robbery? Where?"

"Where's a black and white?" Ben muttered as he reached for the radio. "Dammit, all I want's some sweet and sour pork."

"Pork's poison." Ed unlatched his own belt.

Ben snapped into the radio. "Unit six-oh. We have a five-oh-nine in progress on Third and Douglas. Any available units. We have a civilian in the car. Ah, damn, he's coming out. Requesting backup. Perpetrator's heading south. White male, five-ten, a hundred eighty. Black jacket, jeans." The radio squawked back at him. "Yeah, we're on him."

Ed revved the engine and rounded the corner. From the backseat, Tess stared, fascinated.

She saw the husky man in the black jacket come out of the liquor store and head up the street at a jog. The minute he turned his head and saw the Mustang, he broke into a run.

"Shit, he made us." Ben pulled out the Kojak light. "Just sit tight, Doc."

"Making for the alley," Ed said mildly. He brought the car to a halt, fishtailing it. Before Tess could open her mouth, both men were out of opposite sides and running.

"Stay in the car!" Ben shouted at her.

She listened to him for about ten seconds. Slamming the door behind her, she raced to the mouth of the alley herself.

Ed was bigger, but Ben was faster. As she watched, the man they were chasing reached into his jacket. She saw the gun and only had an instant to freeze before Ben caught him at the knees and sent him sprawling into a line of garbage cans. There was a shot over the clatter of metal. She was halfway down the alley when Ben dragged the man to his feet. There was blood, and the scent of rotting food from the metal cans which were emptied regularly but rarely cleaned. The man didn't struggle, probably because he saw Ed and the police issue in his hand. He spat a stream of blood-tinged saliva.

It wasn't like television, Tess thought as she looked at the man who would have shot Ben in the face if the timing had been a little different. Nor was it like a novel. It wasn't even like the eleven o'clock news, where all the details were neatly tied up and delivered with rapid-fire detachment. Life was full of smelly alleys and spittle. Her training and work had taken her there before, but only emotionally.

She took a deep breath, relieved that she wasn't frightened, only curious. And maybe a little fascinated.

With two snaps Ben had the robber's hands cuffed behind his back. "Haven't you got more brains than to shoot at a police officer?"

"Got grease on your pants," Ed pointed out as he secured his gun.

Ben looked down and saw the long skid mark running from ankle to knee. "Goddammit. I'm with Homicide, jerk," he announced in his prisoner's face. "I don't like getting grease on my pants. In fact, getting grease on my pants really pisses me off." Disgusted, Ben passed him to Ed as he brought out his badge. "You're under arrest, sucker. You have the right to remain silent. You have—Tess, dammit, didn't I tell you to stay in the car?"

"He had a gun."

"The bad guys always have guns." As he looked at her, wrapped in a powder-blue cashmere coat, he could smell the sweat from the petty thief. She looked as though she were on her way to have cocktails on Embassy Row. "Go back to the car, you don't belong here."

Ignoring him, she studied the thief. He had a good-sized scrape on his forehead where he'd connected with concrete. That explained the slightly glazed expression. Minor concussion. His skin and the whites of his eyes had a yellow tinge. There was sweat on his face, though the wind cutting through the alley billowed his jacket. "Looks like he might have hepatitis."

"He'll have plenty of time to recover." He heard the sirens and looked over her shoulder. "Here comes the cavalry. We'll let the uniforms read him his rights."

When Ben took her arm, Tess shook her head. "You were running after him, and he had a gun."

"So did I," Ben pointed out as he pulled her back up the alley. He flashed his badge at the uniforms before continuing on to the car.

"You didn't have it out. He was going to shoot you."

"That's what the bad guys do. They do the crime, we go after them, and they try to get away."

"Don't act like it was a game."

"It's all a game."

"He was going to kill you, and you were mad because you got your pants dirty."

Reminded, Ben glanced down again. "Department's going to get the bill too. Grease never comes out."

"You're crazy."

"Is that a professional opinion?"

There had to be a good reason why she wanted to laugh. Tess decided to analyze it later. "I'm working one up."

"Take your time." The adrenaline from the collar was still pumping Ben up. As he reached the car, he saw they had a three-unit backup for one two-bit hood with hepatitis. Maybe they were all crazy. "Come on, sit down in here while I fill in the uniforms."

"Your mouth is bleeding."

"Yeah?" He wiped the back of his hand over it and looked at the smear. "Yeah. Maybe I need a doctor."

She pulled a tissue out of her pocket and dabbed at the cut. "Maybe you do."

Behind them the man they had arrested began to swear, and a crowd had gathered.

Chapter 6

OVER THE NEXT few days Tess bent under her caseload. Eight- and ten-hour days stretched to twelve and fourteen. She postponed her usual Friday-night dinner with her grandfather, something she would never have done for a date, only for a patient.

The press hounded her, along with a few of her less sensitive associates, such as Frank Fuller. The fact that she was working with the police added just enough mystique to have him hanging around her office at five. Tess began to stay at her desk until six.

She had no new information, only a nagging sense of worry. It wouldn't be long before there was another victim. The more she felt she understood the mind of the killer, the surer she was of that.

But it was Joey Higgins who kept her awake and restless into early Saturday morning, when the streets outside were dark and empty and her eyes were burning from overuse. She slipped off her glasses, sat back and rubbed them.

Why couldn't she get through to him? Why wasn't she making a dent? The session that evening with Joey, his mother, and stepfather had been a disaster. There had been no temper tantrums, no shouting, no accusations. She would have preferred that. There would have been emotion in that.

The boy simply sat there, giving his monosyllabic nonanswers. His father hadn't called. Tess had seen the fury in the mother's eyes, but only blank acceptance in the son's. Joey continued to insist, in his low-key, unshakable way, that he was spending a weekend—Thanksgiving weekend—with his father.

He was going to be let down. Tess pressed her fingers against her eyes until the burning subsided to a dull ache. And when he was let down this time, it could be one time too many.

Joey Higgins was a prime candidate for drink, drugs, or destruction. The Monroes would only see so much, only allow her to go so far. At the mention of hospital care, Tess had been cut off. Joey just needed time, he just needed family structure, he just needed . . . Help, Tess thought. Desperately. She was no longer convinced that a weekly session with her was going to lead to any kind of a breakthrough.

The stepfather, she thought—she might make him see. She might be able to make him understand the necessity of protecting Joey against himself. The next step, she decided, was to get Monroe into her office privately.

Nothing more could be done tonight. She leaned forward to close the file, glancing out the window as she did. On the empty streets a single figure caught her eye. This part of Georgetown, with its tidy edgings of flowers along the sidewalks in front of aging brownstones, didn't lend itself to street people or vagrants. But the man looked as though he had stood there a long time. In the cold, alone. Looking up . . . Looking up at her window, Tess realized, and drew back automatically.

Silly, she told herself, but reached over to switch off

her desk lamp. No one would have a reason to stand on a street corner and stare at her window. Still, with the lights off she got up and went to the edge of the window, drawing the curtain slightly.

He was there, just there. Not moving, but looking. She shuddered with the foolish idea that he was looking right at her, though she was three stories up in a dark room.

One of her patients? she wondered. But she was always so careful to keep her home address private. A reporter. Some of the fear eased with the thought. It was probably a reporter hoping for a new angle on the story. At two A.M.? she asked herself, and let the curtain drop.

It was nothing, she assured herself. She'd imagined he was looking at her window. It was dark, and she was tired. It was just someone waiting for a ride or—

Not in this neighborhood. She started to reach for the curtain again, but couldn't quite bring herself to draw it aside.

He was going to strike again soon. Hadn't that been the thought haunting her? Frightening her? He had pain, pressure, and a mission. Blondes, in their late twenties, small to medium build.

She put a hand to her own throat.

Stop it. Dropping it again, she touched the hem of the curtain. A bit of paranoia was easy to deal with. No one was after her except a sex-crazed psychoanalyst and a few hungry reporters. She wasn't out on the street, but locked in her own home. She was tired, overworked, and imagining things. It was time to call it a night, time to pour a glass of cool white wine, turn on the stereo, and sink into a hot tub filled with bubbles.

But her hand shook a little as she drew the curtain aside.

The street was empty.

As Tess let the curtain fall, she wondered why that didn't ease her mind.

SHE'D looked out at him. He'd known, somehow; he'd known the moment her eyes had focused on him as he stood on the street below. What had she seen? Her salvation?

Almost sobbing against the headache, he let himself into his apartment. The corridor was dark. No one ever watched him come or go. Neither was he worried that she'd seen his face. It had been too dark and too distant for that. But had she seen the pain?

Why had he gone there? He stripped off his coat and let it lie in a heap. The next day he would hang it neatly and tidy the rest of the apartment, as was his habit, but tonight he could hardly think over the pain.

God always tested the righteous.

He found a bottle of Excedrin and chewed two pills, welcoming the dry, bitter taste. His stomach was rolling with a nausea that came every night now and lingered through the mornings. He was dousing himself with over-the-counter drugs just to keep functioning.

Why had he gone there?

Perhaps he was going mad. Perhaps it was all madness. He held out his hand and watched the tremor. If he didn't control himself, they would all know. In the aluminum range hood that he kept clean of grease and grime, as he'd been taught, he saw his distorted reflection. The priest's collar was white beneath his haggard face. If they saw him now, they would all know. Perhaps that would be best. Then he could rest, rest and forget.

Pain sliced through the base of his skull.

No, he couldn't rest, he couldn't forget. Laura needed

him to complete his mission so that she could finally find the light. Hadn't she asked, begged for him to ask God for forgiveness?

Judgment had been quick and harsh for Laura. He'd cursed God, lost his faith, but he'd never forgotten. Now, all these years later, the Voice had come, showing him the way to her salvation. Perhaps she had to die again and again through another lost one, but it was quick, and each time there was absolution. Soon it would be over, for all of them.

Going into the bedroom, he lit the candles. The light flickered on the framed picture of the woman he'd lost, and the women he'd killed. Clipped neatly and lying beneath a black rosary was the newspaper picture of Dr. Teresa Court.

He prayed in Latin, as he'd been taught.

BEN bought her an all-day sucker, swirled with red and yellow. Tess accepted it at the door, gave it a thorough study, then shook her head.

"You know how to keep a woman off balance, Detective. Most men go for chocolate."

"Too ordinary. Besides, I figured you'd probably be used to the Swiss kind, and I—" He broke off, aware that he was going to start rambling if she kept smiling at him over the round hunk of candy. "You look different."

"I do? How?"

"Your hair's down." He wanted to touch it but knew he wasn't ready. "And you're not wearing a suit."

Tess looked down at her wool slacks and oversized sweater. "I don't usually wear suits to a horror-movie double feature."

"You don't look like a psychiatrist anymore."

"Yes, I do. I just don't look like your conception of one." Now he did touch her hair, just a little. She liked the way he did it, in a gesture that was both friendly and cautious.

"You've never looked like my conception of one."

Wanting a moment to align her own thoughts, she set the sucker down on the table beside a Dresden platter, then went to the closet for a jacket. "And what is your conception?"

"Someone pale, thin, and bald."

"Hmmm."

The jacket was suede, and soft as butter. He held it for her as she slipped her arms in. "You don't smell like a psychiatrist either."

She smiled over her shoulder. "What does a psychiatrist smell like? Or do I want to know?"

"Like peppermint, and English Leather aftershave."

She turned to face him. "That's very specific."

"Yeah. Your hair's caught."

He dipped his hand under the collar of her jacket and freed it. He took a step forward, almost without thinking, and had her against the closet door. Her face tilted up, and there was a wariness in her eyes he'd noticed before. She wore little makeup, the sleek, polished look that was so much a part of her image replaced by a warm accessibility a smart man would recognize as dangerous. He knew what he wanted, and was comfortable with the swift rush of desire. The degree of it was another matter. When you wanted too much, too quickly, he thought, it was best to take things slow.

His mouth was close to hers. His hand was still on her hair. "You like butter on your popcorn?"

Tess didn't know whether to laugh or curse. Deciding to do neither, she told herself she was relaxed. "Tons of it."

"Good. Then I don't have to spring for two boxes. It's cold outside," he added, leaning away from her. "You'll need gloves."

He drew out his own scarred black leather ones before he opened the door.

"I'D forgotten just how frightening those movies were." It was dark when Tess settled back in his car, sated with pizza and cheap red wine. The air was biting, stinging her cheeks with the first brush of winter before she slid into Ben's car. Neither the cold nor the media was keeping Washington indoors. The Saturday-night stream of traffic rolled by, on its way to clubs, supper, and parties.

"I've always appreciated the way the cop gets the girl in the *House of Wax*."

"All Vincent needed was a good analyst," she said mildly as Ben adjusted the radio.

"Sure, and he'd have dumped you in the vat, coated you with wax, and turned you into . . ." He turned his head for a narrowed-eyed study. "Helen of Troy, I think."

"Not bad." She pursed her lips. "Of course, some psychiatrists might say you chose that, subconsciously linking yourself with Paris."

"As a cop, I wouldn't romanticize kidnapping."

"Pity." She let her eyes half close, not even aware of how easy it was for her to relax with him. The heater hummed in accompaniment to the moody music from the car radio. She remembered the lyrics and sang them in her head.

"Tired?"

"No, comfortable." As soon as the words were out, she straightened. "I'll probably have a few nightmares. Horror movies are a wonderful escape valve for real tensions. I guarantee no one in that theater was thinking about their next insurance payment or acid rain."

He let out a breezy chuckle as he drove out of the parking lot. "You know, Doc, some people might look at it as simple entertainment. It didn't seem like you were thinking escape valve when you dug holes in my arm when our heroine was running through the fog."

"It must have been the woman on the other side of you."

"I was sitting on the aisle."

"She had a long reach. You missed the turn to my apartment."

"I didn't miss it. I didn't take it. You said you weren't tired."

"I'm not." She wasn't sure she'd ever felt more awake, more alive. The song seemed to be playing just under her skin, promising romance and exquisite heartache. She'd always thought the first was somehow imcomplete without the second. "Are we going somewhere?"

"A little place I know where the music's good and they don't water down the liquor."

She ran her tongue over her teeth. "I'd like that." She was in the mood for music, something bluesy maybe, with the ache of a tenor sax. "I suppose in a professional capacity you're well acquainted with the local bars."

"I've got a working knowledge." He punched in his car lighter. "You're not the bar type."

Interested, she faced him. His profile was in shadows, struck intermittently by streetlights. It was funny how sometimes he looked safe, solid, the kind of man a woman might run to if it were dark. Then the light struck his face another way, and the planes and angles were highlighted. A woman might run from him. She shook off the thought. She'd made a policy not to analyze men she dated. Too often you learned more than you wanted to know.

"Is there a type?"

"Yeah." And he knew them all. "You're not it. Hotel lounge. Champagne cocktails at the Mayflower or the Hotel Washington."

"Now who's doing psychological profiles, Detective?"

"You've got to be able to type people in my business, Doc." He pulled up and maneuvered into a space between a Honda three-wheeler and a Chevette hatchback. Before he turned off the key, he wondered if he was making a mistake.

"What's this?"

"This." He pulled out the keys but left them jingling in his hand. "Is where I live."

She looked out the window at a four-story apartment building with faded red brick and green awnings. "Oh."

"I don't have any champagne."

Her decision. She understood him well enough to understand that. But she understood little else about him. The car was warm and quiet. Safe. Inside, she didn't know what to expect. She knew herself well enough to understand how seldom she took risks. Maybe it was time.

"You have scotch?" She turned back to see his smile.

"Yeah."

"That'll do."

The air snapped cold the moment she stepped from the car. Winter wasn't going to wait for the calendar, she thought, then shuddered, thinking of another calendar, one with the Madonna and Child on the cover. The little twist of fear had her looking up and down the street. A block away a truck let out a blast of exhaust.

"Come on." Ben stood in a pool of light from a streetlamp; the light bounced from the planes of his face. "You're cold."

"Yes." She shivered again when his arm went around her shoulders.

He led her inside. There were about a dozen mail slots against one wall. The pale green carpet was clean but almost threadbare. There was no lobby, no security guard at a desk, only a dim set of stairs.

"It's certainly a quiet building," she said as they climbed to the second floor.

"Everybody here pretty much minds their own business."

There was a faint scent of cooking in the hall when he stopped to unlock his door. The light overhead winked weakly.

His apartment was tidier than she'd expected. It was more than just a general preconception of a man living alone, Tess realized. Ben seemed too relaxed and casual in other areas to bother clearing dust or old magazines. Then she decided she was wrong. The room might be clean, but it did reflect his style.

The sofa was the dominant piece of furniture. Low and far from new, it was plumped with throw pillows. A Dagwood couch, Tess thought. One that simply begged you to relax and take a nap. There were posters rather than paintings. Toulouse-Lautrec's cancan dancers, a single woman's leg standing in a four inch heel, skimmed at the thigh with white lace. There was a Dieffenbachia thriving away in a plastic margarine bowl. And books. One wall was nearly filled with them. Delighted, she pulled out a worn hardbacked copy of *East of Eden*. As Ben's hands went to her shoulders, she opened the flyleaf.

"To Ben." She read the spiky, feminine handwriting. "Kiss, kiss. Bambi." Putting her tongue in her cheek, she closed it. "Bambi?"

"Used bookstore." He removed her jacket. "Fascinating places. Never can tell what you'll pick up."

"Did you pick up the book or Bambi?"

"Never mind." He took the copy from her and stuck it back on the shelf.

"Do you know, one gets an immediate mental image from certain names?"

"Yeah. Scotch, straight up, right?"

"Right." A streak of gray whizzed by and landed on a red pillow. "A cat too?" Amused, Tess strolled over to stroke it. "What's his name?"

"Her. She proved that by having kittens in the bathtub last year." The cat rolled over so Tess could scratch her belly. "I call her D.C."

"As in Washington?"

"As in Dumb Cat."

"It's a wonder she doesn't have a complex." Running her hands over the rounded belly again, Tess wondered if she should warn him he'd be getting another litter of gifts in a month or so.

"She runs into walls. On purpose."

"I could refer you to an excellent pet psychologist."

He laughed, but wasn't entirely sure she was joking. "I'd better get those drinks."

When he went into the kitchen, she rose to look at his view from the window. The streets weren't as quiet as her neighborhood. Traffic moved by at a steady clip, droning and grunting along. He wouldn't take himself far from the action, she thought, and remembered she hadn't paid any attention to what direction he'd taken. She could be anywhere in the city. She expected unease, and instead felt a sense of freedom.

"I promised you music."

She turned and looked at him. The simple dun-colored sweater and faded jeans he wore suited him. She'd thought once that he understood himself very well. Now it would be foolish to deny that she wanted to understand him.

"Yes, you did."

He handed her a glass and thought about how different she was, and how different she looked from any other woman he'd brought here. That quiet class of hers demanded that a man swallow his lust and take the whole person. Wondering if he was ready to, he set down his own glass and flipped through his records.

When he set one on the turntable, Tess heard the brassy heat of jazz. "Leon Redbone," she said.

He shook his head as he turned toward her. "You keep surprising me."

"My grandfather's one of his biggest fans." Sipping her drink, she walked over to pick up the album cover. "It seems the two of you have quite a lot in common."

"Me and the senator?" Ben laughed before he sipped his vodka. "I'll bet."

"I'm serious. You'll have to meet him."

Meeting a woman's family was something he associated with wedding rings and orange blossoms. He'd always avoided it. "Why don't we—" The phone rang and he swore, setting down his glass. "I'd ignore it, but I'm on call."

"You don't have to explain those things to a doctor."

"Yeah." He picked up the phone beside the couch. "Paris. Oh, yeah. Hi."

It didn't take a trained psychiatrist to understand there was a woman on the other end. Tess smiled into her drink and went back to the view.

"No, I've been tied up. Look, sugar—" The minute the word was out, he winced. Tess kept her back to him. "I'm on a case, you know? No, I didn't forget about . . . I didn't forget. Listen, I'll have to get back to you when things lighten up. I don't know, weeks, maybe months. You really ought to try that marine. Sure. See ya." He hung up, cleared his throat, and reached for his drink again. "Wrong number."

It was so easy to laugh. She turned, leaned against the windowsill, and gave in to it. "Oh, really?"

"Enjoyed that, didn't you?"

"Immensely."

"If I'd known you'd get such a kick out of it, I'd have invited her up."

"Ah, the male ego." With one hand crossed over her body, she lifted the drink again. She was still laughing at him. The humor didn't fade when he walked over and took the drink from her hand. The warm, approachable look was back. He felt the pull of it, the danger of it, the need for it.

"I'm glad you're here."

"So am I."

"You know, Doc . . ." He let his fingers play through her hair. The gesture was as friendly as before, but not as cautious. "There's one thing we haven't done together."

She withdrew at that. He sensed it though she hadn't moved away. He continued to toy with her hair as he drew her closer. His breath brushed over her lips.

"Dance," he murmured, and laid his cheek against hers. Whether her sigh was of pleasure or relief, he didn't know, but she was nearly relaxed against him. "There's something I've noticed about you."

"What?"

"You feel good." His lips moved over her ear as they swayed, hardly moving from one spot. "Real good."

"Ben—"

"Relax." He made long slow strokes up her back and down again. "Another thing I've noticed is that you don't relax much."

His body was hard against hers, his lips warm against her temple. "At the moment, it isn't easy."

"Good." He liked the way her hair smelled, fresh and rich without the overlay of scented shampoos, gels, and sprays. From the easy way her body blended with his, he knew she wore nothing but skin under the sweater. He imagined away the layer of material and let the heat rise.

"You know, Doc, I haven't been sleeping well."

Her eyes were nearly closed, but it wasn't because of relaxation. "You've got a lot on your mind with this case."

"Yeah. But there's something else that's been on my mind."

"What?"

"You." He drew her back a little. Eyes open and on hers, he teased her mouth. "I can't stop thinking about you. I think I have a problem."

"I . . . my caseload's pretty heavy right now."

"Private sessions." As he'd wanted to all evening, he slipped his hands under her sweater and let her skin warm him. "Starting tonight."

She felt the ridge of callus below his fingers rub up her spine. "I don't think—" But he stopped her with a kiss, a long, slow melding of lips that had his own heart racing. There was a hesitation in her that licked at his desire. She'd been a challenge from the beginning, and maybe a mistake. He was beyond caring.

"Stay with me, Tess."

"Ben." She drew out of his arms, wanting the distance, and the control. "I think we're rushing this."

"I've wanted you from the start." It wasn't his style to admit it, but this wasn't the usual game.

She dragged a hand through her hair. She thought of the inscription in the book, the phone call. "I don't take sex lightly, I can't."

"I'm not taking you lightly. I wish I could. It's probably a mistake." He looked at her again, fragile, delicate, elegant. It would be, could be, no fling, no easy romp in the sack with no morning repercussions. "I don't give a damn, Tess." Determined, but somehow less sure of himself, he took a step closer to frame her face in his hands. "I don't want to go another night without you." He bent to kiss her. "Stay."

He lit candles in the bedroom. The music had stopped, and it was so quiet she thought she could almost hear the echo of it. She was trembling, and no amount of lecturing herself on being an adult and making her own choices would stop it. Nerves shivered through her. Needs twisted with them until they were one and the same. He came to her and gathered her close.

"You're shaking."

"I feel like a schoolgirl."

"It helps." He buried his face in her hair. "I'm scared to death."

"Are you?" There was a smile on her lips as she put her hands to his face and drew him back.

"I feel, I don't know, like some kid in the backseat of his father's Chevy about to tackle his first bra snaps." He put his hands to her wrists a moment, to hold himself back from touching her. "There's never been anyone like you. I keep worrying that I'll make the wrong move."

Nothing he could have said would have reassured her more. She drew his face down to hers. Their lips met, just a nibble, just a test that threatened to grow to a hungry bite. "So far so good," she murmured. "Make love with me, Ben. I've always wanted you to."

He kept his eyes on hers as he drew up the bulky sweater. Then her hair was pooled over naked shoulders. There was moonlight and candlelight on her skin. He traced his own shadows over it.

She was never sure of herself on this level with a man. There was hesitation as she began to draw his sweater off. Beneath it his torso was lean and firm. A St. Christopher's medal dangled above his breastbone. Tess ran her finger over it and smiled.

"It's just for luck," he told her.

Saying nothing, she pressed her lips to his shoulder. "You've a scar here."

"It's old." He unfastened the snap of her slacks.

Her thumb moved over it. "A bullet," she realized. There was a dull horror in her voice.

"It's old," he repeated, and drew her onto the bed. She lay beneath him, her hair flared out on the dark spread, her eyes heavy, lips parted. "I've wanted you here. I can't tell you how much or how often."

She reached up and touched her fingertips to his face. Along his jawline was the beginnings of his beard. Beneath, just above where his pulse beat, the skin was smooth. "You can show me."

When he grinned, she discovered she was relaxed and waiting for him.

His experience might have been greater, but his need wasn't. Hers had been under tight control and was ripe and hungry now that it was set free. They rolled over the bed, damp and naked, forgetting the civilized, the ordinary.

The spread rumpled and tangled beneath them. He swore at it, then pulled her free and on top of him. Her breasts were small and pale. He cupped one then both in his hands. He heard her murmur of pleasure as he watched her eyes close with it. Then she was pulling him to her, and her mouth was like a fever.

His intention to treat her as a lady, with care and gentleness, was abandoned when her arms and legs wrapped around him. Here, she wasn't the cool and classy Dr. Court, but a woman as passionate and demanding as any man could want. Her skin was soft, fragile to the touch, but slicked with desire. He skimmed his tongue over it, thirsting for her.

She arched against him, letting needs, fantasies, passions have their way. Here and now were all that mattered. What was outside was removed, distant. He was real, and vital, and important. The rest of the world could wait.

Candlelight flickered, gutted, and went out.

Hours later, he awoke, cold. The spread was bundled at the foot of the bed. Tess was curled in a ball beside him, naked, her hair curtaining her face. He rose and pulled the covers over her. Even the moonlight was gone now. For a while he just stood over the bed, looking down at her as she slept. The cat padded into the room as Ben walked quietly out.

Chapter 7

DOCTORS AND COPS. Those in either profession know they will rarely have a day that begins at nine and ends at five. They understand that they've chosen a career where the divorce and burn-out rates are high, the demands many, and the emotional toll extreme. Phone calls spoil dinner parties, sex, and sleep. It's part of the job description.

When the phone rang, Tess reached over automatically. And picked up a candlestick. On the other side of the bed Ben swore, knocked over an ashtray, and found the phone.

"Yeah, Paris." In the dark he ran a hand over his face as if to wipe away sleep. "Where?" Instantly awake, he switched on the lamp. The cat curled on Tess's stomach growled a complaint then leaped aside as she braced herself on her elbows. "Keep him there. I'm on my way." Ben hung up the phone and stared at the light sheen of frost on the window.

"He didn't wait, did he?"

The light fell harshly over his face as he turned to look at her. She gave a quick, involuntary shudder. His eyes were hard—not weary, not regretful, but hard. "No, he didn't wait."

"Do they have him?"

"No, but it looks like we've got a witness." As he rolled out of bed he grabbed his jeans. "I don't know how long I'll be but you can wait here, get some more sleep. I'll fill you in when . . . What are you doing?"

She stood on the opposite side of the bed, dragging on her sweater. "Going with you."

"Forget it." His legs disappeared into the jeans, but he left the pants unsnapped as he pulled open a drawer for a sweater. "There's nothing you can do at a murder scene but get in the way." In the mirror above his dresser he saw her head snap up. "It's still shy of five, for Christ's sake. Go back to bed."

"Ben, I'm involved in this case."

He turned. She wore only the sweater that skimmed her thighs. He remembered the material had been thick and soft when he'd drawn it off her. Her slacks were balled in her hands and her hair was rumpled from the pillow, but it was the psychiatrist facing him, not the woman. Something inside of him curdled. He yanked his own sweater on, then walked to the closet for his shoulder holster. "This is a homicide. It's not like going to look at somebody's who's been painted up nice to lie in a casket."

"I'm a doctor."

"I know what you are." He checked his gun, then hitched the holster on.

"Ben, it's possible I could see something, some detail that would give me a clue to his mind."

"Fuck his mind."

Saying nothing, she shook out her slacks, stepped into them, then fastened them in place. "I understand how you feel, and I'm sorry."

"Yeah?" He sat down to pull on his boots but continued to watch her. "You think you know how I feel? Well, let me tell you anyway. There's a dead woman a few miles from here. Somebody put a scarf around her neck and pulled until she couldn't breathe anymore. She'd have kicked and pulled at the scarf with her hands and tried to scream, but she wouldn't have been able to. So she's dead, but she's not a name on a list yet. She's still a person. For a little while longer she's still a person."

She would have reached out to him if she'd thought there was a chance he'd accept it. Instead she fastened her belt and kept her voice neutral. "Don't you think I understand that?"

"I'm not sure you do."

They studied each other a moment longer, each dedicated, each frustrated, each coming from different backgrounds and beliefs. It was Tess who accepted it first. "I either go with you now or I call the mayor and end up five minutes behind you. Sooner or later you've got to start working with me."

He'd just spent the night with her. He'd poured himself into her three times during the night. He'd felt her body rock and buck and shudder. Now they were talking murder and politics. The femininity, the softness, even the shyness he'd taken to bed were still there, but beneath was a core of toughness, a self-possession he'd recognized from the first. Studying her, he saw she would go no matter what he said, what he did.

"All right. You go with me and get an up-close look. Maybe after you see her, you'll stop letting your heart bleed for the man who did her."

She bent for her shoes. The bed was between them, but it was as if they'd never shared it. "I suppose it's no use reminding you I'm on your side." He was reaching for his wallet and shield, and said nothing. Tess saw her earrings on his nightstand, a little thing of great intimacy. She scooped them up and dropped them in her pocket. "Where are we going?"

"An alley near Twenty-third and M."

"Twenty-third and M? That's only a couple of blocks from my place."

He didn't bother to look at her. "I know."

THE streets were deserted. The bars would have closed at one. Most private parties would have waned by three. Washington was a political town, and though its night spots ranged from the elite to the sleazy, it didn't have the energy of a New York or Chicago. Drug deals around Fourteenth and U were a life-style away. Even the hookers would have called it a night.

Now and then the leaves that had fallen rushed along the sidewalk then stopped, victims of the sporadic wind. They drove past blank storefronts and boutiques with neon sweaters in the windows. Ben lit a cigarette and let the familiar taste of Virginia tobacco ease some of the tension.

He didn't want her there. Doctor or no doctor, he didn't want her to be a part of the hopeless ugliness of this part of his job. She could share in the paperwork, the fitting together of the puzzle, the step-by-step logic of an investigation, but she shouldn't be here.

She had to be here, Tess thought. It was time to face the results, and maybe, just maybe, get a better understanding of the motivation. She was a doctor. It was irrelevant that she wasn't the kind of doctor who prodded fingers in the human body. She was trained, she was capable, and she understood death.

Tess saw the blue and red lights of the first police car and began to school her breathing to long inhales, slow exhales.

The alley and several feet on all sides were roped off, though there was no one on the predawn streets. Cruisers sat with their lights blinking and their radios on. A community of workers was already inside the official area.

Ben pulled up to the curb. "You stay with me," he told Tess, but still didn't look at her. "We have a policy against civilians wandering around homicide scenes."

"I don't intend to get in your way. I intend to do my job. You'll find I'm as good at it as you are at yours." She pushed open her door and nearly collided with Ed.

"Sorry, Dr. Court." Her hands were icy. He patted them without thinking. "You're going to want your gloves." He stuck his own in his pockets as he looked at Ben.

"What have we got?"

"Lab boys are in there now. Sly's getting pictures. Coroner's en route." His breath came out in a white puffy steam. The tips of his ears were already red from the cold, but he'd forgotten to button his coat. "Some kid stumbled across her about four-thirty. Uniforms haven't got much out of him yet. He's been pretty busy whooshing up about a half case of beer." He glanced at Tess again. "Sorry."

"Don't apologize," Ben said briefly. "She'll remind you she's a doctor."

"Captain's coming in on this."

"Terrific." Ben shot the butt of his cigarette into the street. "Let's get to work."

They started toward the alley, passed a cruiser where someone sat in the backseat sobbing. Tess glanced over, pulled toward the sound of despair. Then her arm brushed Ben's and she continued toward the alley. A small man with horn-rimmed glasses and a camera stepped out. He took out a blue bandanna and rubbed it over his nose.

"It's all yours. Get him, for Christ's sake. I don't want to photograph any more dead blondes. A man's got to have a little variety in his work."

"You're a riot, Sly." Ben brushed by him, leaving the photographer sneezing into the bandanna.

They'd taken only a few steps into the alley when the scent of death rose up. They all recognized it, that bitter, fetid stench which was both offensive and eerily compelling to the living.

Her body had emptied itself. Her blood had settled. Her arms had been folded neatly across her body, but she didn't look at peace. Sightless, her eyes were locked open. There was a smear of dried blood on her chin. Her own, Tess thought. Sometime during the struggle to live, she had sawed her teeth through her bottom lip.

She'd worn a long, serviceable wool coat in olive drab. The white silk amice stood out starkly against it. It had been taken from around her neck, where bruises had already formed, and smoothed over her breasts.

The note was pinned there, the message the same.

Her sins are forgiven her.

But this time the letters weren't printed neatly. They were wavery, and the paper was crumpled a bit, as though his hands had mashed it. The word *sins* was printed larger than the rest, the markings darker, almost going through the paper. Tess crouched down beside the body for a closer look.

A cry for help? she wondered. Was it a plea for someone to stop him from sinning again? The shaky handwriting was a deviation, however slight, from his routine. It meant, to Tess, that he was losing his hold, perhaps doubting himself even as he fulfilled his mission.

He hadn't been so sure this time, she decided. His mind was becoming a logjam of thoughts, memories, and voices. He must be terrified, she thought, and almost certainly physically ill by now.

Her coat had been left open rather than neatly arranged. There wasn't enough of a breeze in the alley to have flapped it open. So he hadn't tidied it as he had the clothing of the others. Perhaps he hadn't been able to.

Then she saw the lapel pin against the green wool, a gold heart with the name Anne scrolled inside. She had been Anne. A wave of pity washed over her, for Anne, and for the man who had been driven to kill her.

Ben saw the way she studied the body, clinically, dispassionately, without revulsion. He'd wanted to shield her from the reality of death, but also wanted to press her face into it until she'd wept and run the other way.

"If you've gotten yourself a good look, Dr. Court, why don't you back off and let us do our job?"

She looked up at Ben, then rose slowly to her feet. "He's nearly finished. I don't think he's going to be able to take much more."

"Tell that to her."

"Kid puked all over the place," Ed said lightly, and breathed through his mouth to try to combat the stench. With a pencil he flipped open the woman's wallet, which had spilled out of her purse. "Anne Reasoner," he said, reading her driver's license. "Twenty-seven. Lives about a block up on M."

A block up, Tess thought. A block closer to her own apartment. She pressed her lips together and looked out of the alley until the fear passed. "It's a ritual," she said clearly enough. "From everything I've read, ritual, rites, traditions, are an intricate part of the Catholic Church. He's performing his own ritual here, saving them then absolving them and leaving them with this." She indicated the amice. "The symbol of that salvation and absolution. He folds the amice exactly the same way each time. He positions their bodies exactly the same way. But this time he didn't tidy her clothes."

"Playing detective?"

Tess balled her hands in her pockets, fighting to overlook Ben's sarcasm. "This is devotion, blind devotion to the Church, obsession with ritual. But the handwriting shows that he's beginning to question what he's doing, what he's driven to do."

"That's fine." Unreasonable anger rushed into him at her lack of emotional response. Ben turned his back to her and bent over the body. "Why don't you go out to the car and write that up? We'll be sure to pass on your professional opinion to her family."

He didn't see her face, the quick hurt then the slow anger that came into her eyes. But he heard her walk away.

"Little rough on her, weren't you?"

Ben didn't look at his partner either, but at the woman who had been Anne. She stared back at him. Serve and protect. No one had protected Anne Reasoner.

"She doesn't belong here," he murmured, and thought as much of Anne Reasoner as of Tess. He shook his head, still studying the almost saintlike pose of the body. "What was she doing in an alley in the middle of the night?" An alley that was close, too damn close, to Tess's apartment.

"Maybe she wasn't."

Drawing his brows together, Ben lifted up one of her feet. She'd worn loafers. The kind that last through college, your first marriage and divorce. The leather fit her feet like gloves and was well polished. The back of the heel was freshly scraped and scarred.

"So he killed her on the street and dragged her in." Ben looked over at Ed as his partner crouched and examined the other shoe. "He strangled her out on the fucking street. We got streetlights about every ten goddamn feet in this neighborhood. We got black and whites cruising every thirty minutes, and he kills her on the street." He looked at her hands. Her nails were medium length and well shaped. Only three of them were broken. The coral-colored polish was unchipped. "Doesn't look like she put up much of a fight."

THE light was turning gray, a washed-out, milky gray that promised overcast skies and cold autumn rain. Dawn floated over the city without any beauty. Sunday morning. People were sleeping in. Hangovers were brewing. The first church services would begin soon with raw-eyed, weekend-dazed congregations.

Tess leaned against the hood of Ben's car. The suede jacket wasn't warm enough in the chilled dawn, but she was too restless to get inside the car. She watched a round man with a medical bag and blue-paisley pajama bottoms under a flapping overcoat go into the alley. The coroner's day had started early.

From somewhere blocks away came the grinding metallic sound of a truck changing gears. A single cab rode by without slowing down. One of the uniformed cops brought a big Styrofoam cup with steam and the scent of coffee rising off the top, and handed it to the figure in back of the cruiser.

Tess looked toward the alley again. She'd held up, she told herself, though her stomach was roiling now in reaction. She'd been professional, as she'd promised herself she would be. But she wouldn't forget Anne Reasoner for a long time. Death wasn't a neatly printed statistic when you looked it in the face.

She would have kicked and pulled at the scarf with her hands and tried to scream.

Tess took a long gulp of air that hurt her throat, raw from swallowing nausea. She was a doctor. She repeated it over and over until the cramp in her stomach eased. She'd been trained to deal with death. And she had dealt with it.

Turning away from the alley, she faced the empty street. Who was she trying to fool? She dealt with despair, with phobias, neuroses, even violence, but she'd never been face-to-face with the victim of a murder. Her life was ordered, protected because she'd made certain of it. Pastel walls and questions and answers. Even her hours at the clinic were tame compared to the day-to-day violence on the streets of the city where she lived.

She knew about ugliness, violence, and perversion, but she'd always been neatly separated from all of it by her own background. The senator's granddaughter, the bright young student, the cool-headed doctor. She had her degree, her successful practice, and three published papers. She'd treated the helpless, the hopeless, and the pitiful, but she'd never knelt down beside murder.

"Dr. Court?"

She turned back and saw Ed. Instinctively she looked past him and spotted Ben talking to the coroner.

"I wrangled you some coffee."

"Thanks." She took the cup and sipped slowly.

"Want a bagel?"

"No." She laid a hand on her stomach. "No."

"You did okay in there."

The coffee settled and seemed content to stay down. Looking over the cup, she met his eyes. He understood, she realized, and neither condemned nor pitied. "I hope I never have to do it again."

A black plastic bag was carried out of the alley. Tess found herself able to watch as it was loaded into the morgue van.

"It never gets any easier," Ed murmured. "I used to wish it would."

"Not anymore?"

"No. I figure if it gets easier, it means you've lost the edge that makes you want to find out why."

She nodded. Common sense and common compassion in his quiet voice were soothing. "How long have you and Ben been partners?"

"Five, almost six years."

"You suit each other."

"Funny, I was just thinking the same thing about you."

She gave a low, humorless laugh. "There's a difference between attraction and suitability."

"Maybe. There's also a difference between stubbornness and stupidity." His look remained bland as her head came around. "Anyway, Dr. Court," he went on before she had a chance to react. "I was hoping you might talk to the witness for a couple of minutes. He's pretty shook up, and we're not getting anywhere."

"All right." She nodded at the cruiser. "That's him in the car, isn't it?"

"Yeah. Name's Gil Norton."

Tess walked to the car and crouched at the open door. He was hardly more than a boy, she thought. Twenty, maybe twenty-two. While he shivered and gulped coffee, his face was pale, with a high flush of color over the cheekbones. His eyes were puffed and red from weeping, and his teeth clattered. He'd put dents with his thumbs in the sides of the Styrofoam cup. He smelt of beer and vomit and terror.

"Gil?"

After a jolt, he turned his head. She hadn't any doubt he was stone sober now, but she could see a bit too much white around his irises. His pupils were dilated.

"I'm Dr. Court. How are you feeling?"

"I want to go home. I've been sick. My stomach hurts." There was a trace of the whining self-pity of a drunk who'd had cold water dumped in his face. Under it was plain fear.

"Finding her must have been pretty dreadful."

"I don't want to talk about it." His mouth contracted into a thin white line. "I want to go home."

"I'll call someone for you if you like. Your mother?"

Tears began to squeeze out of his eyes again. His hands trembled until the coffee sloshed in his cup.

"Gil, why don't you step out of the car? You might feel better if you stood up in the fresh air."

"I want a cigarette. I smoked all of mine."

"We'll get some." She held out a hand. After a moment's hesitation, he took it. His fingers closed over hers like a vise. "I don't want to talk to the cops."

"Why?"

"I should have a lawyer. Shouldn't I have a lawyer?"

"I'm sure you can if you like, but you're not in trouble, Gil."

"I found her."

"Yes. Here, let me take that for you." Gently she took the half-empty cup before he could spill the remaining coffee over his pants. "Gil, we need you to tell us whatever you know so we can find out who killed her."

He looked around and saw the blue uniforms and impassive faces. "They're going to dump it on me."

"No." She spoke calmly, having anticipated him. Keeping close to his side, she began to lead him toward Ben. "They don't think you killed her."

"I got a record." He said it in a shaky whisper. "Drug bust last year. Just petty shit, a little grass, but the cops'll figure I got a record, I found her, I killed her."

"It's natural to be scared. That's not going to go away until you talk about what happened. Try to be logical, Gil. Has anyone arrested you?"

"No."

"Has anyone asked you if you killed that woman?"

"No. But I was there." He focused on the alley with blank, fascinated horror. "And she was . . ."

"That's what you need to get out. Gil, this is Detective Paris." She stopped in front of Ben but kept her hand on Gil's arm. "He's with Homicide, and too smart to think you killed anyone."

Beneath the words the message was clear. Go easy. Ben's resentment communicated itself just as lucidly. He didn't have to be told how to handle a witness.

"Ben, Gil could use a cigarette."

"Sure." Ben reached for his pack and shook one out. "Rough morning," he commented as he struck a match.

Gil's hands still shook, but he drew greedily on the cigarette. "Yeah." His eyes darted over and up as Ed approached.

"This is Detective Jackson," Tess continued in a soothing, introductory voice. "They need you to tell them what you saw."

"Will I have to go in?"

"We'll need you to sign a statement." Ben shook out a cigarette of his own.

"Man, I just want to go home."

"We'll get you home." Ben looked at Tess through the haze of his smoke. "Just take it easy and tell it from the beginning."

"I was at a party." He stopped dead and looked at Tess. She gave him an encouraging nod. "You can check, it was over on Twenty-sixth. Some friends of mine just got the apartment, see, and it was like a moving-in party. I can give you names."

"That's fine." Ed had his notebook out. "We'll get them from you later. When did you leave the party?"

"I don't know. I had too much to drink and got into it with my girl. She doesn't like it when I party too hard. We had words, you know." He swallowed, drew in smoke again, then let it out on a shuddering breath. "She got pissed and left, that was about one-thirty. Took the car, so I couldn't drive."

"Sounds like she was looking out for you," Ed put in.

"Yeah, well, I was too wasted to see it that way." The rumblings of a heroic hangover were already beginning. Gil preferred it to the nausea.

"What happened after she left?" Ed prompted.

"I hung around. I think I crashed for a while. The party was winding down when I woke up. Lee—it was his apartment, Lee Grimes—he says I can sleep on the couch, but I . . . well, I needed air, you know? I was going to walk home. I guess I was already feeling pretty sick, so I stopped, just across the street there." He turned and pointed. "My head was spinning, and I knew I was going to toss up some beer. I just rested there a minute and got it under control. And I see this guy come out of the alley—"

"You saw him come out," Ben interrupted. "You didn't hear anything? See him go in?"

"No, I swear. I don't know how long I'd been standing there. Not too long, I think, 'cause it was cold as hell. Even drunk I was thinking I had to move to keep warm. I saw him come out, then he leaned up against the lamppost for a minute, like he was sick too. I thought it was kind of funny, two drunks weaving across the street from each other, like something out of a cartoon. And one of the drunks is a priest."

"How do you know that?" Ben paused in the act of offering Gil another cigarette.

"He's wearing this priest's suit—the black dress with the white collar. I was laughing to myself. You know, looks like he's been hitting the communion wine. Anyway, I'm standing there wondering if I'm going to piss in my pants or barf, and he straightens himself up and walks away."

"Which way?"

"Toward M. Yeah, toward M Street. He went around the corner."

"Did you see what he looked like?"

"Man, I saw he was a priest." Gil pounced on the fresh cigarette. "He was white." He pressed his fingers to his eyes. "Yeah, he was a white dude. I think he had dark hair. Look, I was wasted, and he was standing with his face against the lamppost."

"Okay. You're doing good." Ed flipped a page in his notebook. "How about build? Could you tell if he was short, tall?"

Gil screwed his face up in concentration. Though he still consumed the cigarette in great gulps, Tess saw he was calming. "I guess he was pretty tall, not a little guy anyhow. He wasn't fat. Shit, it's like average, you know. About like you, I guess," he said to Ben.

"How about age?" Ben put in.

"I don't know. He wasn't old and feeble. His hair was dark." He said it quickly as it flashed into his memory. "Yeah, I'm sure it was dark, not gray or blond. He had his hands in it like this." He demonstrated, pressing his hands against the side of his head. "Like his head was hurting him pretty bad. His hands were black, but his face was white. Like he had gloves on, you know. It was cold."

He stopped again as the full implication hit him. He'd seen a murderer. Fear doubled back, a personal thing. If he'd seen, he was involved. The muscles in his face began to tremble. "He's the one who's been doing all these women. He's the one. He's a priest."

"Let's finish this up," Ben said easily. "How'd you find the body?"

"Oh, Christ." He closed his eyes, and Tess moved toward him.

"Gil, try to remember it's over. What you're feeling is

going to fade. It'll start to fade a little bit after you say it all out loud. Once you say it out loud, it'll be easier."

"Okay." He reached for her hand and held on. "After the guy left I was feeling a little better, like maybe I was going to keep everything down after all. But I'd had a lot of beer and I had to get rid of some, you know. I still had myself together enough to know I couldn't just piss all over the sidewalk. So I walked over to the alley. I almost tripped over her." He ran the back of his hand under his nose as it started to leak. "I had my hand in my pants and I almost tripped over her. Jesus. There was enough light coming in from the street so that I saw her face, real good. I never saw anyone dead before. Not ever. It's not like the movies, man. It ain't nothing like the movies."

He took a minute, sucking on the cigarette and crushing Tess's fingers. "I gagged. I took a couple of steps trying to get out, and I just started throwing up. I thought my sides would bust before I stopped. My head was going around again, but I got out somehow. I think I fell down on the sidewalk. There were cops. A couple of them stopped their car. I told them . . . I just told them to go in the alley."

"You did good, Gil." Ben took his pack of cigarettes and stuffed it in the boy's pocket. "We're going to have one of the officers take you home, let you get cleaned up and eat something. Then we need you at the station."

"Can I call my girl?"

"Sure."

"If she hadn't taken the car, she'd have been walking home. She might've walked past here."

"Call your girl," Ben told him. "And ease off the beer. Whittaker." Ben signaled to the driver of the first cruiser. "Take Gil home, will you? And give him some time to clean up and pull it together before you bring him in."

"He could use some sleep, Ben," Tess murmured.

He started to snap at her, then cut himself off. The kid looked ready to drop. "Right. Drop him off, Whittaker. We'll send a car for you about noon. Okay?"

"Yeah." He looked at Tess then. "Thanks. I do feel better."

"If what happens gives you some trouble and you want to talk about it, call the station. They'll give you my number."

Before Gil was in the car, Ben had Tess by the arm, leading her away. "The department doesn't approve of soliciting for patients at the scene."

Tess shook off his arm. "Yes, you're welcome, Detective. I'm glad I could help you get a coherent story out of your only witness."

"We'd have gotten it out of him." Ben cupped his hands around a match and lit a fresh cigarette. Out of the corner of his eye he saw Harris arrive on the scene.

"You really hate it that I helped, don't you? Because I'm a psychiatrist, I wonder, or because I'm a woman?"

"Don't psychoanalyze me," he warned, tossed his cigarette into the street, and immediately wished it back.

"I don't have to psychoanalyze to see resentment, prejudice, and anger." She broke off, realizing how close she was to losing control in public and creating a scene. "Ben, I know you didn't want me to come, but I didn't get in the way."

"Get in the way?" He laughed and studied her face. "No, you're a real pro, lady."

"That's it, isn't it?" she murmured. She wanted to shout, to sit down, to just walk away. It took the rest of her control not to do any of those things. Whatever you begin, you finish. That, too, was part of her training. "I walked into that alley with you and stayed on the same level. I didn't fall apart, get sick, run away. I didn't get hysterical at the sight of a body, and that really bothers you."

"Doctors are objective, right?"

"That's right," she said calmly, though Anne Reasoner's face flashed into her mind. "But maybe it'll soothe your ego to know that it wasn't easy for me. I wanted to turn around and walk out of there."

Something inside him jerked, but he ignored it. "You held up pretty good."

"And that strips me of my femininity, maybe even my sexuality. You would have been happier if you'd had to carry me out of that alley. Never mind the interference or inconvenience. That would have been more comfortable for you."

"That's bullshit." He pulled out another cigarette, cursing himself because he realized it was true. "I work with plenty of women cops."

"But you don't sleep with them, do you, Ben?" She said it quietly, knowing she'd hit a button.

Eyes narrowed, he drew in smoke, long and deep. "Watch your step."

"Yes, that's just what I intend to do." She pulled her gloves out of her pockets, realizing for the first time that her hands were freezing. The sun was up now, but the light was still murky. She didn't think she'd ever been so cold. "Tell your captain that he'll have an updated report by tomorrow afternoon."

"Fine. I'll get someone to drive you home."

"I want to walk."

"No." He took her arm before she could turn away.

"You've mentioned that I'm a civilian enough times to know you can't order me."

"Press charges of harassment if you want, but you're getting an escort home."

"It's two blocks," she began, and his grip tightened.

"That's right. Two blocks. Two blocks, and your name and picture have been in the paper." With his free hand he gathered up her hair. It was nearly the same shade as Anne Reasoner's. They both knew it. "Use some of those brains you're so proud of, and think."

"I'm not going to let you frighten me."

"Fine, but you're getting an escort home." He kept his hand on her arm as he walked her to a cruiser.

Chapter 8

THE FIVE DETECTIVES assigned to the Priest homicides logged better than two hundred sixty hours in legwork and paperwork in the week following Anne Reasoner's murder. One of them had a spouse who threatened divorce, another worked through a nasty bout of the flu, and another around a chronic case of insomnia.

The fourth in the series of murders was the top story on both the six and eleven o'clock news, beating out such items as the President's return from West Germany. For the moment Washington was more interested in murder than politics. NBC planned a four-part special.

Incredibly, manuscripts were being peddled to major publishers. More incredibly, offers were being made. Paramount was thinking miniseries. Anne Reasoner—in fact, none of the victims—had ever earned such attention alive.

Anne had lived alone. She had been a CPA attached to one of the city's law firms. Her apartment had shown a taste for the avant garde, with neon, free-form enameled sculptures and DayGlo flamingos. Her wardrobe had reflected her employer, running to softly tailored suits and silk blouses. She'd been able to afford Saks. She'd owned two Jane Fonda workout tapes, an IBM personal computer, and a Cuisinart. There was a man's picture in a frame beside her bed, a quarter ounce of Colombian in her bureau drawer, and fresh flowers—white zinnias—on top of it.

She'd been a good employee. Only three days out sick since the first of the year. But her coworkers knew nothing about her social life. Her neighbors described her as friendly and described the man in the bedside picture as a frequent guest.

Her address book had been neatly ordered and nearly full. Many of the names were passing acquaintances and distant family, along with insurance brokers, an oral surgeon, and an aerobics instructor.

Then they located Suzanne Hudson, a graphic artist who had been Anne's friend and confidante since college. Ben and Ed found her at home, in an apartment above a boutique. She was wearing a terry-cloth robe and carrying a cup of coffee. Her eyes were red and swollen, with bruising shadows down to the cheekbones.

The sound on the television was off, but the *Wheel of Fortune* played on screen. Someone had just solved the puzzle: WHEN IT RAINS IT POURS.

After she let them in, she went to the couch and curled up her feet. "There's coffee in the kitchen if you want it. I'm having a hard time making the effort to be sociable."

"Thanks, anyway." Ben took the opposite end of the couch and left the chair for Ed. "You knew Anne Reasoner pretty well."

"Did you ever have a best friend? I don't mean someone you just called the best, but someone who was?" Her short red hair hadn't been tended to. She combed a hand through it and sent it into spikes. "I really loved her, you know? I still can't quite grip the fact that she's . . ." She bit down on the inside of her lip, then soothed the hurt with coffee. "The funeral's tomorrow."

"I know. Ms. Hudson, it's a hell of a time to bother you, but we need to ask you some questions."

"John Carroll."

"I'm sorry, what?"

"John Carroll." Suzanne repeated the name, then spelled it meticulously when Ed produced his notebook. "You wanted to know why Anne would have been out walking alone in the middle of the night, didn't you?"

The grief and anger were there as she leaned forward and picked up an address book. With the coffee still in her hand, she used her thumb to page through it. "Here's his address." She passed the book to Ed.

"We have a John Carroll, a lawyer who was on staff at the firm Ms. Reasoner worked for." Ed flipped back in his notes and coordinated the addresses.

"That's right. That's him."

"He hasn't come into the office for a couple of days."

"Hiding," she snapped. "He wouldn't have the courage to come out and face what he's done. If he comes tomorrow, if he dares to show his face tomorrow, I'll spit in it." Then she covered her eyes with her hand and shook her head. "No, no, it's not right." Fatigue came through now as she lowered her hand again. "She loved him. She really loved him. They've been seeing each other for almost two years, ever since he joined the firm. Kept it quiet—his idea." She took a big gulp of coffee and managed to keep her emotions in check. "He didn't want office gossip. She went along with it. She went along with everything. You can't imagine how much she swallowed for that man. Anne was the original Miss Independence—I've made it on my own and like it, single is an alternative life-style. She wasn't militant, if you know what I mean, just content to carve out her own space. Until John."

"They had a relationship," Ben prompted.

"If you can call it that. She didn't even tell her parents about him. No one knew but me." She rubbed her eyes. Mascara had been clumped on her lashes and came off in flakes. "She was so happy at first. I guess I was happy for her, but I didn't like the fact that she was . . . well, so controlled by him. Little things, you know. If he liked Italian food, she did. If he was into French movies, so was she."

Suzanne struggled against the bitterness and grief for a moment. Her free hand began to clamp and unclamp over the lapel of her robe. "She wanted to get married. She needed to marry him. All she could think of was bringing their relationship out and registering at Bloomingdale's. He kept putting her off, not saying no, just not yet. Not yet. Anyway, she was sinking pretty low emotionally. She made some demands on him, and he dumped her. Just like that. He didn't even have the guts to say it to her face. He called her."

"When did this happen?"

Suzanne didn't answer Ben for several seconds. She stared blankly at the television screen. A woman spun the wheel and hit Bankrupt. Tough break.

"The night she was killed. She called me that same night, saying she didn't know what she was going to do, how she was going to handle it. It hit her hard. He wasn't just another guy, he was it for Anne. I asked her if she wanted me to come over, but she said she wanted to be alone. I should have gone." She screwed her eyes closed. "I should have gotten in my car and gone over. We could've gotten drunk or high or ordered pizza. Instead she went out walking alone."

Ben said nothing as she wept quietly. Tess would know what to say. The thought came from nowhere and infuriated him. "Ms. Hudson." Ben gave her a moment, then continued. "Do you know if anyone had been bothering her? Had she noticed anyone around the apartment, around the office? Anyone who made her uneasy?"

"She didn't notice anyone but John. She'd have told me." She let out a long breath and rubbed the back of her hand under her eyes. "We'd even talked about this maniac a couple of times, talked about being extra careful until he was caught. She went out because she wasn't thinking. Or maybe because she had too much to think about. She'd have pulled herself out—Anne was tough. She just never had the chance."

They left her on the couch staring at the Wheel and went to see John Carroll.

He had a duplex in a part of town that catered to young professionals. There was a gourmet market around the corner, a liquor store that would carry obscure brands, and a shop specializing in athletic wear, all tucked within reasonable walking distance of the residential area. A dark blue Mercedes sedan was parked in his driveway.

He answered the door after the third knock. He was wearing an undershirt and jogging pants and carrying a fifth of Chevas Regal. There was little resemblance to the young, successful lawyer on his way up. Three days' worth of beard shadowed his chin. His eyes were swollen and the skin had folded into pockets that drooped beneath. He smelled like a vagrant who had crawled into an alley on Fourteenth to sleep it off. He took a cursory look at the badges, hefted the bottle for another swig, and turned away, leaving the door open. Ed closed it.

The duplex had wide-planked oak floors partially covered with a couple of Aubussons. In the living area the sofa was long and low; the upholstery on it and the chairs ran to masculine colors, grays and blues. State-of-the-art electronic equipment was displayed on one wall. Along another was a collection of toys—antique slots, banks, trains.

Carroll collapsed on the sofa in the center of the room. Two empty bottles and an overflowing ashtray were on the floor. A blanket was tossed over the cushions. Ben calculated he hadn't moved much beyond that spot since he'd been notified.

"I can come up with a couple of clean glasses." His voice was husky but not slurred, as though the liquor had quit doing its job some time before. "But you can't drink, can you? On duty." He lifted the bottle again and sucked. "I'm not on duty."

"We'd like to ask you some questions about Anne Reasoner, Mr. Carroll." There was a chair behind him, but Ben didn't sit.

"Yeah, I figured you'd get around to it. I told myself if I didn't pass out, I'd talk to you." He looked at the bottle that was barely three-quarters full. "Can't seem to pass out."

Ed took the bottle from his fingers and set it aside. "Doesn't help, really, does it?"

"Something's got to." He pressed the heels of his hands against his eyes, then began to search the littered smoked-glass coffee table for a cigarette. Ben lit one for him. "Thanks." He drew hard and kept most of the smoke in his lungs. "I quit two years ago," he said, and drew again. "Didn't gain any weight, though, because I cut out starch."

"You and Miss Reasoner had a relationship," Ben began. "You were one of the last people to talk to her."

"Yes. Saturday night. We were supposed to go to the National. *Sunday in the Park with George*. Anne's fond of musicals. I prefer straight drama myself, but—"

"You didn't go to the theater?" Ben interrupted.

"I was feeling pressured. I called her to break the

date and told her I wanted to let the relationship cool for a while. That's how I said it." He looked up, over the cigarette, and met Ben's eyes. "It should cool for a while. It sounded reasonable."

"Did you have fight?"

"A fight?" He laughed at that and choked on smoke. "No, we didn't fight. We never fought. I don't believe in it. There's always a logical and reasonable solution to any problem. This was a reasonable solution, and it was for her own good."

"Did you see her that night, Mr. Carroll?"

"No." He looked around absently for the bottle, but Ed had put it out of reach. "She asked me to come over, to talk it out. She was crying. I didn't want to have one of those tearful scenes, so I said no. I told her I thought it best if we gave it a little time. In a week or two we could have drinks after work and talk about it calmly. In a week or two." He stared straight ahead. The ash from his cigarette fell on his knee. "She called me later."

"She phoned you again?" Ed balanced his notepad on his palm. "What time was that?"

"It was 3:35. My clock radio's right beside the bed. I was annoyed with her. I shouldn't have been, but I was. She was high. I can always tell when she's had a joint. She didn't have an outrageous habit, just burned a joint now and then to ease tension, but I didn't like it. It's so childish, you know," he added. "I figured she'd done it to irritate me. She told me she'd come to some decisions. She wanted me to know that she didn't blame me. She was going to take responsibility for her own emotions, and not to worry about her causing any scenes at the office."

When he sat back and closed his eyes, his dark blond hair fell over his forehead. "I was relieved at that, because I worried a bit about it. She said she had a lot of thinking to do, a lot of reevaluating before we talked again. I said that was fine and I'd see her Monday. When I hung up it was 3:42. That's seven minutes."

Gil Norton had seen the murderer come out of the alley sometime between four and four-thirty. Ed noted the times on his pad, then put it in his pocket.

"You're probably not in the mood for advice, Mr. Carroll, but you'd be better off if you went up to bed and got some sleep."

He focused on Ed, then looked at the litter of bottles at his feet. "I loved her. How come I didn't know it until now?"

BEN stepped outside and hunched his shoulders against the cold. "Christ."

"I don't think Suzanne Hudson would feel like spitting in his face now."

"So what have we got?" Ben walked to the car and took the driver's seat. "A selfish, self-indulgent lawyer, who doesn't fit Norton's description. A woman trying to pull back from a bad affair, who goes for a walk. And a psychopath who just happens to be there when she does."

"A psychopath who wears a cassock."

Ben stuck the key in the ignition but didn't turn it. "You think he's a priest?"

Instead of answering, Ed sat back and stared at the sky through the windshield. "How many sort of tall, dark-haired priests you figure there are in the city?" Ed took out a plastic bag of trail mix.

"Enough to keep us busy for six months. We haven't got six months."

"It wouldn't hurt to talk to Logan again."

"Yeah." He dipped his fingers into the plastic bag Ed offered without thinking. "How about this? A former priest, one who dropped out because of some

Church-oriented tragedy. Logan might be able to get us a few names."

"Another crumb. In her report, Dr. Court says he's cracking, that this last murder probably left him disabled for a couple of days."

"I read it. What the hell is this? Bark and twigs?" Ben twisted the key and pulled out from the curb.

"Raisins, almonds, some granola. You ought to call her, Ben."

"I'll handle my personal life, partner." He turned the corner and went a block before he swore. "Sorry."

"No problem. You know, I saw this special. It pointed out that in current society, men really have it made. Women have taken the pressure off them to be the sole support—the Mr. Macho who has to handle all the problems and bring home the bacon. Women are generally waiting longer to look for marriage if they look for marriage at all, which leaves men with more choices. Today's woman isn't looking for Prince Charming on a white charger. The funny thing is, a lot of men are still threatened by strength and independence." He plucked out a raisin. "Pretty amazing."

"Kiss ass."

"Dr. Court strikes me as being pretty independent."

"Good for her. Who wants a woman who hangs all over you?"

"Bunny didn't hang exactly," Ed remembered. "She sort of draped."

"Bunny was comic relief," Ben muttered. And Bunny had been one of his standard three-month affairs where you meet, share a few dinners, have a few laughs, bounce around in the sheets, and call it quits before anyone gets any ideas. He thought of Tess leaning back against his windowsill and laughing. "Look, when you're in our business you need a woman who doesn't make you think all the time. Who doesn't make you think about her all the time."

"You're making a mistake." Ed leaned back. "But I figure you're smart enough to see it for yourself."

Ben made the turn toward Catholic University. "Let's hit Logan before we go back in."

❧

AT five P.M. all the detectives assigned to the Priest homicides but Bigsby were spread out in the conference room. Harris had a copy of all the reports in front of him, but went over each point by point. They traced Anne Reasoner's movements on the final night of her life.

At 5:05 P.M. she had left her regular beauty salon, where she'd had a trim, color touch-up, blow-dry, and manicure. She'd been in excellent spirits and had tipped her operator ten dollars. At five-fifteen she had picked up her dry cleaning. One gray suit, with vest, two linen blouses, and a pair of gabardine slacks. At approximately five-thirty she had arrived home. Her next-door neighbor had spoken to her in the hall. Anne had mentioned going to the theater that evening. She'd carried fresh flowers.

At seven-fifteen John Carroll had called her and broken their date and their relationship. They had spoken for roughly fifteen minutes.

At eight-thirty Anne Reasoner had called Suzanne Hudson. She'd been upset, tearful. They had talked for nearly an hour.

Around midnight the next-door neighbor had heard Reasoner's television. She'd noticed it because she was coming in for the evening herself and hadn't expected Reasoner to be home.

At 3:35 Reasoner had phoned Carroll. Two roaches

of marijauna had been found beside the phone. They had talked until 3:42. None of the neighbors heard Reasoner leave the building.

Sometime between four and four-thirty A.M. Gil Norton had seen a man dressed as a priest exit the alley two blocks from Reasoner's apartment. At 4:36 Norton attracted the attention of two patrolmen and reported the body.

"Those are the facts," Harris said. Behind him was a map of the city with the murder sights flagged with blue pins. "From the map we can see that he's confined himself to an area less than seven square miles. All the murders have occurred between one and five A.M. There is no sexual assault, no robbery. From the pattern Monsignor Logan established, we expect him to hit again on December eighth. Street patrols will be working double shifts from now until then.

"We know that he is a man of average or above average height, that he has dark hair and dresses as a priest. From Dr. Court's psychiatric profile and reports, we know that he is psychopathic, possibly schizophrenic, with religious delusions. He kills only young, blond women, who apparently symbolize an actual person who is or was in his life.

"Dr. Court feels that due to the break in pattern of the murder, and the disorder of the printing on the note left on the body, that he is nearing a crisis in his psychosis. The last murder may have cost him more than he can afford."

He dropped the file on the table, thinking it was more than any of them could afford. "It's her opinion that he would have had a physical reaction, headaches, nausea, that would have debilitated him. If he is still able to function on a normal level for periods of time, it's placing an enormous strain on him. She believes it would show in fatigue, loss of appetite, inattention."

He paused a moment, to make certain everyone in the room was taking it in. The room was separated from the squad room by windows and venetian blinds that were yellowing with age. Beyond them could be heard the steady hum of activity, phones, footsteps, voices.

There was a coffee machine in the corner and a jumbo-sized plastic cup for cops with a conscience to drop in twenty-five cents a shot. Harris walked over to it, poured a cup, and added a spoonful of the powdered cream he detested. He drank and looked at his staff.

They were restless, overworked, and frustrated. If they didn't start cutting down to an eight-hour day, he was going to lose some of them to the flu. Lowenstein and Roderick were already popping decongestants. He couldn't afford to have them off sick, and he couldn't afford to pamper them. "We have in this room over sixty years of police experience. It's time we put those sixty-odd years on the line and catch one sick religious fanatic who probably can't keep his breakfast down in the morning anymore."

"Ed and I talked to Logan again." Ben pushed aside his plastic cup of coffee. "Since the guy dresses like a priest, we thought we'd start treating him like one. As a psychiatrist, Logan talks to and treats fellow priests who are having any kind of emotional problems. He's not going to give us a list of his patients, but he's going through his files, checking for anything—anyone who might fit. Then there's a matter of the confessional."

He stopped for a moment. Confession was part of the Catholic ritual that had always given him a problem. He could remember well kneeling in that dark little room with the screened panel, confessing, repenting, atoning. Go and sin no more. But, of course, he had.

"A priest has to confess to somebody, and it has to be another priest. If Dr. Court's right, and he's beginning to think of what he's done as a sin, he's going to have to confess."

"So we start interviewing priests," Lowenstein put in. "Look, obviously I don't know a lot about Catholics, but isn't there something about the sanctity of the confessional?"

"We probably wouldn't get a priest to finger anyone who came to him in the confessional," Ben agreed. "But maybe we'd get another location. Chances are he'd stick with his own parish. Tess—Dr. Court—said he probably attended church regularly. We might be able to find out what church. If he's a priest, or was one, he'd probably be drawn to his own church." He rose and went to the map. "This area," he said, circling the blue flags, "includes two parishes. I'm betting he's been to one or both of these churches, maybe standing on the altar."

"You figure he's going to show up on Sunday," Roderick put in. He clamped his thumb and forefinger on the bridge of his nose to relieve some pressure. "Especially if Dr. Court was right and he was too sick to make it last week. He'll need the support of the ceremony."

"I think so. Masses run Saturday evening too."

"I thought that was our province," Lowenstein commented.

"Catholics are flexible." Ben dipped his hands in his pockets. "And they like to sleep late on Sunday like everybody else. The thing is, I'm betting this guy is a traditionalist. Sunday morning is for mass, the mass should still be said in Latin, and you don't eat meat on Friday. Church rules. I think Court's got something when she says the guy's obsessed with Church rules."

"So we cover the two churches on Sunday. In the meantime, we've got a couple of days to interview priests." Harris looked at each of his detectives. "Lowenstein, you and Roderick take one parish,

Jackson and Paris the other. Bigsby will—where the hell is Bigsby?"

"He said he had a lead on the amices, Captain." Roderick rose and poured a cup of ice water, knowing there was too much coffee in his system already. "Look, I don't want to throw a wrench in the works, but suppose he does show up during one of the masses on Sunday. What makes any of us think we can pick him out of the congregation? The guy isn't a freak, he isn't going to come in speaking in tongues or frothing at the mouth. Dr. Court points out that he's just like anyone else except for the fact that he's troubled."

"It's all we've got," Ben stated, annoyed at having his own doubts stated by someone else. "We've got to go with whatever advantage we have; at the moment it's location. We check out the men who come alone. Court also thinks he's a loner, so he's not going to come in with the wife and kids. Logan takes it one step further and sees him as devout. A lot of people come to mass and nod off or at least space out. He wouldn't do either."

"Spending the day in church gives us the opportunity to try something else." Ed finished a note then looked up. "Pray."

"It couldn't hurt," Lowenstein said under her breath as Bigsby swung into the room.

"I've got something." He held a yellow pad in his hand, and his red and watery eyes were bulging. He'd been spending his nights with Nyquil and a hot-water bottle. "One dozen white silk amices, invoice number 52346-A, ordered on June fifteenth from O'Donnely's Religious Suppliers, Boston, Massachusetts. Delivery July thirty-first, Reverend Francis Moore. The address is a post office in Georgetown."

"How'd he pay for it?" Harris's voice was calm as he worked through the next steps.

"Money order."

"Track it down. I want a copy of the invoice."

"It's on its way."

"Lowenstein, get to the post office." He checked his watch and nearly swore in frustration. "Be there when it opens in the morning. Find out if he still has the box. Get a description."

"Yes, sir."

"I want to know if there's a priest in the city whose name is Francis Moore."

"There'd be a list of all the priests in the Archdiocese. We should be able to get it from their main office."

Harris nodded at Ben. "Check it out. Then check out the rest of the Francis Moores."

He couldn't argue with basic police work, but Ben's instincts told him to concentrate on the area of the murders. He was there. Ben was sure of it. And now maybe they had his name.

Back in the squad room the detectives hit the phones.

An hour later Ben hung up and looked at Ed over the rubble on top of his desk. "We got one Father Francis Moore in the Archdiocese. Been here two-and-a-half years. He's thirty-seven."

"And?"

"He's black." Ben reached for his cigarettes and found the pack empty. "We check him out anyway. What have you got?"

"I've got seven." Ed looked down at his neatly detailed list. Someone sneezed behind him and he winced. The flu was going through the station like brushfire. "A high school teacher, a lawyer, a clerk at Sears, a currently unemployed, a bartender, a flight attendant, and a maintenance worker. He's an ex-con. Attempted rape."

Ben checked his watch. He'd been on duty just over ten hours. "Let's go."

THE rectory made him uncomfortable. The scent of fresh flowers competed with the scent of polished wood. They waited in a parlor with an old, comfortable sofa, two wing chairs, and a statue of a blue-robed Jesus with one hand raised in benediction. There were two copies of *Catholic Digest* on the coffee table.

"Makes me feel like I should've polished my shoes," Ed murmured.

Both men were conscious of the guns under their jackets, and didn't sit. From somewhere down the hall a door opened long enough to let out a few strains of Strauss. The door closed again and the waltz was replaced by footsteps. The detectives looked over as Reverend Francis Moore walked in.

He was tall and built like a fullback. His skin was the color of glossy mahogany and his hair was clipped close around a round face. Against the black of his priest's robe was a white sling. His right arm was in a plaster cast riddled with signatures.

"Good evening." He smiled, apparently more curious than pleased to have visitors. "I apologize for not shaking hands."

"Looks like you've had some trouble." Ed could almost feel his partner's disappointment. Even if Gil Norton had been off on the description, there was no getting around that cast.

"Football a couple of weeks ago. I should have known better. Won't you sit down?"

"We need to ask you a few questions, Father." Ben drew out his badge. "About the strangulation of four women."

"The serial killings." Moore bowed his head a moment, as if in prayer. "What can I do?"

"Did you place an order with O'Donnely's Religious Supplies in Boston last summer?"

"Boston?" Moore's free hand toyed with the rosary at his belt. "No. Father Jessup is in charge of supplies. He orders what we need from a firm here in Washington."

"Do you keep a post office box, Father?"

"Why, no. All our mail is delivered to the rectory. Excuse me, Detective . . ."

"Paris."

"Detective Paris. What is this all about?"

Ben hesitated a moment, then decided to push whatever buttons were available. "Your name was used to order the murder weapons."

He saw the fingers on the rosary tighten. Moore's mouth opened then closed. He reached out and gripped the left wing of a chair. "I—you suspect me?"

"There's a possibility you know or have been in contact with the murderer."

"I can't believe it."

"Why don't you sit down, Father?" Ed touched him gently on the shoulder and eased him into the chair.

"My name," Moore murmured. "It's hard to take it in." Then he laughed shakily. "The name was given to me in a Catholic orphanage in Virginia. It's not even the one I was born with. I can't tell you that one because I don't know it."

"Father Moore, you're not a suspect," Ben told him. "We have a witness who says the murderer is white, and you've got your arm in a cast."

Moore wriggled his dark fingers, which disappeared into plaster. "A couple of lucky breaks. Sorry." He drew a breath and tried to pull himself together. "I'll be honest with you, these murders have more than once been a topic of conversation here. The press calls him a priest."

"The police have yet to determine that," Ed put in.

"In any case, we've all searched our souls and strained our minds trying to find some answers. I wish we had some."

"Are you close to your parishioners, Father?"

Moore turned to Ben again. "I wish I could say yes. There are some, of course. We have a church supper once a month, then there's the youth group. Right now we're planning a Thanksgiving dance for the Teen Club. I'm afraid we don't pack them in."

"Is there anyone who concerns you, someone you might consider emotionally unstable?"

"Detective, I'm in the business of comforting the troubled. We've had some drug and alcohol abuse, and an unfortunate case of wife beating a few months ago. Still, there's no one I would even consider capable of these murders."

"Your name might have been pulled out of a hat, or it might have been used because the killer identified with you, as a priest." Ben paused, knowing he was stepping onto the hard-packed unmovable ground of the sanctified. "Father, has anyone come to you in the confessional and indicated in any way that he knew something about the murders?"

"Again I can be honest and say no. Detective, are you certain it was my name?"

Ed took out his notepad and read from it. "Reverend Francis Moore."

"Not Francis X. Moore?"

"No."

Moore passed his hand over his eyes. "I hope relief isn't a sin. When I was given my name and was old enough to learn to write it, I always used the *X* for Xavier. I thought having a middle name that began with *X* was exotic and unique. I never got out of the habit. Detectives, every piece of identification I have uses my middle initial. Everything I sign includes it. Everyone who knows me, knows me as Reverend Francis X. Moore."

Ed noted it down. If he'd gone with instinct, he would have said good night and gone on to the next address on the list. Procedure was more demanding and infinitely more boring than instinct. They interviewed the three other priests in the rectory.

"Well, it only took us an hour to come up with nothing," Ben commented as they walked back to the car.

"We gave those guys something to talk about tonight."

"We put in yet another hour of overtime this week. Accounting's going to hit the roof."

"Yeah." Ed smiled a little as he eased into the passenger's seat. "Lousy bastards."

"We could give them a break, or we can go see the ex-con."

Ed considered a moment, then pulled out the rest of his trail mix. It should hold him until he could get a meal. "I've got another hour."

THERE were no fresh flowers in the one-room apartment in South East. The furniture, what there was of it, hadn't been polished since it had been bought from the Salvation Army. A Murphy bed no one had bothered to tuck back into the wall took up most of the room. The sheets weren't clean. The unpleasant odors of sweat, stale sex, and onions hung in the room.

The blonde had an inch of brown root showing in her frizzed mop of hair. She opened the door with the slow, wary stare of the knowing when Ben and Ed showed their badges. She wore snug jeans over a well-shaped rear, and a pink sweater that was cut low enough to show breasts that were starting to sag.

Ben gauged her to be about twenty-five, though there were lines already dug deep at the sides of her mouth. Her eyes were brown, and the left one was set off by a bruise that had rainbowed into mauve, yellow, and gray. He judged she'd taken the hit three or four days earlier.

"Mrs. Moore?"

"No, we ain't married." The blonde dug a cigarette out of a pack of Virginia Slims. You've come a long way, baby. "Frank went out for beer. He'll be back in a minute. Is he in trouble?"

"We just need to talk to him." Ed gave her an easy smile, and decided she needed more protein in her diet.

"Sure. Well, I can tell you he's been keeping out of trouble. I've seen to that." She found a pack of matches, lit her cigarette, then used the pack to squash a small roach. "Maybe he drinks a little too much, but I make sure he does it here, where he can't get in trouble." She looked around the pitiful room and drew deep on the cigarette. "It don't look like much, but I'm putting money aside. Frank's got a good job now, and he's dependable. You can ask his super."

"We're not here to hassle Frank." Ben decided against sitting. You couldn't be sure what might be crawling under the cushions. "Sounds like you've got him pretty much in line."

She touched her bruised eye. "I give as good as I get."

"I bet. What happened?"

"Frank wanted another five for beer on Saturday. I've got a budget."

"Saturday?" Ben came to attention. The night of the last murder. The woman facing him was a blonde, of sorts. "I guess you two got into it, then he stomped out so he could go down to the bar and bitch with the boys."

"He didn't go anywhere." She grinned and tapped her ash into a plastic dish that invited you to PUT YOUR BUTT HERE. "He got a shot in, and the neighbors downstairs were beating with that damn broomstick on the ceiling. I got a shot right back." She let the smoke trail lightly out of her mouth and up her nose. "Frank respects that sort of thing in a woman. He likes it, you know. So we . . . made up. He didn't think about beer anymore Saturday night."

The door opened. Frank Moore had arms like cinder blocks, legs like tree trunks, and stood maybe five feet five. He was wearing a black trench coat that had moth holes in the shoulder, and was carrying a six-pack of the King of Beers.

"Who the hell are you?" he demanded. His free arm was already flexed.

Ben pulled out his badge. "Homicide."

Frank dropped his arm. Ben noticed the inch-long scratch on his cheek as he leaned over to read the badge. It was scabbed over and looked every bit as nasty as the blonde's bruise.

"The system eats shit," Frank announced, and slammed the six-pack onto the counter. "That slut tells the judge I tried to rape her, I end up doing three years, then when I get out I got cops hanging around. I told you the system eats shit, Maureen."

"Yeah." The blonde helped herself to a beer. "You told me."

"Why don't you just tell us where you were last Sunday morning, Frank," Ben began. "About four A.M."

"Four in the morning. Jesus, I was in bed like everybody else. And I wasn't alone neither." He jerked a thumb at Maureen before he popped the top on a Bud. Beer fizzled through the opening and added one more smell to the room.

"You Catholic, Frank?"

Frank wiped the back of his hand over his mouth, belched, and drank again. "Do I look Catholic?"

"Frank's daddy was Baptist," Maureen supplied.

"Shut your face," Frank told her.

"Kiss ass." She only smiled when he lifted an arm. Ed had taken only one step forward when Frank dropped it again.

"You want to tell the cops everything, fine. My old man was Baptist. No cards, no drinking, no-fucking-around Baptist. He kicked my ass plenty, and I kicked his once before I left home. That was fifteen years ago. A two-bit whore railroaded me into prison. I did three years, and if I ever saw her again, I'd kick her ass too." He pulled a pack of Camels out of his shirt pocket and lit it with a battered Zippo. "I got a job washing floors and cleaning toilets. I come home every night so this bitch can tell me I only got five dollars for beer. I ain't done nothing illegal. Maureen'll tell you." He swung a loving arm around the woman he'd just called a bitch.

"That's right." She took a swig from her beer.

He didn't fit the description, not the physical one, nor the psychiatric one. Still Ben persisted. "Where were you August fifteenth?"

"Jesus, how am I supposed to remember?" Frank chugged the rest of the beer down and crushed the can. "You guys got a warrant to be in here?"

"We were in Atlantic City." Maureen didn't blink when Frank tossed the can and missed the trash bag by inches. "Remember, Frank? My sister works up there, you know. She got us a good deal at the hotel where she does housekeeping. The Ocean View Inn. It ain't on the strip or nothing, but it's close. We drove up on August fourteenth and spent three days. It's in my diary."

"Yeah, I remember." He dropped his arm and turned on her. "I was playing craps and you came down and started bitching at me."

"You'd lost twenty-five bucks."

"I'd've won it back, and twice that much, if you'd left me be."

"You stole the money out of my purse."

"Borrowed it, you cunt. Borrowed it."

Ben jerked his head toward the door as the argument heated up. "Let's get out of here."

Chapter 9

"Mr. Monroe, I appreciate you coming by to talk with me." Tess greeted Joey Higgins's stepfather at the door to her office. "My secretary's gone for the day, but I can fix us some coffee if you like."

"Not for me." He stood, uncomfortable as always in her presence, and waited for her to make the first move.

"I realize you've already put in a full day," she began, not adding she'd put in one of her own.

"I don't mind the extra time if it helps Joey."

"I know." She smiled, gesturing him to a chair. "I haven't had many opportunities to speak to you privately, Mr. Monroe, but I want to tell you that I can see how hard you're trying with Joey."

"It isn't easy." He folded his overcoat on his lap. He was a tidy man, organized by nature. His fingers were neatly manicured, his hair combed into place, his suit dark and conservative. Tess thought she understood how inscrutable he would find a boy like Joey.

"It's harder on Lois, of course."

"Is it?" Tess sat behind her desk, knowing the distance and the impersonal position would make it easier for him. "Mr. Monroe, coming into a family after a divorce and trying to be a father figure to a teenage boy is difficult under any circumstances. When the boy is as troubled as Joey, the difficulties are vastly multiplied."

"I'd hoped by now, well . . ." He lifted his hands, then laid them flat again. "I'd hoped we could do things together, ball games. I even bought a tent, though I have to admit I don't know the first thing about camping. But he's not interested."

"Doesn't feel he can allow himself to be interested," Tess corrected. "Mr. Monroe, Joey has linked himself with his father to a very unhealthy degree. His father's failures are his failures, his father's problems his problems."

"The bastard doesn't even—" He cut himself off. "I'm sorry."

"No, don't apologize. I know it appears that Joey's father doesn't care, or can't be bothered. It stems from his illness, but that isn't what I wanted to speak with you about. Mr. Monroe, you know I've tried to discuss intensifying Joey's treatment. The clinic I mentioned in Alexandria specializes in emotional illness in adolescents."

"Lois won't hear of it." As far as Monroe was concerned, it ended there. "She feels, and I have to agree, that Joey would think we'd abandoned him."

"The transition would be difficult, there's no denying that. It would have to be handled by all of us in such a way that Joey understands he isn't being punished or sent away, but offered another chance. Mr. Monroe, I have to be candid with you. Joey is not responding to treatment."

"He's not drinking?"

"No, he's not drinking." How could she convince him that the alleviation of one symptom was far from a cure? She'd already seen in their family therapy sessions that Monroe was a man who saw results much more clearly than he saw causes. "Mr. Monroe, Joey is an alcoholic, will always be an alcoholic whether he drinks or not. He's one of twenty-eight million children of alcoholics in this country. One third of them become alcoholics themselves, as Joey has."

"But he's not drinking," Monroe persisted.

"No, he's not." She linked her fingers, laid them on the blotter, and tried again. "He is not consuming alcohol, he's not altering his reality with alcohol, but he has yet to deal with his dependency, and more importantly, the reasons for it. He is not getting drunk, Mr. Monroe, but the alcohol was a cover-up and an offshoot of other problems. He can't control or blanket those problems with liquor anymore, and now they're overwhelming him. He shows no anger, Mr. Monroe, no rage, and very little grief, though it's all bottled inside of him. Children of alcoholics often take on the responsibility for their parent's illness."

Uncomfortable and impatient, Monroe shifted in his chair. "You've explained that before."

"Yes, I have. Joey resents his father, and to a great extent he resents his mother because both of them let him down. His father with his drinking, his mother with her preoccupation with his father's drinking. Because he loves them, he's turned this resentment onto himself."

"Lois did her best."

"Yes, I'm sure she did. She's a remarkably strong woman. Unfortunately, Joey doesn't have her strength. Joey's depression has reached a dangerous stage, a critical stage. I can't tell even you what was discussed or what was said in our recent sessions, but I can tell you I'm more concerned than ever over his emotional state. He's in such pain. At this point I'm doing little more than soothing the pain so that he can get through the week until I can soothe it again. Joey feels his life is worthless, that he's failed as a son, as a friend, as a person."

"The divorce—"

"Divorce batters the children involved. The extent of which depends on the state of mind the children are in at the time, the way the divorce is handled, the emotional strength of the individual child. For some it can be as devastating as a death. There's usually a period of grief, of bitterness, even of denial. Self-blame is common. Mr. Monroe, it's been nearly three years since your wife separated from Joey's father. His obsession with the divorce and his part in it isn't normal. It's become a springboard for all of his problems."

She paused a moment, and linked her hands together again. "His alcoholism is painful. Joey feels he deserves the pain. In fact, he appreciates it in the way a small child appreciates being disciplined for breaking the rules. The discipline, the pain, makes him feel a part of society, while at the same time, the alcoholism itself makes Joey feel isolated from society. He's learned to depend on this isolation, on seeing himself as different, not quite as good as everyone else. Particularly you."

"Me? I don't understand."

"Joey identifies with his father, a drunk, a failure both in business and in family life. You are everything his father, and therefore Joey, is not. Part of him wants to cut himself off from his father and model himself on you. The rest of him simply doesn't feel worthy, and he's afraid to risk another failure. It's gone beyond that even, Mr. Monroe. Joey is fast reaching a point where he's too tired to bother at all with life."

His fingers were clenching and unclenching. When he spoke, it was his calm, board of director's voice. "I don't follow you."

"Suicide is the third highest cause of death among teenagers, Mr. Monroe. Joey has definite suicidal tendencies. He's already playing with the idea, circling around it with his fascination with the occult. It would take very little at this point in his life to push him over the line—an argument that leaves him feeling rebellious, a test in school that makes him feel inadequate. His father's ambivalent behavior."

Though her voice was calm, the underlying urgency was communicating to him. Tess leaned forward, hoping to take it to the next step. "Mr. Monroe, I can't stress how vital it is that Joey begin structured, intensified treatment. You trusted me enough to bring him here, to allow me to treat him. You have to trust me enough to believe me when I say I'm not enough for him. I have information here on the clinic." She pushed a folder across the desk. "Please discuss this with your wife, ask her to come in and talk it over with me. I'll rearrange my schedule so that we can meet any time it's convenient. But, please, make it soon. Joey needs this, and he needs it now, before something pushes him over."

He took the folder, but didn't open it. "You want us to send Joey to a place like this, but you didn't want us to have him change schools."

"No, I didn't." She wanted to pull the pins out of her hair, run her hands through it until the pressure at her temples was gone. "At that time I felt, I hoped, I could still reach him. Since September Joey's been pulling away more and more."

"He saw the change in schools as another failure, didn't he?"

"Yes. I'm sorry."

"I knew it was a mistake." He let out a long breath. "When Lois was making the arrangements to transfer him, he looked at me. It was as if he was saying, please, give me a chance. I could almost hear him. But I backed her up."

"There's no blame here, Mr. Monroe. You and your wife are dealing with a situation where there are no easy answers. There is no absolute right or wrong."

"I'll take the papers home." He rose then, slowly, as though the folder in his hand were weighty and leaden. "Dr. Court, Lois is pregnant. We haven't told Joey."

"Congratulations." She offered her hand while her mind weighed how this news might affect her patient. "I think it would be nice if you told him together, making it a family affair. The *three* of you are expecting a baby. It would be very important to Joey to be made to feel included rather than replaced. A baby, the anticipation of a baby, can bring a great deal of love into a family."

"We've been afraid he might resent it—us."

"He might." Timing, she thought—emotional survival could so often depend on timing. "The more he's brought into the process, into the planning, the more he'll feel a part of it. Do you have a nursery?"

"We have a spare bedroom we thought we might redecorate."

"I imagine Joey would be pretty good with a paintbrush, given the chance. Please call me after you've discussed the clinic. I'd like to go over it with Joey myself, perhaps take him there so that he can see it."

"All right. Thank you, Doctor."

Tess closed the door behind him, then pulled out the pins in her hair. The band of tension eased, leaving only a dull ache. She wasn't sure she could rest easy until Joey was being treated in the clinic. At least they were turning in the right direction, she told herself. Monroe hadn't been enthusiastic about her suggestion, but she believed he would push for it.

Tess locked away Joey's file and his tapes, holding on to the cassette from their last session a moment longer. He'd spoken of death twice during the session, both times in a matter-of-fact way. He hadn't termed it as dying but as opting out. Death as a choice. She kept the last tape out, and decided to phone the director of the clinic in the morning.

When her phone rang she nearly groaned. She could leave it. Her answering service would pick it up after the fourth ring and contact her if it was important. Then she changed her mind, holding Joey's tape in her hand as she crossed over and picked it up.

"Hello, Dr. Court."

In the silence that followed she heard labored breathing and the sounds of traffic. Automatically she pulled a pad over and picked up a pencil.

"This is Dr. Court. Can I help you?"

"Can you?"

The voice was only a whisper. She heard not the panic she was half expecting, but despair. "I can try. Would you like me to?"

"You weren't there. If you'd been there, it might have been different."

"I'm here now. Would you like to see me?"

"Can't." She heard the deep, gulping sob. "You'd know."

"I can come to you. Why don't you tell me your name and where you are?" She heard the click.

Less than a block away, the man in the dark coat leaned against the pay phone and wept in pain and confusion.

"Damn." Tess glanced down at the notes she'd made of the conversation. If he'd been a patient, she hadn't recognized his voice. On the off chance that the phone would ring again, she stayed another fifteen minutes, then gathered up her work and left the office.

Frank Fuller was waiting in the hall.

"Well, there she is." He slipped his breath spray back into his pocket. "I was beginning to think you'd moved out of the building."

Tess glanced back at her door. Her name and profession were neatly printed on it. "No, not yet. Working a bit late tonight, Frank?"

"Oh, you know how it goes." Actually, he'd spent the last hour trying to drum up a date. He hadn't been successful. "Apparently this police-consultant business has kept you pretty tied up."

"Apparently." Even for someone whose manners were as ingrained as Tess's, small talk after the day she'd put in was stretching things. Her thoughts drifted back to the phone call as she waited for the elevator.

"You know, Tess . . ." He used his old trick of resting his hand against the wall and surrounding her. "You might find it beneficial, professionally speaking, to consult with a colleague on this. I'd be glad to make some room on my calendar."

"I appreciate that, Frank, but I know how busy you are." When the elevator doors slid open, she stepped inside. She pressed the button for the ground floor and shifted her briefcase as he stepped in beside her.

"Never too busy for you, Tess, professionally or otherwise. Why don't we discuss it over drinks?"

"I'm afraid I'm not at liberty to discuss it at all."

"We can find something else to discuss then. I have this bottle of wine, a cocky little Zinfandel I've been saving for the right occasion. Why don't we go back to my place, pop the cork, and put up our feet?"

So he could start nibbling her toes, Tess thought, and sent up a quiet prayer of thanksgiving when the doors opened again. "No thanks, Frank."

She made tracks across the lobby, but didn't shake him.

"Why don't we stop in at the Mayflower, then, a quiet drink, a little music, and no shop talk?"

Champagne cocktails at the Mayflower. Ben had told her that was her style. Perhaps it was time to prove to him, and Frank Fuller, that it wasn't. "The Mayflower's a bit staid for my taste, Frank." She flipped up her collar as they stepped into the chilly darkness of the parking lot. "But in any case, I haven't the time for socializing. You should try that new club around the corner, Zeedo's. From what I hear, it's almost impossible not to score if you dig in for the evening." She pulled out her keys and slipped one into the lock of her car door.

"How do you know about—"

"Frank." She clucked her tongue then patted his cheek. "Grow up." Delighted with herself and his astounded expression, she slid into the car. She glanced over her shoulder as she reversed, but barely spared a glance at the man standing in the shadows at the edge of the lot.

She'd hardly gotten through the door and shed her coat and shoes, when someone knocked. If it was Frank, she'd stop being polite, Tess promised herself, and give it to him right between the eyes.

Senator Jonathan Writemore stood in his Saville Row overcoat, holding a red cardboard box of chicken and a slim paper bag.

"Grandpa." Most of the tension Tess hadn't been aware of having slipped away. She drew a deep breath and all but tasted the spices. "I hope you're not on your way to a hot date."

"I'm on my way right here." He dropped the box of chicken into her hands. "It's still hot, little girl. I got extra spicy."

"My hero. I was about to fix myself a cheese sandwich."

"Figures. Get the plates, and plenty of napkins."

She slipped into the kitchen, setting the chicken on the table as she went by. "Does this mean I'm not invited to dinner tomorrow?"

"This means you eat two decent meals this week. Don't forget the corkscrew. I have a bottle of wine here."

"As long as it's not Zinfandel."

"What?"

"Never mind." Tess returned carrying plates, linen napkins, two of her best wineglasses, and a corkscrew. She set the table, lit the candles, then turned to give her grandfather a bear hug. "I'm so glad to see you. How did you know I needed a boost tonight?"

"Grandfathers are born knowing." He kissed both her cheeks, then scowled at her. "You're not getting enough rest."

"I'm the doctor."

He gave her a swat on the rear. "Just sit down, little girl." He turned his attention to the wine bottle when she obeyed. Tess lifted the lid while he dealt with the cork. "Give me one of those chicken tits."

She giggled like a girl, and placed the fast food on her mother's best English bone china. "Think how shocked your constituents would be if they heard you talking about chicken tits." She chose a drumstick and was delighted to discover a box of fries. "How's the Senate business?"

"It takes a lot of shit to grow flowers, Tess." He drew the cork. "I'm still lobbying to get the Medicaid Reform bill passed. I don't know if I can pull off enough support before we adjourn for the holidays."

"It's a good bill. It makes me proud of you."

"Flatterer." He poured her wine, then his own. "Where's the ketchup? Can't eat fries without ketchup. No, don't get up, I'll get it. When's the last time you've been to the store?" he asked the minute he opened the refrigerator.

"Don't start," she said, and took a bite of chicken. "Besides, you know I'm the expert on takeout and eat-ins."

"I don't like to think of my only granddaughter forever eating out of a carton." He came back in with a bottle of ketchup, easily ignoring the fact that they were both eating out of a carton. "If I wasn't here, you'd be over at that desk with a cheese sandwich and a stack of files."

"Did I say I was glad to see you?" Tess lifted her wineglass and smiled at him.

"You're overworking."

"Maybe."

"How about I buy two tickets for Saint Croix and we take off the day after Christmas? Have ourselves a week of fun in the sun."

"You know I'd love to, but the holidays are the roughest on some of my patients. I have to be here for them."

"I've been having second thoughts."

"You?" Bypassing the ketchup, she began to nibble on fries and wondered if she had room for a second piece of chicken. "About what?"

"Getting you involved with these homicides. You're looking worn out."

"It's only partly that."

"Having a problem with your sex life?"

"Privileged information."

"Seriously, Tess, I've spoken with the mayor. He's told me how involved you are with the police investigation. All I had in mind was the profile, maybe showing off my smart granddaughter a bit."

"Vicarious thrills, huh?"

"The thrill takes on a different complexion after the fourth murder. Only two blocks from here."

"Grandpa, that would have happened whether I was involved with the investigation or not. The point now is, I want to be involved." She thought of Ben, his accusations, his resentment. She thought of her own well-ordered life and the sudden small twinges of dissatisfaction. "Maybe I need to be involved. Things have been pretty cut and dried for me up to now in my life, and my career. My part in this has shown me a different aspect of myself, and of the system."

She took up her napkin, but only kneaded it in her hands. "The police aren't interested in the workings of his mind, in his emotional motivation, yet they'll use the knowledge to try to catch him, and to punish him. I'm not interested in seeing him punished, yet I'll use what I can learn of his mind, his motivation, to try to have him stopped and helped. Which of us is right, Grandpa? Is justice punishment or is it treatment?"

"You're talking to a lawyer of the old school, Tess. Every man, woman, and child in this country is entitled to representation and a fair trial. The lawyer might not believe in the client, but he has to believe in the law. The law says that this man has the right to be judged by the system. And usually the system works."

"But does the system, the law, understand the diseased mind?" Shaking her head, she set the napkin down again, recognizing her kneading as nerves. "Not guilty by reason of insanity. Shouldn't it be not responsible? Grandpa, he is guilty of murdering those women. But responsible, no."

"He's not one of your patients, Tess."

"Yes, he is. He has been all along, but I didn't understand that until last week—the last murder. He hasn't asked me for help yet, but he will be asking for it. Grandpa, do you remember what you said to me the day I opened my office?"

He studied her, seeing that even with her intense and troubled eyes, the candlelight made her beautiful. She was his little girl. "Probably said too many things. I've been alive a long time."

"You said that I'd chosen a profession that would

allow me into people's minds, and that I could never forget their hearts. I haven't forgotten."

"I was proud of you that day. I still am."

She smiled and picked up her napkin. "You've got ketchup on your chin, Senator," she murmured, and wiped it off.

❧

THREE and a half miles away Ben and Ed had had more than one drink. The club was decorated with wine bottles, had its fair share of regulars and a blind piano player who sang low-key rock. His tip jar was only half full, but the evening was young. Their table was roughly the size of a place mat squeezed in among a line of others. Ed worked his way through a pasta salad. Ben settled on the beer nuts.

"You eat enough of those," Ben commented with a nod at Ed's plate. "You turn into a yuppie."

"Can't be a yuppie if you don't drink white wine."

"Sure?"

"Absolutely."

Taking him at his word, Ben plucked up a rotini noodle.

"What was the word when you called in?"

Ben picked up his glass and watched a woman in a short leather skirt slide past their table. "Bigsby went by the drugstore where he bought the money order. Nothing. Who's going to remember a guy buying a money order three months ago? Aren't you going to put any salt on that?"

"Are you kidding?" Ed signaled for another round. Neither of them were drunk yet, but not for lack of trying.

"You going over to Kinikee's Saturday to watch the game?"

"I've got to look at apartments. I've got to be out by the first of December."

"You should forget an apartment," Ben said as he switched to his fresh drink. "Rent money's money down the tube. You ought to be thinking about buying your own place, investing your money."

"Buying?" Ed picked up a spoon and stirred his drink. "You mean a house?"

"Sure. You've got to be crazy to toss money out the window every month on rent."

"Buy? You thinking of buying a house?"

"On my salary?" Ben laughed and tipped the chair back the full inch he had.

"Last I looked, I was bringing home the same as you."

"I tell you what you need to do, partner. You need to get married." Ed said nothing, but drained half his drink. "I'm serious. You find a woman, make sure she has a good job—I mean, like a career, so she won't be thinking about dumping it after. It would help if you found one you didn't mind looking at for long periods of time. Then you combine your salaries, you buy a house, and you stop throwing away rent money."

"They're turning my apartment building into condos, so I have to get married?"

"That's the system. Let's ask an unbiased party." Ben leaned over to the woman beside him. "Excuse me, but do you believe with today's social and economic climate that two can live as cheaply as one? In fact, considering the buying power of a two-income family, that two can almost always live more cheaply than one?"

The woman set down her spritzer and gave Ben a considering look. "Is this a pickup?"

"No, this is a random poll. They're turning my partner's apartment into a condo."

"The dirty bastards did the same thing to me. Now it takes me twenty minutes on the Metro to get to work."

"You have a job?"

"Sure. I manage Women's Better Dresses at Woodies."

"Manage?"

"That's right."

"Here you go, Ed." Ben leaned toward him. "Your future bride."

"Have another drink, Ben."

"You're blowing a perfect opportunity. Why don't we switch places so you can . . ." He trailed off as he spotted the man approaching their table. Instinctively he straightened in his chair. "Evening, Monsignor."

Ed turned and saw Logan just behind him, wearing a gray sweater and slacks. "Nice to see you again, Monsignor. Want to squeeze in?"

"Yes, if I'm not interrupting." Logan managed to draw a chair up to the corner of the table. "I called the station and they told me you'd be here. I hope you don't mind."

Ben ran a finger up and down the side of his glass. "What can we do for you, Monsignor?"

"You can call me Tim." Logan signaled to the waitress. "I think that would make us all more comfortable. Bring me a St. Pauli Girl, and bring another round for my associates." Logan glanced over as the piano player went into one of Billy Joel's ballads. "I don't have to ask if you two have had a hard day. I've been in contact with Dr. Court, and I had a brief discussion with your captain a couple of hours ago. You're trying to pin down a Francis Moore."

"Trying's the word." Ed pushed aside his empty plate so the waitress would clear it when she served the drinks.

"I knew a Frank Moore. Used to teach in seminary down here. Old school. Unshakable faith. The kind of priest I imagine you're more accustomed to, Ben."

"Where is he?"

"Oh, in God's light, I'm sure." He picked up a handful of nuts. "He died a couple of years ago. Bless you, child," Logan said when his beer was in front of him. "Now old Frank wasn't a raving fanatic, he simply wasn't flexible. Today we have a lot of young priests who question and search, who debate such horny—you should forgive the pun—issues as celibacy and a woman's right to give the sacraments. It was easier for Frank Moore, who saw things in black and white. A man of the cloth doesn't lust for wine, women, or silk underwear. Cheers." He lifted his glass and drained what was left of the beer. "I'm telling you this because I thought I might tug on a few connections, talk to some people who would remember Frank and some of the students under him. I did some counseling at the seminary myself, but that was nearly ten years ago."

"We'll take what we can get."

"Good. Now that that's settled, I think I'll have another beer." He caught the waitress's eye, then turned back to smile at Ben. "How many years of Catholic school?"

Ben dug for his cigarettes. "Twelve."

"The whole route. I'm sure the good sisters gave you an admirable foundation."

"And a few good shots across the knuckles."

"Yes, bless them. They aren't all Ingrid Bergmans."

"No."

"I don't have much in common with Pat O'Brien myself." Logan hefted his fresh beer. "Of course, we're both Irish. Lecheim."

"Father Logan—Tim," Ed quickly corrected. "Can I ask you a religious question?"

"If you must."

"If this guy, any guy, came to you in the confessional

and told you he'd done someone, murdered someone, would you turn him in?"

"That's a question I can answer equally as a psychiatrist and as a priest. There aren't many." He studied his beer a moment. There were times when Logan's superiors considered him too flexible, but his faith in God and in his fellow man was unwavering. "If someone who had committed a crime came to me in the confessional, or sought my professional help, I would do my best to persuade him to turn himself in."

"But you wouldn't push the button?" Ben persisted.

"If someone came to me as a doctor, or seeking absolution, they'd be looking for help. I'd see that they got it. Psychiatry and religion don't always see eye to eye. In this case they do."

There was nothing Ed liked better than a problem with more than one solution. "If they don't see eye to eye, how can you do both?"

"By struggling to understand the soul and the mind—in many ways, seeing them as one and the same. You know, as a priest I could argue the subject of creation for hours, I could give you viable reasons why Genesis stands solid as a rock. As a scientist I could do precisely the same thing with evolution and explain why Genesis is a beautiful fairy tale. As a man I could sit here and say, what the hell difference does it make, we're here."

"Which do you believe?" Ben asked him. He preferred one solution, one answer. The right answer.

"That depends, in a matter of speaking, on what suit I'm wearing." He took a long drink and realized if he had a third beer, he'd be pleasantly buzzed. While enjoying the second, he began to look forward to the third. "Unlike what old Francis Moore used to teach, there are no blacks and whites, Ben, not in Catholicism, not in psychiatry, and certainly not in life. Did God create us out of his goodness and generosity, and perhaps a sense of the ridiculous? Or did we invent God because we have a desperate, innate need to believe in something larger, more powerful, than ourselves? I argue with myself often." He signaled for another round.

"None of the priests I knew ever questioned the order of things." Ben swallowed the rest of his vodka. "It was right or it was wrong. Usually it was wrong and you had to pay for it."

"Sin in its infinite variety. The Ten Commandments were very clear. Thou shalt not kill. Yet we've been warriors since before we could speak. The Church doesn't condemn the soldier who defends his country."

Ben thought of Josh. Josh had condemned himself. "To kill one-to-one is a sin. To drop a bomb, with an American flag on it, on a village, is patriotic."

"We are ridiculous creatures, aren't we?" Logan said comfortably. "Let me use a more simplistic example of interpretation. I had a young student a couple of years ago, a bright young woman who, I'm embarrassed to say, knew her Bible better than I could ever hope to. She came to me one day on the question of masturbation." He turned a little in his chair and jogged the waitress's elbow. "Excuse me, dear." He turned back. "She had a quote, I'm sure I won't get it quite right, but it had to do with it being better that a man cast his seed into the belly of a whore than to spill it onto the ground. A pretty strong stand, one might say, against, ah, self-servicing."

"Mary Magdalene was a whore," Ed mumbled as the booze began to catch up with him.

"So she was." Logan beamed at him. "In any case, my student's point was that the female has no seed to cast anywhere or to spill on the ground. Therefore, it must only be a sin to masturbate if you're a male."

Ben remembered a couple of sweaty, terrifying

sessions during puberty. "I had to say the whole damn rosary," he muttered.

"I had to say it twice," Logan put in, and for the first time saw Ben relax with a grin.

"What did you tell her?" Ed wanted to know.

"I told her the Bible often speaks in generalities, that she should search her conscience. Then I looked up the quote myself." He took a comfortable drink. "Damned if I didn't think she had a point."

Chapter 10

THE GREENBRIAR ART Gallery was a small, fussy pair of rooms near the Potomac that stayed in business because people always buy the ridiculous if the price tag is high enough.

It was run by a crafty little man who rented the ramshackle building for a song and promoted his eccentric reputation by painting the outside puce. He favored long, unstructured jackets in rainbow hues, with half boots to match, and he smoked pastel cigarettes. He had an odd, moon-shaped face and pale eyes that tended to flutter when he spoke of the freedom and expression of art. He tucked his profits tidily away in municipal bonds.

Magda P. Carlyse was an artist who became trendy when a former first lady had purchased one of her sculptures as a wedding present for the daughter of a friend. A few art critics had suggested that the first lady must not be too fond of the newlyweds, but Magda's career had been launched.

Her showing at the Greenbriar Gallery was a huge success. People crammed into the room dressed in furs, denim, spandex, and silks. Cappuccino was served in thimble-sized cups, along with mushroom quiches the size of quarters. A seven-foot black man wrapped in a purple cloak stood mesmerized by a sculpture of sheet metal and feathers.

Tess took a long look at it herself. It made her think of the hood of a truck that had passed through a migration of unfortunate geese.

"A fascinating combination of mediums, isn't it?"

Tess rubbed a finger over her bottom lip before she glanced up at her date. "Oh, absolutely."

"Powerfully symbolic."

"Frightening," she agreed, and lifted her cup to disguise a giggle. She'd heard of Greenbriar, of course, but had never found the time or the energy to explore this trendy little gallery. Tonight she was grateful for the distraction this gathering provided. "You know, Dean, I'm really delighted you thought of this. I'm afraid I've been neglecting my interest in popular, ah, art."

"Your grandfather tells me you've been working too hard."

"Grandpa worries too much." She turned away to study a two-foot phallic tube that strained toward the ceiling. "But an evening here certainly takes your mind off everything else."

"Such emotion, such insight," a man in yellow silk bubbled to a woman in sable. "As you can see, the use of the broken light bulb symbolizes the destruction of ideas in a society that is driven toward a desert of uniformity." Tess shifted away as the man gestured dramatically with his cigarette then glanced at the sculpture he raved about.

It had a G.E. seventy-five-watt bulb with a jagged hole just off center. The bulb was screwed into a plain wooden base of white pine. That was it, except for the fact that the little blue sticker indicated it had been sold. The price had been twelve hundred seventy-five dollars.

"Amazing," Tess murmured, and was rewarded by a generous beam from Mr. Yellow Silk.

"It is quite innovative, isn't it?" Dean smiled down at the bulb as if he'd created it himself. "And daringly pessimistic."

"Words escape me."

"I know just what you mean. The first time I saw it, I was struck dumb."

Deciding against making the obvious comment, Tess merely smiled and moved on. She could do a paper, she thought, on the psychological implications—mass hysteria—that prompted people to actually pay for esoteric junk. She stopped by a glass square that had been filled with various size and color buttons. Square, round, enameled, and cloth covered, they huddled and bumped together in the sealed box. The artist had called it "Population, 2010." Tess figured a Girl Scout could have put it together in about three and a half hours. The price tag read a whopping seventeen hundred fifty.

With a shake of her head she started to turn back to her date, when she saw Ben. He was standing by another display, his hands in his back pockets and a look of unconcealed amusement on his face. His jacket was open. Under it he wore a plain gray sweatshirt and jeans. A woman in five-thousand-dollars worth of diamonds swept up beside him to study the same piece of sculpture. Tess saw him mumble something under his breath just before he glanced up and saw her.

They stared as people passed between them. The woman in diamonds blocked the way for a moment, but when she walked on, neither of them had moved. Tess felt something loosen inside her, then grow tight and uncomfortable again before she made herself smile at him and nod in a friendly, casual greeting.

". . . don't you agree?"

"What?" She jerked herself back to Dean. "I'm sorry, my mind was wandering."

A man who lectured hundreds of college students a year was used to being ignored. "I said, don't you think this particular sculpture shows the true conflict and eternal cycle of the man-woman relationship?"

"Hmmm." What she saw was a jangle of copper and tin that may or may not have been welded into metallic copulation.

"I'm thinking of buying it for my office."

"Oh." He was a sweet and absolutely harmless English professor whose uncle played an occasional game of poker with her grandfather. Tess felt an obligation to lead him away from the sculpture, as a mother might lead a child whose allowance was hot in his hand away from a shelf of plastic, overpriced model cars. "Don't you think you should look around a bit, consider some of the other . . ." What did one call them? "Pieces first?"

"The stuff's selling like hotcakes. I don't want to miss out." He glanced around the sardine-packed room then began to edge toward the owner. Greenbriar was hard to miss in an electric-blue suit with headband to match. "Excuse me, just a minute."

"Hello, Tess."

Cautious, calm, she looked up at Ben. The fingers around the minuscule handle of her cup dampened. Tess told herself it was the body heat in the overcrowded room.

"Hello, Ben. How are you?"

"Terrific." He was lousy, had been lousy for exactly one week. She stood in the midst of what he considered the pomp and the pompous and looked as cool and virginal as a vase of violets among a forest of orchids. "Interesting gathering."

"At least." Then her gaze slid over to the woman at his side.

"Dr. Court, Trixie Lawrence."

Trixie was an Amazon in red leather. In heeled boots, she stood an inch over Ben, with a mane of improbable red hair that exploded around her head in spikes, corkscrews, and kinks. The army of bracelets on her arm jingled as she shifted. On her left breast was a tattoo of a rose that peeked out from the low V of her vest.

"Hello." Tess smiled and offered her hand.

"Hi. So you're a doctor?" For all her size, Trixie's voice was only a breathless squeak.

"I'm a psychiatrist."

"No shit?"

"No shit," Tess agreed as Ben made a business of clearing his throat.

Trixie took one of the quarter-sized quiches and swallowed it like an aspirin. "I had a cousin in the loony bin once. Ken Launderman. Maybe you know him."

"No, I don't think so."

"Yeah, I guess you see a lot of people with their batteries low."

"More or less," Tess murmured, and glanced over at Ben. No trace of embarrassment there, she noted. He was grinning like a fool. Her own lips twitched before she lifted her cup. "I'm surprised to see you here."

Ben rocked back on the heels of worn tennis shoes. "Just impulse. I busted Greenbriar about seven years ago. Little artistic business with checks. When he sent me the invitation, I thought I'd drop in and find out how he was doing." He glanced over to see his host embrace the woman in diamonds. "Seems to be doing just fine."

Tess tasted her cooling cappuccino and wondered if Ben kept on such friendly relations with everyone he'd arrested. "So, what do you think of the show?"

Ben looked over at the case of buttons. "Such blatant mediocrity, in a society that has singles' night at the supermarket, is bound to be rewarded with tremendous financial gain." He watched the light bloom in her eyes, wishing he could touch her. Just once. Just for a moment.

"That's what makes America great."

"You look terrific, Doc." He yearned. It was the first time he believed he understood the true meaning of the word.

"Thanks." With the clear-minded intensity she hadn't felt since childhood, she wished she looked terrific.

"I've never been to singles' night at the supermarket," Trixie put in as she inhaled a plateful of quiches.

"You'll love it." Ben's smile faded a bit when he looked over Tess's shoulder and saw the man she'd been standing with before. "Friend of yours?"

Tess turned her head, then waited until Dean worked his way through the crowd. Her neck was long, slender, circled by pearls that made her skin seem only more delicate. Ben could smell her cool, quietly sexual scent over everything else.

"Dean, I'd like you to meet Ben Paris and Trixie Lawrence. Ben's a detective with the local police."

"Ah, one of the city's finest." Dean gave him a hearty handshake.

The guy looked like a cover of *Gentlemen's Quarterly* and smelled like a Brut commercial. Ben had an irrational urge to grip his hand Indian-wrestle style and go a round. "You one of Tess's colleagues?"

"No, actually I'm on the staff at American University."

College professor. It figured. Ben stuck his hands in his pockets again and took a small, telling step away from Tess. "Well, Trix and I just walked in. We haven't had a chance to absorb yet."

"It's almost too much to take in in one evening."

Dean cast a proprietary eye at the mangle of copper beside him. "I've just bought this piece. It's a bit risqué for my office, but I couldn't resist."

"Yeah?" Ben looked at it, then stuck his tongue in his cheek. "You must be thrilled. I'm going to stroll around and see if I can pick up something for my den. Nice meeting you." He slipped an arm around Trixie's sturdy waist. "See you, Doc."

"Good night, Ben."

It was still shy of eleven when Tess stepped into her apartment alone. The headache she'd used as an excuse to cut the evening short had only been half a lie. Normally she enjoyed her occasional dates with Dean. He was an undemanding, uncomplicated man, the kind of man she deliberately dated in order to keep her personal life equally undemanding and uncomplicated. But tonight she just hadn't been able to face a late supper and discussion of nineteenth-century literature. Not after the art gallery.

Not after seeing Ben, she made herself admit, and slipped out of her shoes two feet inside the door. Whatever progress she'd made in soothing her ego and alleviating the tension since that last morning she'd seen him had been blown, quite simply, to smithereens.

So she'd start from scratch. A hot cup of tea. She took off her fur jacket and hung it in the hall closet. She'd spend the evening in bed with Kurt Vonnegut, camomile, and Beethoven. The combination would take anyone's mind off their problems.

What problems? she asked herself as she stood listening to the quiet of the apartment she came home to night after night. She had no real problems because she'd made certain she wouldn't. A nice apartment in a good neighborhood, a dependable car, a light and consistently casual social life. That was precisely how she'd planned things.

She'd taken step A, and made certain it led to step B, and so on until she'd reached the plateau that satisfied her. She was satisfied.

She took off her earrings and dropped them on the dining room table. The sound of stone hitting wood echoed dully in the empty room. The mums she'd bought earlier in the week were beginning to go. Bronzed petals lay fading against the polished mahogany. Absently Tess picked them up. Their scent, sharp and spicy, went with her to the bedroom.

She wouldn't look at the files on her desk tonight, she told herself as she pulled down the zipper of her ivory wool dress. If she had a problem, it was that she didn't allow herself enough time. Tonight she would pamper herself, forget about the patients who would come to her office on Monday morning, forget about the clinic where she would have to face the anger and resentment of drug withdrawal two afternoons next week. She'd forget about the murder of four women. And she'd forget about Ben.

In the full-length mirror inside the closet, her reflection leaped out at her. She saw a woman of average height, slim build, in an expensive and conservatively cut ivory wool dress. A choker of three strands of pearls and a fat amethyst lay against her throat. Her hair was caught back at the temples with pearl-trimmed ivory combs. The set had been her mother's, and as quietly elegant as the senator's daughter had been.

Her mother had worn the choker as a bride. Tess had pictures in the leather-bound album she kept in her bottom dresser drawer. When the senator had given the pearls to his granddaughter on her eighteenth birthday, they had both wept. Every time Tess wore them, she felt both a pang and pride. They were a symbol of who she was, where she had come from, and in some ways, what was expected of her.

But tonight they seemed too tight around her throat. She slipped them off, and the pearls lay cool in her hand.

Even without them the image changed little. Studying herself, she wondered why she had chosen such a simple, such a *suitable* outfit. Her closet was full of them. She turned to the side and tried to imagine how she would look in something daring or outrageous. Like red leather.

She caught herself. Shaking her head, she slipped out of the dress and reached for a padded hanger. Here she was—a grown woman, a practical, even sensible woman, a trained psychiatrist—standing in front of a mirror and imagining herself in red leather. Pitiful. What would Frank Fuller say if she went to him for analysis?

Grateful she could still laugh at herself, she reached for her warm, floor-length chenille robe. On impulse she bypassed it and took out a flowered silk kimono. A gift, rarely worn. Tonight she was going to pamper herself, silk against her skin, classical music, and it would be wine not tea she took to bed with her.

Tess put the choker on her dresser then pulled out the combs and lay them beside it. She turned down the bed and fluffed the pillows in anticipation. Another impulse had her lighting the scented candles beside her bed. She drew in a whiff of vanilla before she headed toward the kitchen.

The phone stopped her. Tess sent it an accusing glance, but went to her desk and picked it up on the third ring.

"Hello."

"You weren't home. I've waited such a long time, and you weren't home."

She recognized the voice. He'd called her before, at

her office on Thursday. The thought of a self-indulgent evening at home slipped away as she picked up a pencil. "You wanted to talk to me. We didn't finish talking before, did we?"

"It's wrong for me to talk." She heard him draw in a painful breath. "But I need . . ."

"It's never wrong to talk," she said soothingly. "I can try to help you."

"You weren't there. That night you never came, you never came home. I waited. I watched for you."

Her head jerked up so that her gaze was frozen to the dark window beyond her desk. Watched. She shivered, but deliberately moved closer to look out at the empty street. "You watched for me?"

"I shouldn't go there. Shouldn't go." His voice trailed off, as if he were talking to himself. Or someone else. "But I need. You're supposed to understand," he blurted out quickly, accusingly.

"And I'll try to. Would you like to come to my office and talk to me?"

"Not there. They'd know. It's not time for them to know. I haven't finished."

"What haven't you finished?" There was only silence as he dragged his breath in and dredged it out again. "I could help you more if you'd meet with me."

"I can't, don't you see? Even talking to you is . . . Oh, God." He began to mumble. Tess couldn't understand. She strained her ears. Perhaps Latin, she thought, and put a question mark on the pad, circling it.

"You're in pain. I'd like to help you deal with the pain."

"Laura was in pain. Terrible pain. She was bleeding. I couldn't help her. She died in sin, before absolution."

The hand on the pencil faltered. Tess found it necessary to ease herself into the chair. When she found herself staring blindly at the window, she forced herself to look down at her pad again, and her notes. Training clicked into place, and she schooled herself to breathe deeply and keep her voice calm. "Who was Laura?"

"Beautiful, beautiful Laura. I was too late to save her. I hadn't the right then. Now I've been given the power, and the duty. The will of God is hard, so hard." He almost whispered here, then his voice became strong. "But just. The lambs are sacrificed and the clean blood washes sin away. God demands sacrifices. Demands them."

Tess moistened her lips. "What kind of sacrifices?"

"A life. He gave us life and he takes it. 'Your sons and daughters were eating and drinking wine in the house of their eldest brother, when suddenly a great wind came across the desert and smote the four corners of the house. It fell upon the young people and then smote them; and I alone have escaped to tell you.' I alone," he repeated in the same terrible blank voice he had used to quote. "But after the sacrifices, after the trials, God rewards those who remain innocent."

As if she would be graded on them, Tess concentrated on making her notes clear and even. Her heart hammered away in her throat. "Does God tell you to sacrifice the women?"

"Save and absolve. I have the power now. I lost faith after Laura, turned my back on God. It was a blind, terrible time of selfishness and ignorance. But then He showed me that if I were strong, if I sacrificed, we would all be saved. My soul is tied to hers," he said quietly. "We're bound together. You didn't come home that night." His mind was swinging back and forth. Tess could hear it in the shifts of his voice as much as in the content of his words. "I waited, I wanted to talk to you, to explain, but you spent the night in sin."

"Tell me about that night. The night you waited for me."

"I waited, I watched for the light in your window. It never came. I walked. I don't know how long, where. I thought it was you coming toward me, or Laura. No, I thought it was you, but it wasn't. Then I—I knew she must be the one. . . . I put her in the alley, out of the wind. So cold. It was so cold. Put her out of sight," he said in a terrible hiss. "Put her out of sight before they could come and take me away. They are ignorant and defy the ways of the Lord." His breath came in jagged gasps now. "Pain. Sick. My head. Such enormous pain."

"I can help the pain. Tell me where you are, and I'll come."

"Can you?" A frightened child being offered a night-light during a storm. "No!" His voice boomed out, suddenly powerful. "Do you think you can tempt me to question God's will? I am His instrument. Laura's soul is waiting for the remaining sacrifices. Only two more. Then we'll all be free, Dr. Court. It isn't death that's to be feared, but damnation. I'll watch for you," he promised, almost humbly. "I'll pray for you."

Tess didn't move when the phone clicked in her ear, but sat perfectly still. Outside the stars were clear and close and bright. Cars moved by on the street at a sedate pace. Streetlights pooled onto the sidewalk. She saw no one, but wondered, as she sat near the window, if she was seen.

There was sweat on her forehead, cold and sticky. She took a tissue from the corner of the desk and carefully dried it.

He'd been warning her. She wasn't sure if even he was fully aware of it, but he'd called to warn her as much as to ask for help. She would be next. Her fingers trembled as they lifted to where the pearl choker had lain. She couldn't swallow.

Slowly, and with infinite care, she drew the chair

back and eased out of it, and out of the sight of the window. She'd put a hand to the curtain to draw it closed when the knock on her door made her slam back against the wall in an animal panic she'd never before experienced. Terror swam into her as she looked around for a means of defense, a place to hide, a way to escape. She fought it back as she reached for the phone—911. She had only to dial it, give her name and address.

But when the knock came again, she looked at the door and saw she'd forgotten to put on the chain.

She was across the room in seconds, heaving her weight against the door and fumbling with the chain, which suddenly seemed too big and unwieldly to fit into the slot. Half sobbing, she threw it home.

"Tess?" The knock came again, louder, more demanding. "Tess, what's going on?"

"Ben. Ben, oh, God." Her fingers were even clumsier as she pulled to release the chain. Her hand slipped on the knob once, then she yanked open the door and threw herself against him.

"What is it?" He felt her fingers dig into his coat as he tried to draw her back. "Are you alone?" Instinct had him reaching for his weapon, closing a hand over it as he looked around for someone, anyone who might have tried to hurt her. "What happened?"

"Close the door. Please."

Keeping one arm around her, he closed it and dealt with the chain. "It's closed. You'd better sit down, you're shaking. Let me get you a drink."

"No. Just hold me a minute. I thought, when you knocked, I thought . . ."

"Come on, you need some brandy. You're like ice." Trying to soothe, to stroke, he started to steer her toward the sofa.

"He called me."

The fingers on her arm tightened as he turned her

around to face him. Her cheeks were white, her eyes enormous. Her right hand still gripped his coat. He didn't have to ask who. "When?"

"Just now. He called me at the office before, but I didn't realize it was him. Not then. He's been outside. I saw him one night, on the corner, just standing on the corner. I thought I was being paranoid. A good psychiatrist knows the symptoms." She laughed, then covered her face with her hands. "Oh, God, I have to stop this."

"Sit down, Tess." He relaxed his fingers on her arm and kept his voice calm; the same tone he'd use to interrogate a shaky witness. "You got some brandy around here?"

"What? Oh, it's in the buffet there, the right door."

When she was sitting, he went to the buffet, what his mother would have called a server, and found a bottle of Rémy Martin. He poured a double into a snifter and brought it to her. "Drink some of this before you start over."

"Okay." She was already pulling herself back, but drank to help things along. The brandy shot into her system and dulled the remaining fear. Fear had no place in her life, Tess reminded herself. Only clear thought and careful analysis. When she spoke again, her voice was level, without the bubble of hysteria. She gave herself only a moment to be ashamed of it.

"Thursday night I had a late appointment at the office. When it was over and I was packing up for the day, I got a call. He sounded very troubled, and though I didn't think it was a current patient, I tried to draw him out a bit. I didn't get anywhere, he just hung up." Brandy sloshed gently as she moved the bowl of the snifter around and around in her hands. "I waited a few minutes, but when he didn't call back, I filed it away and went home. He called back tonight."

"You're sure it was the same man?"

"Yes, I'm sure. The same man who called before. The same man you've been looking for since August." She sipped the brandy again, then set the snifter down. "He's falling apart, rapidly."

"What did he say to you, Tess? Tell me everything you remember."

"I wrote it down."

"You—" He stopped and made a quick movement with his head. "Of course you did. Let's have a look."

She rose, steady again, and went to the desk. Tess brought the yellow pad over and handed it to Ben. Here was something positive, something constructive. As long as she could think of it as a case, she wouldn't fall apart again.

"I may have skimmed on a few words when he was talking quickly, but I got most of it."

"It's in shorthand."

"Yes. Oh, I'll read it to you." She started at the beginning, making sure her voice was detached. Words were there to give the psychiatrist a clue to the mind. She remembered that and pushed back the horror of knowing they'd been directed at her. After the biblical quote, she stopped. "It sounds like the Old Testament. I imagine Monsignor Logan could place it."

"Job."

"What?"

"It's out of Job." His gaze was on the far wall as he lit a cigarette. Twice he'd read the Bible through, when Josh had been sick. Looking for answers, Ben remembered, to questions he hadn't even formed. "You know, the guy who had everything going for him."

"And then God tested him?"

"Yeah." He thought of Josh again, then shook his head. Josh had everything going for him, before 'Nam. "Too happy, Job? How about some boils?"

"I see." Though it was painfully obvious she didn't

know the Bible as well as he, she saw the parallel. "Yes, it makes sense. His life was well set, he was content, in all likelihood a good Catholic."

"Never had his faith tested," Ben murmured.

"Yes, then it was tested in some way, and he failed."

"The 'some way' would have to do with this Laura." He glanced down at the pad again, frustrated not to be able to read it himself. "Let's have the rest."

As he listened to her read, Ben fought to think like a cop and not a man caught between infatuation and something deeper. A killer had been watching her. Ben's stomach tightened into a maze of tiny knots. He'd been waiting for her the night Anne Reasoner was killed, the night Tess had spent in his own bed. The cop recognized the warning as quickly as the doctor had.

"He's focused on you."

"Yes, that seems to be the situation." Abruptly cold, she tucked her legs up under her before she set the yellow tablet aside. It was a case. Tess knew it was vital to think of it, to analyze it as a case. "He's drawn to me because I'm a psychiatrist and part of him knows how desperately he needs help. And he's drawn to me because I fit the physical description of Laura."

It had been the voice, she remembered, that had been the most frightening. The way it had swung from pitiful to powerful, in quietly determined madness. She folded her hands together, tight. "Ben, what I want you to understand is that it was like talking to two people. One of them was weepy, desperate, almost pleading. The other—the other was aloof, fanatical, and determined."

"He's only one person when he strangles women." He rose and walked toward the phone. "I'm calling in. We'll want to put a tap on your phone, here and at your office."

"At the office? Ben, I often talk to patients over the phone. I can't jeopardize their right to confidentiality."

"Don't give me grief on this, Tess."

"You have to understand—"

"No!" He whirled to face her. "You have to understand. There's a maniac out there killing women, and he decided to call you. Your phones get wired, with your permission or with a court order, but they get wired. Four other women didn't have the chance. Captain? This is Paris. We got a break."

IT took less than an hour. Two cops in suits and ties came in, did what seemed to be a few minor adjustments to her phone, and politely refused the offer of coffee. One of them picked up the receiver, punched a few numbers, and tested the tap. They took Tess's spare key to her office and went out again.

"That's it?" she asked when she and Ben were alone again.

"These are the days of the microchip. I'll take some of that coffee."

"Oh, sure." With a last glance at the phone, she went into the kitchen. "It makes me feel exposed, knowing that whenever the phone rings, someone with a set of headphones is listening to everything I say."

"It's supposed to make you feel protected."

When she came back in with the coffee, Ben was standing by the window, looking out. She saw him deliberately close the curtain when he heard her behind him.

"I can't be sure he'll call back. I was frightened, I'm sure he sensed it, and dammit, I didn't handle it very well."

"I guess you lose your standing as supershrink." He took the coffee, and her hand. "Aren't you having any?"

"No. I'm already too wired up."

"You're tired." He rubbed his thumb over her knuckles. She looked so fragile all at once, so pale and beautiful. "Look, why don't you go in, get some rest? I'll bunk out on the couch."

"Police protection?"

"Just part of our campaign to improve community relations."

"I'm glad you're here."

"So am I." He released her hand to run a fingertip down the closure of her silk kimono. "Nice."

"I've missed seeing you."

The movement of his finger stopped. He looked at her again and remembered that earlier in the evening she'd worn earrings, and a stone at her throat that had matched her eyes. And he'd wanted to touch her so badly that it had hurt, bone deep. Now, as he had before, Ben backed off.

"Got an extra blanket?"

She knew withdrawal when it smacked her in the face. As he had, she took a step back. "Yes, I'll get it."

When she'd gone, he swore at himself and stood straining against his own contradictions. He wanted her. He didn't want to get involved with anyone like her. She pulled at him. He pushed back. She was cool and lovely, in the way of pink-and-white delicacies behind bakery store windows. He'd already had a taste of her, and knew certain delicacies could be habit-forming. Even if he had room for her in his life, which he didn't, she would never fit. But he remembered again how she'd leaned against his windowsill, laughing.

She carried a blanket and pillow back in and began to make up the sofa.

"You don't act like you want an apology."

"For what?"

"For last week."

Though she'd been determined not to mention it herself, Tess had wondered if he'd bring it up. "Why would I want an apology?"

He watched her tuck the ends of the blanket neatly under the cushion. "We had a pretty fair argument going. Most of the women I—most women I know want to hear the old 'I'm sorry I was a jerk.' "

"Were you?"

"Was I what?"

"A jerk."

He had to admit she'd maneuvered him very nicely. "No."

"Then it would be foolish for you to say you were, just to hold up tradition. There, that should do," she added as she gave the pillow a final fluff.

"All right, dammit, I feel like an idiot about the way I acted the last time."

"You were an idiot." Tess turned from the sofa to smile at him. "But it's all right."

"I meant a lot that I said."

"I know you did. So did I."

Opposite sides, Ben thought. Opposite ends. "So where does that leave us?"

If she'd known, she wasn't sure she could have told him. Instead she kept her voice friendly. "Why don't we just leave it that I'm glad you're here, with all this . . ." Her gaze drifted to the phone.

"Don't dwell on that now. Let me take it from here."

"You're right." She linked her hands together, then pulled them apart. "If you think about something like this too much, you go—"

"Crazy?" he suggested.

"To use a loose, inaccurate term." She moved away then, tidying the desk to keep her hands busy. "I was surprised to see you tonight, at the gallery. I know it's a small town, but—" It struck her then; the confusion and panic had obscured it before. "What are you doing here tonight? I thought you had a date."

"I did. I told her I had an emergency. I wasn't far off. What about yours?"

"My what?"

"Your date."

"Oh, Dean. I, ah, told him I had a headache. I almost did. But you didn't tell me why you came by."

He shrugged that off and picked up her paperweight, a crystal pyramid that ran with colors as he turned it. "Looked like a real upstanding citizen. College professor, huh?"

"Yes." Something began to settle inside of her. It took Tess a moment to recognize it as pleasure. "Your Trixie. Her name was Trixie, wasn't it?"

"That's right."

"She looked charming. Loved her tattoo."

"Which one?"

Tess only lifted a brow. "Did you enjoy the show?"

"I'm fond of pretentious bullshit. Apparently, so's your professor. Great suit. And that natty little tie bar with the little gold chain was so distinguished." He set the paperweight down hard enough to make her pencils jump. "I wanted to push his nose into his forehead."

She beamed at him. "Thanks."

"Don't mention it." After a gulp of coffee, he set the cup on the desk. It would leave a ring, but she said nothing. "I haven't been able to think of anything but you for days. Got a name for that?"

She met his angry look with a smile. "I like *obsession*. Such a nice ring." She walked closer. There was no need for nerves any longer, or for pretenses. When his hands came up and took her shoulders, she continued to smile.

"I guess you think this is pretty damn funny."

"I guess I do. And I guess I could take a calculated

risk and tell you I've missed you. I've missed you a great deal. Would you like to tell me why you're angry?"

"No." He pulled her against him, felt her lips curve then soften, then yield against his. The silk of her kimono rustled as his arms went around her. If he could have walked away then, he would have, without a backward glance. But he'd known when he found himself at her door that it was already too late.

"I don't want to sleep on that frigging couch. And I'm not leaving you alone."

She made the effort to open her eyes, but for the first time in memory she would have been willing to be swept away. "I'll share the bed with you on one condition."

"Which is?"

"That you make love with me."

He drew her against him so that he could smell her hair, feel the way it brushed over his skin. "You drive a hard bargain, Doc."

Chapter 11

THE SCENT OF coffee woke her. Tess turned from her side to her back and lay dozing with the homey, comforting smell. How many years had it been since she'd woken to the scent of coffee already brewing? When she'd lived in her grandfather's house with its high ceilings and tiled foyer, she would come down the arching staircase in the mornings to find her grandfather already behind a huge plate of eggs or hotcakes, the newpaper open, and the coffee already poured.

Miss Bette, the housekeeper, would have set the table with the everyday dishes, the ones with the little violets around the edges. Flowers would have depended on the season, but they would always be there, jonquils or roses or mums in the blue porcelain vase that had been her great-grandmother's.

There would have been the quiet whoosh of Trooper's tail, her grandfather's old golden retriever, as he sat beneath the table hoping for a windfall.

Those had been the mornings of her youth—steady, secure, and familiar—of her young womanhood, just as her grandfather had been the strong central figure in her life.

Then she had grown up, moved into her own apartment, into her own practice. She brewed her own coffee.

With a sigh, she turned lazily, hoping for another dream. Then she remembered, and sat up straight in bed. It was empty, but for her. Pushing her hair out of her eyes, she touched the sheet beside her.

He'd stayed with her and kept the bargain. They had rolled and tossed and loved each other into the night until exhausted sleep had been the only alternative. No questions, no words, and the only answer had been what they had both needed. Each other and oblivion. He'd needed that too. She'd understood that he'd needed a few hours without tension, without puzzles, without responsibilities.

Now it was morning, and each had a job to face.

Tess rose, then slipped into the kimono that had been discarded onto the floor. She wanted a shower, a long, hot one, but she wanted the coffee more.

She found Ben in the little el of her dining room, with a map of the city, a tangle of notes, and her own yellow tablet spread over the table. "Good morning."

"Hi." He said it absently, then glanced up and focused. Though he smiled, she saw that his eyes were shadowed and intense as they studied her face. "Hi," he repeated. "I was hoping you'd sleep longer."

"It's after seven."

"It's Sunday," he reminded her, then rose as if to separate her from what he was doing at the table. "Hungry?"

"Are you cooking?"

"Are you squeamish?"

"Not particularly."

"Then you can probably stomach one of my omelettes. Game?"

"Yeah, I'm game." She went with him into the kitchen and poured a cup of coffee. From the look of the pot, he'd already had several. "Have you been up long?"

"Little while. How often do you shop for food?"

She glanced behind him, into the now open refrigerator. "When my back's to the wall."

"Consider it there." He pulled out a carton of eggs that was less than half full and a miserly chunk of cheddar. "We can still manage the omelettes. Just."

"I've got an omelette pan. Second shelf in the cabinet to your right."

He sent her a mild, pitying glance. "All you need's a hot skillet and a light hand."

"I stand corrected."

She sipped coffee while he cooked. Impressive, she thought, and certainly better than she could do with gourmet utensils and a detailed recipe in front of her. Interested, she leaned over his shoulder and earned a silent stare. Tess split an English muffin, popped it in the toaster, and left the rest up to him.

"It's good," she decided when they sat at the table and she'd swallowed the first bite. "I'm pretty pathetic in the kitchen, which is why I don't keep a lot of food around that obliges me to deal with it."

He shoveled into his own with the easy enthusiasm of a man who considered food one of life's top physical pleasures. "Living alone's supposed to make you self-sufficient."

"But it doesn't perform miracles." He cooked, kept a tidy apartment, was obviously proficient at his job, and apparently had little trouble with women. Tess topped off her coffee and wondered why she was more tense now than when she'd gone to bed with him.

Because she wasn't as handy with men as he was with women. And because, she thought, she wasn't in the habit of sharing a casual breakfast after a frantic night of sex. Her first affair had been in college. A disaster. Now she was nearly thirty and had kept her relationships with men carefully in the safe zone. The occasional side trip had been pleasant but unimportant. Until now.

"Apparently you're self-sufficient."

"You like to eat, you learn how to cook." He moved his shoulders. "I like to eat."

"You've never married?"

"What? No." He swallowed hard, then reached for his half of the muffin. "It tends to get in the way of—"

"Philandering?"

"Among other things." He grinned at her. "You butter a great muffin."

"Yes, that's true. I'd say another reason you've never . . . let's say, settled is that your work comes first." She glanced at the papers he'd pushed to the end of the table. "Police work would be demanding, time-consuming, and dangerous."

"The first two anyway. Homicide's sort of the executive end. Desk work, puzzle work."

"Executive," she murmured, remembering very clearly the ease with which he had once strapped on his gun.

"Most of the guys wear suits." He'd nearly polished off his omelette and was already wondering if he could talk Tess out of some of hers. "Generally, you come in after the deed's been done and then put pieces together. You talk to people, make phone calls, push paper."

"Is that how you got that scar?" Tess scooted the rest of her omelette around her plate. "Pushing paper?"

"I told you before, that's old news."

Her mind was too analytical to let it go at that. "But you have been shot, and probably shot at more than once."

"Sometimes you go into the field and people aren't too happy to see you."

"All in a day's work?"

When he realized she wasn't going to let it drop, he set down his fork. "Tess, it isn't like the flicks."

"No, but it isn't like selling shoes either."

"Okay. I'm not saying you never run into a situation where things might get hot, but basically this kind of police work is on paper. Reports, interviews, head work. There are weeks, months, even years of incredible drudge work, even boredom as opposed to moments of actual physical jeopardy. A rookie in a uniform is likely to deal with more heat in a year than I am."

"I see. Then you aren't likely to encounter a situation, in the normal scheme of things, where you use your gun."

He didn't answer for a moment, not liking where the conversation was going. "What are you getting at?"

"I'm trying to understand you. We've spent two nights together. I like to know who I'm sleeping with."

He'd been avoiding that. Sex was easier if it wore blinders. "Benjamin James Matthew Paris, thirty-five in August, single, six feet one-half inch, a hundred seventy-two pounds."

She rested her elbows on the table, setting her chin on her linked hands as she studied him. "You don't like to talk about your work."

"What's there to talk about? It's a job."

"No, not with you. A job is where you clock in every morning, Monday through Friday. You don't carry your gun like a briefcase."

"Most briefcases aren't loaded."

"You have had to use it."

Ben drained his coffee. His system was already primed. "I doubt many cops get around to collecting their pensions without drawing their weapons at least once."

"Yes, I understand that. On the other hand, as a doctor I'd deal more with the results afterward. The grief of the family, the shock and trauma of the victim."

"I've never shot a victim."

There was an edge to his voice that interested her. Perhaps he liked to pretend to her, even to himself, that the violent aspects of his job were occasional, an expected side effect. He'd consider anyone he shot in the line of duty, as he'd put it, the bad guy. And yet she was sure there was a part of him that thought of the human, the flesh and blood. That part of him would lose sleep over it.

"When you shoot someone in self-defense," she said slowly, "is it like in a war, where you see the enemy as a symbol more than a man?"

"You don't think about it."

"I don't see how that's possible."

"Take my word for it."

"But when you're in a situation that calls for that kind of extreme defensive action, you aim to wound."

"No." On the flat answer, he rose and picked up his plate. "Listen, you draw your weapon, you're not the Lone Ranger. There's no grazing your silver bullet over the bad guy's gun hand. Your life, your partner's life, some civilian's life is on the line. It's black and white."

He took the plates away. She didn't ask if he'd killed. He'd already told her.

She glanced at the papers he'd been working on. Black and white. He wouldn't see the shades of gray she saw there. The man they sought was a killer. The state of his mind, his emotions, perhaps even his soul, didn't matter to Ben. Maybe they couldn't.

"These papers," she began when he came back. "Is there something I can help with?"

"Just drudge work."

"I'm an expert drudge."

"Maybe. We can talk about it later. Right now I've got to get moving if I'm going to make nine o'clock Mass."

"Mass?"

He grinned at her expression. "I haven't gone back to the fold. We think our man might show up at one of two churches this morning. We've been covering the masses at both of them since six-thirty. I got a break and drew the nine, ten, and eleven-thirty services."

"I'll go with you. No, don't," she said even as he opened his mouth. "I really could help. I know the signs, the symptoms."

There was no point in telling her he'd wanted her to come. Let her think she'd talked him into it. "Don't blame me if your knees give out."

She touched a hand to his cheek, but didn't kiss him. "Give me ten minutes."

THE church smelled of candle wax and perfume. The pews, worn smooth by the sliding and shifting of hundreds of cloth-covered haunches, were less than half full for the nine o'clock service. It was quiet, with the occasional cough or sniffle echoing hollowly. A pleasant, religious light came through the stained-glass windows on the east wall. The altar stood at the head of the church, draped with its cloth and flanked by candles. White for purity. Above it hung the Son of God, dying on the Cross.

Ben sat with Tess in the back pew and scanned the congregation. A few older women were scattered among the families toward the front. A young couple sat in the pew across from them, choosing the rear, Ben thought, because of the sleeping infant the woman carried. An elderly man who had come in with the help of a cane sat alone, two private feet away from a family of six. Two young girls in their Sunday best sat and whispered together, and a boy of about three knelt backward on the pew and ran a plastic car quietly over the wood.

Ben knew he was making the sounds of the engine and screeching tires in his head.

There were three men sitting alone who fit the general description. One was already kneeling, his thin, dark coat still buttoned, though the church was warm. Another sat, passing idly through the hymnal. The third was in the front of the church, and sat unmoving. Ben knew Roderick had the front, and the rookie, Pilomento, was situated in the middle.

A movement beside Tess had Ben stiffening. Logan slid in beside her, patted her hand, and smiled at Ben. "Thought I'd join you." His voice was a bit wheezy. He coughed quietly into his hand to clear it.

"Nice to see you, Monsignor," Tess murmured.

"Thank you, my dear. I've been a little under the weather lately and wasn't sure I'd make it. I was hoping you'd be along. You'd have a sharp eye." His gaze traveled around the half-empty church. Mostly the old and young, he thought. Those in the middle of their lives rarely thought God needed an hour of their time. After digging a Sucret out of his pocket, he looked at Ben again. "I hope you don't mind my volunteering. If you happen to get lucky, I might be of help. After all, I have what we might call house advantage."

For the first time since Ben had met him, Logan wore the white clerical collar. Seeing it, Ben only nodded.

The priest entered, the congregation rose. The service began.

Entrance Rite. The Celebrant in green vestments, stole, alb, the amice worn harmlessly under the flowing robes, the gangly altar boy in black and white, ready to serve.

Lord have mercy.

A baby five pews up began to cry lustily. The congregation murmured the responses in unison.

Christ have mercy.

The old man with the cane was working his way through the rosary. The young girls giggled and tried desperately to stop. The little boy with the plastic car was shushed by his mother.

A man with a white silk amice next to his skin felt the drumming in his head ease with the familiar flow of Celebrant and congregation. His palms were sweaty, but he kept them clasped in front of him.

The Lord be with you.

And with your spirit.

It was the Latin he heard, the Latin of his childhood, of his priesthood. It soothed, and the world stayed steady.

The Liturgy. The congregation sat with shuffles, murmurs, and creaks. Ben watched, not really hearing the priest's words. He'd heard them all so many times before. One of his earliest memories was of sitting on a hard pew, his hands between his knees, the starched collar of his best shirt rubbing against his neck. He'd been five, or perhaps six. Josh had been an altar boy.

The man in the thin black coat was slumped back in his seat as if exhausted. Someone cheerfully blew his nose.

"For the wages of sin is death," the priest intoned, "but God's gift is eternal life in Christ Jesus, our Lord."

The amice was cool against his skin, against his heart, as he murmured the response. "Thanks be to God."

They rose for the Gospel. Matthew 7:15–21. "Be on your guard against false prophets."

Isn't that what the Voice had told him? His head began to ring with the power of it as he sat very still. Excitement, fresh and clean, sang through his tired body. Yes, be on your guard. They wouldn't understand, they wouldn't let you finish. She pretended to understand. Dr. Court. But she only wanted to have him put in a place where he couldn't finish.

He knew the kind of place—white walls, all those white walls and white nurses with their bored and wary looks. A place like his mother had been those last terrible years.

"Take care of Laura. She breeds sin in her heart and listens to the devil." His mother's skin had been pasty, her cheeks flaccid. But her eyes had been so dark and bright. Bright with madness and knowledge. "You're twins. If her soul's damned, so is yours. Take care of Laura."

But Laura had already been dead.

He heard the last of the gospel. It spoke to him. "Lord, Lord, who will enter into the kingdom of heaven, but he who does my heavenly Father's will?"

He bowed his head, accepting. "Praise to you, O Christ."

They sat for the sermon.

Ben felt Tess's hand slip over his. He linked fingers, aware that she knew he was uncomfortable. He'd resigned himself to sitting through Mass again, but it was a different story when a priest sat a foot away. It reminded him, clearly, of the few times he'd gone to church as a boy and discovered, to his embarrassment, Sister Mary Angelina sitting in the pew ahead of his family. Nuns weren't as tolerant as mothers when little boys played with their fingers and hummed to themselves during Mass.

"You were daydreaming during Mass again, Benjamin." He remembered the trick Sister Mary Angelina had had of slipping her white hands into the black sleeves of her habit so that she looked like one of those egg-shaped, bottom-heavy toys you couldn't knock down. "You should try to be more like your brother, Joshua."

"Ben?"

"Hmmm?"

"The man there." Tess's voice was light as a feather near his ear. "The one in the black coat."

"Yeah, I saw him before."

"He's crying."

The congregation stood for the Creed. The man in the black coat continued to sit, weeping silently over his rosary. Before the prayer was finished, he rose unsteadily then hurried out of the church.

"Stay here," Ben ordered, and slipped out to follow. When she made a move to go with him, Logan pressed her hand.

"Relax, Tess. He knows his job."

He didn't come back through the Offertory prayers or the washing of hands. Tess sat with her hands clasped in her lap and her spine trembling. Ben knew his job, she agreed silently, but he didn't know hers. If they'd found the man, she should be out with him. He'd need to talk. She stayed where she was, acknowledging fully for the first time that she was afraid.

Ben returned, his expression grim as he leaned over the back of the pew and touched Logan's shoulder. "Could you come out here a minute?"

Logan went without question. Tess found herself taking a deep breath before she followed them into the vestibule.

"The guy's sitting out there on the steps. His wife died last week. Leukemia. I'd say it's been a pretty rough time. I'm going to check him out anyway, but—"

"Yes, I understand." Logan glanced toward the closed doors of the church. "I'll take care of him. Let me know if anything changes." He smiled at Tess and patted her hand. "It was lovely seeing you again."

"Good-bye, Monsignor."

They watched him walk outside into the crisp bite of the November morning. In silence, they went back into the church. On the altar was the Consecration. Fascinated, Tess sat to watch the ritual of the bread and wine.

For this is My body.

Heads bowed, accepting the symbol and the gift. She found it beautiful. The priest, his vestments making him large and wide at the altar, held the round white wafer up. Then the gleaming silver chalice was consecrated and lifted as offering.

As sacrifice, Tess thought. He had spoken at length of sacrifice. The ceremony she found beautiful, even a little pompous, would only mean sacrifice to him. His God was the Old Testament God, righteous, harsh, and thirsty for the blood of submission. The God of the Flood, of Sodom and Gomorrah. He wouldn't see the lovely ceremony as a bond between the congregation and a God of mercy and kindness, but as a sacrifice to the demanding.

She reached for Ben's hand. "I think he'd feel . . . full here."

"What?"

She shook her head, not sure how to explain.

From the altar came the solemn words, ". . . as you were pleased to accept the offering of holy Abel and the sacrifice of our father Abraham, and that of your high priest Melchisedec, a holy sacrifice, a spotless victim."

"A spotless victim," Tess repeated. "White for purity." She looked at Ben with a dull horror. "Not saving. Not saving so much as sacrificing. And when he's here, he twists all this so that it reinforces what he's doing. He wouldn't fall apart here, not here. He feeds off this in the most unhealthy way."

She watched the priest consume the wafer, then after the sign of the cross, drink the wine. Symbols, she thought. But how far had one man taken them beyond symbols to flesh and blood?

The priest held up the host and spoke in a clear voice. "Behold the Lamb of God, behold Him who takes away the sins of the world. Lord, I am not worthy that You should come under my roof. Speak but the word and my soul will be healed."

Members of the congregation began to shift out of pews and shuffle down the aisle to receive communion.

"Do you think he'd take communion?" Ben murmured, watching the slow-moving line.

"I don't know." She suddenly felt cold, cold and unsure. "I think he'd need to. It's renewing, isn't it?"

The body of Christ.

"Yeah, that's the idea."

The man who'd been paging through the hymnal rose to go to the altar. The other man Ben had watched kept his seat, with his head bent either in prayer or a light doze.

There was another who felt the need and the longing rise up urgently inside him. His hands nearly trembled with it. He wanted the offering, the flesh of his Lord to fill him and wash away all stain of sin.

He sat as the church filled with voices.

"You're born in sin," his mother had told him. "You're born sinful and unworthy. It's a punishment, a righteous one. All of your life you'll fall into sin. If you die in sin, your soul is damned."

"Restitution," Father Moore had warned him. "You must make restitution for sin before it can be forgiven and absolved. Restitution. God demands restitution."

Yes, yes, he understood. He'd begun restitution. He'd brought four souls to the Lord. Four lost, seeking souls to pay for the one Laura had lost. The Voice demanded two more for full payment.

"I don't want to die." Laura, in delirium, had gripped his hands. "I don't want to go to hell. Do something. Oh, please, God, do something."

He wanted to clasp his hands over his ears, to fall on his knees at the altar and take the host into himself. But he wasn't worthy. Until his mission was finished, he wouldn't be worthy.

"The Lord be with you," the priest said clearly.

"Et cum spiritu tuo," he murmured.

TESS let the freshening breeze outside play on her face and revive her after over three hours of services. The frustration was back as she watched the stragglers from late Mass stroll to their cars; frustration and a vague, nagging feeling that he'd been close all along.

She linked her arm with Ben's. "What now?"

"I'm going into the station, make a few calls. Here's Roderick."

Roderick came down the steps, nodded to Tess, then sneezed three times into his handkerchief. "Sorry."

"You look terrible," Ben commented, and lit a cigarette.

"Thanks. Pilomento's checking out a license plate. Said a guy across from him mumbled to himself through the last service." He tucked the handkerchief away and shivered a bit in the wind. "I didn't know you'd be here, Dr. Court."

"I thought I might be able to help." She looked at his reddened eyes, sympathizing when he was wracked with a fit of coughing. "That sounds bad. Have you seen a doctor?"

"No time."

"Half the department's down with flu," Ben put in. "Ed's threatened to wear a face mask." Thinking of his partner, he looked back at the church. "Maybe they had better luck."

"Maybe," Roderick agreed, wheezing. "You going in?"

"Yeah, I've got some calls to make. Do me a favor.

Go home and take something for that. Your desk's upwind from mine."

"I've got a report."

"Screw the report," Ben said, then shifted as he remembered he stood a couple of yards from the church. "Keep your germs home for a couple of days, Lou."

"Yeah, maybe. Give me a call if Ed came up with anything."

"Sure. Take it easy."

"And see a doctor," Tess added.

He managed a weak smile and headed off.

"Sounds to me like it's heading into his lungs," she murmured, but when she turned back to Ben, she saw his mind was already on other things. "Look, I know you're anxious to make calls. I'll take a cab home."

"What?"

"I said I'll take a cab home."

"Why? Tired of me?"

"No." To prove it, she brushed her lips over his. "I know you've got work you want to do."

"So come with me." He wasn't ready to let her go yet, or give up whatever private, uncomplicated time might be left of the weekend. "After I tie things up, we can go back to your place and . . ." He bent down and nipped her earlobe.

"Ben, we can't make love all the time."

With his arm around her, he walked to the car. "Sure we can. I'll show you."

"No, really. There are biological reasons. Trust me, I'm a doctor."

He stopped by the car door. "What biological reasons?"

"I'm starving."

"Oh." He opened the door for her then went around to the driver's side. "Okay, so we'll make a quick stop at the market on the way. You can fix lunch."

"I can?"

"I fixed breakfast."

"Oh, so you did." She settled back, finding the idea of a cozy Sunday afternoon appealing. "All right, I'll fix lunch. I hope you like cheese sandwiches."

He leaned close, so that his breath feathered over her lips. "Then I'll show you what people are supposed to do on Sunday afternoons."

Tess let her eyes flutter half closed. "And what's that?"

"Drink beer and watch football." He kissed her hard, and started the car as she laughed.

He watched them huddled together in the car. He'd seen her in church. His church. It was a sign, of course, that she should come to pray in his church. At first it had upset him a little, then he'd realized she'd been guided there.

She would be the last one. The last, before himself.

He watched the car pull out, caught a glimpse of her hair through the side window. A bird landed in the branch of the denuded tree beside him and looked down with bright black eyes, his mother's eyes. He went home to rest.

Chapter 12

"I THINK I found a place."

Ed sat solidly at his desk, hammering away two finger-style at his typewriter.

"Oh, yeah?" Ben sat at his own, the map of the city in front of him again. Patiently, he drew lines with a pencil to connect the murder scenes. "A place for what?"

"To live."

"Umm-hmm."

Someone opened the refrigerator and complained loudly that their A & W had been stolen. No one paid any attention. The staff had been whittled down by the flu and a double homicide near Georgetown University. Someone had taped a cardboard turkey onto one of the windows, but it was the only outward sign of holiday cheer. Ben put a light circle around Tess's apartment building before he glanced over at Ed.

"So when are you moving?"

"Depends." Ed frowned at the keys, hesitated, then found his rhythm again. "Have to see if the contract goes through."

"You having someone killed so you can rent their apartment?"

"Contract of sale. Shit, this typewriter's defective."

"Sale?" Ben dropped his pencil and stared. "You're buying a place? *Buying?*"

"That's right." Ed patiently applied Liquid Paper to his last mistake, blew on it, then typed the correction. He kept a can of Lysol spray at his elbow. If anyone who looked contagious walked by, he sprayed the area. "You suggested it."

"Yeah, but I was only—Buying?" To cover his tracks, Ben pushed some excess paper into his trash basket on top of the empty can of A & W. "What kind of dump can you afford on a detective's pay?"

"Some of us know how to save. I'm using my capital."

"Capital?" Ben rolled his eyes before folding the map. He wasn't getting anywhere. "The man has capital," he said to the station at large. "Next thing you know, you'll be telling me you play the market."

"I've made a few small, conservative investments. Utilities mostly."

"Utilities. The only utilities you know about is the gas bill." But he studied Ed with an uncertain eye. "Where is this place?"

"Got a few minutes?"

"I've got some personal time coming."

Ed pulled his report out of the typewriter, cast a wary glance over it, then set it aside. "Let's take a drive."

It didn't take long. The neighborhood was on the outer and rougher edges of Georgetown. The row houses looked more tired than distinguished. The fall flowers had simply given up for lack of interest, and stood faded among tangles of unraked leaves. Someone had chained a bike to a post. It had been stripped down of everything portable. Ed pulled up to the curb.

"There it is."

Cautious, Ben turned his head. To his credit, he didn't groan.

The house was three stories high, and narrow, with its front door hardly five paces from the sidewalk. Two of the windows had been boarded up, and the shutters that hadn't fallen off tilted drunkenly. The brick was old and softly faded, except for where someone had spray painted an obscenity. Ben got out of the car, leaned on the hood, and tried not to believe what he was seeing.

"Something, isn't it?"

"Yeah, something. Ed, there aren't any gutters."

"I know."

"Half the windows are broken."

"I thought I might replace a couple of them with stained glass."

"I don't think the roof's been reshingled since the Depression. The real one."

"I'm looking into skylights."

"While you're at it you ought to try a crystal ball." Ben stuck his hands in the pockets of his jacket. "Let's have a look inside."

"I don't have a key yet."

"Jesus." With a mutter, Ben walked up three broken concrete steps, pulled out his wallet, and found a credit card. The pitiful lock gave without complaint. "I feel like I should carry you over the threshold."

"Get your own house."

The hall was full of cobwebs and droppings from assorted rodents. The wallpaper had faded to gray. A fat, hard-backed beetle crawled lazily across it. "When does Vincent Price come down the steps?"

Ed glanced around and saw a castle in the rough. "It just needs a good cleaning."

"And an exterminator. Are there rats?"

"In the basement, I imagine," Ed said carelessly, and walked into what had once been a charming parlor.

It was narrow and high ceilinged, with the openings of what would be two five-foot windows boarded up.

The stone of the fireplace was intact, but someone had ripped out the mantel. The floors, under a coating of dust and grime, might very well have been oak.

"Ed, this place—"

"Terrific potential. The kitchen has a brick oven built into the wall. You know what bread tastes like out of a brick oven?"

"You don't buy a house to bake bread." Ben walked back into the hall, watching the floor for any signs of life. "Christ, there's a hole in the ceiling back here. It's fucking four feet wide."

"That's first on my list," Ed commented as he came to join him. They stood for a moment in silence, looking up at the hole.

"You're not talking about a list. You're talking about a lifetime commitment." As they watched, a spider the size of a man's thumb dropped down and landed at their feet with a noticeable plop. More than a little disgusted, Ben kicked it aside. "You can't be serious about this place."

"Sure I am. A man gets to a point he wants to settle down."

"You didn't take me seriously about getting married too?"

"A place of his own," Ed continued placidly. "A workroom, maybe a little garden. There's a good spot for herbs in the back. A place like this would give me a goal. I figure on fixing up one room at a time."

"It'll take you fifty years."

"I got nothing better to do. Want to see upstairs?"

Ben took another look at the hole. "No, I want to live. How much?" he asked flatly.

"Seventy-five."

"Seventy-five? Seventy-five *thousand*? Dollars?"

"Real estate's at a premium in Georgetown."

"Georgetown? Christ on a raft, this isn't Georgetown." Something bigger than the spider skuddled in the corner. He reached for his weapon. "The first rat I see is going to eat this."

"Just a field mouse." Ed put a soothing hand on Ben's shoulder. "Rats stick to the basement or the attic."

"What, do they have a lease?" But he left his weapon secured. "Listen, Ed, the realtors and developers push back the borders so they can call this Georgetown and take idiots like you for seventy-five-thousand dollars."

"I only offered seventy."

"Oh, that's different. You only offered seventy." He started to pace but ran into a magnificent cobweb. Swearing, he fought himself free. "Ed, it's those sunflower seeds. You need red meat."

"You feel responsible." Ed smiled, terrifically pleased before he strolled into the kitchen.

"No, I don't." Ben jammed his hands into his pockets. "Yes, dammit, I do."

"That's the yard. My yard," Ed pointed out when Ben trailed after him. "I figure I can grow basil, some rosemary, maybe some lavender in that little spot right outside the window."

Ben saw a patch of knee-high grass nearly wide enough for two swipes of a lawn mower. "You've been working too hard. This case is making us all loony. Ed, listen carefully to these words, see if they ring a bell. Dry rot. Termites. Vermin."

"I'm going to be thirty-six."

"So?"

"I've never owned a house."

"Hell, everybody's going to be thirty-six once, but not everybody has to own a house."

"Shit, I never even lived in one. We always had apartments."

The kitchen smelled of decades of grease, but this time Ben said nothing.

"There's an attic. The kind you see in shows where there're trunks and old furniture and funny hats. I like that. I'm going to do the kitchen first."

Ben stared out at the pitiful clump of grass. "Steam," he said. "That's the best way to strip this old wallpaper."

"Steam?"

"Yeah." Ben pulled out a cigarette and grinned. "You're going to need plenty of it. I dated this woman who worked at a paint store. Marli . . . yeah, I think her name was Marli. She'd probably still give me a discount."

"Date anyone who works at a lumberyard?"

"I'll check. Come on, I have to make a call."

They stopped at a phone booth a few miles away. Ben found a quarter and dialed Tess's office number while Ed went into the 7-Eleven.

"Dr. Court's office."

"Detective Paris."

"Yes, Detective, just a moment."

There was a click, then silence, then another click. "Ben?"

"How are you, Doc?"

"I'm fine." As she spoke she was clearing her desk. "Just on my way out to the clinic."

"What time do you finish there?"

"Usually five-thirty, maybe six."

He glanced at his watch and shifted the rest of his schedule. "Fine. I'll pick you up."

"But you don't need—"

"Yes, I do. Who's on you today?"

"I beg your pardon?"

"Who's watching you at the office?" Ben explained,

and tried to find a corner in the phone booth where the wind wouldn't reach.

"Oh, Sergeant Billings."

"Good." He cupped his hands around a match as he lit a cigarette, and wished like hell he'd remembered his gloves. "Have Billings drive you to the clinic."

There was silence. In it he heard her temper, and was tempted to smile at it. "I don't see any reason why I can't drive myself to the clinic as I've done every week for the last several years."

"I'm not asking you to see a reason, Tess. I've got plenty of them. See you at six."

He hung up, knowing she'd hold the phone, and her temper, until she could replace it quietly. She wouldn't want to do something as childish, and typical, as slamming it down.

❧

HE was right. Tess counted backward from five, slowly, then quietly replaced the receiver. She'd hardly set it down when Kate buzzed her again.

"Yes?" It took effort not to bite the word off.

"You have another call on line two. He won't give his name."

"All right, I—" The nerves in her stomach tangled, and she knew. "I'll take it, Kate."

She stared at the slowly blinking button. Her finger was steady when she pushed it. "This is Dr. Court."

"I saw you in church. You came."

"Yes." The instructions she'd been given raced through her head. Try to keep him on the line. Keep him calm and on the line. "I was hoping to see you there so we could talk again. How are you feeling?"

"You were there. Now you understand."

"What do I understand?"

"You understand the greatness." His voice was calm. A decision reached, faith confirmed. "The sacrifices we're asked to make are so small compared to the rewards of obedience. I'm glad you were there, so that you understand. I had doubts."

"What kind of doubts?"

"About the mission." His voice dropped, as if even whispering of doubt was a sin. "But not anymore."

Tess took a chance. "Where is Laura?"

"Laura." She could hear the tears. "Laura waits in purgatory, suffering, until I atone for her sins. She's my responsibility. She has no one but me and the Blessed Mother to intercede for her."

So Laura was dead. Now she could be sure of it. "You must have loved her very much."

"She was the best part of me. We were joined before birth. Now I must make restitution for her before we can be joined after death. You understand now. You came. Your soul will join the others. I will absolve you in the name of the Lord."

"You can't kill again. Laura wouldn't want you to kill again."

There was silence . . . three, four, five seconds. "I thought you understood."

Tess recognized the tone, the accusation, the betrayal. She was going to lose him. "I think I do. If I don't, I need you to explain things to me. I want to understand, I want you to help me understand. That's why I want to come talk to you."

"No, it's lies. You're full of sin and lies." She heard him begin to mumble the Lord's Prayer before the connection was broken.

WHEN Ben walked back into the squad room, Lowenstein was standing by her desk. She signaled to him, cradling the phone against her ear so her hands would be free.

"She can't keep away from me," Ben told Ed. He started to slip an arm around her, not aiming for her waist, but for the bag of chocolate-covered raisins on her desk.

"He called Court again," Lowenstein told him. His hand froze.

"When?"

"Call came through at 11:21."

"The trace?"

"Yeah." She lifted a pad from her desk and handed it to him. "They pinned it to that area. Had to be within those four blocks. Goldman said she did real good."

"Christ, we were just there." He tossed the pad back on her desk. "We might have driven right past him."

"The captain's sent out Bigsby, Mullendore, and some uniforms to comb the area and look for witnesses."

"We'll give them a hand."

"Ben. Ben, wait." He stopped, turning back with impatience. Lowenstein pressed the mouthpiece of the phone against her shoulder. "They're sending up a transcript of the call for the captain. I think you'll want to see it."

"Fine, I'll read it when I get back."

"I think you'll want to see it now, Ben."

A few hours' work at the Donnerly Clinic was enough to take Tess's mind off her own nerves. The patients there ranged from manic-depressive businessmen to street junkies who were withdrawing. Once a week, twice if her schedule permitted, she came to the clinic to work with the staff doctors. Some of the patients she would only see once or twice, others she would see week after week, month after month.

She gave her time there, when she could, because it wasn't an elite hospital where the rich came when their problems or addictions became too much to cope with. Neither was it a street-side clinic run by idealists on a shoestring. It was a struggling and capable institution which took in the emotionally and mentally ill from all walks of life.

There was a woman on the second floor with Alzheimer's disease who sewed dolls for her grandchildren, then played with them herself when she forgot she had grandchildren. There was a man who thought he was John Kennedy and spent most of his day harmlessly writing speeches. The more violent patients were kept on the third floor, where security was tighter. Thick glass doors were locked and windows were barred.

Tess spent most of the afternoon there. By five she was nearly wrung dry. For the better part of an hour she'd been in session with a paranoid schizophrenic who had hurled obscenities then his lunch tray at her, before he'd ultimately been restrained by two orderlies. Tess had given him an injection of Thorazine herself, but not without regret. He'd be on medication for the rest of his life.

When he was quiet again, Tess left him to catch a few moments of quiet in the staff lounge. She still had one more patient to see: Lydia Woods, a thirty-seven-year-old woman who had run a household with three children, held down a full-time job as a stock broker, and worked as president of the PTA. She had cooked gourmet meals, attended every school function, and had been named Businesswoman of the Year. The new woman, who could have and handle it all.

Two months before, she had fallen violently apart at a school play. There had been convulsions, and a seizure many of the horrified parents had taken for epilepsy.

When she'd been taken to the hospital it was discovered she'd been in a withdrawal as serious as one from heroin addiction.

Lydia Woods had held together her perfect world with Valium and alcohol until her husband had threatened divorce. To prove her strength, she'd gone cold turkey and had ignored her physical reactions in a desperate attempt to keep her life as she had structured it.

Now, though the physical illness was well under control, she was being forced to deal with the causes, and the results.

Tess took the elevator down to the first floor, where she requested Lydia's file. After studying it, Tess tucked it under her arm. Her room was at the end of the hall. Lydia had left the door open, but Tess knocked before going in.

The curtains were drawn, the room dim. There were flowers beside the bed, pink carnations. Their scent was light and sweet and hopeful. Lydia herself was on the bed, curled up to face the blank wall. She didn't acknowledge Tess's presence.

"Hello, Lydia." Tess set the file on a small table and glanced around the room. The clothes Lydia had worn the day before were heaped in a corner. "It's dark in here," she said, and moved to the curtain.

"I like it dark."

Tess glanced at the figure on the bed. It was time to push. "I don't," she said simply, then drew the curtain open. When light spilled in, Lydia rolled over and glared. She hadn't bothered with her hair and makeup. There was a drawn, bitter look around her mouth.

"It's my room."

"Yes, it is. From what I hear you've been spending too much time alone in it."

"And what the hell are you supposed to do around this place? Weave baskets with the fruits and nuts?"

"You might try going for a walk on the grounds." Tess sat, but didn't touch the file.

"I don't belong here. I don't want to be here."

"You're free to go any time." Tess watched her sit up and light a cigarette. "This isn't a prison, Lydia."

"Easy for you to say."

"You signed yourself in. When you feel you're ready, you can sign yourself out."

Lydia said nothing, smoking in brooding silence.

"I see your husband was in to see you yesterday."

Lydia glanced at the flowers, then away. "So?"

"How did you feel about seeing him?"

"Oh, I loved it," she snapped. "I loved having him come in here to see me looking like this." She grabbed a handful of her unwashed hair. "I told him he should bring the kids so they can see what a pitiful hag their mother is."

"Did you know he was coming?"

"I knew."

"You have a shower in there. Shampoo, makeup."

"Aren't you the one who said I was hiding behind things?"

"Using prescription drugs and alcohol as a crutch isn't the same as making the effort to look nice for your husband. You wanted him to see you this way, Lydia. Why, so he'd go away feeling sorry for you? Guilty?"

The arrow hit home and started the blaze, as she'd hoped. "Just shut up. It's none of your business."

"Did your husband bring you those flowers? They're lovely."

Lydia looked at them again. They made her want to cry, lose the edge of bitterness and failure that was her defense now. Picking up the vase, she hurled it and the flowers against the wall.

From out in the hall where he'd been told to wait,

Ben heard the crash. He was out of his chair and heading toward the open door when a nurse stopped him.

"I'm sorry, sir, you really can't go in. Dr. Court's with a patient." Blocking his way, she went to the door herself.

"Oh, Mrs. Rydel." Ben heard Tess's voice, cool and unruffled. "Would you bring a dustpan and a mop so Mrs. Woods can clean this up?"

"I won't!" Lydia shouted at her. "It's my room and I won't clean it up."

"Then I'd be careful where I walked, so I didn't cut my feet on the glass."

"I hate you." When Tess didn't even wince, Lydia shouted it more loudly. "I hate you! Did you hear me?"

"Yes, I hear you very well. But I wonder if you're shouting at me, Lydia, or yourself."

"Who the hell do you think you are?" Her hand worked up and down like a jack hammer to crush out her cigarette. "You come in here week after week with your smug self-righteous looks and your pretty, upscale suits and wait for me to strip my soul. Well, I won't. Do you think I want to talk to some ice maiden who has her life all worked out? Miss Perfect Society who treats basket cases as a hobby then goes to her just-so home and forgets about them."

"I don't forget about them, Lydia."

Tess's voice was quiet, a direct contrast, but in the hall, Ben heard it.

"You make me sick." Lydia heaved herself off the bed for the first time that day. "I can't stand the sight of you with your Italian shoes and little gold pins and that 'I never sweat' perfection."

"I'm not perfect, Lydia, none of us is. None of us has to be to earn love and respect."

The tears started, but Tess didn't rise to offer comfort. It wasn't time. "What do you know about mistakes?

What the hell do you know about how I lived? Dammit, I made things work. *I* did."

"Yes, you did. But nothing works forever if you refuse to allow for flaws."

"I was as good as you. I was better. I had clothes like yours, and a home. I hate you for coming in here and reminding me. Get out. Just get out and leave me alone."

"All right." Tess rose, taking the file with her. "I'll be back next week. Sooner, if you ask for me." She walked to the door and turned. "You still have a home, Lydia." The nurse stood in the doorway, holding the dustpan and mop. Tess took them and set them against the inside wall. "I'll have them send down a fresh vase for those flowers."

Tess walked out the door and shut her eyes a moment. That kind of violent dislike, even when it came from illness and not from the heart, was never easy to take.

"Doc?"

Tess shook herself back and opened her eyes. Ben was there, a few steps away. "You're early."

"Yeah." He came to her and wrapped a hand around her arm. "What the hell are you doing in a place like this?"

"My job. You'll have to wait a minute. I have to enter some things in this file." She walked down to the nurses' station, checked her watch, and began to write.

Ben watched her. Right now she seemed totally unaffected by the nasty little scene he'd overheard. Her face was calm as she wrote in what he was sure was a very professional hand. But he'd seen that one quick unguarded moment when she'd stepped into the hall. Not unaffected, but impossibly controlled. He didn't like it, just as he didn't like this place with its clean white walls and blank, miserable faces.

She handed the file back to the nurse, in an undertone said a few things he assumed referred to the woman who'd just berated her, then glanced at her watch again.

"I'm sorry you had to wait," Tess said when she came back. "I have to get my coat. Why don't you meet me outside?"

When she came out, he was standing at the edge of the grass, smoking steadily. "You never gave me a chance on the phone to tell you I didn't want you to bother with all this. I've been getting myself to and from the clinic for a long time."

He dropped the cigarette and carefully crushed it. "Why did you take all that crap from her?"

Tess drew a long breath before she linked her arm with his. "Where are you parked?"

"That's psychiatrist shit, answering questions with questions."

"Yes. Yes, it is. Look, if she didn't attack me, I wouldn't be doing my job. It's the first time we've really gotten anywhere since I've started seeing her. Now, where are you parked? It's cold."

"Over here." More than happy to leave the clinic behind, he began to walk with her. "He called you again."

"Yes, right after you did." She wanted badly to treat that with the same professional ease she had the patients in the clinic. "Were they able to trace it?"

"Narrowed it down to a couple blocks. No one saw anything. We're still working on it."

"His Laura is dead."

"I figured that much out." He put his hand on the car door, then released it again. "The same way I figured out you're his next target."

She didn't grow pale or shudder. He hadn't expected her to. She simply nodded, accepting, then put her hand on his arm. "Would you do me a favor?"

"I can give it a shot."

"Let's not talk about it tonight. At all."

"Tess—"

"Please. I have to go to the station with you tomorrow and meet with Captain Harris. Isn't that soon enough to hash all this over?"

He put cold, ungloved hands on her face. "I'm not going to let anything happen to you. I don't care what I have to do."

She smiled, lifting her hands to his wrist. "Then I don't have anything to worry about, do I?"

"I care about you," he said carefully. It was as close to a declaration as he'd ever come with a woman. "I want you to know that."

"Then take me home, Ben." She turned her lips into his palm. "And show me."

Chapter 13

THE MAINTENANCE MAN was glumly mopping up a mud-colored puddle in the hallway outside the squad room. Under the heavy scent of pine cleaner hung trails of more human odors. The machine that dispensed coffee black, coffee light, and when its mood was generous, hot chocolate, leaned like a wounded soldier against its companion which handled Hershey bars and Baby Ruths. A platoon of Styrofoam cups littered the tile. Ben steered Tess around the worst of it.

"Coffee machine blow up again?"

The man with dusty gray overalls and dusty gray hair looked over the handle of his mop. "You guys gotta quit kicking these machines. Look at that dent." He slopped more coffee and Lysol as he gestured. "Criminal."

"Yeah." Ben sent a look of dislike at the candy machine. He'd added a fresh dent there himself after he'd lost another fifty cents the day before. "Somebody ought to investigate. Watch your shoes, Doc." He led her into the squad room, where at eight o'clock phones were already shrilling.

"Paris." Lowenstein chucked a paper cup toward her

trash basket where it caught the rim and flipped in. "Captain's daughter had her baby last night."

"Last night?" He stopped by his desk to look for messages. The one from his mother reminded him that it had been nearly a month since he'd checked in.

"At 10:35 P.M."

"Shit, couldn't she have waited a couple of days? I had the fifteenth in the pool." There was still a chance, he figured, if she'd cooperated and had a boy. "What'd she have?"

"Girl, seven pounds, seven ounces. Jackson hit it on the nose."

"Figures."

She rose, giving Tess a quick professional sweep. Lowenstein judged the price of the snakeskin bag in the ballpark of a hundred fifty and felt a small, harmless tug of envy. "Good morning, Dr. Court."

"Good morning."

"Ah, if you'd like coffee or anything, we're getting it out of the conference room until things are cleared up. We'll be meeting in there in a few minutes." The perfume was French, the real stuff, Lowenstein deduced as she took a quick, discreet sniff.

"Thanks, I'll wait."

"Why don't you have a seat until the captain's ready?" Ben suggested, glancing around for a clean chair. "I've got to return a couple of these calls."

There was a sudden spurt of obscenities from the hall, then a metallic crash. Tess turned to see the dirty water from the bucket stream down the hall. Then all hell broke loose.

A stringy black man with his hands cuffed behind him got as far as the doorway when a man in an overcoat caught him in a headlock.

"Look at my floor!" Almost dancing with fury, the

maintenance man jumped into view. He swung his mop, spraying everything. "I'm going to the union. See if I don't."

The prisoner bucked and squirmed like a landed trout while the officer in charge tried to hang on. "Get that wet mop out of my face." Panting and a bit red-faced, he tried to avoid the next shower while the black man sent up a high, keening wail.

"Shit, Mullendore, can't you control your prisoners?" Without hurry Ben walked over to assist when the black man managed to sink his teeth into Mullendore's hand. There was a low growl of a curse before the prisoner burst free and ran headlong into Ben. "Jesus, give me a hand, will you? This guy's an animal." Mullendore made a grab, sandwiching the prisoner between them. For a moment they looked as though they were ready to rhumba. Then all three men lost their footing on the damp floor and went down in a heap.

Beside Tess, Lowenstein watched with her hands comfortably on her hips.

"Shouldn't you break it up?" Tess wondered aloud.

"The guy's cuffed and weighs maybe a hundred pounds. They'll just be a minute."

"You ain't putting me in a cell!" The black man rolled and squirmed and screamed, and managed to bring his knee solidly into Ben's groin. In reflex, Ben jerked his elbow and caught him under the chin. As his body went limp, Ben collapsed on it, with Mullendore panting beside them.

"Thanks, Paris." Mullendore held up his wounded hand to study the teeth marks. "Christ, I'm probably going to need a shot. The guy went crazy when we walked into the building."

Ben managed to rise to his hands and knees. His breath whistled as he sucked it in, and left a hole burning in his gut. He tried to speak, dragged in another whistling breath, and tried again. "Sonofabitch put my balls into my stomach."

"I'm real sorry about that, Ben." Mullendore took out a handkerchief and wrapped it around the bite. "He looks real peaceful now, though."

With a grunt Ben pushed himself off to sit on the floor, braced by the wall. "For Christ's sake get him into holding before he comes to."

He sat there as Mullendore hefted the unconscious prisoner. The cold, coffee-stained wash water had soaked through the knees and thighs of his jeans and splattered his shirt. Even when it soaked through the seat, he continued to sit, wondering why the knee that had connected with his pride had been so bony.

As he headed down the hall for a fresh batch of soapy water, the maintenance man rattled his mop in his bucket. "I'm talking to the shop steward. I had that floor almost finished."

"Tough break." Ben spared him a look as the pain between his legs sang its way up to his head.

"Don't worry about it, Paris." Lowenstein leaned on the doorway, carefully avoiding the small river. "Chances are you're still a stallion."

"Kiss my ass."

"Honey, you know my husband's a jealous man."

Tess crouched down beside him, giving him a sympathetic tut-tut. Her hand was gentle as she patted his cheek, but her eyes were lit with laughter. "Are you all right?"

"Oh, I'm terrific. I like absorbing my coffee through my skin."

"Executive branch, right?"

"Yeah, right."

"Want to get up?"

"No." He resisted reaching a hand between his legs to make certain everything was in place.

The laugh wasn't quite muffled as she pressed a hand to her mouth. The long, narrowed look he gave her only made it worse. Her voice hitched and bubbled. "You can't sit here all day. You're sitting in a puddle, and you smell like the floor of a café that hasn't been washed over the weekend."

"Great bedside manner, Doc." He took her arm as she fought a losing war against laughter. "One good tug and you're down here with me."

"Then you'd have all those guilt ramifications to deal with. Not to mention the cleaning bills."

Ed walked down the hall, still bundled in his outdoor gear. As he avoided the worst of the wet, he dug the rest of his breakfast yogurt out of the carton. Licking the spoon, he stopped in front of his partner. "Morning, Dr. Court."

"Good morning." She rose, still swallowing laughter.

"Nice day."

"Yes, a little cold though."

"Weatherman said it should hit fifty this afternoon."

"Oh, you two are a riot," Ben told them. "A real riot."

Tess cleared her throat. "Ben . . . Ben had a little accident."

Ed's bushy brows lifted as he looked at the stream running down the hall.

"Just keep your sophomoric humor to yourself," Ben warned.

"Sophomoric." Ed rolled the word around on his tongue, impressed. He handed his empty carton to Tess, then hooking his hands under Ben's armpits, hauled his partner effortlessly to his feet. "Your pants are wet."

"I was restraining a prisoner."

"Yeah? Well, things like this happen in the midst of all that tension and excitement."

"I'm going to my locker," he muttered. "Make sure the doctor hasn't hurt herself laughing." He sloshed, a little spread-legged, down the hall.

Ed took the empty carton and plastic spoon from Tess. "Want some coffee?"

"No," she managed, strangling a bit on the word. "No, I think I've had enough."

"Give me just a minute, and I'll take you in to Captain Harris."

THEY met in the conference room. Though the heater sent out a hopeful mechanical buzz, the floors remained chilly. Harris had lost his annual campaign for carpet. The blinds were closed in a fruitless attempt to insulate the windows. Someone had tacked up a poster urging America to conserve energy.

Tess sat at a table, with Ed lounging beside her. The light scent of jasmine steamed out of his tea. Lowenstein balanced on the edge of a small desk, idly swinging one leg. Bigsby hunched in a chair, an economy-sized box of Kleenex on his lap. Every few minutes he blew his already red nose. Roderick's flu had him in bed.

Harris stood beside a green chalkboard on which the names and other pertinent information on the victims had been aligned in neat columns. A map of the city stretched over the wall, pierced with four blue flags. There was a corkboard beside that. Black-and-white glossies of the murdered women were tacked to it.

"We all have transcripts of the phone calls Dr. Court received."

It sounded so cold, so businesslike, she thought. Transcripts. They couldn't hear the pain or the sickness in transcripts. "Captain Harris." Tess shifted her own notes in front of her. "I've brought you an updated report, with my own opinions and diagnosis. But I feel it might be helpful if I explained these phone calls to you and your officers."

Harris, with his hands linked behind his back, only nodded. The mayor, the media, and the commissioner were snapping at his ankles. He wanted it over, long over, so he could spend some time doting on his new granddaughter. Seeing her behind the nursery window had almost made him believe that life had its points.

"The man who contacted me called because he was frightened, of himself. He is no longer controlling his life, but is being controlled by his illness. The last . . ." Her gaze was drawn to the photograph of Anne Reasoner. "The last murder was not part of the plan." She moistened her lips, glancing over only briefly as Ben walked in. "He was waiting for me—me specifically. We can't be certain how he focused in on the other victims. In the case of Barbara Clayton we can be all but certain it was coincidence. Her car broke down. He was there. In my case it's much more fine-tuned. He's seen my name and picture in the paper."

She paused a moment, expecting Ben to slip into the chair beside her. Instead he stayed back, leaning against the closed door, separated from her by the table.

"The rational part of his mind, the part that keeps him functioning on a daily basis, was drawn. Here was help, someone who hasn't condemned him out of hand. Someone who claims to understand at least some of the pain. Someone who looks enough like his Laura to trigger feelings of love and complete despair.

"I think it's accurate to say that he waited for me the night of Anne Reasoner's murder because he wanted to talk to me, to explain why before he . . . before he did what he's being driven to do. From your own investigations I think it's also accurate to say that he didn't feel this need to explain with any of the others. In your transcripts you'll see that time and time again he asks me to understand. I'm a hinge at this point. His door is swinging both ways." She put her palms together, moving them back and forth to demonstrate. "He's asking for help, then his illness takes over and he only wants to finish what he's started. Two more victims," she said calmly. "Or in his mind, two more souls to be saved. Me, then himself."

Ed made small, neat notes in the margin of his transcripts. "What's to stop him from going off, taking someone else down because he can't get to you?"

"He needs me. At this point he's contacted me three times. He's seen me in church. He deals in signs and symbols. I was in church—his church. I resemble his Laura. I've told him I want to help. The closer he feels to me, the more necessary it would be for him to complete his mission with me."

"You still think he'll target for December eighth?" Lowenstein had the transcript in her hands, but she wasn't looking at it.

"Yes. I don't think he could break pattern again. Anne Reasoner took too much out of him. The wrong woman, the wrong night." Tess's stomach shuddered once before she drew herself straight and controlled it.

"Isn't it possible," Ed began, "that because he's homed in on you this way, that he could go for you sooner?"

"It's always possible. Mental illness has few absolutes."

"We'll be continuing our twenty-four-hour protection," Harris put in. "You'll have the wire on your phone and the guards until he's caught. In the meantime, we want you to continue your office and personal routine. He's been watching you, so he'll know what they are. If you look accessible, we might draw him out."

"Why don't you give her the bottom line?" From the door Ben spoke quietly. His hands were in his pockets, his voice relaxed. Tess only had to look in his eyes to see what was going on inside. "You want her for bait."

Harris stared back. His voice didn't change in volume or tone when he spoke again. "Dr. Court has been singled out. What I want doesn't matter as much as what the killer wants. That's why she's going to have people on her at home, in her office, and at the damn grocery store."

"She should be in the safe house for the next two weeks."

"That's been considered and rejected."

"Rejected?" Ben pushed himself away from the door. "Who rejected it?"

"I did." Tess folded her hands on her file, then sat very still.

Ben barely glanced at her before he poured his rage on Harris. "Since when do we use civilians? As long as she's in the open, she's in jeopardy."

"She's being guarded."

"Yeah. And we all know how easily something can go wrong. One misstep and you'll be tacking her picture up there."

"Ben." Lowenstein reached out for his arm, but he shook her off.

"We've got no business taking chances with her when we know he's going to go for her. She goes in the safe house."

"No." Tess gripped her hands together so tight the knuckles whitened. "I can't treat my patients unless I go to my office and the clinic."

"You can't treat them if you're dead either." He spun to her, slamming both palms flat on the table. "So take a vacation. Buy yourself a ticket to Martinique or Cancún. I want you out of this."

"I can't, Ben. Even if I could walk away from my patients for a few weeks, I can't walk away from the rest."

"Paris—Ben," Harris amended in a quieter tone. "Dr. Court is aware of her options. As long as she's here, she'll be protected. It's Dr. Court's own opinion that he'll seek her out. Since she's decided to cooperate with the department, we'll be able to keep her under tight surveillance and cut him off when he makes his move."

"We get her out, and we plant a policewoman in her place."

"No." This time Tess rose, slowly. "I'm not going to have someone die in my place again. Not again."

"And I'm not going to find you in some alley with a scarf around your neck." He turned his back on her. "You're using her because the investigation's stalled, because we've got one jerky witness, a religious outlet in Boston, and a ream of psychiatric guesswork."

"I'm accepting Dr. Court's cooperation because we've got four dead women." It was the burning in his own stomach that kept Harris from raising his voice. "And I need every one of my officers at top level. Pull yourself together, Ben, or you'll be the one out of it."

Tess gathered up her papers and quietly slipped out. Ed was less than ten seconds behind her. "Want some air?" he asked when he found her standing miserably in the hall.

"Yes. Thanks."

He took her elbow in a way that would normally have made her smile. As he pushed open the door, the blast of November wind buffeted them. The sky was a hard, cold blue, without a cloud to soften it. Both of them remembered it had been August, hot steamy August, when it had begun. Ed waited while Tess buttoned her coat.

"I think we might get some snow by Thanksgiving," he said conversationally.

"I suppose." She dipped into her pocket and found her gloves, but only stood running them through her hands.

"I always feel sorry for the turkeys."

"What?"

"The turkeys," Ed repeated. "You know, Thanksgiving. I don't guess they're very grateful to be a tradition."

"No." She found she could smile after all. "No, I guess not."

"He's never been tangled up with a woman before. Not like this. Not like you."

Tess let out a long breath, wishing she could find the answer. She'd always been able to find the answer. "It just gets more complicated."

"I've known Ben a long time." Ed pulled a peanut out of his pocket, cracked it, and offered the meat to Tess. When she shook her head, he popped it into his mouth. "He's pretty easy to read, if you know how to look. Right now he's scared. He's scared of you and he's scared for you."

Tess looked out over the parking lot. One of the cops wasn't going to be happy when he came out and found his right-front tire flat. "I don't know what to do. I can't run away from this, though part of me, deep down, is terrified."

"Of the phone calls or Ben?"

"I'm beginning to think you should be in my business," she murmured.

"If you're a cop long enough, you learn a little bit of everything."

"I'm in love with him." It came out slowly, like a test. Once it was said, she took a shaky breath. "That would be hard enough under normal circumstances, but now . . . I can't do what he wants."

"He knows that. That's why he's scared. He's a good

cop. As long as he's looking out for you, you're going to be okay."

"I'm counting on it. He's got a problem with what I do for a living." She turned to face him. "You know about that. You know why."

"Let's say I know enough to say he's got his reasons, and when he's ready, he'll let you know about them."

She studied his wide, wind-reddened face. "He's lucky to have you."

"I'm always telling him."

"Bend down a minute." When he did, she brushed her lips over his cheek. "Thanks."

His color rose a little higher. "Don't mention it."

Ben watched them through the glass door a moment before he pushed it open. He'd used up most of his temper on Harris. All that was left was a dull ache in the center of his gut. He knew enough of fear to recognize it.

"Moving in on my time?" he asked mildly.

"If you're stupid enough to make room." Ed smiled down at Tess and handed her some peanuts. "Take care of yourself."

Tess jiggled the nuts in her hand and said nothing as Ed disappeared inside.

His jacket unzipped, Ben stood beside her, looking, as she did, out over the parking lot. The wind sent a small brown bag racing across the asphalt. "I've got a neighbor who'll look after my cat for a while." When Tess remained silent, he shifted. "I want to move in with you."

She stared hard at the flat tire. "More police protection?"

"That's right." And more, a whole lot more. He wanted to be with her, day and night. He couldn't explain, not yet, that he wanted to live with her, when he'd never lived with another woman. That kind of commitment had been dangerously close to a permanency he didn't consider himself ready for.

Tess studied the peanuts in her hand before slipping them into her pocket. As Ed had said, he was easy enough to read if you knew how to look. "I'll give you a key, but I won't cook breakfast."

"How about dinner?"

"Now and then."

"Sounds reasonable. Tess?"

"Yes?"

"If I told you I wanted you to go because . . ." He hesitated, then put his hands on her shoulders. "Because I don't think I could handle it if anything happened to you, would you go?"

"Would you come with me?"

"I can't. You know I have to—" He broke off, struggling with frustration as she looked up at him. "All right. I should know better than to argue with someone who plays Ping-Pong with brain cells. You'll do what you're told, though, right down the line."

"I have a vested interest in making this case easier for you, Ben. Until it's over, I'll do what I'm told."

"That has to do." He backed off just enough for her to realize it was the cop now, much more than the man, who stood with her. "Two uniforms are following you to your office. We've arranged for the guard in the lobby to take a vacation, and have already replaced him with one of ours. We'll have three men taking turns in your waiting room. Whenever it can be arranged, I'll pick you up and take you home. When it can't, the uniforms will follow you. We're using an empty apartment on the third floor as a base, but when you get in, your door stays locked. If you have to go out for any reason, you call in and wait until it's cleared."

"It sounds thorough."

He thought about the four glossies on the corkboard.

"Yeah. If anything, I mean *anything*, happens—a guy cuts you off at a light, somebody stops you on the street for directions—I want to know about it."

"Ben, it's no one's fault that things have taken this turn. Not yours, not Harris's, not mine. We just have to see it through."

"That's what I intend to do. There're the uniforms. You'd better get going."

"All right." She went down the first step, then stopped and turned back. "I guess it would be improper conduct for you to kiss me here, while you're on duty."

"Yeah." He bent down, and in the way that never failed to make her limbs weak, cupped her face in his hands. Eyes open and on hers, he lowered his mouth. Her lips were chilled, but soft, generous. Her free hand gripped the front of his coat for balance, or to keep him there an extra moment. He watched in fascination as her lashes fluttered, then lowered slowly to shadow her cheeks.

"Can you remember just where you were for about eight hours?" Tess murmured.

"I'll make a point of it." He drew away, but kept her hand in his. "Drive carefully. We wouldn't want the uniforms to be tempted to give you a ticket."

"I'd just have it fixed." She smiled. "See you tonight."

He let her go. "I like my steak medium-well."

"I like mine rare."

He watched her get into her car then pull competently out of the lot. The uniforms stayed a car length behind.

❧

TESS knew she was dreaming, just as she knew there were solid and logical reasons for the dream. But it didn't stop her from knowing fear.

She was running. The muscles in her right calf were knotted with the effort. In sleep she whimpered quietly in pain. Corridors sprang up everywhere, confusing her. As much as she was able, she kept to a straight route, knowing there was a doorway somewhere. She had only to find it. In the maze her breathing bounced back heavily. The walls were mirrored now, and threw dozens of her reflections at her.

She was carrying a briefcase. She looked down at it stupidly, but didn't set it aside. When it became too heavy for one hand, she dragged it with both and continued to run. As she lost her balance, she thrust out a hand and connected with a mirror. Panting, she looked up. Anne Reasoner stared back at her. Then the mirror melted away into another corridor.

So she ran on, taking the straight path. The weight of the briefcase hurt her arms, but she pulled it with her. Muscles strained and burned. Then she saw the door. Almost sobbing with relief, she dragged herself to it. Locked. She looked desperately for the key. There was always a key. But the knob turned slowly from the other side.

"Ben." Weak with relief, she reached out a hand for him to help her over that final step to safety. But the figure was black and white.

The black cassock, the white collar. The white silk of the amice. She saw it come up, knotted like pearls, and reach for her throat. Then she started to scream.

"Tess. Tess, come on, baby, wake up."

She was gasping, reaching up for her throat as she dragged herself out of the dream.

"Relax." His voice came calm and soothing out of the dark. "Just breathe deep and relax. I'm right here."

She clung hard, with her face pressed into Ben's shoulder. As his hands moved up and down her back, she fought to focus on them and let the dream fade.

"I'm sorry," she managed when she caught her breath. "It was just a dream. I'm sorry."

"Must have been a beaut." Gently, he brushed the hair from her face. Her skin was clammy. Ben pulled the covers up and wrapped them around her. "Want to tell me about it?"

"Just overworked." She drew her knees up to rest her elbows on them.

"Want some water?"

"Yes, thanks."

She rubbed her hands over her face as she listened to the tap run in the bathroom. He left the light on so that it slanted through the door. "Here you go. You have nightmares often?"

"No." She sipped to ease her dry throat. "I had some after my parents died. My grandfather would come in and sit with me, and fall asleep in the chair."

"Well, I'll sit with you." After he got into bed again, he put an arm around her. "Better?"

"A lot. I guess I feel stupid."

"Wouldn't you say, psychiatrically speaking, that under certain circumstances it's healthy to be scared?"

"I suppose I would." She let her head rest on his shoulder. "Thanks."

"What else is bothering you?"

She took a last sip of water before setting the glass aside. "I was making an effort not to let it show."

"Didn't work. What is it?"

Tess sighed and stared at the slant of light on the bedroom floor. "I have a patient. Or I had one, anyway. This young boy, fourteen, alcoholic, severe depression, suicidal tendencies. I wanted his parents to put him into a clinic in Virginia."

"They won't go for it."

"Not only that, but he missed his session today. I

called, got the mother. She tells me that she feels Joey's progressing just fine. She didn't want to discuss the clinic, and she's going to let him take a breather from his sessions. There's nothing I can do. Nothing." It was that, most of all, that had slapped her down. "She won't face the fact that he isn't progressing. She loves him, but she's put blinders on so she doesn't have to see anything that isn't in straight focus. I've been slapping a Band-Aid on him every week, but the wound's not healing."

"You can't make her bring the boy in. Maybe a breather will help. Let the wound get some air."

"I wish I could believe that."

It was the tone of her voice that made him shift, and bring her closer. When he'd woken to her screams, his blood had run cold. Now it was pumping warm again. "Look, Doc, both of us are in the business where we can lose people. It's the kind of thing that wakes you up at three in the morning, has you staring at walls or out windows. Sometimes you've just got to turn it off. Just turn the switch."

"I know. Rule number one is professional detachment." His hair brushed her cheek as she turned her face to his. "What turns the switch best for you?"

In the shadowed light she saw him grin. "You really want to know?"

"Yes." She ran a hand down his side until it rested comfortably at his hip. "Right now I especially want to know."

"This usually works." In one easy move he rolled her on top of him. He felt the give of firm breasts pressing against him, smelled the fragrance of her hair as it curtained his face. He took a handful and brought her mouth down to his.

How well she seemed to fit. The thought ran through his head. The brush of her fingertips on his skin was like a blessing. There was something about her hesitancy that had his own excitement drumming. If he ran his own fingers along her inner thigh, she shivered, just enough to let him know she wanted him but was still unsure.

He didn't know why or how it should seem so fresh with her. Each time he found himself holding her in the dark, in the quiet, it was like the first time. She was bringing something to him he hadn't known he'd missed and was no longer certain he could do without.

Her mouth moved lightly over his face. He wanted to roll her over on her back, pump himself into her until they both exploded. With most women it had always been that last, split second of insanity that had washed everything else away. With Tess it was a touch, a murmur, a quiet brush of lips. So he pushed back that first rage of desire and let them both drift.

He could be so gentle, she thought hazily. At times when they made love, it was all speed, all urgency. And then . . . When she least expected it, he would be tender, almost lazy, until her heart was ready to break from the sweetness of it. Now he let her touch the body she had come to know as well as her own.

There were sighs. Sighs of contentment. There were murmurs. Murmurs of promises. He buried his hands in her hair as she tasted, almost shyly at first, then with growing confidence. There were muscles to be discovered. She found them taut, and delighted in the knowledge that she caused the tension.

There were bones in his hips, long and narrow. When her tongue glided over them, he arched like a bow. The trail of her finger along the crease of his thigh had his long body shuddering. She sighed as her lips followed the path. There was no more thought of nightmares.

He'd had women touch him. Maybe too many women.

But none of them had made his blood hammer like this. He wanted to lie there for hours and absorb each separate sensation. He wanted to make her sweat and shake as he was.

He sat up, grabbing her hands at the wrist. For a moment, a long moment, they stared at each other in the narrow beam of light. His breath came in pants. His eyes were dark, glazed with passion. The scent of desire hung heavy in the room.

He lowered her slowly, until she lay on her back. With his hands still gripping her wrists, he used his mouth to drive her to the edge. Narrow, delicate, her hands strained against his hold. Her body twisted, arched, not in protest, but in a delirium of pleasure. His tongue slid over her, into her, until she thought her lungs would balloon and explode from the pressure. He felt her go rigid and call out as she came. Her scent spilled into the room. She was limp, boneless, when he filled her.

"I'm going to watch you go up again."

He braced himself over her, and though each muscle trembled with the effort, went slowly, exquisitely slowly. She moaned, then opened her eyes as the sensations and pleasure began to build again. Her lips trembled open as she started to say his name. Then her fingers dug into the rumpled sheets.

Ben buried his face in her hair and cut himself loose.

Chapter 14

"I APPRECIATE YOUR making time to see me, Monsignor." Tess took a seat in the front of Logan's desk and had a quick, not entirely comfortable flash of how her patients must feel during their initial consultation.

"It's my pleasure." He was settled comfortably, his tweed jacket draped over the back of his chair, his shirt-sleeves rolled up to reveal sturdy forearms sprinkled with hair just beginning to gray. She thought again that he seemed to be a man more accustomed to the rugby field or racquetball court than vespers and incense. "Would you like some tea?"

"No. Nothing, thank you, Monsignor."

"Since we're colleagues, why don't you call me Tim?"

"Yes." She smiled, ordering herself to relax, starting with her toes. "That would make things easier. My call to you today was on impulse, but—"

"When a priest is troubled, he seeks out another priest. When an analyst is troubled . . ." As he trailed off, Tess found her conscious effort to relax was working.

"Exactly." The fingers on her purse loosened their grip. "I guess that means you get hit from both ends."

"It also means I have two roads to choose from

when I have problems of my own. That's a matter which has its pros and cons, but you didn't come to discuss Christ versus Freud. Why don't you tell me what's troubling you?"

"At this point, a number of things. I don't feel like I've found the key to the mind of . . . of the man the police are looking for."

"And you think you should have?"

"I think being as involved as I am now, I should have more." She lifted one hand in a gesture that spoke of frustration and uncertainty. "I've talked to him three times. It bothers me that I can't get through my own fear, maybe my own self-interest, to push the right buttons."

"Do you think you know those buttons?"

"It's my job to know them."

"Tess, we both know the psychotic mind is a maze, and the routes leading to the core can shift and shift again. Even if we had him under intensive therapy in ideal conditions, it might take years to find the answers."

"Oh, I know. Logically, medically, I know that."

"But emotionally is a different story."

Emotionally. She dealt with other people's emotions on a daily basis. It was different, and much more difficult, she discovered, to open her own to someone else. "I know it's unprofessional, and that worries me, but I'm past the point where I can be objective. Monsignor Logan—Tim—that last woman who was killed was meant to be me. I saw her in that alley. I can't forget."

His eyes were kind, but she saw no pity in them. "Transferring guilt won't change what happened."

"I know that too." She rose and went to the window. Below, a group of students rushed across the grass to make their next class.

"May I ask you a question?"

"Naturally. I'm in the answer business."

"Does it bother you that this man may be, or may have been, a priest?"

"On a personal level, you mean, because I'm a priest?" To consider it, he sat back with his hands steepled. As a young man he'd boxed both in and out of the ring. His knuckles were fat and spread. "I can't deny a certain discomfort. Certainly the idea of the man being a priest rather than, say, a computer programmer, makes the entire business more sensational. But the simple truth is that priests are not saints, but as human as a plumber, a right fielder, or a psychiatrist."

"When he's found, will you want to treat him?"

"If I were asked," Logan said slowly. "If I believed I could be of use, then perhaps. I wouldn't feel obliged or responsible, as I believe you do."

"You know, the more afraid I am, the more essential it becomes to me to help him." She turned to the window again. "I had a dream last night. A rather dreadful one. I was lost in these corridors, this maze, and I was running. Even though I knew I was dreaming I was still terrified. The walls became mirrors and I could see myself over and over again." Unconsciously she put a hand to the glass of the window, as she had to the mirror in the dream. "I was carrying my briefcase, dragging it really, because it was so heavy. I looked in one of the mirrors and it wasn't my reflection, but Anne Reasoner's. Then she was gone and I was running again. There was a door. I just had to get on the other side of that door. When I got there, it was locked. I looked frantically for the key, but I didn't have it. Then the door opened on its own. I thought I was safe. I thought—then I saw the priest's frock and the amice."

She turned back, but couldn't bring herself to sit. "Oh, I could sit down and write a very detailed and comprehensive analysis of that dream. My fear of being out of control in this situation, overwork, and my refusal to cut down on that workload. Guilt over Anne Reasoner. My frustration at not finding the key to this case and my ultimate, my very ultimate failure."

She hadn't mentioned fear for her life. Logan considered it a very interesting and telling omission. Either she had not yet brought herself to face it, or she linked the possibility with her dread of failing.

"You're so sure you're going to fail?"

"Yes, and I detest the idea." The admission brought a self-deprecating smile. Tess ran her fingers over the cover of the antique Bible and found the carving deep and smooth. "There's something in here about pride going before a fall."

"I tend to think that depends on the pride. You've given the police everything a trained psychiatrist could, Tess. You haven't failed."

"I never have, you know. Not really. Not on a personal level. I did well in school, played hostess very properly for my grandfather until my practice cut back on my free time. As far as men were concerned, after one minor disaster in college I always made sure I called the shots. Things have been very safe and tidy until . . . well, until a few months ago."

"Tess, as far as this case is concerned, you were brought in as a consultant. It's the police department's responsibility to find this man."

"Maybe I could have left it at that. Maybe," she murmured, running a hand through her hair. "I'm not totally sure. But now, how can I? He's turned to me. When he spoke to me, there was a desperation, a plea. How could I, how could any doctor try not to answer that?"

"Treating him at some later date isn't the same thing

as feeling responsible for the results of his illness." A frown of concern entered his eyes as he linked his fingers and rested them on the desk. "If I had to speculate out of hand, before a thorough reading of this report, I would say he's drawn to you because he senses compassion, and a certain vulnerability. You have to be careful not to give so much of the first that you fall victim to the second."

"It's difficult for me to follow the rules on this one. Ben—Detective Paris—wanted me to go out of town. When he suggested it, for a minute I thought, I'll go. I'll get on a plane and go down to, I don't know, Mazatlán, and when I come back this will all be over and my life will be as neat and tidy as it used to be." She paused and met Logan's quiet, patient gaze. "I really detest myself for that."

"Don't you consider it a normal reaction to the stress of the situation?"

"For a patient," she said, and smiled. "Not for me."

"There is such a thing as overachievement, Tess."

"I don't smoke. I'm a very light drinker." She came back to sit. "I figure I'm entitled to a vice."

"I don't have sex," Logan said contemplatively. "I suppose that's why I feel entitled to smoke and drink." He looked back, pleased that she seemed more at ease. Confession, he knew well, was good for the soul. "So you're staying in Georgetown and cooperating with the police. How do you feel about that?"

"Nervous," she told him immediately. "It's an uneasy feeling to know someone's watching you all the time. I don't mean just—" Shaking her head, she broke off. "I have such a difficult time knowing what to call him."

"Most people would call him a killer."

"Yes, but he's also a victim. In any case, it's not just knowing he might be watching that unnerves me. It's knowing the police are. At the same time I feel satisfied that it's the right thing. I didn't cut and run. I want to help this man. It's become very important to me to help him. In the dream, when I was faced with him I fell apart. Therefore I failed him and myself. I'm not going to let that happen."

"No, I don't think you will." Logan picked up his letter opener, running the hilt through his hands. It was old and a bit tacky, a souvenir from a trip to Ireland during his youth. He was fond of it, as he was of many foolish things. Though he didn't consider Tess foolish, he was becoming fond of her as well. "Tess, I hope you don't take offense if I suggest that after all this is over, you do get away for a while. Stress and overwork can break even the strongest of us."

"I won't take offense, but I might take it as doctor's orders."

"Good girl. Tell me, how is Ben?" When she gave him a blank stare, he smiled. "Oh, come, even a priest can smell romance in the air."

"I suppose you could say Ben is another problem."

"Romance is supposed to be a problem." He put the letter opener down. "Are you calling the shots this time, Tess?"

"It doesn't seem as though either of us is. We're just fumbling around. He—I think we care for each other a great deal. We just haven't gotten around to trusting each other yet."

"Trust takes time if it's going to be solid. I've had a couple of professional discussions with him, and one rather drunken meeting at a little bar downtown."

"Oh, really? He didn't mention it."

"My dear, a man doesn't like to mention he got drunk with a priest. In any case, would you like my opinion of Detective Paris?"

"Yes, I think I would."

"I'd say he's a very good man, dependable. The kind

of man who probably calls his mother once a month even when he'd rather not. Men like Ben bend rules but very rarely break them, because they appreciate structure, they understand the concept of law. There's an anger in him he keeps well buried. He didn't give up the Church because of laziness, but because he found too many flaws. He gave up the Church, Tess, my dear, but he's Catholic right down to his toes." Tim sat back, pleased with himself. "Sixty-second analysis is my speciality."

"I believe it." She pulled a file out of her briefcase. "I hope you have as much luck with this. I cleared it with Captain Harris. This is my updated report. You'll also find the transcripts of my phone calls. I'd appreciate a miracle."

"I'll see what I can do."

"Thanks for listening."

"Any time." He rose to go to the door with her. "Tess, if you have any more nightmares, give me a call. It never hurts to ask for a little help."

"Where have I heard that before?"

Logan watched her go through the outer office before he closed the door.

HE watched her exit the building. It was dangerous to follow her, but he knew the time for caution was almost over. She paused by her car, looking for her keys. Her head was bent, as if in prayer. The need billowed up inside him until his head rang. Groping, he found the white silk in his coat pocket. Cool, soft. It steadied him. Tess pushed the key into the lock.

If he was quick enough, sure enough, it could be over in minutes. His fingers clutched and unclutched on the amice while his heart thudded in his throat. A few forgotten leaves, dry as dust, rustled around her ankles. He saw the wind blow wisps of hair around her face. She looked troubled. Soon, very soon, she would be at peace. They would all be at peace.

He watched her get into her car, heard the door close, then the sound of the engine. A puff of smoke spurted out of the tailpipe. The car made a gentle sweep of the parking area, then turned onto the road.

He waited until the police car made the turn before he went to his own car. She would go to her office now, and he would continue the vigil. The moment hadn't arrived. There was still time to pray for her. And himself.

❦

TESS hung up the phone, leaned back in her chair, and shut her eyes. She was batting about .500. In her game, that wasn't nearly good enough.

Joey Higgins. How could she treat the boy if she couldn't talk to him? His mother had taken a stand. Joey was no longer drinking, therefore, Joey was fine and no longer needed the embarrassment of a psychiatrist. It had been a painful and ultimately fruitless conversation. She had one more shot. She had to make it good.

Leaning forward, Tess buzzed her secretary. "Kate, how much time do I have before the next appointment?"

"Ten minutes."

"All right. Please get Donald Monroe on the line for me."

"Right away."

While she waited, Tess looked over Joey's file. Their last session remained very clear in her mind.

"Dying's not such a big deal."

"Why do you say that, Joey?"

" 'Cause it's not. People are always dying. You're supposed to."

"Death's inevitable, but that doesn't make it an answer. Even very old people, very sick people, cling to life because it's precious."

"People say when someone dies, they're at peace."

"Yes, and most of us believe there is something after life. But each of us is here for a reason. Our life is a gift, not always easy, certainly not always perfect. Making it better for ourselves and for the people around us takes some effort. What's your favorite thing to eat?"

He gave her a blank look. "Spaghetti, I guess."

"Meat balls or meat sauce?"

The smile was quick, but it was there. "Meat balls."

"Suppose you'd never tasted spaghetti and meat balls. The sky would probably still be blue, Christmas would still come once a year, but you'd be missing something pretty terrific. And if you weren't here, say you'd never been born, we'd still have the sky and Christmas, but something pretty terrific would be missing."

Her buzzer brought her back to the present. "Mr. Monroe on one."

"Thank you, Kate. Mr. Monroe."

"Dr. Court. Is there a problem?"

"Yes, Mr. Monroe, I feel there's a big problem. I'm strongly opposed to Joey withdrawing from treatment."

"Withdrawing? What do you mean?"

"Mr. Monroe, are you aware that Joey missed his last session?"

There was a pause before she caught just a whisper of a weary sigh. "No. I suppose he decided to take off on his own. I'll discuss it with Lois."

"Mr. Monroe, I've already spoken to your wife. She's decided to take Joey out of therapy. I take it you weren't informed."

"No, I wasn't." Another pause, then he drew a long breath. "Dr. Court, Lois wants Joey to resume a normal life, and he does seem a great deal better. We told him about the baby, and his reaction was encouraging. He's going to help me paint the nursery."

"I'm glad to hear that, Mr. Monroe. My feeling is, however, that he's far from ready to pull out of therapy. In fact, I still believe he would be helped a great deal by some time in the clinic we discussed."

"Lois is completely opposed to the clinic. I'm sorry, Dr. Court, and I do appreciate your concern, but I have to back her on this."

Anger surged, barely controlled. Couldn't he see it was the boy he had to back up? That they both had to back up? "I understand that you feel you should show Joey a united front. But, Mr. Monroe, I can't stress enough how vital it is for Joey to continue to receive consistent professional help."

"And, Dr. Court, there's also the risk of overanalyzing. Joey isn't drinking, he isn't hanging around with the same crowd he was when he was drinking. He hasn't even mentioned his father in two weeks."

The last statement had alarm bells ringing in her head. "The fact that he hasn't mentioned his father only means he's repressing his feelings. His emotional state at this point is very tenuous. Can you understand, when there is little self-esteem, suicide becomes almost easy? I'm afraid—no, I'm terrified of what he might do."

"Dr. Court, I can't help but think you're overreacting."

"I promise you, I'm not. Mr. Monroe, I don't want to see Joey become a statistic. What I want, more than anything, is for his therapy to stop, when he's ready. It's both my professional opinion and my gut instinct that he's not."

"I'll see if I can convince Lois to bring him back for another session." But even as he said it, Tess recognized the dismissal. Some other boy might slash his wrists or swallow a bottle of pills, but not Joey.

"Mr. Monroe, has anyone asked Joey if he wants to continue seeing me?"

"Dr. Court, I can only promise to look into this." Impatience came through now, with a trace of annoyance. "I'll use whatever influence I have to see that Joey comes back for at least one more session. I think you'll see for yourself how much better he is. You've been very helpful, Doctor, but if we feel Joey is well, then the sessions should be stopped."

"Please, before you do anything, would you get a second opinion? Perhaps you're right not to take my word for it. I can recommend several excellent psychiatrists in the area."

"I'll talk to Lois. We'll consider it. Thank you, Dr. Court, I know you've helped Joey a great deal."

Not enough, she thought as the connection broke. Not nearly enough.

"Dr. Court. Mr. Grossman is here."

"All right, Kate. Send him in." She took Joey's file, but didn't put it away. Instead she set it aside on her desk, within easy reach.

IT was nearly five when the last patient left for the day. Kate stuck her head in the door. "Dr. Court, Mr. Scott didn't schedule his next appointment."

"He doesn't need one."

"Really?" Kate relaxed against the door. "You did good work there, Dr. Court."

"I like to think so. You can take his file out of current patients."

"It's a pleasure."

"Do it tomorrow, Kate. If you hurry you can get out of here exactly one minute early."

"Watch me. Good night, Dr. Court."

"Good night, Kate." When the phone rang she

reached for it herself. "I've got it. Go on home, Kate." With her hand on the receiver, she took a long breath. "Dr. Court."

"Hi, Doc."

"Ben." A layer of tension dissolved. She heard background noises of phones, voices, and typewriters. "Still at work?"

"Yeah. I wanted you to know I'd be a while yet."

"You sound tired. Did something happen?"

He thought of the day he'd put in and the stench he wasn't sure would ever wash off his skin. "It's been a long one. Look, why don't I pick up some pizza or something? Things should be wrapped up here in another hour or so."

"Okay. Ben, I'm a good listener."

"I'll keep that in mind. Go straight home and lock the door."

"Yes, sir."

"See you later, smartass."

It wasn't until she hung up that Tess realized how quiet the office was. Normally she would have appreciated an hour in the evening to herself. Her desk could be put in order, paperwork could be finished up. Now the quiet seemed too close and too thick. Calling herself a fool, she picked up the Scott file to close it out. Success was satisfying.

She took the files and tapes from her late-afternoon patients and locked them away. Joey Higgins's file remained on her desk. Knowing she was spinning her wheels, Tess put it in her briefcase to take home.

Three times she caught herself looking toward her door with her pulse throbbing.

Ridiculous. Determined not to be a fool, she checked the next day's appointments. There were two policemen outside, she reminded herself, and one in the lobby. She was perfectly safe.

But each time she heard the elevator hum in the hall outside, she felt a jolt.

If she went home now, the apartment would be empty. She didn't want to face solitude there now, not now that she was sharing the apartment with Ben.

What was she getting into? Sighing, she began to gather the rest of her things. She was over her head with Ben Paris. Just how did the eminent Dr. Court deal with falling in love? Very poorly, she decided as she went to the closet for her coat.

If it were spring, she'd have an excuse for daydreaming and smiling at nothing in particular. Smart people fell in love in spring, she thought, when everything was fresh and seemed as though it would stay that way.

She stopped at the window. The trees that marched along the street in front of the buildings were dark and naked. What patches of grass could be seen were already yellowed and tired. People huddled inside their coats, heads bowed against the wind. It wasn't spring, she thought, feeling foolish. And everyone's hurrying home.

Then she saw him. He stood very still in his black coat, just in back of a group of young trees. Her breath caught. Her knees trembled. Watching—he was waiting and watching. Instinctively, she swung around for the phone, grabbing it from her desk. She'd call downstairs, she thought as she began to punch buttons. She'd call and tell the police that he was outside, watching. Then she'd go down too. She'd go because she'd promised herself that much.

But when she turned back to look, he was gone.

She stood there a moment, the phone in her hand, the number half dialed. He was gone.

Just someone on his way home, Tess told herself. A doctor or lawyer or bank executive walking home to keep fit. She forced herself to walk back to her desk and calmly replace the phone. She was jumping at shadows. Because her legs were still unsteady, she sat on the edge of the desk. Layer by layer she rebuilt control.

Diagnosis, acute paranoia.

Prescription, hot bath and quiet evening with Ben Paris.

Feeling better, she drew on her cashmere coat, hefted her briefcase, and tossed her purse strap over her shoulder. After locking her office, she turned and saw the knob on the reception-area door turn.

The keys in her hand slipped out of nerveless fingers. She took a step back into the door she'd just locked. The door opened an inch. The scream backed up in her throat, bubbling hot. Frozen, she stared as the door opened a bit more. There was no maze to run through, no place to go. She took a deep breath, knowing she was on her own.

"Anybody home?"

"Oh, Jesus, Frank." Her knees felt like butter as she braced herself against her office door. "What are you doing sneaking around the halls?"

"I was walking down to the elevator and saw the light under your door." He smiled, delighted to find her alone. "Don't tell me you're taking work home again, Tess." He stepped inside, strategically closing the outer door at his back.

"No, I keep my laundry in here." She bent to retrieve her keys, furious enough with herself to let him feel the backlash. "Look, Frank, I've had a long day. I'm not in the mood for your fumbling attempts at seduction."

"Why, Tess." His eyes widened, and so did his smile. "I had no idea you could be so . . . so aggressive."

"If you don't get out of my way, you're going to get a close-up view of the nap of this carpet."

"How about a drink?"

"Oh, for God's sake." She pushed past him, took

hold of the freshly pressed sleeve of his jacket, and yanked him into the hall.

"Dinner at my place?"

Setting her teeth, Tess switched off the light, closed the door, and locked it. "Frank, why don't you take your sexual delusions and write a book? It might keep you out of trouble." She whipped past him and punched the button for the elevator.

"You could be chapter one."

She took a long breath, counted backward from ten, and discovered, to her amazement, that it did nothing to calm her. When the doors slid open she stepped inside, turned, and blocked the opening. "If you like the shape of your nose, Frank, don't try to get on this elevator with me."

"How about dinner and a hot tub?" he said as the doors started to close. "I know a great place for Chicken Kiev."

"Stuff it," she muttered, then leaned against the back wall.

She was nearly home before she started to laugh. It was possible, if she put her mind to it, to forget about the police car behind her, to block out the fact that on the third floor of her building cops were drinking coffee and watching the early news. A two-car accident on Twenty-third held her up an extra fifteen minutes but didn't spoil the mood she was building.

She was humming when she unlocked the door to her apartment. After wishing briefly that she'd thought to pick up fresh flowers, she went straight to the bedroom and stripped. She chose the silk kimono again, then dumped a double shot of bubble bath under the stream of water pulsing into the tub. She took the time to put an album on the stereo. Phil Collins bounced out, happy to be alive and in love.

So was she, Tess thought as she lowered herself into

the steaming water. And tonight she was going to enjoy every minute of it.

When Ben used his key to get in, he felt he was home. The furniture wasn't his, and he hadn't picked out the paintings, but he was home. The cardboard box was warm on the bottom, where he held it. He set it on the dining room table, on top of the linen placement he imagined had taken some little French nun the better part of a week to embroider, and wished he could crawl into bed and sleep around the clock.

He put the paper bag he carried next to the pizza before he stripped out of his coat and let it fall over the back of a chair. Peeling off his shoulder holster, he dropped it on the seat.

He could smell her. Even here, barely three steps inside the door, he could smell her. Soft, subtle, elegant. Drawing her in, he found fatigue warring against a need he'd yet to find a way to curb.

"Tess?"

"Back here. I'm in the tub. I'll be out in a minute."

He followed her scent and the sound of water. "Hi."

When she glanced up at him, he believed he saw her color rise a bit. Funny lady, he thought as he moved over to sit on the edge of the tub. She could make a man pant in bed, but she blushed when he caught her in a bubble bath.

"I didn't know how long you'd be." She stopped herself from sinking farther under the cover of bubbles.

"Just had to tie up a few things."

Embarrassment faded as quickly as it had come. "It was a rough one, wasn't it? You look exhausted."

"Let's just say it was one of the less pleasant days on the job."

"Want to talk about it?"

He thought of the blood. Even in his business you didn't often see that much. "No, not now."

She sat up to reach over and touch his face. "There's room in here for two, if you're friendly. Why don't you take Dr. Court's reliable prescription for overwork?"

"The pizza'll get cold."

"I love cold pizza." She began to unbutton his shirt. "You know, I had a rather strange day myself, ending with an invitation for Chicken Kiev and a hot tub."

"Oh?" He rose to unsnap his pants. The feeling that went through him was ugly, and unrecognizable to a man who'd never experienced basic jealousy before. "Doesn't seem too smart to turn that down for cold pizza and bubbles."

"More fool me for refusing an evening with the handsome, successful, and excruciatingly boring Dr. Fuller."

"More your type," Ben muttered, sitting on the john to pull off his shoes.

"Boring's more my type?" Tess lifted a brow as she leaned back. "Thank you very much."

"I mean the doctor, the three-piece suits, the Gold American Express Card."

"I see." Amused, she began to soap her leg. "You don't have a gold card?"

"I'm lucky Sears still lets me charge my underwear."

"Well, in that case, I don't know if I should invite you into my tub."

He stood, naked but for the jeans riding low at his hips. "I'm serious, Tess."

"I can see that." She took a handful of bubbles and studied them. "I guess that means you see me as a shallow, materialistic, status-minded woman who's willing to slum it occasionally for good sex."

"I don't mean anything like that." Frustrated, he sat on the lip of the tub again. "Look, I've got a job that means I deal with slime almost on a daily basis."

Her hand was wet and very gentle when she set it on his. "It was a filthy day, wasn't it?"

"That has nothing to do with it." He took her hand in his a moment, studying it. It was rather small and narrow, delicate at the wrist. "My father sold used cars in a dealership that was barely on the right side of the tracks in the suburbs. He owned three sport coats and drove a DeSoto. My mother baked cookies. If a cookie could be baked, she did it. Their idea of a night on the town was the Knights of Columbus hall. I punched my way through high school, crammed my way through college for a couple of years then the Academy, and I've spent the rest of my life looking at dead bodies."

"Are you trying to convince me that you're not good enough for me because of cultural, educational, and genealogical differences?"

"Don't start that shit with me."

"All right. Let's try another approach." She pulled him into the tub.

"What the hell are you doing?" He spit out bubbles. "I'm still dressed."

"I can't help it if you're slow." Before he could regain his balance, she slid her arms around him and closed her mouth over his. Often, even a psychiatrist knows it's action rather than words that gets to the core. She felt the tension ebb and flow before he reached for her. "Ben?"

"Hmm?"

"Do you think it's relevant, at the moment, that your father sold used cars and mine didn't?"

"No."

"Good." She drew back, and laughing, brushed bubbles from his chin. "Now, how are we going to manage to get your pants off?"

THE pizza was stone cold, but they didn't leave a crumb. Ben waited until she'd dumped the carton.

"I bought you a present."

"You did?" Surprised, and foolishly pleased, she looked at the paper bag he offered. "Why?"

"Questions, always questions." Then he drew it back as she reached for it. "You really want to know?"

"Yes."

He moved closer, close enough to slip an arm around her waist. The scent of the bath was on both of them. Her hair was pinned up and damp. "Well, I think I'm going out of my head. Yes, I think I'm going out of my head, over you."

She let her eyes close slowly for the kiss. "Little Anthony," she murmured, playing the tune over in her head. "Was it 1961, '62?"

"I figured you being a shrink, you'd fall for that approach."

"You're right."

"Don't you want your present?"

"Umm-hmm. But I think you have to let me go so I can open the bag."

"Then don't take too long." He gave it to her, watching her expression as she looked inside. It couldn't have been better—the blank frown, the surprise, then the amusement.

"A dead bolt. God, Ben, you know how to sweep a woman off her feet."

"Yeah, it's a real talent."

Her lips curved as she pressed them against his. "I'll always treasure it. If it was a little less bulky, I'd wear it next to my heart."

"It's going to be in your door in less than an hour. I put my tools in the kitchen closet the other day."

"Handy too."

"Why don't you see if there's something you can do for a while. Otherwise, I'll make you watch."

"I'll come up with something," she promised, and left him to it.

While he worked, Tess edited a lecture she was to give at George Washington University the following month. The buzz of the drill and clank of metal against wood didn't disturb her. She began to wonder how she had ever tolerated the total silence of her life before him.

When her lecture was in order and the files she'd brought home dealt with, she turned to see him just finishing up. The lock looked bright and secure.

"That should do it."

"My hero."

He shut the door, held up a pair of keys, then set them on the table. "Just use it. I'll put my tools away and wash up. You can sweep the floor."

"Sounds fair." As she walked toward the door, she paused to turn on the television for the news.

Though there seemed to be more mess than the small lock warranted, Tess swept the sawdust into the pan without complaint. She was straightening up, the pan and broom still in her hands, when the top story came on.

"Police discovered the bodies of three people in an apartment in North West. Responding to the concern of a neighbor, police broke into the apartment late this afternoon. The victims had been stabbed repeatedly while bound with clothesline. Identified were Jonas Leery, Kathleen Leery, his wife, and Paulette Leery, their teenaged daughter. Robbery is thought to be the motive. We'll switch to Bob Burroughs on the scene for more details."

A husky, athletic-looking reporter appeared on the screen, holding a microphone and gesturing at the brick building behind him. Tess turned and saw Ben just outside the kitchen doorway. She knew immediately that he'd seen the inside of the building himself.

"Oh, Ben, it must have been dreadful."

"They'd been dead ten, maybe twelve hours. The kid couldn't have been more than sixteen." The memory of it had the acid burning in his stomach. "They'd carved her up like a piece of meat."

"I'm sorry." She set everything aside and went to him. "Let's sit down."

"You get to a point," he said, still watching the screen, "you get to a point where it's almost, almost routine. Then you walk into something like that apartment today. You walk in and your stomach turns over. You think, God, it's not real. It can't be real because people can't do that kind of thing to each other. But you know, deep down, you know they can."

"Sit down, Ben," she murmured, easing them both onto the couch. "Do you want me to turn it off?"

"No." But he rested his head in his hands for a minute, then dragged them through his hair before he straightened. The on-the-scene reporter was talking to a weeping neighbor.

"Paulette used to baby-sit my little boy. She was a sweet girl. I can't believe this. I just can't believe it."

"Those bastards'll go down," Ben said half to himself. "There was a coin collection. A fucking coin collection worth eight hundred, maybe a thousand. Fenced, it might bring half that. They butchered those people for a bunch of old coins."

She glanced back at the lock, now firmly in her door, and understood why he'd brought it to her tonight. She drew him close, and in the way women have of offering comfort, rested his head against her breast.

"They'll pawn the coins, then you'll trace them."

"We've got a couple other leads. We'll have them tomorrow, the day after at the latest. But those people, Tess . . . sweet Christ, as long as I've been in this, I still can't believe anything human could do that."

"I can't tell you not to think about it, but I can tell you I'm here for you."

Knowing it, knowing it was just that simple, dulled the horror of the day. She was there for him, and for tonight, for a few hours, he could make that all that mattered.

"I need you." He shifted, bringing her over into his lap so that he could nuzzle at her throat. "It scares the hell out of me."

"I know."

Chapter 15

"TESS, I DON'T know. I'm not at my best with senators." Ben sent Lowenstein a snarl as she grinned over at him, then turned his back, cradling the phone between shoulder and jaw.

"He's my grandfather, Ben, and really rather sweet."

"I've never heard anyone call Senator Jonathan Writemore a sweetheart."

Pilomento called him from across the room, so Ben nodded and gestured with a finger to hold him off.

"That's because I'm not doing his P.R. In any case, it's Thanksgiving, and I don't want to disappoint him. And you did tell me your parents live in Florida."

"They're over sixty-five. Parents are supposed to move to Florida when they hit sixty-five."

"So you don't have any family to have Thanksgiving dinner with. I'm sure Grandpa would like to meet you."

"Yeah." He tugged at the neck of his sweater. "Look, I've always had this policy about going to meet family."

"Which is?"

"I don't do it."

"Oh? Why is that?"

"Questions," he muttered under his breath. "When I

was younger my mother always wanted me to bring the girl I was seeing home. Then my mother and the girl would get ideas."

"I see." He could hear the smile in her voice.

"Anyway, I made a policy—I don't take women to see my mother, and I don't go to see theirs. That way nobody gets the idea to start picking out silver patterns."

"I'm sure you have a point. I can promise that neither my grandfather nor I will discuss silver patterns if you join us for dinner. Miss Bette makes a terrific pumpkin pie."

"Fresh?"

"Absolutely." A smart woman knew when to back off. "You've got some time to think about it. I wouldn't have bothered you with it now, but with everything that's been going on, I'd forgotten the whole thing myself until Grandpa called a few minutes ago."

"Yeah, I'll give it some thought."

"And don't worry. If you decide against it, I'll still bring you a piece of pie. I've got a patient waiting."

"Tess—"

"Yes?"

"Nothing. Nothing," he repeated. "See you later."

"Paris."

"Sorry." He hung up the phone and turned. "What you got?"

Pilomento handed him a sheet of paper. "We finally tracked down that name the neighbor gave us."

"The guy who was hanging around the Leery girl?"

"Right. Amos Reeder. Not much of a description because the neighbor only saw him come by once. Creepy looking was about the upshot, but she admitted she only saw him go to the Leerys' once, and there wasn't any trouble."

Ben was already picking up his jacket. "We always check out creepy looking."

"I got an address and rap sheet."

Before he stuffed his pack of cigarettes into his pocket, he noted with some disgust that he only had two left. "What'd he do time for?"

"When he was seventeen he carved another kid up for pocket money. Reeder had a nickle bag of pot in his pocket and a line of needle marks on his arm. Other kid pulled through, Reeder was tried as a minor, got drug rehab. Harris said you and Jackson should have a talk with him."

"Thanks." Taking the papers, he headed to the conference room, where Ed had his head together with Bigsby on the Priest homicide. "Saddle up," Ben said briefly, and started toward the door.

Ed lumbered beside him, already bundling into his coat. "What's up?"

"Got a lead on the Leery case. Young punk who likes knives was hanging around the girl. Thought we might chat awhile."

"Sounds good." Ed settled comfortably in the car. "How about Tammy Wynette?"

"Kiss ass." Ben punched in a cassette of *Goat's Head Soup*. "Tess called a few minutes ago."

Ed opened one eye. He considered it best to handle the Rolling Stones blind. "Problem?"

"No. Well, yeah, I guess. She wants me to have Thanksgiving dinner with her grandfather."

"Whoa, turkey with Senator Writemore. Think he needs a caucus to decide whether it's going to be oyster or chestnut dressing?"

"I knew I was going to get grief on this." More for spite than out of desire, Ben pulled out a cigarette.

"It's okay, I got it out of my system. So you're going to have Thanksgiving dinner with Tess and her granddaddy. What's the problem?"

"First it's Thanksgiving, then before you know it, it's

Sunday brunch. Then Aunt Mabel's coming over to check you out."

Ed dug in his pocket, decided to save the yogurt-covered raisins for later, and settled for sugarless gum. "Does Tess have an Aunt Mabel?"

"Try to follow the trend here, Ed." He downshifted and brought the car to a halt at a stop sign. "You turn around twice and you're invited to her cousin Laurie's wedding and her Uncle Joe is punching you in the ribs with his elbow and asking when you're going to take the plunge."

"All that because of mashed potatoes and gravy." Ed shook his head. "Amazing."

"I've seen it happen. I tell you, it's scary."

"Ben, you've got bigger things to worry about than if Tess has an Aunt Mabel. Scarier things."

"Oh, yeah, like what?"

"Do you know how much undigested red meat is clogging up your intestines?"

"Jesus, that's disgusting."

"You're telling me. My point here, Ben, is that you can worry about nuclear waste, acid rain, and your own cholesterol intake. Keep these things in the front of your mind and join the senator for dinner. If he starts looking like he's ready to welcome you into the family, do something to throw him off."

"Such as?"

"Eat your cranberry sauce with your fingers. Here's the place."

Ben pulled up at the curb then tossed his cigarette through the crack of his window. "You've been a big help, Ed. Thanks."

"Any time. How do you want to handle this?"

From the car Ben studied the building. It had seen better days. Much better days. There were a couple of broken windows with newspapers clogging the holes.

Graffiti was splashed lavishly on the east wall. Cans and broken bottles were in more profusion than grass.

"He's in 303. Fire escape's on the third floor. If he bolts, I don't want to chase him all over his own territory."

Ed dug a dime out of his pocket. "We flip to see who goes in and who covers the back."

"Fine. Heads I go in, tails I climb up the fire escape and cover the window. Oh, no, not in here." Ben put a hand on Ed's arm before his partner could flip the coin. "Last time you flipped in here I ended up having bean sprouts for lunch. We do it outside, where we've got some room."

In agreement, they got out and stood on the sidewalk. Ed took off his gloves, pocketing them before he flipped the coin.

"Heads," he announced, showing the coin. "Give me time to get in position."

"Let's go." Ben kicked the glass neck of a beer bottle out of his way and started into the building. Inside it smelled like baby puke and old whiskey. Ben unzipped his jacket as he climbed to the third floor. He took a long, slow look up and down the hall before he knocked on 303.

The door was opened a crack by a teenager with matted hair and a missing front tooth. Even before he got the first whiff of pot, Ben saw by his eyes that he was high. "Amos Reeder?"

"Who wants him?"

Ben flipped open his badge.

"Amos ain't here. He's out looking for work."

"Okay. I'll talk to you."

"Man, you got a warrant or something?"

"We can talk in the hall, inside, or downtown. You got a name?"

"I don't have to tell you nothing. I'm in here minding my own business."

"Yeah, and I smell enough grass coming through this door to show probable cause. Want me to come in and take a look around? Vice is having a special this week. For every ounce of pot I turn in, I get a free T-shirt."

"Kevin Danneville." Ben saw sweat begin to pearl on the kid's forehead. "Look, I got rights. I don't have to talk to no cops."

"You look nervous, Kevin." Ben pressed a hand to the door to keep the crack open. "How old are you?"

"I'm eighteen, if it's any of your fucking business."

"Eighteen? You look more like sixteen to me, and you're not in school. I might have to take you down to juvie. Why don't you tell me about a little girl whose daddy had a coin collection?"

It was the shifting of Kevin's eyes that saved Ben's life. He saw the change of expression, and on instinct whirled. The knife came down, but instead of severing his jugular, made a long slice through his arm as he fell against the door and crashed into the apartment.

"Christ, Amos, he's a cop. You can't kill a cop." Kevin, rushing to get out of the way, crashed into a table and sent a lamp shattering to the floor.

Reeder, flying on the PCP he'd just scored, only grinned. "I'm going to cut the motherfucker's heart out."

Ben had time enough to see that his assailant was barely old enough to be out of high school before the knife swung toward him again. He dodged, fighting to free his weapon with his left hand as blood poured out of the right. Kevin scooted over the floor like a crab and whimpered. Behind them the window crashed in.

"Police." Ed stood outside the window, legs spread, revolver level. "Drop the knife or I'll shoot."

Spittle ran out of the side of Amos's mouth as he focused on Ben. Incredibly, he giggled. "Gonna slice you up. Slice you into little pieces, man." Hefting the knife over his head, he made a leap. The .38 caliber, blunt-nosed wadcutter caught him in the chest and jerked his body back. For a moment he stood, eyes wide, blood pumping out of the hole in his chest. Ed kept his finger wrapped around the trigger guard. Then Reeder went down, taking a folding table with him. The knife slipped out of his hand with a quiet clatter. He died without a sound.

Ben stumbled and went down to his knees. By the time Ed climbed through the broken window, he'd managed to free his gun. "Flinch," Ben said between gritted teeth as he aimed his service revolver at Kevin. "Just one good flinch is considered resisting arrest."

"Amos did it. Amos did all of them," Kevin said as he began to blubber. "I just watched. I swear, I just watched, that's all."

"Just one good flinch, you little sonofabitch, and I'll blow your balls off before you learn how to use them."

Ed made a routine and unnecessary check of Amos before he crouched beside Ben. "How bad's the arm?"

The pain was incredibly hot and had already made a trip into his stomach to trigger nausea. "I had to pick heads. Next time I toss."

"Fine. Let's have a look."

"Just call someone in to clean up this mess, and get me to the hospital."

"Didn't hit an artery or you'd be gushing out A Positive."

"Oh, that's okay then." He sucked in his breath as Ed revealed the wound. "How about a round of golf?"

"Just keep this on it, hold the pressure steady."

Ed took Ben's gun then clamped his hand onto the bandanna he'd put on the gash. The smell of his own blood drifted up to him. Where he sat, his feet were only inches from Amos's. "Thanks."

"It's okay, it's an old bandanna."

"Ed." Ben spared a glance at Kevin, who'd curled into the fetal position with his hands over his ears. "He's got a picture of Charles Manson over the bed."

"I saw it."

❧

BEN sat on the edge of the table in Emergency and counted nurses to keep his mind off the needle going in and out of his flesh. The doctor who stitched him up chatted amiably about the Redskins' chances against the Cowboys on Sunday. In the curtained enclosure beside them a doctor and two nurses worked on a nineteen-year-old girl fighting off a crack overdose. Ben listened to her sobbing and wished for a cigarette.

"I hate hospitals," he muttered.

"Most people do." The doctor sewed as neatly as a maiden aunt. "The defensive line's like a brick wall. If we keep it on the ground, Dallas is going to be standing around sucking their thumbs by the third quarter."

"Not a pretty sight." Ben's concentration wavered long enough for him to feel the pull and tug on his flesh. He focused his attention on the sounds behind the curtain. The kid was hyperventilating. A sharp, authoritative voice was ordering her to breathe into a paper bag. "You get many like her in here?"

"More every day." The doctor knotted off another suture. "We put them back on their feet, if they're lucky, so they can go to the first street corner and buy another vial. There, that's a very nice seam, if I say so myself. What do you think?"

"I'll take your word for it."

Tess rushed through the automatic glass doors of Emergency. After a quick glance around the waiting area, she headed toward the examining rooms. She stopped, staring blankly as an orderly wheeled away a gurney with a shrouded figure on top. Her blood drained down to her feet. A nurse came out of a curtained area and took her by the arm.

"I'm sorry, miss, you don't belong back here."

"Detective Paris. Stabbing."

"He's getting his arm stitched up back there." The nurse kept her grip firm. "Now, why don't you go back to the waiting room and—"

"I'm his doctor," Tess managed, and tore her arm away. She didn't run. There was enough control left so that she walked steadily enough past a broken arm, a second-degree burn, and a mild concussion. An old woman lay on a gurney in the hall, trying miserably to sleep. Tess passed the last curtained area and found him.

"Why, Tess." The doctor looked over, pleased and surprised. "What are you doing here?"

"Oh. John. Hello."

"Hello yourself. It's not often I get beautiful women to visit me at the office," he began, then saw the way she looked at his patient. "Oh, I see." His considerable ego took only a slight bruise. "I take it you two know each other."

Ben shifted on the table and would have stood if the doctor hadn't held him still. "What are you doing in here?"

"Ed called me at the clinic."

"He shouldn't have."

Now that her images of him bleeding to death were put to rest, her knees went weak. "He thought I might be concerned, and didn't want me to hear about it on a news bulletin. John, how bad is it?"

"It's no big deal," Ben answered.

"Ten stitches," the doctor added as he secured the bandage. "No apparent muscle damage, some blood loss but nothing major. To quote the Duke, it's just a scratch."

"The guy had a goddamn butcher knife," Ben muttered, annoyed at having someone else downplay his injury.

"Fortunately," John went on as he turned to the tray beside him, "the detective's jacket and fancy footwork prevented the wound from being any deeper. Without it, we'd have been stitching up both sides of his arm. This will sting a bit."

"What will?" Automatically Ben shot out a hand to grab the doctor's wrist.

"Just a little tetanus shot," John said soothingly. "After all, we don't know where that knife has been. Come on now, bite the bullet."

He started to protest again, but Tess took his hand. The sting in his arm came, then dulled.

"There now." John left the tray for a nurse to deal with. "That ties things up. Forgive the pun. No tennis or sumo wrestling for a couple of weeks, Detective. Keep the area dry and come back for a return visit the end of next week. I'll yank those stitches out for you."

"Thanks a lot."

"Your good health and medical insurance are thanks enough. Nice seeing you, Tess. Give me a call the next time you're in the mood for saki and sea urchin."

"Bye, John."

"John, huh?" Ben eased himself off the table. "Did you ever date anyone but doctors?"

"Whatever for?" A light answer seemed best when she'd spotted the blood-soaked linen on the tray. "Here's your shirt. Let me help you."

"I can do it." But his arm was stiff and painful. He managed one sleeve.

"It's all right. You're entitled to be cranky after ten stitches."

"Cranky?" He shut his eyes as she eased his shirt on. "Jesus Christ. Four-year-olds are cranky if they don't have a nap."

"Yes, I know. Here, I'll button it." She intended to. She told herself she would button his shirt, keep the conversation brisk. She'd nearly done two before she dropped her forehead on his chest.

"Tess?" He brought his hand to her hair. "What is it?"

"Nothing." She drew herself away and with her head bent finished buttoning his shirt.

"Tess." With a hand under her chin, he lifted her face. Tears swam in her eyes. He brushed one from her lashes with his thumb. "Don't."

"I'm not going to." But her breath hitched before she pressed her cheek to his. "Just a minute, okay?"

"Yeah." He put his good arm around her and absorbed the basic pleasure of being cared about. Some women had been turned on by his job, others repulsed by it, but he wasn't sure he'd ever had anyone who just cared.

"I was scared," she admitted, her voice muffled against him.

"Me too."

"Later, will you tell me about it?"

"If I have to. A guy hates to admit to his woman that he was a jerk."

"Were you?"

"I was sure the little sonofabitch was inside. Ed had the window, I had the door. Very simple." When he drew away, he saw her gaze go to his ripped and bloodstained shirt. "You think this is bad, you should see my jacket. I just bought it two months ago."

In control again, she took his arm and led him down the hall. "Well, maybe Santa will bring you a new one for Christmas. Do you want me to drive you home?"

"No, thanks. I've got a report to file. And if the other kid hasn't spilled his guts by now, I want to be in on the interrogation."

"So there were two."

"There's only one now."

She thought of the shrouded figure on the gurney. Because she could smell the dried blood on Ben's shirt, Tess said nothing. "There's Ed."

"Oh, God, he's reading."

Ed glanced up, gave his partner a quick but very thorough study, then smiled at Tess. "Hi, Dr. Court. I must have missed you when you came in." He didn't mention the fact that when she'd arrived, he'd been donating a pint of blood. Both he and Ben were A Positive. Setting the magazine aside, he gave Ben his jacket and holster. "Too bad about the coat. It should only take the department till April to process the papers and replace it."

"Ain't it the truth?" With Ed's help Ben managed to heft on his holster and the damaged jacket.

"You know, I just read this fascinating article about kidneys."

"Save it," Ben advised, and turned to Tess. "You going back to the clinic?"

"Yes, I left in the middle of a session." It wasn't until that moment that Tess fully realized she had put him ahead of a patient. "Speaking as a doctor, I'd advise you to go home and rest after you've filed your report. I'll be home around six-thirty, and could probably be persuaded to pamper you."

"Define pamper."

Ignoring him, she turned to Ed. "Why don't you come to dinner, Ed?"

Initially he looked perplexed by the invitation, then pleased. "Well, I—Thanks."

"Ed's not used to articulating to women. Come on

over, Ed. Tess'll fix you bean curds." He stepped outside, grateful for the rush of cold air. His arm was no longer numb, but beginning to throb like a toothache. "Where are you parked?" He was already scanning the lot for the black and white.

"Just over there."

"Walk the lady to her car, will you, Ed?" Taking her by the front of her coat, he kissed her hard. "Thanks for coming by."

"You're welcome."

She waited until he'd started toward the Mustang before she turned with Ed. "You'll look out for him?"

"Sure."

Digging her keys out of her pocket, she nodded. "The man who stabbed Ben is dead?"

"Yeah." He took the keys from her, and in a gesture she found sweet, unlocked the car himself. Tess looked at his face and saw, as clearly as if he'd spoken, who had fired the shot. Her values, the code she lived by, warred briefly with a new awareness. Putting a hand on his collar, she drew him down and kissed him. "Thanks for keeping him alive." She got in the car, smiling up at him before she shut the door. "See you at dinner."

Half in love with her himself, Ed walked back to his partner. "You don't go to Thanksgiving dinner, you're one dumb sonofabitch."

Ben shook off grogginess as Ed slammed the car door. "What?"

"And you shouldn't need her Uncle Joe to punch you in the ribs." Ed started the engine with a roar.

"Ed, did you get a bad piece of granola?"

"You better start looking at what's in front of your face, partner, before you end up tripping over the saw."

"Saw? What saw?"

"Farmer's sawing wood," Ed began as he drove off the lot. "City slicker's watching him. Dinner bell rings and the farmer starts moving but he trips over the saw. He just picks himself up and starts cutting wood again. Slicker asks him why he doesn't go in to dinner and the farmer says, since he tripped over the saw, it's no use going in. There won't be anything left."

Ben sat in silence for a full ten seconds. "That explains it. Why don't you turn back around, we'll go into the hospital and have them take a look at you?"

"The point is, if you fuck around when opportunity is staring you in the face, you miss it. You got a hell of a woman, Ben."

"I think I know that."

"Then you better be damn careful you don't trip over the saw."

Chapter 16

IT WAS JUST beginning to snow when Joey walked out of the back door. Knowing the storm door rattled, he pulled it carefully closed until it latched. He'd remembered to take his gloves, and had even pulled his blue ski cap over his head. Rather than changing to boots, he kept on his high tops. They were his favorite.

No one saw him leave.

His mother was in the den with his stepfather. He knew they'd been arguing about him, because their voices had been pitched low and had carried that thin, nervous tone their voices carried whenever they argued about him.

They didn't think he knew.

His mother had roasted a turkey with all the trimmings. Throughout the meal she had chatted brightly, too brightly, about it being nice to have Thanksgiving with just the family. Donald had joked about leftovers and bragged about the pumpkin pie he'd baked himself. There'd been cranberry sauce and real butter and the little crescent rolls that popped up fluffy in the oven.

It had been the most miserable meal of Joey's life.

His mother didn't want him to have any problems.

She wanted him to be happy, do well in school, and go out for basketball. Normal. That was the word Joey had heard her use in an urgent undertone to his stepfather. *I just want him to be normal.*

But he wasn't. Joey guessed his stepfather sort of understood that, and that's why they argued. He wasn't normal. He was an alcoholic, just like his father.

His mother said his father was NO GOOD.

Joey understood that alcoholism was a disease. He understood addiction and that there was no cure, only a continuing period of recovery. He also understood that there were millions of alcoholics, and that it was possible to be one and live the normal life his mother wanted so badly for him. It took acceptance and effort and change. Sometimes he got tired of making the effort. If he told his mother he was tired, she would get upset.

He knew, too, that alcoholism could often be inherited. He'd inherited his from his father, the same way he'd inherited the NO GOOD.

The streets were quiet as he headed out of the nice, tidy neighborhood. Snowflakes fluttered in the beam of streetlights like the fairy dancers in storybooks he remembered his mother reading him years before. He could see the illumination in windows where people were eating their Thanksgiving meal or resting after the effort in front of the TV.

His father hadn't come for him.

He hadn't called.

Joey thought he understood why his father didn't love him anymore. He didn't like to be reminded about the drinking and the fighting and the bad times.

Dr. Court said his father's disease hadn't been Joey's fault. But Joey figured if he'd gotten the sickness from his father, then maybe, somehow, his father had gotten the sickness from him.

He remembered lying in bed, knowing it was late,

and hearing his father shout in that thick nasty voice he used when he'd been drinking a lot.

"All you think about is that kid. You never think about me. Everything changed after we had him."

Then later he had heard his father cry, big, wet sobs which were somehow even worse than the temper.

"I'm sorry, Lois. I love you, I love you so much. It's the pressure that makes me like this. Those bastards at work are always on my back. I'd tell them all to get fucked tomorrow, but Joey needs a new pair of shoes every time I turn around."

Joey waited for a car to rumble past, then crossed the street and headed for the park. Snow was falling thickly now, a white curtain buffeted by the wind. The air whipped healthy pink into his cheeks.

Once he'd thought if he hadn't needed new shoes, his father wouldn't need to get drunk. Then he'd realized things would be easier on everyone if he just wasn't there. So he'd run away when he'd been nine. It had been scary because he'd gotten lost and it had been dark and there'd been noises. The police had found him in a few hours, but to Joey it had seemed like days.

His mother had cried and his father had held him so tight. Everyone had made promises they had meant to keep. For a while things had been better. His father had gone to AA and his mother had laughed more. That was the Christmas Joey had gotten his two-wheeler and his father had spent hours running beside the bike with his hand hooked under the seat. He hadn't let Joey fall, not even once.

But just before Easter his father had started coming home late again. Joey's mother's eyes had stayed red, and the laughter had stopped. One night Joey's father had taken the turn into the driveway too wide and hadn't seen the two-wheeler. His father had come in the house shouting. Joey had woken up to the swearing, the accusations. His father had wanted to get Joey out of bed and take him outside to show him what his negligence had done. His mother had blocked the way.

That was the first night he'd heard his father strike his mother.

If he'd put the bike away instead of leaving it on the lawn beside the driveway, his father wouldn't have hit it. Then his father wouldn't have gotten so angry. His father wouldn't have hit his mother and given her a bruise on her cheek she tried to hide with makeup.

That was the first night Joey tried alcohol.

He hadn't liked the taste. It had hurt his mouth and made his stomach rise up uncomfortably. But when he'd sipped from the bottle three or four times, he felt strangely as if he'd slipped on a thin plastic shield. He didn't feel like crying anymore. There had been a nice, quiet buzz in his head as he climbed back into his bed. He'd fallen dreamlessly to sleep.

From that night Joey had used alcohol as an anesthetic whenever his parents fought.

Then the divorce had come in a horrible culmination of arguments, shouting, and name calling. One day his mother had picked him up at school to drive him to a small apartment. There she explained to him as gently as possible why they wouldn't be living with his father any longer.

He'd been ashamed, horribly ashamed, because he'd been glad.

They'd started their new life. His mother had gone back to work. She cut her hair and no longer wore her wedding ring. But Joey noticed from time to time the thin circle of white skin the band had covered for over a decade.

He could still remember how anxious, how pleading

her eyes had been when she'd explained to him about the divorce. She'd been so afraid he would blame her, so she'd justified a move that left her riddled with guilt and uncertainty by telling him what he already knew. But hearing it from her had shattered whatever thin defenses he'd had left.

He could remember, too, how hard she'd cried the first time she came home from work to find her eleven-year-old son drunk.

The park was quiet. On the ground a thin, pretty layer of white had already formed. In another hour no one would notice his footprints. Joey thought that was the way it should be. Snow was falling now in big, soft flakes which clung to the branches of trees and lay glistening and fresh on bushes. Flakes melted on his face, making his skin damp, but he didn't mind. He wondered, only briefly, if his mother had gone up to his room yet and discovered him gone. He was sorry she was going to be upset, but he knew what he was doing would make things easier for everyone. Especially himself.

He wasn't nine years old this time. And he wasn't afraid.

He'd gone to Alateen and Alanon meetings with his mother. They didn't reach him. He didn't let them reach him because he didn't want to admit he was ashamed to be like his father.

Then Donald Monroe had come along. Joey wanted to be glad his mother was happy again, then felt guilty because he was so close to accepting a replacement for his father. His mother was happy again, and Joey was glad because he loved her so much. His father grew more and more bitter, and Joey resented the change because he loved his father so much.

His mother married and her name changed. It was no longer the same as Joey's. They moved into a house in a quietly affluent neighborhood. Joey's room overlooked the backyard. His father complained about the child-support payments.

When Joey had begun to see Tess, he was finding a way to get drunk every day, and he'd already begun to contemplate suicide.

He hadn't liked going to see her at first. But she hadn't pulled at him or pressured or claimed to understand. She'd just talked. When he stopped drinking, she gave him a calendar, what she had called a perpetual calendar that he could use forever.

"You have something to be proud of today, Joey. And every day when you get up in the morning, you'll have something to be proud of."

Sometimes, he'd believed her.

She never gave him that quick, sharp look when he walked into the room. His mother still did. Dr. Court had given him the calendar and believed in him. His mother still waited for him to disappoint her. That's why she'd taken him out of his school. That's why she wouldn't let him hang around with his friends.

You'll make new friends, Joey. I only want the best for you.

She only wanted him not to be like his father.

But he was.

And when he grew up he might have a son, and his son would be like him. It would never stop. It was like a curse. He'd read about curses. They could be passed from generation to generation. Sometimes they could be exorcised. One of the books he kept under his mattress explained the ceremony for exorcizing evil. He'd followed it point by point one night when his mother and stepfather had been at a business dinner. When he was finished, he didn't feel any different. It proved to him that the evil, the no good inside of him, was stronger than the good.

That's when he'd begun to dream of the bridge.

Dr. Court wanted to send him to a place where people understood dreams about death. He'd found the brochures his mother had thrown away. It looked like a nice place, quiet. Joey had saved the brochures, thinking it might be a better place than the school he hated. He'd nearly worked up the nerve to talk to Dr. Court about it when his mother said he didn't need to see the doctor anymore.

He'd wanted to see Dr. Court, but his mother had that bright, nervous smile on.

Now they were home arguing about it, about him. It was always about him.

His mother was going to have a new baby. She was already picking out colors for the nursery and talking about names. Joey thought it might be nice to have a new baby in the house. He'd been glad when Donald asked him to help paint the nursery.

Then one night he'd dreamed that the baby had been dead.

He wanted to talk to Dr. Court about it, but his mother said he didn't need to see her anymore.

The surface of the bridge was slippery with its coating of snow. Joey's footprints were long, sliding marks. He could hear the rush of traffic below, but walked on the side that overlooked the creek and the trees. It was a high, exhilarating feeling to walk up here, above the tops of the trees, with the sky so dark above his head. The wind was frigid, but the walk had kept his muscles warm.

He wondered about his father. The night, this last Thanksgiving night, had been a test. If his father had come, if he'd been sober and had come to take Joey with him for dinner, Joey would have tried one more time. But he hadn't come because it was too late for both of them.

Besides, he was tired of trying, tired of seeing those sharp, uncertain looks on his mother's face, of seeing the anxious concern on Donald's. He couldn't stand being to blame anymore, for any of it. When he was finished, there wouldn't be any reason for Donald and his mother to fight about him. He wouldn't have any reason to worry that Donald would leave his mother and the new baby because he couldn't tolerate Joey any longer.

His father wouldn't have to make child-support payments.

The rail of the Calvert Street Bridge was slick, but he got a good purchase with his gloves.

All he wanted was peace. Dying was peaceful. He'd read all about reincarnation, about the chance of coming back to something better, as someone better. He was looking forward to it.

He could feel the wind tossing snow, cold, almost sharp snow, against his face. He could see his breath puff out slow and steady in the dark. Below him now were the white-tipped trees and the icy flow of Rock Creek.

He'd decided quite calmly against other forms of suicide. If he slashed his wrists, the sight of his own blood might make him too weak to finish. He'd read where people who tried to overdose on pills often vomited them up and just got sick.

Besides, the bridge was right. It was clean. For a moment, for one long moment, it would feel like flying.

He balanced himself a moment and prayed. He wanted God to understand. He knew that God didn't like people to make a choice to die. He wanted them to wait until He was ready.

Well, Joey couldn't wait, and he hoped God and everyone else would understand.

He thought of Dr. Court and was sorry that she was going to be disappointed. Joey knew his mother would be upset, but she had Donald and the new baby. It wouldn't take her long to see that it was all for the best. And his father. His father would just get drunk again.

Joey kept his eyes open. He wanted to see the trees rush up at him. He took a long breath, held it, and dove.

"MISS Bette has outdone herself again." Tess sampled the rich dark meat her grandfather had carved. "Everything's spectacular, as always."

"Nothing the woman likes better than to fuss with a meal." The senator added steaming gravy to a mound of creamy white potatoes. "I've been barred from my own kitchen for two days."

"Did she catch you sneaking in for samples again?"

"Threatened to make me peel potatoes." He swallowed a healthy forkful, then grinned. "Miss Bette has never subscribed to the notion that a man's home is his castle. Have some more dressing, Detective. It's not every day a man gets to indulge himself."

"Thanks." Because the senator held the bowl over his plate, Ben had little choice but to take it. He'd already had two helpings, but it was difficult to resist the senator's cheerful insistence. After an hour in the company of Senator Writemore, Ben had discovered the old man was vibrant, both in looks and speech. His opinions were hard as granite, his patience slim, and his heart undeniably lay in his granddaughter's hands.

What relieved Ben was that after that hour he wasn't nearly as uncomfortable as he'd been prepared to be.

Initially the house had made him uneasy. From the outside it had merely been quietly elegant, distinguished. Inside it had been like a trip around the world in a first-class cabin. Turkish rugs faded just enough to show their age and durability, were spread over black-and-white checkerboard tile on the hall floor. An ebony cabinet, high as a man's shoulders and magnificently painted with peacocks, stood under a long curve of stairs.

In the parlor, where a silent Oriental had served before-dinner drinks, two Louis Quinze chairs flanked a long rococo table. A cabinet fronted with etched glass held a treasure trove. Venetian glass almost thin enough to read through was stained with color. A glass bird caught and reflected the light from the fire. Guarding the white marble hearth was a porcelain elephant the size of a terrier.

It was a room that reflected the senator's background and, Ben realized, Tess's. Comfortable wealth, a knowledge of art and style. She'd sat on the dark green brocade of the sofa in a pale lavender dress that had made her skin glow. The pearl choker lay against her throat, its glinting center stone pulsing with light and the heat from her body.

To Ben she'd never looked more beautiful.

There was a fire in the dining room as well. This one had been banked to simmer and pop through the meal. Light came from the prisms of the tiered chandelier above the table. Wedgwood plates, delicately tinted, Georgian silver, heavy and gleaming, Baccarat crystal waiting to be filled with cool white wine and sparkling water, Irish linen soft enough to sleep on. Bowls and platters were heaped. Oysters Rockefeller, roast turkey, buttered asparagus, fresh crescent rolls, and more; their scents mixed into a delightful potpourri with candles and flowers.

As the senator carved the turkey, Ben had thought back on the Thanksgivings he'd experienced as a child.

Because they had always eaten at midday rather than evening, he'd woken to the enticing smells of roasting fowl, sage, cinnamon, and the sausage his mother had browned and crumbled into the stuffing. The television had stayed on through the Macy's parade and football. It was one of the few days of the year when he or his brother hadn't been drafted to set the table. That was his mother's pleasure.

She'd take out her best dishes, the ones used only when his Aunt Jo visited from Chicago or his father's boss came to dinner. The flatware hadn't been sterling, but a more ornate stainless. She'd always taken pride in arranging the napkins into triangles. Then his father's sister would arrive with her husband and brood of three in tow. The house would be full of noise, arguments, and the scent of his mother's honey bread.

Grace would be said while Ben ignored his cousin Marcie, who became more disagreeable every year, and who, for reasons of her own, his mother would insist on seating next to him.

Bless us O Lord with these Thy gifts which we are about to receive from Thy bounty through Christour-lordamen.

The last of the prayer always ran together as greed became overwhelming. The minute the Sign of the Cross was completed, hands began to reach out for whatever was closest.

There had never been a silent Oriental seeing the glasses were full of Pouilly-Fuissé.

"I'm glad you could join us tonight, Detective." Writemore helped himself to another serving of asparagus. "I often feel guilty about keeping Tess all to myself over the holidays."

"I appreciate the invitation. Otherwise I'd probably be eating a taco in front of the television."

"A profession like yours doesn't leave time for many quiet meals, I'd imagine. I'm told you're a rare breed, Detective, being dedicated." When Ben only lifted a brow, the senator gave him a bland smile and gestured with his wineglass. "The mayor's been keeping me informed on the ins and outs of your case, as my granddaughter's involved."

"What Grandpa means is that he gossips with the mayor."

"That too," Writemore agreed easily. "Apparently you didn't approve of Tess being brought in to consult."

Blunt, Ben decided, is best met with blunt. "I still don't."

"Try some of these pear preserves on that roll." Genially, the senator passed the dish. "Miss Bette puts them up herself. Do you mind if I ask if you disapproved of consulting with a psychiatrist or of consulting with Tess."

"Grandpa, I don't think Thanksgiving dinner is an appropriate place for a grilling."

"Nonsense, I'm not grilling the boy, just trying to see where he stands."

Taking his time, Ben spread the preserves on the bread. "I didn't see the point in a psychiatric profile that involved more time and paperwork. I prefer basic police work, interviews, legwork, logic." He glanced over at Tess, and saw her studying her wine. "As far as law enforcement is concerned, it doesn't matter to me if he's psychotic or just mean. This dressing's incredible."

"Yes, Miss Bette has quite a hand." As if to corroborate, Writemore took another forkful. "I'm inclined to see your opinion, Detective, without wholly agreeing. That's what we in politics call diplomatic bullshit."

"We call it the same thing in law enforcement."

"Then we understand each other. You see, I'm of the opinion that it's always wise to understand your opponent's mind."

"Insofar as it helps you stay a step ahead of him." Ben turned his attention to Writemore. The senator sat at the table's head in a black suit and stiff white shirt. The dark tie was held in place by a single unadorned diamond. His hands were big and rough looking against the elegant crystal. It surprised Ben to note that his own grandfather's hands, the old butcher's hands, had been much the same—worked, thick at the knuckle, wide backed. He wore a plain gold band on his left hand, the sign of a commitment to the wife who had died more than thirty years before.

"Then you don't feel Tess's work as a psychiatrist has helped you in this particular case?"

As if she were sublimely unconcerned, Tess continued to eat.

"I'd like to say that," Ben answered after a moment. "Because if I did it might be easier to convince her, or to convince you to convince her to stay out of it from here on. But the fact is, she's helped us establish a pattern and a motive."

"Would you pass me the salt?" Tess smiled as Ben lifted the lead crystal dish. "Thank you."

"You're welcome," he said, but grudgingly. "That doesn't mean I approve of her being involved."

"Then I take it you've come to realize that my granddaughter is both a dedicated and stubborn woman."

"I've gotten the picture."

"I consider it an inheritance," Tess said, and covered the senator's big hand with hers. "From my grandfather."

Ben saw the hands link and hold. "Thank God you didn't get my looks." Then, in the same genial tone, "I'm told you've moved in with my granddaughter, Detective."

"That's right." Preparing for the inquisition he'd been expecting all evening, Ben fell back on the pear preserves.

"I wonder if you're charging the city overtime."

Tess laughed and sat back in her chair. "Grandpa's

trying to see if he can make you sweat. Here, darling." She passed the senator more turkey. "Indulge yourself. The next time you gossip with the mayor, tell him that I'm receiving the very best in police protection."

"What else should I tell him you're receiving?"

"Whatever else I'm receiving is none of the mayor's business."

Writemore dropped another slab of turkey on his plate before he reached for the gravy. "And I suppose you're going to tell me it's none of mine either."

"I don't have to." Tess spooned cranberry sauce onto his plate. "You've just said so yourself."

At five feet and a hundred forty pounds, Miss Bette shuffled into the room and cast an approving eye on the dent made in the feast she'd prepared. She wiped small, pudgy hands on her apron. "Dr. Court, there's a call for you."

"Oh, thank you, Miss Bette. I'll take it in the library." After she rose, she leaned down to kiss the senator's cheek. "Don't be a nuisance, Grandpa. And make sure I get a piece of that pie."

Writemore waited until Tess was out of the room. "A beautiful woman."

"Yes, she is."

"You know, when she was younger, people often underestimated her because of her looks, her size, her sex. After you've lived more than half a century, you don't take much on face value. She was just a bit of a thing when she moved in here with me. We only had each other. People would assume that I got her through the rough times. The truth was, Ben, she got me through. I think I would have crumbled up and died without Tess.

"I'm closing in on three quarters of a century." Writemore smiled as if the thought pleased him. "When you do that, you start to look at each day in sharp focus. You start to appreciate little things."

"Like feeling your feet on the ground in the morning," Ben murmured, then catching the senator's look, shifted uncomfortably. "Something my grandfather said."

"Obviously an astute man. Yes, like feeling your feet on the ground in the morning." Holding his wineglass, he leaned back, studying Ben. It relieved him that he liked what he saw. "Human nature forces a man to appreciate those things, even after he's lost his wife and his only child. Tess is all I have left besides those small pleasures, Ben."

Ben discovered he was no longer uncomfortable, no longer waiting to be backed into a corner. "I'm not going to let anything happen to her. Not just because I'm a cop and it's my duty to shield and protect, but because she matters."

When he leaned away from the table, the diamond in Writemore's tie glinted from the light. "You follow football?"

"Some."

"When neither of us have to worry about Tess, you come to a game with me. I've got season tickets. We'll have a few beers and you can tell me about yourself, things I didn't learn from copies of your departmental record." He grinned, showing a white set of teeth which were almost all his own. "She's all I've got, Detective. I could tell you what your score was last week at target practice."

Amused, Ben polished off his wine. "How'd I do?"

"Good enough," Writemore told him. "Damn good enough."

Surprisingly in tune, both men turned as Tess entered the room again. Ben only had to see her face to be out of his chair. "What's wrong?"

"I'm sorry." Her voice was calm, without a tremor, but her cheeks were very pale. She stretched out a hand as she walked to her grandfather. "I've got to go, Grandpa. I have an emergency at the hospital. I don't know if I'll make it back."

Because her hand was cold, her grandfather covered it with both of his. Better than anyone, he understood how much emotion she kept locked inside. "A patient?"

"Yes. Attempted suicide. He's been taken to Georgetown, but it doesn't look good." Her voice was cool and flat, a doctor's voice. Ben studied her carefully, but other than the lack of color, he could see no emotion. "I'm sorry to leave you like this."

"Don't you worry about me." The senator had already risen. His arm was draped around her as he walked her from the room. "You give me a call tomorrow, let me know how you are."

Something inside her trembled and shook, but she held steady. She pressed her cheek to his, wanting to draw a bit of his strength. "I love you."

"I love you, too, little girl."

As they walked into the snow-swathed night, Ben took her arm to keep her from slipping on the stairs. "Can you tell me what happened?"

"A fourteen-year-old boy decided life was too much to handle. He jumped off the Calvert Street Bridge."

Chapter 17

THE SURGICAL FLOOR smelled of antiseptic and fresh paint. With the staff halved for the holiday, the halls were almost empty. Someone had covered a mincemeat pie in Saran Wrap and left it at the nurse's station. It looked cheerful and miserably out of place. Tess stopped there as the nurse on duty filled out a report.

"I'm Dr. Teresa Court. Joseph Higgins, Jr., was admitted a short time ago."

"Yes, Doctor. He's in surgery."

"What's his condition?"

"Massive trauma, hemorrhaging. He was comatose when they took him up. Dr. Bitterman's operating."

"Joey's parents?"

"Down the end of the hall and to the left, in the waiting area, Doctor."

"Thank you." Steeling herself, Tess turned to Ben. "I don't know how long this might take, and it won't be pleasant. I'm sure I can arrange for you to wait in the doctor's lounge. You'd be more comfortable."

"I'll go with you."

"All right." Unbuttoning her coat as she went, Tess

started down the hall. Their footsteps sounded like gunfire in the tiled silence of the corridor. As she approached the door to the waiting area, she heard the muffled sobs.

Lois Monroe was huddled close against her husband. Though it was overwarm in the room, neither of them had taken off their coats. She cried quietly, with her eyes open and unfocused. A Thanksgiving special danced soundlessly from the television mounted high on the wall. Tess motioned for Ben to stay back.

"Mr. Monroe."

At the sound of her voice his eyes shifted from the wall to the door. For a moment he stared at her as if he didn't know who she was, then a seizure of pain ran through him, reflecting briefly, poignantly, in his eyes. She could almost hear the thoughts.

I didn't believe you. I didn't understand. I didn't know.

Responding to that even more than to the weeping, Tess went to them to sit beside Lois Monroe.

"She went up to see if he wanted some more pie," Monroe began. "He—he was gone. There was a note."

Because she understood need, Tess reached out and held his free hand. He gripped it tight, swallowed, then went on.

"It said he was sorry. That he—he wished he could be different. It said everything would be better now, and that he was going to come back in another life. Someone saw him . . ." Monroe's fingers vised on hers while he closed his eyes and fought for control. "Someone saw him jump and called the police. They came—they came to the house just after we realized he was gone. I didn't know what to do, so I called you."

"Joey's going to be just fine." With her hands kneading together, Lois shifted farther away from Tess. "I've always taken care of him. He's going to be fine, then we're going to go home together." Maintaining the distance, she turned her head enough to look at Tess. "I told you he didn't need you anymore. Joey doesn't need you or any clinic or more treatment. He just needs to be left alone for a little while. He's going to be fine. He knows I love him."

"Yes, he knows you love him," Tess murmured as she took Lois's hand. The pulse was rapid and thready. "Joey knows how hard you've tried to make things good for him."

"I have. Everything I've done has been to try to protect him, to try to make things better. All I've ever wanted was for Joey to be happy."

"I know that."

"Then why? You tell me why this happened." Tears dried up. Her voice went from wavery to venomous. Lois struggled away from her husband to grab Tess by the shoulders. "You were supposed to heal, you were supposed to make him well. You tell me why my boy's bleeding on that table. You tell me why."

"Lois, Lois, don't." Already grieving, Monroe tried to gather her close, but she sprang up, dragging Tess with her. Instinctively Ben started forward, but was stopped by a furious shake of Tess's head.

"I want an answer. Damn you, I want you to give me an answer!"

Rather than block the fury, Tess accepted it. "He was hurting, Mrs. Monroe. And the hurt was deep, deeper than I could reach."

"I did everything I could." Though her voice was quiet, almost level, Lois's fingers dug deep into Tess's flesh. Bruises would show the next day. "I did everything. He wasn't drinking," she said with a hitch in her voice. "He hadn't had a drink in months."

"No, he wasn't drinking. You should sit down, Lois." Tess tried to ease her back on the sofa.

"I don't want to sit." Fury that was fear spewed out until each word was like a bullet. "I want my son. I want my boy. All you did was talk and talk, week after week just talk. Why didn't you *do* something? You were supposed to make him better, make him happy. Why didn't you?"

"I couldn't." In a wave, the grief washed over her. "I couldn't."

"Lois, sit down." Strengthened by her need, Monroe took her by the shoulders and brought her to the sofa. As his arm went around her again, he looked at Tess. "You told us this could happen. We didn't believe you. We didn't want to. If it's not too late, we can try again. We can—"

Then the door swung open, and they all knew it was too late.

Dr. Bitterman still wore his surgical scrubs. He'd pulled down his mask so that it hung by its strings. The sweat on it hadn't dried. Though his time in the operating room had been relatively brief, there were lines of strain and fatigue around his eyes and mouth. Before he spoke, before he moved over to the Monroes, Tess knew they had both lost a patient.

"Mrs. Monroe, I'm sorry. There was nothing we could do."

"Joey?" She looked blankly from the doctor to her husband. One hand was already clawing at Monroe's shoulder.

"Joey's gone, Mrs. Monroe." Because the hour he'd spent trying to sew the boy back together had left him sick and defeated, Bitterman sat beside her. "He never regained consciousness. He had a massive head injury. There was nothing that could be done."

"Joey? Joey's dead?"

"I'm sorry."

The sobbing started, harsh, guttural sounds that poured out of her into the room. She cried with her mouth open, her head back, in an agony of grief that twisted Tess's stomach. No one could truly understand the measure of joy a mother received from giving birth to a child. No one could truly understand the devastation a mother experienced upon losing one.

An error in judgment, a desire to keep her family whole with her own strength, had cost her her son. There was nothing Tess could do for her now. There was no longer anything she could do for Joey. With her own grief clogging her lungs, she turned and walked from the room.

"Tess." Ben caught her arm as she started down the hall. "You aren't staying?"

"No." Her voice was strong and icy as she continued to walk. "Seeing me now only makes it more painful for her, if possible." She pushed the button for the elevator then jammed her hands into her pockets, where they curled and uncurled.

"That's it?" Dull and centered in his gut, the anger began to spread. "You just cross it off?"

"There's nothing more I can do here." She stepped into the elevator, fighting to breathe calmly.

It was snowing hard on the way home. Tess didn't speak. Tasting bitterness in his own throat, Ben remained as coldly silent as she. Though the car heater poured out warmth, she had to struggle not to shiver. Failure, grief, and anger were so twined together that it made one hard knot of emotion that wedged in her throat; she could taste it. Control was often hard won, but never so vital as it seemed to her at that moment.

By the time they stepped into her apartment, the pressure in her chest was so strong she had to consciously school every breath. "I'm sorry you got dragged into this," she said carefully. She needed to get away, away from him, from everyone until she'd pulled herself back together. The throbbing in her head was building to a roar. "I know it was difficult."

"You seem to be handling it just fine." After yanking off his jacket, he tossed it into a chair. "You don't have to apologize to me. I'm in the business, remember?"

"Yes, of course. Listen." She had to swallow the bubbling heat in her throat. "I'm going to have a bath."

"Sure, go ahead." He walked to the liquor cabinet and reached for the vodka he'd stored. "I'm going to have a drink."

She didn't bother to go into the bedroom to change. When the door was closed quietly behind her, Ben heard the sound of water rushing against porcelain.

He hadn't even known the kid, Ben told himself as he splashed vodka into a glass. There was no reason for him to feel this ugly squeeze of resentment. It was one thing to feel sorrow, pity, even anger at the useless loss of a life, a young life, but there was no reason for this helpless, shaking rage.

She'd been so detached. So goddamned untouched.

Just like Josh's doctor.

The bitterness lodged deep for years swirled into his throat. Ben lifted the vodka to wash the taste away, then slammed it, untouched, onto the cabinet. Not sure what he was going to do, he went down the hall and pushed the bathroom door open.

She wasn't in the tub.

Like thunder, the water hit the porcelain full force, then whirled down the drain she hadn't bothered to close. Steam was rising, already sweating on the mirror. Fully dressed, using the sink for support, Tess wept violently into her hands.

For a moment Ben stood silently in the open doorway, too stunned to go in, too shocked to close the door and leave her the privacy she'd sought.

He'd never seen her as the helpless victim of her own emotions. In bed there were times she seemed utterly guided by her own passion. Occasionally he'd seen her temper flare, teetering briefly on full blossoming. Then she snapped it back, always. Now it was grief, and the grief was total.

She hadn't heard him open the door. Slowly, her body rocked back and forth in a rhythm of mourning. Self-comfort. Ben's throat tightened, driving back the bitterness. He started to touch her, then hesitated. It was harder, he discovered, unbelievably harder to comfort someone who really mattered.

"Tess." When he did touch her, she jolted. When his arms went around her, she went board stiff. He could feel her fighting to block off the tears, and him. "Come on, you should sit down."

"No." Humiliation washed through her already weakened system. She'd been caught in her lowest and most private moment, stripped naked, without the strength to cover herself. She wanted only solitude, and the time to rebuild. "Please just leave me alone for a while."

It hurt—her resistance, her rejection of the comfort he needed to give. It hurt enough that he started to draw away. Then he felt the shudder pass through her, a shudder more poignant, more pitiful than even the tears. In silence he moved over and shut off the tap.

She'd uncovered her face to wrap her fingers around the lip of the sink. Her back was ramrod straight, as if she were braced to ward off a blow or a helping hand. Drenched, her eyes met his. Her skin was already streaked and reddened from tears. He didn't say a word, didn't think of the angles as he lifted her into his arms and carried her from the room.

He expected a struggle, some fierce and furious words. Instead her body went limp as she turned her face into his throat and let herself cry.

"He was just a child."

Ben sat on the edge of the bed and gathered her closer. The tears were hot on his skin, as if they had burned behind her eyes for too long. "I know."

"I couldn't reach him. I should have been able to. All the education, all the training, the self-analysis, the books and lectures, and I couldn't reach him."

"You tried."

"That's not good enough." The anger sprang out, full-blown and vicious, but it didn't surprise him. He'd been waiting for it, hoping for it. "I'm supposed to heal. I'm supposed to help, not just talk of helping. I didn't just fail to complete his treatment, I failed to keep him alive."

"Are psychiatrists required to have godlike egos?"

Like a slap in the face, his words jarred her away from him. In an instant she was on her feet. The tears were still drying on her face, her body still trembling, but she didn't look as though she would collapse. "How dare you say that to me? A young boy is dead. He'll never have a chance to drive a car, to fall in love, to start a family. He's dead, and the fact that I'm responsible hasn't anything to do with ego."

"Doesn't it?" Ben rose as well, and before she could turn away, took her shoulders. "You're supposed to be perfect, always in control, always having the answers, the solutions? This time you didn't have them and you weren't quite indestructible. You tell me, could you have stopped him from going to that bridge?"

"I should've been able to." The sob was dry and shaky as she pressed the heel of her hand between her brows. "No. No, I couldn't give him enough."

With his arm around her again, he drew her back to the bed. For the first time in their relationship he felt needed, leaned on. In the normal course of events it would have been his cue to make for the door. Instead he sat with her, taking her hand as her head rested on his shoulder. Complete. It was odd and a little frightening to feel complete.

"Tess, this is the boy you told me about before, isn't it?"

She remembered the night of her dream, the night she'd woken to find Ben warm, and willing to listen. "Yes. I've been worried about what he might do for weeks."

"And you told his parents?"

"Yes, I told them, but—"

"They didn't want to hear it."

"It shouldn't have made any difference. I should have been able to—" She broke off when he turned her face to his. "No," she said on a long breath, "they didn't want to hear it. His mother pulled him out of therapy."

"And cut the strings."

"It might have pushed him a bit further inward, but I don't think it was the final factor that drove him to suicide." The grief was still there, cold and hard in her stomach, but her mind was clearing enough for her to see past her own involvement. "I think something else happened tonight."

"And you think you know what it was?"

"Maybe." She rose again, unable to sit. "I've been trying to contact Joey's father for weeks. His phone's disconnected. I even went by his apartment a few days ago, but he'd moved without leaving a forwarding address. He was supposed to spend this weekend with Joey." Tess rubbed tears from her cheeks with the backs of her hands. "Joey had been counting on it, too heavily. When his father didn't come for him, it was another brick on his back. Maybe the last one he could carry. He was a beautiful boy, a young man really." Fresh tears started, but this time the grief loosened and came clean. "He'd had such a tough time, and yet there was this warmth just under the surface, this great need to be loved. He just didn't believe he deserved to have anyone really care about him."

"And you cared."

"Yes. Maybe too much."

It was strange, but the small, hard ball of resentment coated with a thin layer of bitterness that he'd carried in his gut since his brother's death began to break apart. He looked at her—the aloof, the objective psychiatrist, the poker and prodder of minds—and saw the real and human scars of grief, not just for the patient, but for the boy.

"Tess, what his mother said back at the hospital . . ."

"It doesn't matter."

"Yes, it does. She was wrong."

Tess turned away, and in the dim light from the hallway saw her own reflection in the mirror above her dresser. "Only partly. You see, I'll never know if I'd pushed in a different direction, tried another angle, whether it would have made a difference."

"She was wrong," Ben repeated. "A few years ago I said some of those same things. Maybe I was wrong too."

In the glass her gaze shifted and met his. He was still sitting on the bed, in the shadows. He looked alone. It was strange, because she had considered him a man constantly surrounded by friends, good feelings, his own self-confidence. She turned, but not certain he wanted her to reach out, remained where she was.

"I've never told you about Josh, my brother."

"No. You've never told me much about your family. I didn't know you had a brother."

"He was almost four years older than me." It didn't take the use of the past tense to tell her Josh was dead. She'd known it as soon as Ben had said the name. "He was one of those people who have gold on the ends of their fingers. No matter what he did, he did it better than anyone else. When we were kids we had this set of Tinker Toys. I'd built a little car, Josh would build a sixteen-wheeler. In school I'd maybe pull a B if I studied until my eyes dropped out. Josh would ace a test without opening a book. He just absorbed. My mother used to say he was blessed. She kept hoping he'd be a priest, because once he was ordained, he'd probably be able to perform miracles."

It wasn't said with the resentment many siblings might have felt, but with a trace of humor, and more than a little admiration.

"You must have loved him very much."

"Sometimes I hated him." It was said with a shrug, from a man who understood that hate was often the heat that tempered real love. "But mostly yes, I thought he was terrific. He never bullied me, not that he couldn't have. He was a hell of a lot bigger, but he just didn't have that kind of temperament. Not that he was holy or anything. He was good, just basically, deep down good.

"We shared a room when we were growing up. Once Mom found my stash of *Playboys*. She was prepared to whale the lust as well as the tar out of me. Josh told her they were his, that he was doing a report on pornography and its sociological effects on teenagers."

Unable to resist, Tess laughed. "And she bought it?"

"Yeah, she bought it." Even now, remembering made him grin. "Josh never lied to cover his own ass, only when he thought it was the best thing to do. In high school he was quarterback on the football team. The girls all but threw themselves on the ground in front of him. He was healthy enough to get some pleasure out of that, but he fell hard for one girl. It was like him to focus in on one instead of, well, picking the tree dry. Still, she was the one big mistake I ever thought he made. She was gorgeous, smart, and from one of the better families. She was also shallow. But he was crazy in love, and in his senior year he took his savings and bought her a diamond. Not just a little chip, but a real rock. She used to go around flashing it to make the other girls drool.

"They fought about something. He never would say what it was, but it was a real fallout. Josh had an academic scholarship to Notre Dame, but the day after graduation he enlisted in the Army. Kids were protesting 'Nam, smoking pot, and wearing peace signs, but Josh decided to give his country a few years of his time."

For the first time since he'd begun, Ben reached for and lit a cigarette. The tip glowed red in the shadowed light that fell over him. "My mother cried buckets, but my father was bust-button proud. His son wasn't a draft dodger or a pot-headed college student, but a real American. My father's a simple man, that's the way he thought. For myself, I leaned more toward the left. I'd be starting high school myself in the fall, so I figured I already knew about everything I needed to know. I spent an all-night session with Josh trying to talk him out of it. Of course, the papers were signed and it was too late, but I figured there must be a way out. I told him he was stupid to toss three years of his life away because of a girl. The trouble was, it had gone beyond that. As soon as Josh had enlisted, he'd decided he was going to be the best soldier in the United States Army. They'd already talked to him about Officer's Training. The way Johnson was escalating things over there, we needed smart, capable officers leading the troops. That's how Josh saw himself."

She heard it then, the splinter of pain that worked its way into his voice. Leaving the light for the shadows, Tess went to him. He hadn't realized he'd needed it, but when her hand touched his, Ben held on.

"So he went." He drew deep on his cigarette and let smoke out with a sigh. "He got on the bus, young, I guess you could say beautiful, idealistic, confident. From his letters it seemed he was thriving in Basic. It was the discipline, the challenge, the camaraderie. He made friends easily, and it wasn't any different there. He got his orders for 'Nam less than a year later. I was in high school bluffing my way through Algebra and finding out how many cheerleaders I could rack up. Josh shipped out a Second Lieutenant."

He lapsed into silence. Tess sat beside him, his hand in hers, waiting for him to go on.

"My mother went to church every day he was over there. She used to go in and light a candle then pray to the Blessed Virgin to intercede to her Son for Josh's safety. Every time she got a letter, she'd read it until she knew every word. But it didn't take long for the letters to change. They got shorter, the tone was different. He stopped mentioning his friends. We didn't know until later that two of his best buddies had been splattered all over the jungle. We didn't know that until he'd come back and started having nightmares. He didn't get killed over there. My mother must have lit enough candles for that, but he died. The part of him that made him what he was died. I need a drink."

Before he could rise, Tess put a hand to his arm. "I'll get it." She left him, and wanting to give him the time he needed, poured two warming brandies. When she went back in, he'd lit another cigarette, but hadn't moved.

"Thanks." He drank, and found that while the brandy didn't fill the hole grief had left, it no longer had to bypass that ball of bitterness. "Nobody was giving hero's welcomes back then. The war had turned sour. Josh came back with medals, commendations, and a time bomb in his head. It seemed okay for a while. He was quiet, withdrawn, but we figured nobody could come through that without some change. He moved back into the house, got a job. He didn't want to talk about going back to school. We all figured, well, he just needs some time.

"It took almost a year before the nightmares started. He'd wake up screaming and sweating. He lost his job. He told us he'd quit, but Dad found out he'd picked a fight and gotten himself fired. It took about another year before things really deteriorated. He couldn't keep a job for more than a few weeks. He started coming home drunk, or not coming home at all. The nightmares got violent. One night I tried to bring him out of one and he knocked me across the room. He started shouting about ambush and snipers. When I stood up and tried to calm him down, he came at me. When my father came in, Josh was strangling me."

"Oh, God, Ben."

"Dad managed to bring him out, and when he realized what he'd done, what he'd almost done, Josh just sat down on the floor and cried. I've never seen anyone cry like that. He couldn't stop. We took him to the V.A. They assigned him a psychiatrist."

The ash on his cigarette had grown long. Crushing it out, Ben went back to the brandy. "I was in college by then, so I'd drive him sometimes when I had a light afternoon schedule. I hated that office; it always made me think of a tomb. Josh would go in. Sometimes you could hear him crying. Other times you couldn't hear anything at all. Fifty minutes later he'd come out. I kept waiting for him to walk out that door one day and be the way I remembered."

"Sometimes it's as hard, even harder on the family, than it is on the one who's ill," Tess said, keeping her hand near his, letting him take or reject the contact. "You feel helpless when you want so badly to help . . . confused when you need so badly to think clearly."

"My mother broke down one day. It was a Sunday. She'd been fixing a pot roast. All of a sudden she just dumped it all in the sink. If it was cancer, she said, they'd find a way to cut it out of him. Can't they see what's inside him is eating him up? Why don't they find a way to cut it out of him?"

He stared down into his brandy, the image of his mother standing over the sink, sobbing, as clear as if it had happened yesterday.

"For a while he really seemed to get better. Because he was under psychiatric care and his job record was shaky, it was hard for him to find work. Our pastor applied a little pressure, some good old-fashioned Catholic guilt, and got him a job at a local gas station as a mechanic. He'd had a scholarship to Notre Dame five years before, and now he was changing spark plugs. Still, it was something. The nightmares slowed down. None of us knew he was eating barbiturates to keep them that way. Then it was heroin. That got by us too. Maybe if I'd been home more, but I was in college, and for the first time in my life serious about making it work. My parents were totally naive about drugs. It got by the doctor too. He was a major, regular Army, had done a tour of Korea and 'Nam, but he didn't see that Josh was pumping himself full of smack to get through the night."

Ben dragged a hand through his hair before he finished off the brandy. "I don't know, maybe the guy was overworked, or maybe he burned out. Anyway, the upshot was, after two years of therapy, after thousands of candles and prayers to the Blessed Virgin, Josh went up to his room, put on his combat fatigues and his medals, and instead of picking up his syringe, loaded his service revolver and ended it."

"Ben, saying I'm sorry isn't enough, isn't nearly enough, but there's nothing else I can say."

"He was only twenty-four."

And you'd have been only twenty, she thought, but rather than say it, put her arm around him.

"I thought about blaming the whole U.S. Army—better yet, the entire military system. I figured it made more sense to focus on the doctor who was supposed to be helping him. I remember sitting there when the police were upstairs, in the room I'd shared with Josh, and thinking that the bastard was supposed to do something. He was supposed to make him better. I even thought about killing him for a while, then the priest came and distracted me. He wouldn't give Josh last rites."

"I don't understand."

"It wasn't our pastor, but this young, straight-out-of-the-seminary rookie who turned green at the thought of going upstairs to Josh. He said Josh had willingly and knowingly taken his life, dying in mortal sin. He wouldn't give him absolution."

"That's wrong. Worse, it's cruel."

"I threw him out. My mother stood there, tight-lipped, dry-eyed, then she went up to the room where her son's brains were splattered on the wall and she prayed for his absolution herself."

"Your mother's strong. She must have tremendous faith."

"All she'd ever done was cook." He drew Tess closer, needing the soft, feminine scent. "I don't know if I could have walked up those stairs a second time, but she did. When I watched her do that, I realized that no matter how much she hurt, no matter how much she'd grieve, she believed and would always believe that what happened to Josh was God's will."

"But you didn't."

"No. It had to be someone's fault. Josh had never hurt anyone in his life, not until 'Nam. Then what he'd done there was supposed to be right because he was fighting for his country. But it wasn't right, and he couldn't live with it anymore. The psychiatrist was supposed to show him that no matter what he'd done over there, he was still decent, still worthwhile."

As she had been supposed to show Joey Higgins he was worthwhile. "Did you ever talk to Josh's doctor afterward?"

"Once. I think I still had it in my head I should kill him. He sat there behind his desk, with his hands folded." Ben looked down at his own, watching them curl into fists. "He didn't feel anything. He said he was sorry, explained how extreme Delayed Stress Syndrome could be. Then he told me, while he kept his hands folded on the desk and his voice just two shades away from being involved, that Josh hadn't been able to cope with what had happened in 'Nam, that coming home and trying to live up to what he'd been before had created more and more pressure, until finally the lid had blown off."

"I'm sorry, Ben. Probably a great deal of what he told you was true, but he could have done it in a different way."

"It could have meant a damn to him."

"Ben, I'm not defending him, but a lot of doctors, medical or psychiatric, hold themselves back, don't let themselves in too close, because when you lose someone, when you aren't able to save them, it hurts too much."

"The way losing Joey hurt you."

"That kind of grief and guilt rips at you, and if it rips at you too often, there's nothing left, not for you or for the next patient."

Maybe he understood that, or was beginning to. But he couldn't see Josh's regular Army shrink closing himself in the bathroom and sobbing. "Why do you do it?"

"I guess I have to look for answers, the same way you do." Turning, she touched his face. "It does hurt when it's too little, or too late." She remembered how he'd looked when he'd told her about three strangers who'd been murdered for a handful of coins. "We're not as different as I once thought."

He turned his lips into her palm, comforted by it. "Maybe not. When I saw you tonight, I felt the same way I did when I saw you looking at Anne Reasoner in that alley. You seemed so detached from the tragedy of it, so completely in control. Just the way that major had been, with his hands folded on the desk, telling me why my brother was dead."

"Being in control isn't the same as being detached. You're a cop, you have to know the difference."

"I wanted to know you felt something." Sliding his hand down to her wrist, he held it firm while he looked into her eyes. "I guess what I really wanted was for you to need me." And that was perhaps one of the most difficult confessions of his life. "Then, when I walked into the bathroom and saw you crying, I knew you did, and it scared the hell out of me."

"I didn't want you to see me like that."

"Why?"

"Because I didn't trust you enough."

He dropped his gaze long enough to study his hand over her slender, impossibly delicate wrist. "I've never told anyone but Ed about Josh. Until now, he's the only one I've trusted enough." He brought her fingers to his lips, brushing them lightly. "So what happens now?"

"What do you want to happen?"

A laugh, even when quiet and reluctant, can be cleansing. "Psychiatrist's cop-out." Thoughtfully, he fingered the pearls around her neck. He unhooked them. Her throat was fragrant and silky. "Tess, when this is over, if I asked you to take off for a few days, a week, and go somewhere with me, would you?"

"Yes."

Amused, and more than a little surprised, he looked at her. "Just like that?"

"I might ask where when the time comes, so I'd know whether to pack a fur coat or a bikini." She took the pearls from him to set them on the bedside table.

"They should be in a safe."

"I'm sleeping with a cop." Her voice was light, but she saw him brooding and thought she understood where his thoughts had taken him. "Ben, it will be over soon."

"Yeah." But when he brought her close, when he began to fill himself with her, he was afraid.

It was November twenty-eighth.

Chapter 18

"You don't step foot out of the apartment until I give you the okay."

"Absolutely not," Tess agreed while Ben watched her pin up her hair. "I have enough work at home to keep me chained to my desk all day."

"You don't even take out the garbage."

"Not even if the neighbors write up a petition."

"Tess, I want you to take this seriously."

"I am taking it seriously." She chose ribbed gold triangles and clipped them to her ears. "I'm not going to be alone for a minute today. Officer Pilomento will be here at eight."

Ben looked at the dove-gray slacks and soft, cowl-necked sweater she wore. "Is that who you're getting all dressed up for?"

"Of course." When he came to stand behind her, she smiled at their twin reflections. "I've developed a penchant for the police lately. It has all the earmarks of becoming an obsession."

"Is that right?" He bent to brush his lips over the back of her neck.

"I'm afraid so."

He dropped his hands to her shoulders, wanting to remain close, touching. "Worried about it?"

"No." Still smiling, she turned into his arms. "I'm not worried a bit. Not about that or anything else." Because there was a frown between his brows, Tess lifted a finger to smooth it away. "I wish you weren't."

"It's my job to worry." For a moment he just held her, knowing it was going to be hard, unreasonably hard, to walk out the door that morning and trust her to someone else's care. "Pilomento's a good man," he told her, as much to appease himself as her. "He's young but he's by-the-book. Nobody's going to get in the door while he's here."

"I know. Come on, let's have some coffee. You've only got a few more minutes."

"Lowenstein relieves him at four." As they walked into the kitchen, he ran over the schedule, though they both knew every move. "She's the best. She might look like a nice suburban wife, but there's nobody I'd rather have backing me up in a hairy situation."

"I won't be alone at all." Tess took down two mugs. "Cops will still be taking shifts on the third floor, the phone's wired, there'll be a unit parked across the street at all times."

"It won't be a black and white. If he makes his move, we don't want to scare him off. Bigsby, Roderick, and Mullendore will switch off with Ed and me on surveillance."

"Ben, I'm not worried." After handing him his coffee, she took his arm to walk to the dining room table. "I've thought this through. Believe me, I've thought this through. Nothing can happen to me as long as I'm inside and inaccessible."

"He won't know you're being guarded. When I return at midnight, I'll come in the back and use the stairs."

"He has to make his move tonight, that I'm sure of. When he does, you'll be there."

"I appreciate the confidence, but I tell you I'd feel a little less edgy if you were a little more so. Look, no grandstanding." He took her arm for emphasis, before she could lift the coffee. "When we've got him, he goes back to the station for interrogation, you don't."

"Ben, you know how important it is to me to talk to him, to try to get through."

"No."

"You can only block me on this so long."

"As long as it takes."

Tess backed off and tried another tack, one that had woken her in the early hours and kept her awake. "Ben, I think you understand this man better than you know. You know what it is to lose someone who's an intricate part of your life. You lost Josh, he lost his Laura. We don't know who she was, but we can be sure that she mattered a great deal to him. You told me that when you lost Josh, you considered killing his doctor. Wait," she said before he could speak. "You wanted to blame someone, to hurt someone. If you hadn't been a strong man emotionally, you might very well have done so. Still, the resentment and the pain stayed with you."

The words, and the truth behind them, made him uncomfortable. "Maybe they did, but I didn't start killing people."

"No, you became a cop. Maybe part of the reason you did was because of Josh, because you needed to find answers, to make things right. You're healthy, self-confident, and were able to turn what might have been the biggest tragedy in your life into something constructive. But if you weren't healthy, Ben, if you didn't have a strong self-image, a strong sense of right and wrong, something might have cracked inside you. When Josh died you lost your faith. I think he lost his over Laura.

We don't know how long ago it might have been—a year, five years, twenty—but he's picked up the pieces of his faith and put them back together. Only the pieces aren't fitting true; the edges are jagged. He kills, sacrifices to save Laura. Laura's soul. What you told me last night made me wonder. Perhaps she died in what the Church considers mortal sin and was refused absolution. He's been taught all of his life to believe that without absolution, the soul is lost. In his psychosis he murders, sacrifices women who remind him of Laura. But he still saves their souls."

"Everything you say may be right. None of it changes the fact that he's killed four women and is aiming for you."

"Black and white, Ben?"

"Sometimes that's all there is." It frustrated him more because he was beginning to understand, even to feel some of what she was saying. He wanted to continue to look at it straight-on, without any angles. "Don't you believe that some people are just born evil? Does a man tell his wife he's going out to hunt humans then drive to the local McDonald's and shoot kids because his mother beat him when he was six? Does a man use a college campus for target practice because his father cheated on his mother?"

"No, but this man isn't the kind of mass murderer you're talking about." She was on her own ground here and knew her steps. "He isn't killing randomly and motivelessly. An abused child is as likely to become a bank president as a psychotic. And neither do I believe in the bad seed. We're talking about an illness, Ben, something more and more doctors are coming to believe is caused by a chemical reaction in the brain that destroys rational thought. We've come a long way since the days of demon possession, but even sixty years ago schizophrenia was treated by tooth extraction. Then it was injections of horse serum, enemas. And in the last quarter of the twentieth century, we're still groping. Whatever triggered his psychosis, he needs help. The way Josh did. The way Joey did."

"Not for the first twenty-four hours," he said flatly. "And not until the paperwork clears. He might not want to see you."

"I've thought of that, but I believe he will."

"None of this matters until we get him."

When the knock came, Ben's hand reached slowly for his weapon. His arm was still stiff, but usable. He'd have no problem holding his Police Special. He moved toward the door, but stood beside it. "You ask who it is." As she started to move forward, he held up a hand. "No, ask from over there. You don't stand in front of the door." Though he doubted the means would change from amice to bullet, he wasn't taking chances.

"Who is it?"

"Detective Pilomento, ma'am."

Recognizing the voice, Ben turned and pulled the door open.

"Paris." Pilomento knocked snow from his shoes before he stepped inside. "The roads are still a mess. We got about six inches. Morning, Dr. Court."

"Good morning. Let me take your coat."

"Thanks. Freezing out there," he said to Ben. "Mullendore's in position out front. Hope he wore his long underwear."

"Don't get too comfortable watching game shows." Ben reached for his own coat as he took a last look around the room. There was only one entrance, and Pilomento would never be more than about twenty-five feet from her. Still, even as he bundled into his coat, he didn't feel warm. "I'll be in periodic contact with the surveillance teams. Now, why don't you go into the kitchen and pour yourself some coffee?"

"Thanks. I just had one in the car on the way over."

"Have another."

"Oh." He looked from Ben to Tess. "Yeah, sure." Whistling between his teeth, he walked off.

"That was rude, but I don't mind." With a low laugh Tess slipped her arms around Ben's waist. "Be careful."

"I make a habit of it. See that you do."

He drew her close, and the kiss was long and lingering. "You going to wait up for me, Doc?"

"Count on it. You'll call if . . . well, if anything happens?"

"Count on it." Taking her face in his hands, he held it a moment, then pressed a kiss to her forehead. "You're so lovely." It was the quick surprise in her eyes that made him realize that he hadn't made use of all his clever and slick compliments with her as he had with other women. The realization caught him off balance. To cover it, he tucked her hair behind her ear, then backed away. "Lock the door."

He pulled it shut behind him, wishing he could shake the uneasy feeling that things weren't going to go as neatly as planned.

HOURS later he was huddled inside the Mustang, watching Tess's building. Two kids were putting the finishing touches on an elaborate snowman. Ben wondered if their father knew they'd copped his fedora. The day had gone even slower than he'd imagined.

"Days're getting shorter," Ed commented. Sprawled in the passenger's seat, he was warm as a bear in a union suit, corduroys, flannel shirt, sweater, and an L.L. Bean parka. The cold had long since numbed its way through Ben's boots.

"There's Pilomento."

The detective came out of the building, paused only

a heartbeat on the sidewalk, and flipped up the collar of his coat. It was the signal that Lowenstein was inside and things were tight. Ben's muscles relaxed only fractionally.

"She's fine, you know." Ed stretched a bit and began isometric exercises to keep his legs from cramping. "Lowenstein's mean enough to hold off an army."

"He isn't going to move until dark." Because his face froze if he cracked the window for too long, Ben substituted a Milky Way for the cigarette he wanted.

"You know what that sugar's doing to the enamel of your teeth?" Never one to give up the battle, Ed drew out a small plastic container. Inside was a homemade snack of raisins, dates, unsalted nuts, and wheat germ. He'd made enough for two. "You gotta start reeducating your appetite."

Ben took a large, deliberate bite of his candy bar. "When Roderick relieves us, we're stopping by the Burger King on the way in. I'm getting a Whopper."

"Please, not while I'm eating. If Roderick, Bigsby, and half the station had a proper diet, they wouldn't have been down with the flu."

"I didn't get sick," Ben said over a mouthful of chocolate.

"Blind luck. By the time you hit forty, your system's going to revolt. It won't be pretty. What's this?" Ed sat up straight as he watched the man across the street. His long black coat was buttoned high. He walked slowly. Too slowly, too cautiously.

Both detectives had one hand on their weapons and one on the door handles when the man suddenly broke into a run. Ben had already pushed the car door open when the man scooped up one of the little girls playing in the snow and tossed her high. She let out a quick, ringing laugh, and called out, "Daddy!"

As the breath pushed out of his body, Ben sat back

down. Feeling foolish, he turned to Ed. "You're as jumpy as I am."

"I like her. I'm glad you decided to risk eating turkey with her granddaddy."

"I told her about Josh."

Ed's brows lifted, disappearing into the seaman's cap he'd pulled over his head. That, he knew, was more of a commitment than even he'd believed Ben could make. "And?"

"And I guess I'm glad I did. She's the best thing that's happened in my life. God, that sounds corny."

"Yeah." Content, Ed began to munch a date. "People in love tend to be corny."

"I didn't say I was in love." That came out quickly, the reflex action on the trap door. "I just mean she's special."

"Certain people have difficulty admitting to emotional commitment because they fear failing in the long haul. The word *love* becomes a stumbling block that once uttered is like a lock, blocking off their privacy, their singleness, and obliging them to perceive themselves as one half of a couple."

Ben tossed the candy wrapper on the floor. "*Redbook?*"

"No, I made it up. Maybe I should write an article."

"Look, if I was in love with Tess, with anybody, I wouldn't have any trouble saying it."

"So? Are you?"

"I care about her. A lot."

"Euphemism."

"She's important to me."

"Evasions."

"Okay, I'm crazy about her."

"Not quite there, Paris."

This time he did crack the window and pull out a cigarette. "All right, so I'm in love with her. Happy now?"

"Have a date. You'll feel better."

He swore, then heard himself laugh. Tossing out the cigarette, he bit into the date Ed handed him. "You're worse than my mother."

"That's what partners are for."

❧

INSIDE Tess's apartment time went just as slowly. At seven she and Lowenstein shared a supper of canned soup and roast beef sandwiches. For all her talk about not being worried, Tess managed to do little more than stir the chunks of beef and vegetables around in her bowl. It was a cold, miserable night. No one who didn't have to would want to be out in it. But the fact that she couldn't move beyond her own door left her with a feeling of being caged.

"You play canasta?" Lowenstein asked.

"I'm sorry, what?"

"Canasta." Lowenstein glanced at her own watch and figured her husband would be giving their youngest a bath. Roderick would be in position out front, Ben and Ed would be sweeping the area before they returned to the station, and her oldest daughter would be complaining about being stuck with the dishes.

"I'm being lousy company."

Lowenstein set half a sandwich back on the pale green glass plate she'd admired. "You're not supposed to entertain me, Dr. Court."

But Tess pushed her plate aside and made the effort. "You have a family, don't you?"

"A mob, actually."

"It's not easy, is it, managing a demanding career and taking care of a family?"

"I've always thrived on complications."

"I admire that. I've always avoided them. Can I ask you a personal question?"

"Okay, if I can ask you one afterward."

"Fair enough." With her elbows on the table, Tess leaned forward. "Does your husband find it difficult being married to someone whose job is not only demanding, but potentially dangerous?"

"I guess it's not easy. I know it's not," Lowenstein corrected. She took a pull from the Diet Pepsi Tess had served in thin, scrolled glasses Lowenstein would have kept on display. "We've had to work through a lot of it. A couple of years ago we had a trial separation. It lasted thirty-four-and-a-half hours. The bottom line is, we're nuts about each other. That usually cuts through everything else."

"You're lucky."

"I know. Even when I feel like pushing his head in the toilet, I know. My turn."

"All right."

Lowenstein gave her a long, measuring look. "Where do you get your clothes?"

She was only too surprised to laugh for a few seconds. For the first time all day, Tess relaxed.

OUTSIDE, Roderick and a stocky black detective known as Pudge shared a thermos of coffee. A bit cranky with a head cold, Pudge shifted every few minutes and complained.

"I don't think we're going to see a sign of this dude. Mullendore's got the late shift. If anyone makes the collar, it'll be him. We'll just sit here freezing our asses off."

"It has to be tonight." Roderick poured Pudge another cup of coffee before going back to study Tess's windows.

"Why?" Pudge let out a huge yawn and cursed the antihistamines that left his nose and his mind clogged.

"Because it was meant to be tonight."

"Christ, Roderick, no matter what shit-shoveling duty you pull, you never complain." On another yawn, Pudge slumped against the door. "God, I can hardly keep my eyes open. Goddamn medication whips you."

Roderick took another sweep of the street, up, then down. No one stirred. "Why don't you sleep awhile? I'll watch."

" 'Preciate it." Already half there, Pudge closed his eyes. "Just give me ten, Lou. Mullendore takes it in an hour anyway."

With his partner snoring lightly, Roderick kept watch.

TESS was learning the fine points of canasta from Lowenstein when the phone rang. The relaxed girl talk ended with a snap. "Okay, you answer it. If it's him, keep calm. Stall if you can, agree to meet him if you have to. See if you can pin him down to a location."

"All right." Though her throat dried up, Tess picked up the receiver and spoke naturally. "Dr. Court."

"Doctor, this is Detective Roderick."

"Oh, Detective." Her muscles went limp as she turned and shook her head at Lowenstein. "Yes? Is there any news?"

"We've got him, Dr. Court. Ben picked him up less than two blocks from your building."

"Ben? Is he all right?"

"Yes, don't worry. It's nothing serious. He wrenched his shoulder some during the arrest. He asked me to call you and let you know you can relax. Ed's taking him to the hospital."

"Hospital." She remembered the tray with the blood-soaked bandages. "Which one? I want to go."

"He's being taken to Georgetown, Doctor, but he didn't want you to bother."

"No, it's no bother. I'll leave right away." Remembering the woman breathing down her neck, Tess turned to Lowenstein. "You should talk to Detective Lowenstein. I appreciate you calling."

"We're all just glad it's over."

"Yes." She squeezed her eyes shut a moment, then handed the phone to Lowenstein. "He's been caught." Then she dashed into the bedroom for her purse and car keys. When she hurried back in for her coat, Lowenstein was still pulling details out of Roderick. Impatient, Tess tossed her coat over her arm and waited.

"Sounds like a clean collar," Lowenstein said when she hung up. "Ben and Ed decided to do a few more sweeps of the area and saw this guy come out of an alley and head toward your building. He had his coat open. They could see he was wearing a cassock. He didn't protest when they stopped him, but when Ben found the amice in his pocket, he apparently lost it, started fighting and calling for you."

"Oh, God." She wanted to see him, talk to him. But Ben was on his way to the hospital, and Ben came first.

"Lou said Ben got a little banged up, doesn't sound serious."

"I'll feel better when I see for myself."

"I know what you mean. Do you want me to take you to the hospital?"

"No, I'm sure you want to get back to the station and tie up the loose ends. It doesn't look as though I need police protection any longer."

"No, but I'll walk you down to your car anyway. Tell Ben I said good work."

As Ben crossed the parking lot to the station house, Logan pulled in behind him and hurried out of his car.

"Ben." Hatless, gloveless, dressed as he rarely was in a cassock, he caught up with them on the steps. "I was hoping I'd find you here."

"Not a good night for priests to go walking around, Tim. We got a lot of nervous cops out tonight. You could find yourself cuffed."

"I was saying late Mass for the sisters and didn't have time to change. I think I have something."

"Inside," Ed said, pushing open the door. "Your fingers are going to fall off."

"I was in such a hurry." Absently, Logan began to rub his fingers together for warmth. "For days I've been going over everything. I knew you were fixed on the use of the name Reverend Francis Moore and were checking it out, but I couldn't get my mind off the Frank Moore I'd known at the seminary."

"We're still digging there." Impatient, Ben looked at his watch.

"I know, but I was with him, you see, I knew that he bordered between being a saint and a fanatic. Then I remembered a seminarian who'd been under him and had left after a celebrated row with Moore. I remembered him because the young man had gone on to become a well-known writer. Stephen Mathias."

"I've heard of him." As excitement began to drum, Ben edged closer. "You think Mathias—"

"No, no." Frustrated by his inability to speak quickly or coherently enough, Logan took a deep breath. "I didn't even know Mathias personally, since I was already established in the university when all that went on. But I remembered the gossip that there was nothing, and no one, Mathias didn't know about in the seminary. In fact, he used plenty of inside stuff for his first couple of books. The more I thought about that, the more things clicked. And I remembered reading one novel in particular that mentioned a young student who had suffered a breakdown and had left the seminary after his sister—his twin sister—had died as the result of an illegal abortion. Apparently there was a tremendous scandal. It was discovered that the boy's mother was confined to an institution and that he had been treated himself for schizophrenia."

"Let's track down Mathias." Ben was already heading down the hall when Logan stopped him.

"I've already done that. It only took me a few calls to locate him.. He's living in Connecticut, and he remembered the incident perfectly. The seminarian had been unusually devout, as devout to Moore as he was to the Church. In fact, he served as his secretary. Mathias said his name was Louis Roderick."

It was possible for the blood to freeze, for the heart to stop pumping, and for the body to remain alive. "Are you sure?"

"Yes, Mathias was positive, but when I asked, he went back through his old notes and checked on it. He's willing to come down and give you a description. With that and a name, you should be able to find him."

"I know where he is." Ben spun around into the squad room and grabbed the first phone he reached.

"You know him?" Logan grabbed on to Ed before he lost him as well.

"He's a cop. He's one of us, and right now he's heading up the outside surveillance on Tess's building."

"Sweet God." As the room in front of him humped into action, Logan began to pray.

Units were dispatched to Roderick's address, others to back up Tess's apartment. Logan was on Ben's heels as they headed to the door. "I want to go with you."

"This is police business."

"Seeing a priest might calm him."

"Don't get in the way." They hit the glass door and nearly ran over Lowenstein.

"What the hell's going on here?"

Half wild with fear, Ben caught her by the collar of her coat. "Why aren't you with her? Why did you leave her alone?"

"What's wrong with you? Once Lou called to verify it had gone down, there was no reason for me to hang around."

"When did he call?"

"Twenty minutes ago. But he said you were on your way—" Though her mind rejected it, the expression on Ben's face told her everything. "Oh, God, not Lou? But he's—" A cop. A friend. Lowenstein kicked herself back. "He called twenty minutes ago, telling me there had been a clean arrest and to pull off the guard and come in. I never questioned it. God, Ben, I never thought to verify with headquarters. It was Lou."

"We've got to find him."

She grabbed Ben's arm before he could push past her. "Georgetown Hospital. He told her you'd been taken to Emergency."

Nothing else was needed to have him streaking down the steps to his car.

TESS pulled up in the parking lot after a frustrating twenty-minute drive. The roads were all but clear, but that hadn't stopped the fender benders. She told herself the good part was that Ben was already fixed up and waiting. And it was over.

Slamming her door, she dropped her keys into her pocket. On the way home they were going to pick up a bottle of champagne. Two bottles, she corrected. Then they were going to spend the rest of the weekend in bed drinking them.

The idea was so pleasant, she didn't notice the figure melt out of the shadows and into the light.

"Dr. Court."

Alarm came first, with her hand flying up to her throat. Then, with a laugh, she lowered it and started forward. "Detective Roderick, I didn't know you'd—"

The light glinted on the white clerical collar at his throat. It was like the dream, she thought in a moment of blank panic, when she'd thought herself only a step away from safety only to find her worst fears confirmed. She knew she could turn and run, but he was only an arm's span away and would catch her. She knew she could scream, but she had no doubt he'd silence her. Completely. There was only one choice. To face him.

"You wanted to talk to me." No, it wouldn't work, she thought desperately. Not if her voice was shaking, not when her head was filled with the rushing echo of her own fear. "I've wanted to talk to you too. I've wanted to help you."

"Once I thought you could. You had kind eyes. When I read your reports, I knew you understood I wasn't a murderer. Then I knew you'd been sent to me. You'd be the last one, the most important one. You were the only one the Voice said by name."

"Tell me about the voice, Lou." She wanted to back up, just edge back one foot, but saw by his eyes that even that small movement would trigger the violence. "When did you first hear it?"

"When I was a boy. They said I was crazy, like my mother. I was afraid, so I blocked it out. Later I realized it was a call from God, calling me to the priesthood. I was happy to be chosen. Father Moore said only a few are chosen to carry out the Lord's work, to celebrate the sacraments. But even the chosen are tempted to sin. Even the chosen are weak, so we sacrifice, we do penance. He taught me how to train my body to fight off temptation. Flagellation, fasting."

And one more piece to the puzzle fell into place. An emotionally disturbed boy enters the seminary, to be trained by an emotionally disturbed man. He would kill her. Following the path he saw laid out for him, he would kill her. The parking lot was all but empty, the doors of the Emergency Room two hundred yards away. "How did you feel about becoming a priest, Lou?"

"It was everything. My whole life was formed, do you understand? Formed. For that purpose."

"But you left it."

"No." He lifted his head as if scenting the air, as if listening to something only for his ears. "That was like a blank spot in my life. I didn't really exist then. A man can't exist without faith. A priest can't exist without purpose."

She saw him reach in his pocket, saw the snatch of white in his hand. Her eyes were almost as wild as his when they met again. "Tell me about Laura."

He'd come a step closer, but the name stopped him. "Laura. Did you know Laura?"

"No, I didn't know her." He had the amice in both hands now, but seemed to have forgotten it. Treat, she told herself to hold back a scream. Treat, talk, listen. "Tell me about her."

"She was beautiful. Beautiful in that fragile way that makes you worry if such things can last. My mother worried because Laura enjoyed looking at herself in the mirror, brushing her hair, wearing pretty clothes. Mother could sense the Devil drawing, always drawing Laura into sin and bad thoughts. But Laura only laughed and said she didn't care for sackcloth and ashes. Laura laughed a lot."

"You loved her very much."

"We were twins. We shared life before life. That's what my mother said. We were bound together by God.

It was for me to keep Laura from spurning the Church and everything we'd been taught. It was for me, but I failed her."

"How did you fail Laura?"

"She was only eighteen. Beautiful, delicate, but there wasn't any laughter." The tears began, sobless, to glisten on his cheeks. "She'd been weak. I hadn't been there for her, and she'd been weak. Back-street abortion. God's judgment. But why did God's judgment have to be so harsh?" His breathing quickened and became painfully loud as he pressed a hand to his forehead. "A life for a life. It's fair and just. A life for a life. She begged me not to let her die, not to let her die in such sin that would send her to Hell. I had no power to absolve her. Even as she lay dying in my arms, I had no power. The power came later, after the despair, the dark, blank time. I can show you. I have to show you."

He stepped forward, and even as Tess's instincts had her pull back, he slipped the scarf around her. "Lou, you're a police officer. It's your job, your function to protect."

"Protect." His fingers trembled on the scarf. A policeman. He'd had to drug Pudge's coffee. It would have been wrong to do more, to hurt another officer. Protect. The shepherd protects his flock. "I didn't protect Laura."

"No, it was a terrible loss, a tragedy. But now you've tried to give something back, haven't you? Isn't that why you became a police officer? To give something back? To protect others?"

"I had to lie, but after Laura it didn't seem to matter. Maybe with the police I could find what I'd been looking for in the seminary. That sense of purpose. Vocation. Man's law, not God's law."

"Yes, you swore to uphold the law."

"The Voice came back, so many years later. It was real."

"Yes, to you it was real."

"It isn't always inside my head. Sometimes it's a whisper in the other room, or it comes like thunder from the ceiling over my bed. It told me how to save Laura, and myself. We're bound together. We've always been bound together."

Her hands clenched over the keys in her pocket. She knew if the scarf tightened, she would use them to gouge his eyes. For survival. The need to live surged through her.

"I will absolve you from sin," he murmured. "And you will see God."

"Taking a life is a sin."

He hesitated. "A life for a life. A holy sacrifice." The pain rushed through his voice.

"Taking a life is a sin," she repeated as the blood pounded in her ears. "To kill breaks God's law, and man's. You understand both laws as a police officer, as a priest." When she heard the siren, her first thought was that it was an ambulance coming into Emergency. She wouldn't be alone. She didn't take her eyes from his. "I can help you."

"Help me." It was only a whisper, part question, part plea.

"Yes." Though it trembled, she lifted her hand and placed it on his. Her fingers brushed over the silk.

Doors slammed behind them, but neither of them moved.

"Get your hands off her, Roderick. Take your hands off her and move aside."

Keeping her fingers around Roderick's, Tess turned to see Ben no more than ten feet behind them, spread-legged, his gun held in both hands. Beside him and to the left, Ed mirrored his position. Sirens still screamed and lights flashed as cars poured into the lot.

"Ben, I'm not hurt."

But he didn't look at her. His eyes never left Roderick, and in them she saw that core of violence he strapped down. She knew if she stepped aside now, he'd cut it loose.

"Ben, I said I'm not hurt. He wants help."

"Move out of the way." If he'd been certain Roderick wasn't armed, he would have rushed forward. But Tess turned her body and used it as a shield.

"It's over, Ben."

After a quick hand signal, Ed walked forward. "I have to search you, Lou. Then I have to cuff you and take you in."

"Yes." Dazed and docile, he lifted his arms to make it simpler. "That's the law. Doctor?"

"Yes. No one's going to hurt you."

"You have the right to remain silent," Ed began when he'd removed Roderick's police issue from under his coat.

"That's all right, I understand." As Ed snapped on the handcuffs, Roderick's attention focused on Logan.

"Father, did you come to hear my confession?"

"Yes. Would you like me to go with you?" As he spoke, Logan put his hand over Tess's and squeezed.

"Yes. I'm so tired."

"You can rest soon. Come with us now, and I'll stay with you."

With his head bowed, he began to walk between Ed and Logan. "Bless me, Father, for I have sinned."

Ben waited until they'd passed him. Tess stood where she was, watching him, not certain her legs would carry her if she moved forward. She saw him holster his gun before he was across the pavement to her in three strides.

"I'm all right, I'm all right," she repeated over and over as he crushed her against him. "He wasn't going to go through with it. He couldn't."

Ben only drew her away to yank the scarf from

around her and toss it in a mound of snow. He ran his own hands over her throat to make certain it was unmarked. "I could have lost you."

"No." She pressed herself against him again. "He knew. I think he knew all along I could stop him." As tears of relief began, she tightened her arms around him. "The trouble was, I didn't. Ben, I've never been so frightened."

"You stood between us and blocked me."

Sniffling, she drew away only far enough to find his lips with hers. "Protecting a patient."

"He's not your patient."

She had to take the chance that her legs would hold her a few minutes longer. Stepping back, she faced him. "Yes, he is. And as soon as the paperwork clears, I'll start tests."

He grabbed her by the front of her coat, but when she touched a hand to his face, he could only drop his forehead on hers. "Damn you, I'm shaking."

"Me too."

"Let's go home."

"Oh, yeah."

With arms hooked tight around waists, they walked to the car. She noticed, but didn't comment, that he'd run over the curb. Inside the car she huddled against him again. No one had ever been so solid or so warm.

"He was a cop."

"He's ill." Tess linked her fingers with his.

"He's been one step ahead of us all along."

"He's been suffering." She closed her eyes a moment. She was alive. This time she hadn't failed. "I'm going to be able to help him."

For a moment he said nothing. He would have to live with this, her need to give herself to people. Maybe someday he'd come to believe that both the sword and words could bring about justice.

"Hey, Doc?"

"Mmmm?"

"Do you remember talking about us getting away for a few days?"

"Yes." Sighing, she imagined an island with palm trees and fat orange flowers. "Oh, yes."

"I've got some time coming."

"How soon do you want me packed?"

He laughed, but continued to jiggle the keys nervously in his hand. "I was thinking we could go down to Florida for a while. I want you to meet my mother."

Slowly, not wanting to take a leap when a step was indicated, she lifted her head from his shoulder to look at him. Then he smiled, and his smile told her everything she needed to know.

"I'd love to meet your mother."

NEW YORK TIMES BESTSELLING AUTHOR OF THREE FATES
NORA
ROBERTS
BRAZEN
VIRTUE
BANTAM BOOKS
"Roberts is indeed a word artist, painting her story and characters with vitality and verve." —Daily News of Los Angeles

BRAZEN VIRTUE

on sale now

GRACE HEARD THE low, droning buzz and blamed it on the wine. She didn't groan or grumble about the hangover. She'd been taught that every sin, venial or mortal, required penance. It was one of the few aspects of her early Catholic training she carried with her into adulthood.

The sun was up and strong enough to filter through the gauzy curtains at the windows. In defense, she buried her face in the pillow. She managed to block out the light, but not the buzzing. She was awake, and hating it.

Thinking of aspirin and coffee, she pushed herself up in bed. It was then she realized the buzzing wasn't inside her head, but outside the house. She rummaged through one of her bags and came up with a ratty terry-cloth robe. In her closet at home was a silk one, a gift from a former lover. Grace had fond memories of the lover, but preferred the terry-cloth robe. Still groggy, she stumbled to the window and pushed the curtain aside.

It was a beautiful day, cool and smelling just faintly of spring and turned earth. There was a sagging chain-link fence separating her sister's yard from the yard next door. Tangled and pitiful against it was a forsythia bush. It was struggling to bloom, and Grace thought its tiny yellow flowers looked brave and daring. It hadn't occurred to her until then how tired she was of hothouse flowers and perfect petals. On a huge yawn, she looked beyond it.

She saw him then, in the backyard of the house next door. Long narrow boards were braced on sawhorses. With the kind of easy competence she admired, he measured and marked and cut through. Intrigued, Grace shoved the window up to get a better look. The morning air was chill, but she leaned into it, pleased that it cleared her head. Like the forsythia, he was something to see.

Paul Bunyan, she thought, and grinned. The man had to be six-four if he was an inch and built along the lines of a fullback. Even with the distance she could see the power of his muscles moving under his jacket. He had a mane of red hair and a full beard—not a trimmed little affectation, but the real thing. She could just see his mouth move in its cushion in time to the country music that jingled out of a portable radio.

When the buzzing stopped, she was smiling down at him, her elbows resting on the sill. "Hi," she called. Her smile widened as he turned and looked up. She'd noticed that his body had braced as he'd turned, not so much in surprise, she thought, but in readiness. "I like your house."

Ed relaxed as he saw the woman in the window. He'd put in over sixty hours that week, and had killed a man. The sight of a pretty woman smiling at him from a second-story window did a lot to soothe his worn nerves. "Thanks."

"You fixing it up?"

"Bit by bit." He shaded his eyes against the sun and studied her. She wasn't his neighbor. Though he and Kathleen Breezewood hadn't exchanged more than a dozen words, he knew her by sight. But there was something familiar in the grinning face and tousled hair. "You visiting?"

"Yes, Kathy's my sister. I guess she's gone already. She teaches."

"Oh." He'd learned more about his neighbor in two seconds than he had in two months. Her nickname was Kathy, she had a sister, and she was a teacher. Ed hefted another board onto the horses. "Staying long?"

"I'm not sure." She leaned out a bit farther so the breeze ruffled her hair. It was a small indulgence the pace and convenience of New York had denied her. "Did you plant the azaleas out front?"

"Yeah. Last week."

"They're terrific. I think I'll put some in for Kath." She smiled again. "See you." She pulled her head inside and was gone.

For a minute longer Ed stared at the empty window. She'd left it open, he noted, and the temperature had yet to climb to sixty. He took out his carpenter's pencil to mark the wood. He knew that face. It was both a matter of business and personality that he never forgot one. It would come to him.

Inside, Grace pulled on a pair of sweats. Her hair was still damp from the shower, but she wasn't in the mood to fuss with blow dryers and styling brushes. There was coffee to be drunk, a paper to be read, and a murder to be solved. By her calculations, she could put Maxwell to work and have enough carved out to be satisfied before Kathleen returned from Our Lady of Hope.

Downstairs, she put on the coffee, then checked out the contents of the refrigerator. The best bet was the spaghetti left over from the night before. Grace bypassed eggs and pulled out the neat plastic container. It took her a minute to realize that her sister's kitchen wasn't civilized enough to have a microwave. Taking this in stride, she tossed the top into the sink and dug in. She'd eat it cold. Chewing, she spotted the note on the kitchen table. Kathleen always left notes.

Help yourself to whatever's in the kitchen. Grace smiled and forked more cold spaghetti into her mouth. *Don't worry about dinner, I'll pick up a couple of steaks.* And that, she thought, was Kathleen's polite way of telling her not to mess up the kitchen. *Parent conference this afternoon. I'll be home by five-thirty. Don't use the phone in my office.*

Grace wrinkled her nose as she stuffed the note into her pocket. It would take time, and some pressure, but she was determined to learn more of her sister's moonlighting adventures. And there was the matter of finding out the name of her sister's lawyer. Kathleen's objections and pride aside, Grace wanted to speak to him personally. If she did so carefully enough, her sister's ego wouldn't be bruised. In any case, sometimes you had to overlook a couple of bruises and shoot for the goal. Until she had Kevin back, Kathleen would never be able to put her life in order. That scum Breezewood had no right using Kevin as a weapon against Kathleen.

He'd always been an operator, she thought. Jonathan Breezewood the third was a cold and calculating manipulator who used family position and monied politics to get his way. But not this time. It might take some maneuvering, but Grace would find a way to set things right.

She turned the heat off under the coffeepot just as someone knocked on the front door.

Her trunk, she decided, and snatched up the carton of spaghetti as she started down the hall. An extra ten bucks should convince the delivery man to haul it upstairs. She had a persuasive smile ready as she opened the door.

"G. B. McCabe, right?" Ed stood on the stoop with a hardback copy of *Murder in Style*. He'd nearly sawed a finger off when he'd put the name together with the face.

"That's right." She glanced at the picture on the back cover. Her hair had been styled and crimped, and the photographer had used stark black and white to make her look mysterious. "You've got a good eye. I barely recognize myself from that picture."

Now that he was here, he hadn't the least idea what to do with himself. This kind of thing always happened, he knew, whenever he acted on impulse. Especially with a woman. "I like your stuff. I guess I've read most of it."

"Only most of it?" Grace stuck the fork back in the spaghetti as she smiled at him. "Don't you know that writers have huge and fragile egos? You're supposed to say you've read every word I've ever written and adored them all."

He relaxed a little because her smile demanded he do so. "How about you tell a hell of a story?"

"That'll do."

"When I realized who you were, I guess I wanted to come over and make sure I was right."

"Well, you win the prize. Come on in."

"Thanks." He shifted the book to his other hand and felt like an idiot. "But I don't want to bother you."

Grace gave him a long, solemn look. He was even more impressive up close than he'd been from the window. And his eyes were blue, a dark, interesting blue. "You mean you don't want me to sign that?"

"Well, yes, but—"

"Come in then." She took his arm and pulled him inside. "The coffee's hot."

"I don't drink it."

"Don't drink coffee? How do you stay alive?" Then she smiled and gestured with her fork. "Come on back anyway, there's probably something you can drink. So you like mysteries?"

He liked the way she walked, slowly, carelessly, as though she could change her mind about direction at any moment. "I guess you could say mysteries are my life."

"Mine too." In the kitchen, she opened the refrigerator again. "No beer," she murmured and decided to remedy that at the first opportunity. "No sodas, either. Christ, Kathy. There's juice. It looks like orange."

"Fine."

"I've got some spaghetti here. Want to share?"

"No, thanks. Is that your breakfast?"

"Mmmm." She poured his juice, gesturing casually to a chair as she went to the stove to pour her coffee. "Have you lived next door long?"

He was tempted to mention nutrition but managed to control himself. "Just a couple of months."

"It must be great, fixing it up the way you want." She took another bite of the pasta. "Is that what you are, a carpenter? You have the hands for it."

He found himself pleasantly relieved that she hadn't asked him if he played ball. "No. I'm a cop."

"You're kidding. Really?" She shoved her carton aside and leaned forward. It was her eyes that made her beautiful, he decided on the spot. They were so alive, so full of fascination. "I'm crazy about cops. Some of my best characters are cops, even the bad ones."

"I know." He had to smile. "You've got a feel for police work. It shows in the way you plot a book. Everything works on logic and deduction."

"All my logic goes into writing." She picked up her coffee, then remembered she'd forgotten the cream. Rather than get up, she drank it black. "What kind of cop are you—uniform, undercover?"

"Homicide."

"Kismet." She laughed and squeezed his hand. "I can't believe it, I come to visit my sister and plop right down beside a homicide detective. Are you working on anything right now?"

"Actually, we just wrapped up something yesterday."

A rough one, she decided. There'd been something about the way he'd said it, the faintest change of tone. Though her curiosity was piqued, it was controlled by compassion. "I've got a hell of a murder working right now. A series of murders, actually. I've got . . ." She trailed off. Ed saw her eyes darken. She sat back and propped her bare feet on an empty chair. "I can change the location," she began slowly. "Set it right here in D.C. That's better. It would work. What do you think?"

"Well, I—"

"Maybe I could come down to the station sometime. You could show me around." Already taking her thought processes to the next stage, she thrust her hand into the pocket of her robe for a cigarette. "That's allowed, isn't it?"

"I could probably work it out."

"Terrific. Look, have you got a wife or a lover or anything?"

He stared at her as she lit the cigarette and blew out smoke. "Not right now," he said cautiously.

"Then maybe you'd have a couple of hours now and again in the evening for me."

He picked up his juice and took a long swallow. "A couple of hours," he repeated. "Now and again?"

"Yeah. I wouldn't expect you to give me all your free time, just squeeze me in when you're in the mood."

"When I'm in the mood," he murmured. Her robe dipped down to the floor but was parted at the knee to reveal her legs, pale from winter and smooth as marble. Maybe miracles did still happen.

"You could be kind of my expert consultant, you know? I mean, who'd know murder investigations in D.C. better than a D.C. homicide detective?"

Consultant. A little flustered by his own thoughts, he switched his mind off her legs. "Right." He let out a long breath, then laughed. "You roll right along, don't you, Miss McCabe?"

"It's Grace, and I'm pushy, but I won't pout very long if you say no."

He wondered as he looked at her if there was a man alive who could have said no to those eyes. Then again, his partner Ben always told him he was a sucker. "I've got a couple hours, now and then."

"Thanks. Listen, how about dinner tomorrow? By that time Kath will be thrilled to be rid of me for a while. We could talk murder. I'm buying."

"I'd like that." He rose, feeling as though he'd just taken a fast, unexpected ride. "I'd better get back to work."

"Let me sign your book." After a quick search, she found a pen on a magnetic holder by the phone. "I don't know your name."

"It's Ed. Ed Jackson."

"Hi, Ed." She scrawled on the title page, then unconsciously slipped the pen into her pocket. "See you tomorrow, about seven?"

"Okay." She had freckles, he noticed. A half dozen of them sprinkled over the bridge of her nose. And her wrists were slim and frail. He shifted the book again. "Thanks for the autograph."

Grace let him out the back door. He smelled good, she thought, like wood shavings and soap. Then, rubbing her hands together, she went upstairs to plug in Maxwell.

She worked throughout the day, skipping lunch in favor of the candy bar she found in her coat pocket. Whenever she surfaced from the world she was creating into the one around her, she could hear the hammering and sawing from the house next door. She'd set up her workstation by the window because she liked looking at that house and imagining what was going on inside.

Once she noticed a car pull up in the driveway next

door. A rangy, dark-haired man got out and sauntered up the walk, entering the house without knocking. Grace speculated on him for a moment, then dove back into her plot. The next time she bothered to look, two hours had passed and the car was gone.

She arched her back, then, digging her last cigarette out of the pack, read over a few paragraphs. "Good work, Maxwell," she declared. Pushing a series of buttons, she shut him down for the day. Because her thoughts drifted to her sister, Grace got up to tidy the bed.

Her trunk stood in the middle of the room. The delivery man had indeed carried it upstairs for her, and with the least encouragement from her would have unpacked it as well. She glanced at it, considered, then opted to deal with the chaos inside it later. Instead she went downstairs, found a top-forty station on the radio, and filled the house with the latest from ZZ Top.

Kathleen found her in the living room, sprawled on the sofa with a magazine and a glass of wine. She had to fight back the surge of impatience. She'd just spent the day battling to push something into the minds of a hundred and thirty teenagers. The parent consultation had gotten her nowhere, and her car had begun to make ominous noises on the way home. And here was her sister, with nothing but time on her hands and money in the bank.

With the bag of groceries in her arm, she walked over to the radio and switched it off. Grace glanced up, focused, and smiled. "Hi. I didn't hear you come in."

"I'm not surprised. You had the radio up all the way."

"Sorry." Grace remembered to put the magazine back on the table rather than let it slide to the floor. "Rough day?"

"Some of us have them." She turned and walked toward the kitchen.

Grace swung her feet to the floor, then sat for a minute with her head in her hands. After taking a few deep breaths, she rose and followed her sister into the kitchen. "I went ahead and beefed up the salad from last night. It's still the best thing I cook."

"Fine." Kathleen was already lining a broiling pan with foil.

"Want some wine?"

"No, I'm working tonight."

"On the phone?"

"That's right. On the phone." She slapped the meat onto the broiler pan.

"Hey, Kath, I was asking, not criticizing." When she got no response, Grace reached for the wine and topped off her glass. "Actually, it crossed my mind that I might be able to use what you're doing as an angle in a book."

"You don't change, do you?" Kathleen whirled around. In her eyes, the fury was hot and pulsing. "Nothing's ever private where you're concerned."

"For heaven's sake, Kathy, I didn't mean I'd use your name or even your situation, just the idea, that's all. It was simply a thought."

"Everything's grist for the mill, your mill. Maybe you'd like to use my divorce while you're at it."

"I've never used you," Grace said quietly.

"You use everyone—friends, lovers, family. Oh, you sympathize with their pain and problems on the outside, but inside you're ticking away, figuring out how to make it work for you. Can't you be told anything, see anything without thinking how you can use it in a book?"

Grace opened her mouth to deny, to protest, then closed it again on a sigh. The truth, no matter how unattractive, was better faced. "No, I guess not. I'm sorry."

"Then drop it, all right?" Kathleen's voice was abruptly calm again. "I don't want to argue tonight."

"Neither do I." Making an effort, she started fresh. "I was thinking I might rent a car while I'm here, play tourist a little. And if I was mobile, I could do the shopping and save you some time."

"Fine." Kathleen switched the broiler on, shifting her body enough so that Grace couldn't see her hand wasn't steady. "There's a Hertz place on the way to school. I could drop you off in the morning."

"Okay." Now what, Grace asked herself as she sipped her wine. "Oh, I met the guy next door this morning."

"I'm sure you did." Her voice was taut as she slid the meat under the flame. She was surprised Grace hadn't made friends with everyone in the entire neighborhood by now.

Grace sipped her wine and worked on her temper. It was usually she who lost it first, she remembered. This time she wouldn't. "He's very nice. Turns out to be a cop. We're having dinner tomorrow."

"Isn't that lovely." Kathleen slammed the pot on the stove and added water. "You work fast, Gracie, as usual."

Grace took another slow sip, then set her glass carefully on the counter. "I think I'll go for a walk."

"I'm sorry." With her eyes closed, Kathleen leaned against the stove. "I didn't mean that, I didn't mean to snap at you."

"All right." She wasn't always quick to forgive, but she only had one sister. "Why don't you sit down? You're tired."

"No, I'm on call tonight. I want to get this done before the phone starts ringing."

"I'll do it. You can supervise." She took her sister's arm and nudged her into a chair. "What goes in the pan?"

"There's a package in the bag." Kathleen dug in her purse, pulled out a bottle, and shook out two pills.

Graced dipped in the grocery bag and took out an envelope. "Noodles in garlic sauce. Handy." She ripped it open and dumped it in without reading the directions. "I'd just as soon you didn't jump down my throat again, but do you want to talk about it?"

"No, it was just a long day." She dry-swallowed the pills. "I've got papers to grade."

"Well, I won't be able to do you any good there. I could take the phone calls for you."

Kathleen managed a smile. "No, thanks."

Grace took out the salad bowl and set it on the table. "Maybe I could just take notes."

"No. If you don't stir the noodles, they'll stick."

"Oh." Willing to oblige, Grace turned to them. In the silence, she heard the meat begin to sizzle. "Easter's next week. Don't you get a few days off?"

"Five, counting the weekend."

"Why don't we take a quick trip, join the madness in Fort Lauderdale, get some sun?"

"I can't afford it."

"My treat, Kath. Come on, it'd be fun. Remember the spring of our senior year when we begged and pleaded with Mom and Dad to let us go?"

"You begged and pleaded," Kathleen reminded her.

"Whatever, we went. For three days we partied, got sunburned, and met dozens of guys. Remember that one, Joe or Jack, who tried to climb in the window of our motel room?"

"After you told him I was hot for his body."

"Well, you were. Poor guy nearly killed himself." With a laugh, she stabbed a noodle and wondered if it was done. "God, we were so young, and so stupid. What the hell, Kath, we've still got it together enough to have a few college guys leer at us."

"Drinking sprees and college boys don't interest me. Besides, I've arranged to be on call all weekend. Switch the noodles down to warm, Grace, and turn the meat over."

She obeyed and said nothing as she heard Kathleen setting the table. It wasn't the drinking or the men, Grace thought. She'd just wanted to recapture something of the sisterhood they'd shared. "You're working too hard."

"I'm not in your position, Grace. I can't afford to lie on the couch and read magazines all afternoon."

Grace picked up her wine again. And bit her tongue. There were days she sat in front of a screen for twelve hours, nights she worked until three. On a book tour she was on all day and half the night until she had only enough energy to crawl into bed and fall into a stuporous sleep. She might consider herself lucky, she might still be astonished at the amount of money that rolled in from royalty checks, but she earned it. It was a constant source of annoyance that her sister never understood that.

"I'm on vacation." She tried to say it lightly, but the edge was there.

"I'm not."

"Fine. If you don't want to go away, would you mind if I did some puttering around in the yard?"

"I don't care." Kathleen rubbed her temple. The headaches never seemed to fade completely any longer. "Actually I'd appreciate it. I haven't given it much thought. We had a beautiful garden in California. Do you remember?"

"Sure." Grace had always thought it too orderly and formal, like Jonathan. Like Kathleen. She hated the little stab of bitterness she felt and pushed it aside. "We could go for some pansies, and what were those things Mom always loved? Morning glories."

"All right." But her mind was on other things. "Grace, the meat's going to burn."

Later, Kathleen closed herself in her office. Grace could hear the phone ring, the Fantasy phone, as she'd decided to term it. She counted ten calls before she went upstairs. Too restless to sleep, she turned on her computer. But she wasn't thinking of work or of the murders she created.

The contented feeling that had been with her the night before and most of the day was gone. Kathleen wasn't all right. Her mood swings were too quick and too sharp. It had been on the tip of her tongue to mention therapy, but she'd been too aware of what the reaction would have been. Kathleen would have given her one of those hard, closed-in looks, and the discussion would have ended.

Grace had mentioned Kevin only once. Kathleen had told her she didn't want to discuss him or Jonathan. She knew her sister well enough to realize that Kathleen was regretting her visit. What was worse, Grace was regretting it herself. Kathleen always managed to point out the worst aspects of her, aspects that under other circumstances Grace herself managed to brush over.

But she'd come to help. Somehow, despite both of them, she was going to. But it would take some time, she told herself for comfort, resting her chin on her arm. She could see lights in the windows next door.

She couldn't hear the phone ring now with the office door closed and her own pulled to. She wondered how many more calls her sister would take that night. How many more men would she satisfy without ever having seen their faces? Did she grade papers between calls? It should have been funny. She wished it were funny, but she couldn't stop seeing the tension on Kathleen's face as she'd pushed her food around her plate.

There was nothing she could do, Grace told herself as she rubbed her hands over her eyes. Kathleen was determined to handle things her way.

❧

IT was wonderful to hear her voice again, to hear her make promises and give that quick, husky laugh. She was wearing black this time, something thin and flimsy that a man could tear away on a whim. She'd like that, he thought. She'd like it if he were there with her, ripping off her clothes.

The man she was talking to barely spoke at all. He was glad. If he closed his eyes, he could imagine she was talking to him. And only him. He'd been listening to her for hours, call after call. After a while, the words no longer mattered. Just her voice, the warm, teasing voice that poured through his earphones and into his head. From somewhere in the house a television was playing, but he didn't hear it. He only heard Desiree.

She wanted him.

In his mind he sometimes heard her say his name. Jerald. She would say it with that half laugh she often had in her voice. When he went to her, she would open up her arms and say it again, slowly, breathlessly. Jerald.

They would make love in all the ways she described.

He would be the man to finally satisfy her. He would be the man she wanted above all others. It would be his name she said over and over again, on a whisper, on a moan, on a scream.

Jerald, Jerald, Jerald.

He shuddered, then lay back, spent, in the swivel chair in front of his computer.

He was eighteen years old and had made love to women only in his dreams. Tonight his dreams were only of Desiree.

And he was mad.